L

AND

HOOK, LINE AND
SHOTGUN BRIDE
BY
CASSIE MILES

MILLS
BOON

First published in Great Britain 2011
by Mills & Boon, an imprint of Harlequin (UK) Limited,
Eton House, 18-24 Paradise Road, Richmond, Surrey TW9 1SR

© Kay Bergstrom 2010

ISBN: 978 0 263 88518 7

46-0411

Harlequin (UK) policy is to use papers that are natural, renewable and recyclable products and made from wood grown in sustainable forests. The logging and manufacturing processes conform to the legal environmental regulations of the country of origin.

Printed and bound in Spain
by Blackprint CPI, Barcelona

LOCK, STOCK AND SECRET BABY

BY
CASSIE MILES

Though born and raised in L.A., **Cassie Miles** has lived in Colorado long enough to be considered a semi-native. The first home she owned was a log cabin in the mountains overlooking Elk Creek, with a thirty-mile commute to her work at the *Denver Posy*.

After raising two daughters and cooking tons of macaroni and cheese for her family, Cassie is trying to be more adventurous in her culinary efforts. Ceviche, anyone? She's discovered almost anything tastes better with wine. When she's not plotting Intrigue books, Cassie likes to hang out at the Denver Botanical Gardens near her high-rise home.

Chapter One

Clutter spilled across the desktop in Ray Jantzen's home office: unopened junk mail, books, a running shoe with a broken lace, file folders, research notes for a paper he'd published in the *American Journal of Psychiatry* and…a gun.

Behind a stack of magazines, he located a framed photograph of his late wife, Annie, and their son, Blake. The sight of his beloved Annie's smile wrenched at his heart. She'd passed away two years ago, a month shy of their fortieth anniversary.

With his thumb, Ray wiped a smudge from the glass and focused on the image of his son. Though Blake was only eight in this picture, his dark brown eyes snapped with impatient intelligence. *Gifted* wasn't a sufficient word to describe him. And yet, he hadn't chosen a career where he could concentrate on his intellect. At age twenty-five, Blake was part of a Special Forces team working undercover in undisclosed locations.

Setting aside the photo, Ray opened his laptop and typed an e-mail.

My dear son, I loved you from the moment you emerged from your mother's womb with

a squall and two clenched fists. Forgive me for
what I'm about to disclose…

He was well aware of his pompous phrasing, clearly
a defense mechanism to hide his shame. He should have
told Blake long ago. After four decades as a psychiatrist,
Ray should have been wiser. Unspoken secrets never went
away. The lies one told festered beneath the surface and
arose in times of stress to bite one's ass.

His e-mail ended with: Take care of Eve Weathers.
She needs you.

He hit Send, closed the laptop and took it to the safe
hidden behind the bookshelves. Like the rest of his office,
the interior of the safe had accumulated a great deal of
paper. But these notes were precious; they would tell the
whole truth about the story he hinted at in his e-mail.

After locking the safe and closing the hinged section of
bookshelves, he went to the window. The red, yellow and
magenta tulips in his garden bobbed in the June breezes.
The sun was setting behind the foothills west of Denver.
So beautiful. He should have spent more time outdoors.

The door to his office opened. A melodic voice said,
"Good evening, Dr. Jantzen."

"How did you get inside?"

"Your alarm system is rudimentary. Your locks, pathetic." The extraordinary tonal quality of the intruder's
voice hinted at his immense musical talent. "And this office
is a rat's nest. How do you work?"

"I like it this way."

"And what does that say about your emotional state?
Hmm? Disorganized thinking, perhaps?"

Angered by this mocking analysis, Ray turned away
from the window and faced the intruder. His eyes were
silver, like the barrel of his Beretta.

Ray lunged for his own weapon. It trembled in his hand. He'd never be able to shoot this young man whom he had known literally since birth.

"You're not a killer." The voice was sheer music. "Put down the gun."

Ray sank into the chair behind his desk and reached for the telephone. Still holding the gun, he hit the speed dial for the security service that monitored his "rudimentary" alarm system. They were guaranteed to respond within ten minutes.

"Hang up the phone, Dr. Jantzen."

"Or else?"

"Be reasonable." He aimed the Beretta. "You know what I'm looking for."

Turning over his records wouldn't be enough, and Ray knew it. "I won't remain silent. I can't."

"Then you will die."

Ray squeezed off several shots, aiming high. He hoped to frighten his opponent, though he knew that hope was futile.

Three bullets burned into his chest. Before his eyelids closed, he imprinted his gaze on the photograph of Blake and his beloved Annie.

Eve Weathers had attended many funerals, mostly in the company of her parents, mostly for people she didn't know. Being raised on army bases meant death visited her community with a sad and terrible frequency. But she'd never before stood at the graveside of someone who'd been murdered.

The bright sun of an early June afternoon dimmed, as if a shadow hung over them, as if they all shared in the guilt. The police said Dr. Ray Jantzen had been killed by a burglar. They had no suspects. The killer might even be among them.

While the preacher read from Psalms, she checked out the other graveside mourners. Her mother would have called this a good turnout—close to a hundred people. An eclectic bunch, they appeared to be from all walks of life. There were serious-looking older men who were probably Ray's friends and psychiatrist coworkers, several men in uniform because Ray had worked at the VA hospital, a young man in leather with spiky, black hair and mirrored sunglasses, a couple of teenagers and various family members. Their only common denominator was that Eve didn't know any of them.

Dr. Ray had been in her life for as long as she could remember, literally since she was born. When her parents had applied for an experimental in vitro fertilization program at the army base where her dad had been stationed, Eve had become part of a lifelong study. Every year, she had filled in a questionnaire and had given Dr. Ray an update on her life, both her physical and emotional condition.

They'd only met in person a couple of times before she had moved to Boulder three years ago to take a mathematical engineering position at Sun Wave Labs. For the past two years, she and Dr. Ray had done their updates over dinner. His wife had passed away, and she assumed he was lonely.

The sound of his coffin being lowered startled her. She blinked. Her gaze lit upon a dark-haired man in a black suit who stood beside the preacher. She recognized him from the photo Dr. Ray had carried in his wallet. His son, Blake Jantzen.

She studied Blake with a mathematician's eye, taking his measure. His physical proportions were remarkable. Her mind calculated the inches and angles of his shoulders, his torso and the length of his legs. Though he wasn't splayed out, like Da Vinci's *Vitruvian Man,* Blake Jantzen was close to ideal.

When his gaze met hers, a tremor rippled through her, and she immediately lowered her eyes. She hadn't meant to stare, hadn't intended to intrude on what had to be a terrible day for him. When she looked up again, he was still watching her.

Their eye contact intensified. His dark eyes bored into hers, and that little tremor expanded to a full-blown, pulsating earthquake inside her rib cage. If she didn't look away, it felt as if her heart would explode. This wasn't how she usually reacted to men, even if they were practically perfect.

Pretending to pray, she stared down at her feet. Her toes protruded from her hiking sandals which were really too casual for a funeral, even if they were black. Suddenly self-conscious, she decided her black skirt was too short, showing off way too much of her winter white legs. She buttoned her black cotton jacket over her white tank top, stained with a dribble of coffee from this morning.

Whenever she mingled with the general public, her style seemed inadequate. In the lab, she wore comfortable jeans and T-shirts with nerdy slogans. Her chin-length, wheat-blond hair resembled a bird's nest. None of the guys she worked with cared what she looked like. They were so absorbed in their work that they wouldn't notice if she showed up naked, except perhaps to comment on the small tattooed symbol for pi above her left breast.

The crowd dispersed, and she lost sight of Blake, which was probably for the best. Her mother would have told her that the proper behavior would be to shake his hand and offer condolences, but she didn't trust herself to get that close to him without a meltdown. Was she so desperate for male companionship that she'd hit on a guy at his father's funeral?

She made a beeline for her car. As she clicked the door lock, she heard a voice behind her. "Are you Eve Weathers?"

Without turning around, she knew who that sexy baritone belonged to. "I'm Eve."

"I'm Blake Jantzen. I need to talk to you."

Up close, he was even more amazing. Was there a degree beyond perfection? Most people had incongruities in their facial structure: one eye higher than the other, a bump on the nose or a dimple in one cheek and not the other. Blake had none of those anomalies. Even the shadows of exhaustion beneath his eyes were precisely symmetrical.

She stammered, "I'm s-sorry for your loss."

He acknowledged with a crisp nod. "Come back to the house. My aunt arranged a reception."

"I don't know where you live."

"My father's house," he clarified.

Though she'd planned to return to her office in Boulder, she couldn't refuse without being rude. "I've never been to Dr. Ray's home."

A flicker of surprise registered in his coffee-brown eyes. "I thought you were close to him. He thought highly of you."

"We met for dinner a couple of times, and he was very kind to me. But it was always at a restaurant. He kept his private life, well, private." Her parents never could have afforded her postgrad studies if Dr. Ray hadn't helped her obtain scholarships. "I thought of him as a benefactor."

"Stay here," Blake said. "I'll tell my aunt that I'm riding with you."

Though she obediently slid behind the steering wheel of her hybrid and waited, his attitude irked her. Blake had the arrogant tone of someone who gave orders that must be followed. *A military guy.* An alpha male. The kind of man who demanded too much and gave little in return. If she ever fell in love, she hoped it would be with a guy who at least pretended to treat her as an equal.

Though she doubted that she and Blake would get along, Eve checked her reflection in the visor mirror. She'd shed a couple of tears, but the mascara around her blue eyes wasn't smudged. She pushed her bangs into a semblance of order.

In a matter of minutes, Mr. Perfect returned to her car and climbed into the passenger side. "At the exit from the cemetery, turn right."

Having issued his order, he leaned back in the seat and closed his eyes.

Eve wished there was something she could do or say to comfort him. Her mother was good in these situations; she knew how to show empathy without being too sentimental. Eve lacked those people skills. She could calculate quadratic equations in the blink of an eye, but the art of conversation baffled her. She pinched her lips and remained silent as she drove.

When Blake opened his eyes and leaned forward, he appeared to be completely in control. "What's your birthday?"

An odd question. "June twenty-second. I'll be twenty-six."

"Mine is June thirtieth. Same year," he said. "And you were born in New Mexico."

"At an army base near Roswell."

"Me, too."

"I guess we have something in common."

"More than you know," he said. "Tell me about your relationship with my dad."

Apparently, Mr. Perfect wasn't big on idle chatter. This felt like an interrogation. "I communicated with Dr. Ray once a year, every year. On my birthday, I filled out a status report with forty questions. Some of them were essay questions and took a while to answer."

"Did you ever wonder why?"

"Of course, I did." His terse questions provoked an equally abrupt response from her. "I'm not a mindless idiot."

He gave a short laugh. "I'd bet on the opposite. You're pretty damn smart."

"Maybe."

"Tell me what you know about my dad's status reports."

What was he getting at? He must already know this information. "Your father told me I was part of a study group made up of children with similar backgrounds and key genetic markers. He monitored potential and achievement, which was why he helped me get scholarships."

"Take a right at the next light."

She could feel his scrutiny as he studied her. Though she wasn't sure that she even liked this guy, she responded to him with an unwanted excitement that set her heart racing. Her brain fumbled for something to break the silence. "There was a good turnout for the funeral."

"Did you recognize anybody?"

"Not a soul. I kind of expected to see Dr. Prentice."

"How do you know Prentice?"

"He was the other half of the study your father worked on," she said. "As I'm sure you already know."

"Tell me, anyway."

"Your dad correlated the psychiatric data. And Prentice did medical examinations every few years or so. He contacted me about six weeks ago."

"The date?"

She pulled up her mental calendar. "It was April six-teenth, the day after tax day. Prentice said he needed to see me right away. There was an issue about possible exposure to radiation when I was a child."

"And you were scared."

"Terrified." There had been a similar scare five years ago that Dr. Prentice treated with a brief course of media-tion. "Radiation poisoning isn't something to mess around with. Turns out that I'm fine. Prentice gave me a clean bill of health."

"What do you remember about the testing?"

"It was a thorough physical." She wasn't about to go into details about the pelvic exam or the part where she'd been under anesthetic. "I went to a clinic after work on a Friday, and I didn't get home until after ten o'clock. Dr. Prentice's assistant drove me and made sure I got into bed."

"Any ill effects?"

Come to think of it she hadn't been feeling like her-self lately. Her stomach had been queasy. A couple of times, she'd vomited. "Do you know anything about the testing?"

"Yes," he said curtly.

Her fear returned with a vengeance. What did Blake know? Had he pulled her aside because he had bad news? She might have been poisoned by a childhood exposure, might have some awful disease. Her cells could be turning against her at this very moment. "Why did you say that you needed to talk to me?"

"Pull over."

This had to be bad news. "Why?"

He touched her arm, and she recoiled as if he'd poked her with a cattle prod. She wanted nothing more to do with

Mr. Perfect. He was toying with her, asking inane questions and hinting at dire circumstances.

She yanked the steering wheel and made a hard right onto a side street with wood-frame houses, skimpy trees and sidewalks that blended into the curb. Halfway down the block, she parked and turned off the engine. Eve preferred facts to innuendo. She wanted the truth, no matter how horrible.

"All right, Blake, I'm parked. If you have something to tell me, get on with it."

His eyes flicked as if he was searching her face, trying to gauge her reaction. "It might be better if I gave you more information. Set the framework."

"Just spit it out." She braced herself. "Am I dying?"

He cleared his throat. "Eve, I have reason to believe that you're pregnant."

"That's impossible."

She was a virgin.

Chapter Two

Blake watched her reaction, looking for a sign that Eve Weathers had been complicit in Prentice's scheme. He saw nothing of the kind.

His information had shocked her. She gasped, loudly and repeatedly. Her eyes opened wide. Pupils dilated. She was on the verge of hyperventilation. Her chest heaved against the seat belt. "I can't be pregnant."

"I said it was a possibility."

"Why would you say such a thing? And how the hell would you know?"

"Before he was murdered, my father sent me an e-mail." At the moment the e-mail was sent, Blake had been in a debriefing meeting at the Pentagon. He didn't read the message until two hours later. By then, it was too late. His father was dead.

"What did it say?"

Too much for him to explain right now. Blake cut to the pertinent facts. "My father received information that Dr. Prentice had implanted you with an embryo."

"During the examination? While I was unconscious?" She dragged her fingers through her pale blond hair. "That's sickening. Disgusting."

When she grasped the key in the ignition, he stayed her hand. Gently, he said, "Maybe you should let me drive."

She yanked away from him. "My car. I drive."

"You don't look so good," he said.

"Thanks so much."

"Not an insult." He liked her looks. "I meant that you appear to be in shock. I don't want you to pass out."

"Oh, I'm way too angry to faint." She started the car. "You want out?"

"No." He couldn't let her drive off by herself. In his e-mail, Dad had told Blake to take care of Eve Weathers. That last request could not be ignored.

She punched the accelerator and squealed away from the curb. Halfway down the street, she whipped a U-turn, barely missing a van parked at the curb.

His right foot pushed down on an invisible brake on the passenger-side floorboard. "If you let me drive, we can be at my father's house in ten minutes."

"That's not where we're going."

At the corner, she made an aggressive merge into traffic. Her tension showed in her white-knuckle grip on the steering wheel, but she wasn't reckless. She checked her mirrors before changing lanes and stayed within the speed limit. With a sudden swerve, she drove into the parking lot outside a convenience store.

Without a word, she threw off her seat belt and left the car. He trailed behind her. Inside the store, he asked, "You mind telling me what we're doing here?"

"Maybe I wanted a donut."

Her sarcasm was preferable to the moment of shock when he'd mentioned pregnancy. He should have been more careful, should have expected her reaction, but he wasn't operating at peak efficiency. Eve's problems weren't his primary concern.

His focus was on his father's murder. The cops were satisfied with the lame explanation that a burglar did the crime. *Like hell.* This killing wasn't a random act of violence. Blake was determined to find the son of a bitch who pulled the trigger and the men who sent him.

He stood behind Eve as she stared at shelves packed with an array of over-the-counter medicines. When she spied the pregnancy tests, she grabbed three of them. "Damn, I left my purse in the car."

"I'll pay," he said.

At the counter, the clerk gave them a knowing smirk as he rang up the purchase.

Eve added a pack of gum. "And two jerky sticks and one of these pecan things."

"There's food at the house," he said.

"I have a craving. Isn't that what pregnant women do?"

When she plucked a magazine off the rack below the counter, she set down her car keys. He snatched them. "I'm driving. It's easier than giving you directions."

"Fine," she growled. "You drive."

Back in the car, he adjusted the driver's seat for his long legs and headed toward his father's house while Eve tore open the packaging on the pregnancy tests and read the instructions. "When we get to the house," she said, "I'd appreciate being shown to the nearest bathroom."

He nodded.

"I won't make a scene," she assured him. "I respect your father's memory."

Several other vehicles were already parked on the street outside the long ranch-style house that his mother had loved so much. When they had first moved here fifteen years ago, there had been few other houses in the area. Development had crept closer, but his father's house still commanded an outstanding view. To the south, Pikes Peak was visible on a clear day like today.

No matter where in the world he was stationed, he treasured the memory of home—of translucent, Colorado skies and distant, snowcapped peaks. This vision was his solace and the basis for his daily meditation.

As they went up the sidewalk to the house, he pocketed her keys, not wanting her to have easy access to an escape until she calmed down.

Inside, he skirted the living room where people had gathered and escorted her down a long hallway that bisected the left half of the house. At the end of the hall, he opened the door to his dad's office. Unlike the rest of this well-maintained residence, this room looked like the aftermath of a tornado. In addition to the papers and magazines, a fine coating of fingerprint dust from the police investigation covered many of the surfaces. The supposedly secret safe in the bookshelves hung open in its hinges. His father's blood stained the Persian carpet behind the desk.

When he closed the door, Eve stood very still. "Is this where it happened?"

"Yes."

"You haven't cleaned up."

"Not yet." Valuable information could be hidden somewhere in this room. He'd already searched, but he would search again and again and again, until he found the killer.

IN THE PRIVACY OF THE bathroom, Eve almost yielded to the overwhelming pressure of anger and fear. If ever there had been a time in her life when she wanted to curl up in a ball and cry, this was it. She didn't want to be pregnant. Not now, possibly not ever. Having a baby wasn't on her agenda.

She knew that she'd skipped her last period but hadn't worried because Dr. Prentice told her she might be irregular after her testing. Prentice, that bastard. Why had she believed him? With good reason, damn it. She had twenty-five years of good faith; Prentice and Dr. Ray had been part of her life since birth.

Setting her purse on the counter, she took out the kits from the convenience store: three different brands. Two of the kits had two tests inside the box, and she set the extras aside.

She followed the simple instructions and arrayed the three test sticks on the counter beside the sink. Then, she waited, counting the seconds.

Each test had a different indicator. One showed a plus sign in the window to indicate a positive. Another showed a pink line. The third would turn blue.

Though counting didn't make time go faster, reciting numerical progressions had always soothed her. As a child, she learned to count prime numbers all the way up to 3,571—the first five hundred primes. Five hundred unique numbers, divisible only by themselves and one.

The last time she had seen Dr. Ray over dinner, she'd talked about prime. He had suggested—in his kindly way—that she might want to pursue deeper interpersonal relationships. Make friends, join groups, go on dates, blah, blah, blah.

She had told him that she was happy just as she was. Some people needed others to make them complete, but she was unique. Like a prime number, she was divisible only by herself. Singular.

If she was pregnant, she'd never be alone again.

One of the tests required only one minute to show results. She could look down right now and see. But the others needed five minutes, and she didn't want to peek until all the results were in and could be verified against each other.

But she couldn't wait. She looked down. The first test showed a positive.

Could she trust a kit from a convenience store? It hardly seemed scientific in spite of the claim on the box of ninety-nine percent accuracy in detecting a pregnancy hormone, hCG, released into the body by the placenta.

The second test repeated the positive. And the third.

She was pregnant, pregnant and pregnant.

Tentatively, she touched her lower abdomen. *Hello, in there. Can you hear me?* An absurd question. At this point in development, the fetus wouldn't have ears. But they shared the same body, the same blood. The food she ate nurtured the tiny being that grew within her. The miracle of life. Amazing. Infuriating.

Damn it, this couldn't be happening! She dug into her purse and found her cell phone. Dr. Prentice's private cell phone number was in the memory.

He answered after the fourth ring. "I've been expecting to hear from you, Eve."

"How could you do this to me?"

"I assume you're aware of—"

"I'm aware, damn you. I just took a pregnancy test."

"You're upset."

A mild description of her outrage. "You might as well have raped me."

"Not at all the same thing. Rape is an act of violence. You received the highest quality medical care. My intentions were for your own good. I could have hired a surrogate, you know."

"A what?"

"A surrogate mother. Some women rent out their wombs like cheap motels."

"I know what a surrogate is."

Her voice was louder than she intended. Blake knocked on the bathroom door. "Eve? Are you all right?"

She didn't want to deal with him. This wasn't his problem. Lowering her voice, she demanded, "Why, Dr. Prentice? Why would you do this?"

"Ray's research indicated the optimum condition for development comes when the biological mother carries the fetus and bonds with the infant."

Biological mother? Bonding? None of what he'd just said made sense. "I ought to hire a lawyer and sue you."

"Don't bother. When you came for your examination, you signed a consent form."

With a jolt, she remembered being handed several documents on a clipboard. "You told me it was a routine medical procedure."

"If you like, I can fax you a copy."

He knew her too well, knew that she wouldn't bother to read the fine print. She had trusted him. "I have to know why."

"To create the second generation."

"Second generation of what?"

From outside the bathroom door, she heard Blake. "Who are you talking to, Eve?"

"I'm fine," she told him.

"Unlock the damn door," Blake said.

"In a minute."

She moved to the farthest wall of the bathroom beside the toilet. A magazine stand held back issues of *Psychology Today*. Guest towels with a teal-blue border hung from a pewter rack. She spoke into the phone. "Signed consent form or not, this was wrong."

"What's done is done," he said.

"I'm not ready to be a mother." Everything in her life would have to change. She'd have to find a way to juggle work and child care. There was so much to learn, an over-whelming amount of research. How could she manage? "Maybe I should give the baby up for adoption."

"That would be a mistake."

"It's not your call, Dr. Prentice."

"Let me give you something else to consider. Do you re-member five years ago when I had you on medication?"

The earlier scare about possible radiation poisoning. "Another lie?"

"I'm a scientist," he said archly. "I don't deal in ethics. Five years ago, the medication I gave you was actually a fertility drug that encouraged ovulation. You produced several eggs which I then harvested during your physical exam. I used those eggs to create embryos."

"My egg?" The impact of this new information hit her hard. "You implanted me with my own egg?"

"The fetus you're carrying is biologically your own."

My baby. Her hand rested protectively on her stomach. She felt a deep, immediate connection. *This is my baby.*

"This entire process would have been far less compli-cated," Dr. Prentice said, "if Ray had agreed to facilitate. He had a decent grasp on your psychological development and could have convinced you that having this baby was a good idea. Brilliant, in fact. You're lucky to take part in—"

The room started to spin. Eve never fainted. But her knees went weak. *I'm having a baby.* She collapsed with a thud. The phone fell from her limp hand onto the tiled bathroom floor.

Chapter Three

Eve heard the sharp rap of knuckles against the bathroom door—a faraway sound, like pebbles being tossed down a well.

Blake called through the door, "Are you all right? Eve, answer me."

She wasn't all right. Too many variables swirled inside her head. Nothing made logical sense.

"I'm coming in," Blake said.

The doorknob turned. Through a haze, she saw him come closer. He knelt beside her. His fingers rested on her throat, checking her pulse.

"Locked door," she said. "How did you…"

"Picked the lock," he said. "Can you sit up?"

"I'm fine."

But she wasn't fine. Her eyelids closed, shutting out the light and the intolerable confusion. Her mind careened wildly. How could she be pregnant when she'd never made love? She had the result without the experience. People told her sex was great, but she hadn't tested the theory, didn't know for sure. There was a lot she didn't know, like how to be a mother. Would the baby look like her? A girl baby or a boy? Oh, God, what would she tell her parents?

She was aware of being lifted from the bathroom floor and carried like a little girl. If only she could go back to those more innocent times. Her childhood memories were happy. Not idyllic, but happy. Her parents had loved her, even though she had never quite fit in. She always felt different, like an alien girl who had beamed into their normal world from the planet Nerd.

When she opened her eyes, she was stretched out on the leather sofa in Dr. Ray's office with her feet elevated on a pillow. A crocheted green-and-yellow afghan covered her. Blake pressed a cool washcloth against her forehead.

"I'm going to have a baby," she whispered.

"I know." His smile reached his eyes, deepening the faint, symmetrical lines that radiated from the corners. Though he had no reason to care about her, he seemed concerned. Maybe Mr. Perfect had a heart, after all.

Her hand lingered on her flat stomach. An intuitive urge to protect the baby? She couldn't count on motherly instincts to show her the way. There were books to be read. More information was vital. She'd need a regimen of special vitamins and exercises. "I should go."

"You'll stay here tonight. I have an extra bedroom."

"Is that an order?"

He arched one eyebrow, disrupting the precise balance of his features. "That isn't what I meant."

"I know." She also knew that he couldn't stop himself from being bossy. With an effort, she swung her legs down to the floor and sat up on the sofa. The washcloth fell from her forehead. She wasn't dizzy, but an edge of darkness pressed against her peripheral vision.

He placed a bottle of water into her hand. "Drink."

No objection from her. Rehydrating her body was a very good idea. Tipping the bottle against her lips, she took a couple of sips. The cool liquid tasted amazing. A few drops slid down her chin, and she wiped them away.

Though she didn't feel capable of running a mile, her strength was returning. Arching her neck, she stretched.

"Does anything hurt?" Blake asked.

"Only my pride," she said. "I've never keeled over like that before."

"There's a first time for everything."

"Like being pregnant." Each and every thought circled back to that inevitable theme.

"Who were you talking to on the phone?" he asked.

"Dr. Prentice. That old toad." She still couldn't believe what he'd done to her. "You were right about him implanting an embryo, but here's the kicker. He used one of my own eggs. Biologically, I'm the mother of this baby."

"How did you reach Prentice?"

She shrugged. "I have his cell number."

"I need to talk to him. ASAP." His momentary compassion faded quickly. His jaw was so tense that his lips didn't move when he talked. "I want you to arrange a meeting with Prentice."

"After what he did to me? No way. I'm not getting within a hundred yards of Dr. Edgar Prentice."

"I don't expect you to come along. Set a meeting for me. A face-to-face meeting."

"What's going on?" She took another sip of water. "Is there some other horrible secret you haven't told me yet?"

Instead of responding, he rose to his feet. "You're feeling better. You should eat something."

His quick change of subject worried her. Eve wasn't usually good at reading other people's expressions, but she had a weird connection with Blake. She could tell that he was holding back. "If there's something else, I want to know."

He headed toward the door. "I'll bring a sandwich from the buffet table."

Before she could stop him, he left the office. Moving fast, he almost seemed to be fleeing from her, abandoning her. So much for counting on Blake for support.

Slowly, she rose from the sofa. Her legs steadied as she walked to the bathroom. On the countertop, the three pregnancy test sticks lined up to mock her. She shoved them into the trash and washed her hands. After splashing cold water on her face, she felt more alert, more aware and more certain that Blake was hiding something. What else could be wrong? Was this something to do with the father of her baby? She hadn't even considered that huge question. Prentice had chosen someone as a sperm donor. But who? *Oh, God, do I even want to know?*

She couldn't take much more. Finding out that she was pregnant had been devastating enough. She'd shattered like protons in a super collider. Could she take another life-changing jolt?

There was no other choice. *I need to know everything.* It was time to pull herself together. She picked up her cell phone and tucked it into her purse. She needed answers.

When she returned to the sofa, Blake slipped back into the office with a plate of fruit and a ham sandwich. The sight of food momentarily eclipsed her other concerns. She wolfed down half the sandwich in huge bites. Not the most ladylike behavior but she needed her strength.

"Eating for two?" he asked.

"Apparently so." She swallowed. "I should thank you for helping me when I fainted. You're good at taking care of people."

"I have paramedic training."

The way he'd treated her—elevating her feet, covering her with a blanket and giving her water—was standard procedure for shock. "Your dad mentioned that you're in the military."

"Correct."

"I was an army brat, so I know all about you guys. Let me guess. You're in Special Forces."

"Good guess."

"You're one of those scary dudes who can take out ten armed terrorists with a spoon and a paper clip."

He shrugged. "Not ten. Maybe six."

"I appreciate your ferociousness. I really do. But what I need from you right now doesn't involve physical mayhem. I want answers. There's something you're holding back, something else you haven't told me."

His reluctance showed when he paced away from her and went to the window—putting physical distance between them. "I'm not sure you can handle the truth."

"You're not saying that right. In the movie, it was like this." She made a fist and did a bad Jack Nicholson impression. "You can't handle the truth."

"I loved when he did that."

"Me, too." Laughing, she realized that she was as comfortable with Blake as she was with the guys in the lab. Who would have thought that an antisocial mathematician like her would get along with Mr. Perfect? "Tell me, Blake."

Blake looked down at her from his superior height. He'd shed his suit jacket and necktie. The sleeves of his white shirt were rolled up to the elbow, revealing muscular forearms. "I don't know where to start."

"The beginning?" Biting into an apple slice, she chewed with deliberation, refusing to be distracted by his masculine gorgeousness.

"Before he died, my dad sent me an e-mail. It was like a confession. He'd done something he regretted deeply."

"With Dr. Prentice?"

Blake paced on the worn Persian carpet in front of the desk. "Twenty-six years ago, on that army base near Roswell, Prentice was experimenting with frozen embryos. My mom was in her late thirties and thought she'd never have a baby. Prentice offered my father a solution."

He paused to pick up a framed photograph on the desk. "My mom never knew the truth about me. Biologically, I wasn't her child. I'm the result of an embryo created from two outstanding donors—people with high IQs and exceptional physical ability."

"Genetic engineering." That explained why Blake was so perfect. "Prentice was trying to create superbabies."

"Though he had ethical reservations, my dad agreed to monitor the experiment." He set down the photo and returned to the chair beside the sofa. "He measured the intellectual and psychological development of the supposed superbabies. Using subjects like you."

"Me?" she squeaked.

"You're highly intelligent. Your health is excellent."

"But I'm not perfect. All I have to do is look in a mirror to see that my mouth is too big. My nose has a weird curve at the tip. Besides, if I'm so genetically attractive, why don't I have a slew of boyfriends?"

"You've put all your energy into your intellect," he said. "When other girls were dating, you were studying."

She waved her hands to erase the memory of herself peering out from behind a stack of books to watch the other teenagers flirting and kissing in the library. Not that she'd been a recluse. She had gotten along well with guys and had had boyfriends. But there had always been something that got in the way. Her romantic life had been complicated to the point of nonexistence. "A truly superior specimen should be able to have it all."

"That's the part that fascinated my dad—the effects of nurturing and environment on subjects who started life with a genetic advantage."

"Wait." She hadn't even considered this angle. "If I was genetically engineered, the people who raised me aren't my biological parents. Did they know?"

"None of the parents knew. That was part of the study." He folded his arms across his chest and leaned against his father's desk. "You seem to be taking this well."

"In a sick way, it makes sense. Why not help nature along in the selection process? Why not make sure the most highly evolved people produce offspring?"

"Because it's wrong to manipulate people."

"It's morally shady," she said.

"It's fraud."

"But logical," she said. "Now I understand why Prentice impregnated me. He wants to create a second generation."

"What are you going to do now?"

"I don't know."

All she wanted was to get home, surround herself with silence and figure out how to restructure her life to accommodate a child.

Outside the office door, she heard other mourners arriving. They'd be eating, drinking and sharing memories of Dr. Ray, seeking solace in the company of others. Blake should be out there with his father's friends and colleagues. On the day of his father's funeral, he deserved closure.

She stood and straightened her shoulders. "I'm glad you told me, Blake. I don't blame your father. Not in the least. Dr. Ray was a good man."

"I know."

"Can I have my car keys? I need to go home."

He looked surprised. "I thought you were staying here tonight."

"Thanks for the offer, but I'd rather be alone."

"What about Prentice? I need to get in touch with him."

She took her cell phone from her purse, scanned her contacts and gave him the number for Dr. Prentice's private cell phone. "That's the best I can do."

As he handed over the keys, their hands touched. A spark of static electricity raced up her arm. She wondered if she'd ever see him again.

BLAKE STOOD ON THE PORCH and watched her drive away. He understood her need to be alone. When he had read the e-mail informing him that he wasn't biologically his father's son, Blake had felt as if somebody had punched him in the gut. Eve had a lot more to deal with. Finding out that she was pregnant without her consent or knowledge had to be a hell of a shock. Her life wasn't any of his business, but he hoped she wasn't considering adoption.

A couple of years ago, when he had been in college, his girlfriend had thought she might be pregnant. She'd knocked him for a loop. The only comparable feeling was when he had parachuted for the first time from fifteen thousand feet into enemy territory. He had known his life would be forever changed. That realization had been followed by an irrational sense of awe. Creating a new life? A miracle! When it had turned out to be a false alarm, his relief had mingled with deep regret.

He hoped that Eve would come to see her pregnancy in a positive light. No matter what she decided, he wouldn't abandon her. His dad's dying wish had been for him to take care of her.

Aunt Jean came out to the porch. "Are you coming inside?"

"I need to make a phone call first."

"Well, hurry up. People are asking about you."

His aunt meant well, as did his father's old friends. But Blake didn't see the point in mourning, not while the killer went free. That was why he needed to contact Prentice.

The cops had no leads in solving his dad's murder. They'd found no fingerprints or trace evidence. Because the burglar alarm had been expertly disabled and the safe robbed, they suspected a professional burglar.

Though Blake hadn't revealed the contents of his dad's e-mail, he had mentioned Prentice as a person with a grudge against his father. At his insistence, the homicide detective had spoken to Dr. Edgar Prentice—founder of the world-renowned Aspen IVF and Genetics Clinic in the mountains. Prentice's alibi was airtight; he'd been out of state at the time of the murder.

Of course, he'd cover his butt. Prentice would hire someone else to do his dirty work.

On his military cell phone that wouldn't give away his identity, Blake called the number Eve had given him. Prentice answered immediately. "Who is this?"

"Blake Jantzen. We need to talk."

"How did you get this number?"

"From Eve."

"Thank God you're with her."

Blake hadn't expected that response. The old bastard sounded as if he was concerned about Eve. "Why do you say that?"

"I might have inadvertently put her in danger. Stay with her, Blake. Your father would have wanted—"

"Don't talk to me about my father." *Unless you want to confess to his murder.*

"I should have called, should have made it to the funeral. I'm sorry. Sorry for your loss."

"Where are you?" Blake demanded. "I want to see you."

"That's not possible," Prentice said. "Stay with Eve. Make sure she's safe."

The call was disconnected.

Blake stared at his cell phone as if this piece of plastic and circuitry could tell him the truth. Either Prentice was lying to manipulate him or Eve was truly in danger. He couldn't take chances with her safety.

He ran down the driveway into the cul-de-sac where his father's station wagon was parked across the street. No time to waste. He started the engine.

Earlier, he'd planted a GPS locator on Eve's car in case he needed to find her. It'd be easy to follow her route on the hand-held tracking device he took from his pocket. Activating the system, he saw a reassuring blip. She was taking the back road to Boulder, avoiding traffic on the highway. Would she go to the lab where she worked? Or to her home?

His dad's station wagon wasn't a high performance vehicle, but after he got out of the burbs, he made good time on the two-lane road that ran parallel to the foothills. He passed a pickup and an SUV.

He never should have let her go, should have insisted that she stay at his house. If anything happened to her…

He passed a sedan that was already going over the speed limit. When he hit Boulder, the traffic slowed him down, but he was within a mile of her location when the tracking device showed that she'd parked.

The car in front of him at the stoplight rolled slowly forward. Blake wanted to honk, but he was back in mellow Colorado where car horns were seldom used. He turned right at the next corner and zipped the last few blocks to Eve's house.

Her car was parked at the curb in front of a yellow brick bungalow with a long front yard and mature shade trees on either side. Her unkempt shrubbery—spreading juniper and prickly clumps of potentilla—were good for xeriscaping but too plain for his taste. He preferred his mother's neatly pruned rose garden.

As soon as he opened his car door, he heard a scream.

Chapter Four

Eight minutes ago, Eve had unlocked her front door and entered her house, glad to be home. Her familiar surroundings had greeted her like old, faithful friends. The oversize wingback chair where she did most of her reading had beckoned, and she'd decided to curl up in its cozy embrace and have a cup of tea while her mind wrapped around the complications of being pregnant.

On the way to the kitchen to put on the hot water to boil, she'd patted the back of the comfy sofa with its multicolored throw pillows. She'd passed the round dining-room table.

In the doorway to the kitchen, she froze.

Two men, dressed in suits and neckties, stood between the sink and the refrigerator. Except for their sunglasses, they looked like businessmen at a sales meeting. She desperately wanted to believe that there was a logical reason for them to be here.

Holding her purse in front of her like a shield, she asked, "Who are you? How did you get into my house?"

"The back door was open."

That was probably true. She often forgot to lock up after leaving food for the feral cats that lived in the alley. Still, an unlocked door didn't constitute an invitation to enter. "What do you want?"

"Our employer wants to meet with you."

Were they talking about Prentice? "Who do you work for?"

With a cool smile, the taller man took a step toward her. If he lunged, he could grab her easily. That was when the reality of the situation hit her. These men were a threat.

"It's all right," he reassured her. "We aren't going to hurt you."

Liar! She was in severe danger, and she knew it. Her panicked instincts told her to run, but the men were bigger than she was. Faster. Stronger.

She had to be smarter.

Her mind cleared. She saw the problem as a geometric equation. Her kitchen was a rectangle with the two men in the center. She stood one step inside the doorway. To her left was a table and chairs. To her right, a cabinet jutted into the room. The distance between the corner of the cabinet and the corner of the kitchen table was approximately three feet. If she could block that space, she'd create an obstacle which would slow their pursuit and allow her to escape.

"Come with us, Eve." The tall man spoke in silky tones. "Everything will be explained to your satisfaction."

It took all her self-control to play along with his false civility. "This isn't convenient. Perhaps your employer could call me and make an appointment."

The second man drew a gun from a holster inside his jacket. "Enough playing around. Get over here."

A gun. Oh, God, he had a gun. "Don't shoot me."

Abruptly, she raised one hand over her head. When she lifted the other hand, she swung her arm wide. The tall man was forced to step back or be smacked by her purse. As he shifted his weight, she dropped both hands and yanked a chair from the table to block the three-foot space.

She pivoted and ran. Though she hadn't planned to scream, she heard herself wailing like a siren. Logic told her that she couldn't go faster than a bullet. Would they start shooting? Were they coming after her? She whipped open the front door—fortunately unlocked—and dashed outside. One step from the front stoop, she ran smack into Blake.

Though she was sprinting at full speed, she didn't knock him over. He staggered as he absorbed her velocity. "Are you all right?"

"Two men. One has a gun," she blurted. "We've got to get away."

He reacted forcefully. His left arm wrapped around her midsection, and he yanked her along with him. They were moving back toward the front door. *Wrong way!* They should be fleeing.

"He has a gun," she repeated.

"Heard you the first time."

His calm tone reminded her that he was a commando—specially trained to face danger. She could trust him. Though her pulse pounded and her nerve endings sizzled with fear, she forced herself to stand beside him on the porch instead of running willy-nilly toward her car. "What's next?" she asked.

"Stay."

"You mean, stay here?" She pointed to the concrete of the stoop. "Right here?"

Ignoring her, he was already on the move. He tore open the door to her house and charged inside, directly into the line of fire. His aggressive approach shocked her. He didn't have a weapon. How did he intend to overcome a man with a gun? *He's Special Forces,* she reminded herself. *His aggressive assault must be some sort of tactic.*

She pressed her back against the wall beside the mailbox

and clutched her purse against her chest. *Stay.* It was a simple, unambiguous command. But what if the men in suits left her kitchen and circled around to the front? What if Blake was shot? What if…

Oh, damn. She darted into the house behind him. In her clunky sandals, there was no way she could move stealthily, but she tried not to plod like a rhino. She went right—toward the bookshelves beside the fireplace where she grabbed a poker to use as a weapon. Then she hid behind her wingback reading chair. Peering around the arm, she saw no one. She heard no gunfire.

When Blake entered from the kitchen, his movements were as swift and efficient as a mountain lion on the prowl.

She popped up. "Are they gone?"

He went into attack mode. For a moment, she thought he was going to launch himself at her like a missile. Instead, he waved her toward him. "Come with me. Hurry."

Another quick command, spoken with authority. She jumped to obey. "I couldn't stay on the porch because—"

He grasped her arm and propelled her through the front door, off the porch and across the yard toward a station wagon. He ran around to the driver's side. "Get in."

She barely had time to fasten her seat belt before he was behind the wheel. He flipped the key in the ignition, and the station wagon roared down her quiet residential street like a tank.

"Keep your eyes open," he said. "Look for a black SUV with tinted windows."

"Where were they parked?"

"In the alley behind your house. I saw them pull away."

They were safe. She exhaled slowly, hoping to ease the

tension that clenched every muscle in her body. That brief encounter in her kitchen might have been the scariest thing that had ever happened to her. Though the confrontation only lasted eight minutes, it had felt like hours. According to Einstein, time was relative. Her fear made everything move in slow motion.

She reached into her purse and took out her cell phone. "I should call 911."

"Don't bother," he said. "Getting the cops involved is a waste of time."

Though she had no prior experience with intruders or guns being pointed at her, she was pretty sure he was wrong. "This is a job for the police."

"Did the intruders steal anything?"

"They weren't robbers."

"How do you know?"

"They knew my name and asked me to come with them."

"Not typical of burglars," he said.

"And they were wearing suits and neckties." She shuddered at the memory. "And gloves. The kind of throwaway latex gloves we wear in the lab if we're handling sensitive material."

"Did they break in?"

She frowned. "It wasn't exactly breaking and entering because my back door was unlocked, but they could be charged with…entering."

"You weren't harmed," he said. "What crime would you report to the police?"

"That guy pointed a gun at me. He's dangerous."

"You're right about that." He focused on the road, driving fast through a maze of residential streets. "They could be the men who killed my father."

The unexpectedness of his statement stunned her. The

air squeezed out of her lungs, and she felt herself gasping like a trout out of water. *Those men? Murderers?* She had it fixed in her mind that Dr. Ray was the victim of a burglary gone wrong—being in the wrong place at the wrong time. "You're saying that your father was targeted. That the murderer came after him on purpose. It was premeditated."

"Yes."

She waited for him to explain, but he was too busy watching in all directions and driving too fast. "Could you possibly be more terse?"

"No."

The tires squealed as Blake rounded a corner. "That's them. That's their vehicle."

At the foot of the hill in front of them, about two blocks away, she saw a black SUV. It made a left turn and disappeared from sight, thank goodness. Unless the bad guys doubled back, they were safe.

In a purely counterintuitive manner, Blake zoomed toward the other car. She shouted, "What are you doing?"

"Going after them."

He'd just acknowledged that those men were possibly murderers. "Are you crazy?"

"My dad was murdered. I have few leads and no evidence. Those guys might know something."

"Or they might kill us."

"Try to get the number on their license plate."

He hit the brakes to avoid a collision with a car pulling out of a driveway. At the corner, he had to stop again for schoolkids with backpacks crossing the street.

Finally reaching the corner, he turned in the direction the SUV had headed. This street fed into a main thoroughfare, and the other vehicle had already disappeared in traffic.

"Damn." Blake's right hand clenched into a fist which he pressed against his forehead. His jaw was tight. He winced, and the tiny creases at the corners of his eyes deepened.

She sensed the depth of his frustration. Though she had no desire to ever see either one of those men again, she said, "I'm sorry."

"Me, too."

Dozens of questions popped inside her head. Usually, Eve was good at sorting out variables and assigning rational values, but she didn't have enough information. "Why did you come to my house? Did you know I was in danger?"

"If I'd known, I never would have let you leave. I would never knowingly put you in harm's way."

His military phrasing reassured her; he sounded a bit like her father. "You must have had a reason for showing up on my doorstep."

He made another left turn and drove in the direction of her house. "I called Prentice to set up a meet, and he told me that he might have accidentally put you in danger."

"There are no accidents," she said darkly. If she hadn't been so confused, she would have been furious. Dr. Prentice was at the center of this tornado that had thrown her life into chaos. "Do you think Prentice is involved in your dad's murder?"

"I don't have facts or evidence," he said. "My dad's e-mail talked about the Prentice-Jantzen study. If he went public about the study, Prentice's reputation would be damaged. From what I've learned, the Aspen IVF and Genetics Clinic is big business."

"So your father was a threat."

Blake nodded. "His files pertaining to the study are missing, probably stolen."

"Did the police question Prentice?"

"He has an alibi."

But he could have hired those two men in suits. "You should have told me your suspicions about your father's murder. There's no logical reason for you to withhold information."

He pulled up to a stop sign and turned toward her. His gaze seemed to soften as he placed his hand on her shoulder. "I didn't say anything about the murder because I thought you'd had enough shocks for one day."

"True enough." Finding out that she was pregnant and that her mom and dad weren't her genetic parents were huge issues. "Nonetheless, it might have been useful to know about the potential for danger."

"Don't worry." His voice was gentle. "I won't let anything bad happen to you."

His touch warmed her through the cotton fabric of her jacket as he massaged her shoulder. He gave a light squeeze before turning back toward the road.

While she continued to stare at his perfect profile, the questions inside her head turned to gibberish. She wanted him to hold her and comfort her and tell her that everything was going to be all right. Their brief physical contact had erased her intelligence like a bucket of white paint thrown against a blackboard filled with equations. With one pat on her shoulder, he'd turned her into a dumb blonde.

"When we get back to your house," he said, "I want you to pack a suitcase. You'll be staying with me."

She couldn't put her life on hold. There were important projects at work—schedules to be met and responsibilities to be handled. Though she should have been telling him all those things, all she could manage to say was, "Okay."

Staying with Blake seemed like the most rational plan she'd heard all day.

BACK AT HER HOUSE, Blake stood in the center of her kitchen, which was incredibly clean. Either she was a neat freak or she didn't actually cook. He suspected the latter. He faced her. "I want to reenact what happened while your memory is fresh. They were standing here, right?"

"The shorter one was there. The tall guy was closer." She motioned him toward her. "Move eighteen inches forward."

He did so. "Here?"

"Close enough."

As she explained what had happened, using geometry analogies, he cursed himself for missing his chance to nab these two guys. He should have been faster, should have driven her home and entered her house first.

She pulled the chair down onto the floor and concluded, "Then I ran. And screamed."

"And they didn't come after you?"

Her chin lifted. "Apparently, I outsmarted them by creating an effective obstacle."

Though he had no doubt that her IQ was double that of these two characters, an overturned chair wasn't all that impressive. He motioned for her to start running. "Go ahead and show me what you did next."

When she darted toward the front door, he hurdled the chair. Before her hand was on the doorknob, he caught her arm and spun her around to face him.

Her blue eyes widened as she leaned her back against the closed door and gazed up at him. "You got me."

"And I wasn't even running hard."

"I can explain," she said. "You were ready to chase me, and they weren't. Plus you're taller than them. Longer legs mean you're faster. Or maybe I wasn't moving as fast."

"Or maybe those two guys were incompetent."

They'd taken off like a couple of scared jackrabbits as

soon as they'd realized she wasn't alone. He would have thought Prentice could afford a better grade of thug.

"I still think we should talk to the police," Eve said. "I can identify both of those men. I'm very observant."

"Prove it."

"The taller man was five feet eleven inches tall. He had a gold pinkie ring with an amber stone and his watch had a gold and silver band. Cleft chin. Small ears. High forehead. The other one probably put on some weight recently because the waistband on his trousers was tight."

He watched her lips as she rattled off more details about their shoes and shirts and the cut of their hair. He could have stepped back and given her more space, but he liked being close. "You have a photographic memory."

"It's called eidetic memory or recall, and I'm not one hundred percent. But I'm good with visuals and numbers." She reached toward him and rested the flat of her palm against his chest. "It's a useful skill, especially for investigating. I'm sure we'll find the man who killed your father."

"We?"

"You and me," she said. "With your Special Forces training and my logic, we'll make a really good team."

This plan had to be nipped in the bud. He caught hold of her hand and gently lowered it to her side. No way did he intend to get tied down with a partnership. This was his fight. "I appreciate the offer, but no."

"Why not?"

"The situation is dangerous." He moved away from her. "While I'm investigating, I can't be worried about what's happening to you."

"But you want me to come home with you," she said. "To stay at your house. What am I supposed to be doing while you're investigating?"

His father's last wish was for him to protect Eve. He couldn't put her in jeopardy. "Maybe you could take up knitting."

"And maybe you could go to hell."

"Too late, babe. I'm already there."

"Don't call me babe."

Her eyes flared with righteous anger. He didn't blame her for being ticked off. He hadn't been gentle in rejecting her, but he didn't have time to waste. Clues were fading like footprints on a beach being washed away by the tide. He needed to focus on finding his father's killer. "Pack your things."

"Tell you what, Blake. I'm going to let your condescending, sexist attitude slide for now because I know you're under duress. But make no mistake. My abilities are a valuable resource. You need me."

He watched as she moved past him and turned into the hallway. She was smart, all right. But, in this case, she was wrong. He had never in his life needed anyone.

Chapter Five

No matter how irritated she got, Eve had to accept the fact that Blake was well-trained for situations involving physical violence, and she'd be wise to follow his directions. Still, she didn't want to be totally dependent on him and definitely wanted to have access to her own car while she was staying at his father's house.

When he loaded her suitcase into the back of his station wagon, she said, "I'll drive myself and meet you there."

He slammed the car door closed. "Ever been in a high-speed pursuit?"

"No."

"Do you have training in evasive driving tactics?"

She could see where he was heading. Her shoulders slumped, and she exhaled a sigh. "I'm pretty good at dodging squirrels."

"If those guys see you driving alone, they might try to apprehend you again." He gave her a wink. "You ride with me."

She groaned. Her life had become too dangerous for her to drive her own car. Too dangerous to sleep in her own bed. This was so unfair. When she glanced over her shoulder at her cozy little bungalow with the warm brown bricks and the clean white trim at the windows, an unwanted memory of fear tightened her gut. Those intruders had invaded her privacy, violated her home. Never before had she felt so vulnerable. She wanted bars on the windows and triple locks on the doors. Even then, she didn't know if she'd feel secure. "There's something I need to do before we leave."

She marched up the sidewalk to the front door and went through the living room and dining room to the kitchen where she took a bag of dried cat food from the cupboard. The stray cats in the alley depended on her for food. She couldn't abandon them. Nor could she leave the whole bag by the trash cans in the alley where the raccoons would carry it off.

Later she'd call her neighbor and ask him to take over for her while she was away. And how long would that be? A day? A week? Two weeks? So unfair!

As she went out the back door and down the narrow sidewalk to the gate in the white picket fence, Blake followed. "What are you doing?"

"Taking care of the wildlife. There's a family of cats that live out here."

Instead of scoffing, he spoke in a gentle voice. "You could call animal rescue. I'm sure there are organizations that take care of feral animals."

"I've tried." Four times she'd contacted humane groups. "These little guys don't want to be caught. Even when the cat rescue people manage to pick up one or two, another litter of kittens appears. They multiply like Tribbles."

"Like what?"

She squatted beside a blooming lilac bush and poured cat food into a plastic container. "Tribbles. You know, furry critters that reproduce exponentially. From *Star Trek*."

"You're a Trekkie," he said. "That explains the T-shirt."

When she'd changed out of her too-short skirt, she had

put on black denim jeans and the least obnoxious T-shirt in her closet—blue with a subtle Enterprise emblem above her left breast. If she slipped back into her black jacket, no one would notice the emblem.

"I'm not a psycho fan," she said. "But I've attended a number of science fiction and fantasy cons. You'd probably like them. G.I. Joe is popular again."

As she watched, two gray-striped kittens peeked over the low-hanging lilac boughs and mewed.

"Hi, little guys."

Eve sat back on her heels so she wouldn't scare them. The kittens crept closer to the food, nudging each other. Their yellow eyes were huge in their tiny faces. Their pink noses pushed at the dry food.

Blake squatted beside her. "New members of the feral cat family?"

"I've never seen these two before." The way she figured, there must be a couple of females who were constantly pregnant—no need for frozen embryos with these felines. "Tribbles."

One of the kittens jumped and scurried back into the bushes. The other sat and stared at Eve. A brave little one. Would her child be courageous? And curious?

Slowly, she stretched out her hand, palm up, toward the kitten. The pink nose came closer and closer. With sharp little claws, the kitten batted at her finger, then darted away.

Babies—kittens, puppies and people—had the most remarkable innocence. And so much to learn. Would she be a good teacher? A good mother? Damn it, she couldn't even take care of herself, much less a baby.

Tears welled up, and she bolted to her feet so Blake wouldn't notice that she was crying. He already regarded her as less than useful in terms of his investigation, and she didn't want him to add weepy to his list of complaints.

During the ride back to Denver, she intended to convince him that she ought to be his partner. It was only logical: two minds were better than one.

Sitting in the passenger seat, she waited to speak until they were on the highway and relatively free from the distraction of stop-and-go traffic. Without preface she said, "If Prentice warned you that I was in danger, he must have wanted you to protect me. Therefore, it's unlikely that he sent those two intruders."

Blake stared through the windshield, refusing to respond.

She continued, "Prentice also said that he might have accidentally caused the threat, which implies that he knows who sent them."

Though he still didn't comment, a muscle in his jaw twitched.

"And so," she said, "Prentice must have communicated with someone after he spoke to me. Is there any way we can get his phone records? Or monitor his e-mails?"

Grudgingly, Blake said, "I can't reach him. He won't answer the phone when I call. Supposedly, he's on vacation."

"He talked to me."

"I seriously doubt that he'll set up a meeting with you."

"Probably not." Their conversation hadn't been friendly. "He can't just disappear. Someone at his clinic in Aspen must know where he is."

"They won't rat out their employer. Even if we find him, he's smart enough to use an untraceable phone or encrypted computer."

They were sharing information, and that pleased her. As

long as she didn't talk about his father, she figured Blake would work with her. "When I talked to him, his voice got tense when I hinted that I might give the baby up for adoption. For some reason, Prentice and the person who sent the intruders want me to be a real mother and raise this child. I'd like to find out who was working on this study."

"You think another scientist wants to continue the experiment through you."

"It's possible," she conceded.

But genetic engineering—both the concept and the practice—had greatly evolved over the past twenty-five years. The Prentice-Jantzen study was archaic when compared with new research on the human genome. It simply didn't make scientific sense to continue with an outmoded methodology. "If I give birth to the second generation, who benefits?"

"The father."

His quick response surprised her, though it shouldn't have. The existence of a male sperm donor was, of course, necessary to create a viable embryo. But she had avoided thinking about that part of the equation.

If her child truly was second generation, the father had to be someone else in the initial study. They needed to know the identities of the original superbabies. "We need to see your father's notes on the Prentice-Jantzen study."

"Can't," he said. "That data was stolen in the robbery."

Dr. Ray was murdered and his notes stolen. Surely, not a coincidence.

BY THE TIME THEY GOT BACK to Denver, sunset had colored the skies with fiery red and yellow. A few years ago in Kenya, Blake had seen the body of an elder burned on a funeral pyre in a solemn ceremony. The flames purified and released the soul from the body.

He had buried his father today. And yet, he felt no sense of closure.

Outside his father's house, only a few extra cars were parked on the cul-de-sac. Apparently, most of the mourners had already paid their respects and gone home. "We'll leave your suitcase in the car. It's easier than explaining. I'm pretty sure that Aunt Jean won't approve of you spending the night."

"If you're worried about your reputation," she said coolly, "I'd be happy to tell your aunt that there's no hanky-panky going on."

"Just don't say anything."

"Yes, sir."

She snapped off a sarcastic salute. Oh, yeah, Eve was definitely an army brat. Also a math nerd and genetic genius. And pregnant. His dad had picked one hell of a difficult woman for him to protect.

When he opened the front door for her, he heard *Rhapsody in Blue* being played on the grand piano in the living room. He took two steps on the polished hardwood floor before the music stopped him like an invisible wall of sound. The gliding crescendos held bittersweet memories. "This is one of my dad's favorites."

"Dr. Ray had good taste."

His mom had been the real musician in the family. Almost every day, she practiced at the piano, sometimes Mozart but more often Cole Porter tunes. His dad loved to sing along. Blake remembered the two of them sitting on the piano bench, humming and laughing.

When he was growing up, Mom had tried to include him in their music. First, by teaching him the basics, which he stumbled through. Then, she had learned songs she thought he'd like. He smiled at the memory of her playing Backstreet Boys and Busta Rhymes while she had rapped in her angelic soprano voice.

After she had died, his dad's life had been greatly diminished. Blake should have made more of an effort to get home and spend time with him. Under his breath, he said, "I could have been a better son."

"The down and dirty truth," Eve murmured.

"Did he talk to you about me?"

"He loved you and was proud of you." She tossed her head and her blond hair bounced. "But when you said that you could be better, that was true. Human behavior can always be improved upon."

"Not like math, huh? Numbers are perfect."

Her eyebrows lifted. "You really don't want to get me started on this topic."

The musical selection concluded, and they went into the front room. Seven people stood beside the gleaming rosewood instrument, applauding the pianist. Among the audience, Blake recognized General Stephen Walsh. His close-cropped white hair stood at attention. The array of medals and decorations—evidence of a long, heroic career—dated back to Vietnam when he was an enlisted man. Though General Walsh and his father hadn't seen eye to eye on the treatment of post-traumatic stress disorder in veterans, they had remained friends and occasional golf partners. Walsh was a good man to have as an ally.

The pianist was David Vargas. Blake had only met David briefly but suspected that he might be another of the superbabies in the Prentice-Jantzen Study.

His aunt swooped toward him. "Where on earth have you been? Everyone has been asking about you."

When he introduced Aunt Jean to Eve, his aunt eyed her

casual black denim pants and loafers with disdain. "I saw you at the funeral. And you were at the house earlier."

"I had to leave because I was feeling ill." Eve pulled her black jacket to cover the Trekkie symbol on her T-shirt. "I changed clothes and I'm much better now. Looks like you could use some help putting away the food from the buffet table."

"I certainly could." Aunt Jean smoothed her soft brown hair into the bun at the nape of her long neck. "I'd like to pack most of this up and take it downtown to a mission my church runs. Is that all right with you, Blakey?"

"Sure." He couldn't remember if he'd eaten today. Must have. Aunt Jean had been pushing food at him since he got out of bed.

As the two women carried plates into the kitchen, Blake approached David Vargas, who stood beside the piano.

"You play well," he said. "Professional musician?"

"Music is my hobby," Vargas said. "A way to relax."

He was a sharp dresser—smooth and classy without trying too hard. Though he appeared to be the same age as Blake, his black hair had a streak of white at the right temple. His eyes gleamed like silver dollars.

"How did you know my dad?" Blake asked.

"I was part of a study he did with Dr. Prentice."

Blake's first impression had been correct. "How much do you know about the study?"

"Quite a lot. In my teens, I had an illness that might have been genetic. When my parents consulted with Prentice, I discovered that we didn't share the same DNA."

Blake wondered how many of the others had known the truth about their conception. "Did you learn the identities of your biological parents?"

"Unfortunately, no. It turned out that my illness wasn't

serious and not caused by my DNA. There was no need to track them down."

"Did you continue with the study?"

"I did. I'd like to say that I was motivated by intellectual curiosity, but your father pointed out an emotional reason. He said I have a need for belonging, family and heritage. Though I don't share identical DNA with the other subjects, it felt like we're related, like I have brothers and sisters."

Blake hadn't considered that perspective. Though an only child, he'd never lacked for companions, male and female. When he had joined the army and gone into Special Forces, the men in his platoon had become his brothers. "Did my dad give you any information about the others?"

"He was discreet," Vargas said. "But I'm guessing that you and I share a similar birth history."

"Correct."

They exchanged an assessing gaze. Blake was a couple of inches taller and carried fifteen pounds more muscle. If it ever came to a physical fight between them, he had the clear advantage.

He wondered how Vargas had used his genetic gifts. His clothes were too expensive for an academic, so he probably hadn't gone into teaching or research. Though he held himself with the confidence of a surgeon, he had the kind of charisma that came from working with other people.

"Finance," Vargas said, answering his unspoken question. "I made my first million before I was twenty. Our current economy makes for some fascinating challenges."

"But you're doing okay."

"More than okay."

"Good for you." He didn't want to get competitive,

but he also didn't want to hear about a balance sheet that showed billions in profit.

Vargas glanced toward the buffet table where Eve was trying to carry three casserole dishes at the same time. "What about her? What's her story?"

Blake watched Eve's balancing act, which was definitely not an example of genius. She'd already smeared a glob of melted cheese on the front of her Trekkie T-shirt. "What makes you think she's one of us?"

"Playing the odds. She's the right age and must have had a relationship with your father. What does she do?"

"Mathematician. She works at Sun Wave Labs in Boulder."

"You came in together," Vargas said. "Are you dating?"

"Me and Eve? No." *Hell, no.*

He straightened his shirt collar. "I'd like to get to know her better. Do you mind?"

Hell, yes. Blake's gut clenched. *Back off, Finance Man.* But he had no claim on Eve. "She's all yours."

As he watched, David Vargas moved in like a python coiling around its prey. No way in hell could Eve handle this super-rich, super-charming guy. He'd sweep her off her loafers.

Blake felt as if he should warn her, but Eve's affections weren't his problem. He took his cell phone from his pocket and placed a call to the homicide detective investigating his father's murder. Might as well report the break-in at Eve's house. The detective might get useful fingerprints.

He heard Eve giggle as she talked to Vargas. Blake had no right to feel possessive about her, but he was secretly glad that she'd be spending the night here at his house. Far away from Vargas.

Chapter Six

Eve stood under the light on the porch and watched as David Vargas pulled away from the curb. His hybrid SUV was packed with floral arrangements that he'd promised to drop off at local hospitals and nursing homes, but she really didn't think he'd make those deliveries himself. Vargas presented himself as a very important guy—a legend in his own mind—who had battalions of assistants to take care of life's pesky details.

When he had first started talking to her and helping her clear the buffet table, she'd been puzzled. Why would somebody like him—a rich and powerful mover and shaker—show interest in somebody like her? Guys like Vargas dated supermodels. Why would he waste his considerable charm on a mathematician in a Star Trek T-shirt?

Not being one for subtlety, she'd asked him point-blank. "Why?"

"The Prentice-Jantzen study," he'd said without losing a glimmer of his suavity. "I believe we were both subjects."

Did Blake know about this? She'd wanted to signal him, but he had been deep in conversation with the general. "How much have you found out about the study?"

"Enough to know that we're genetically superior. You and I are unique."

"Except for the others."

"There were twenty-four subjects," he had said. "Only two women."

She'd filed away that bit of information for future reference. "Do you know any of the others?"

"Just you and Blake." The overhead light had glistened on the streak of silver in his hair. "And I only figured that out today when I saw you both at the funeral. You're the right age. You had a connection to Dr. Ray. And there's something remarkable about you."

"Me? I don't think so." There was nothing special about her, except for the pregnant virgin bit.

"I'd like to see you again, Eve."

"Give me a call."

"I will," he had promised.

Apparently, her genetically engineered birth made her a hottie. Might be nice to have Vargas fawning over her. She could do a lot worse than dating a handsome, intelligent, wealthy, musically gifted man.

Aunt Jean bustled outside with her purse slung over her shoulder and her jacket tucked under her arm. "I need to get going before all this food turns bad. Will you be all right?"

"I'm fine." Eve remembered that Blake hadn't wanted his aunt to know she was spending the night. "I'll get Blake to drive me home later."

"I'm worried about him. Losing his father like this, well, it's hard." She made a tsk-tsk noise. "Our Blakey is so big and strong we sometimes forget that he has a sensitive streak. Like his mother."

Though Eve hadn't seen much evidence of sensitivity

in Blake, she didn't object. "It's hard on you, too. Losing a brother."

"Ray and I weren't close. He was ten years older than me." Her lips pinched together, and Eve had the impression that Aunt Jean would have had quite a bit to say if she'd been the sort of woman who spoke ill of the dead. "I'll pray for my brother. And for Blakey. He's the only family I've got left."

He should have been out here on the porch, saying a proper goodbye to his aunt. "I wonder where he's disappeared to."

"He was always like that. Going off by himself." She patted Eve on the arm. "See if you can get him to open up."

Eve seriously doubted that was going to happen. Blake held himself like a closed fist.

After Jean left, she went back into the house and closed the door. With Dr. Ray gone, no one really lived here anymore. The house felt desolate. "Blake?"

If he wanted to slink off by himself, fine with her. But he was supposed to be her bodyguard. If somebody tried to break in, she was totally unprotected.

Her footfalls echoed on the hardwood floor as she went through the living room, turning on the lights that Jean had just extinguished. Where was he? She needed to talk to him, to get this investigation rolling.

On the granite countertop in the kitchen, she found the brown leather condolence book that guests had signed at the funeral service and at the reception. Several pages were filled with signatures and brief remembrances.

Tucked into the back of the book was a note from Aunt Jean. At the top, she'd written emphatically: "Blake, send thank-you cards." Then came a list of names of those who had brought flowers or casseroles. Eve's mother would have done exactly the same thing. It was protocol.

Eve had a different take on the condolence book. Some of the people who had signed could be suspects. She started at the top of the first page and scanned all the names, committing them to memory. Vargas had a strong, dramatic scrawl. General Walsh's handwriting was shaky, causing her to wonder about the state of his health. Someone named Peter Gregory added an odd comment: "Rock on, Dr. Ray." There was another Gregory. Peter's father? Her eyes stopped on Dr. Trevor Latimer. She'd seen that name listed outside the clinic where Prentice had taken her for the supposed examination when he had implanted the embryo.

She knew the clinic address but not the phone number. When she'd arrived to meet Prentice, it had been after closing time. No one but Prentice and his assistant had been there. That clinic might be a good starting point for their investigation.

With the book in hand, she prowled down the hallway toward Dr. Ray's office. No doubt, he had an address file in here. She could start researching these other names.

When she opened the door, she saw Blake sitting on the leather sofa. He was hunched over, elbows on knees, staring into a glass of amber liquid. He drained the dregs and poured more whiskey from an open bottle on the coffee table in front of him. "Are they gone?"

She could have given him a hard time for not treating his aunt with the proper respect, but she could see that he was already doing a fine job of beating himself up. "Everybody's left."

He glared at her with bloodshot eyes. "Even your boyfriend?"

"Who?"

"The financial whiz kid." His upper lip curled in a sneer. "Vargas."

"For your information, Vargas is one of us, one of the superbabies. And he seems to know about the study. Maybe he can help us investigate."

"You and I aren't investigating together. I'm doing this alone."

She thought they'd already gotten around this barrier. "I don't mind you being stubborn, but don't be a jerk. I can't help being involved. Men with guns broke into my house."

"Stubborn, huh?"

"And a jerk."

He rose to his feet, snatched the tumbler and took another aggressive gulp. "You didn't tell Vargas my suspicions about the murder, did you?"

"Give me some credit." She knew a thing or two about strategy. "I know better than to blab. Loose lips sink ships."

"Well said, army brat."

She'd seen her share of troops coming home from battle, struggling for control. Blake was on the edge. He'd buried his father today, and he was deeply troubled by the murder.

She needed for him to focus. Holding up the condolence book, she said, "I have a lead. I started going through the names of people who came to the funeral and—"

"Vargas is the kind of guy who needs to be in charge. He's the boss man."

Not unlike Blake. Both he and David Vargas were alpha males—intelligent and charismatic. Both were natural leaders. "Are you jealous?"

"Of him? No way. Well, maybe I'd like to know his tailor. Or his barber." With his finger, Blake drew a line on his temple. "Maybe I should get myself a silver streak. Skunk hair."

She slammed the condolence book down on the coffee table. The resulting thud was loud enough to compel Blake's attention. Though she empathized with his need to mourn, they didn't have time for self-pity.

Circling the coffee table, she stood before him. "You need to shape up. And we'll start by pouring a gallon of coffee down your throat."

"What if I don't want coffee?" He leaned toward her. "Are you going to make me drink it?"

"Oh. Hell. Yes."

His nose was six inches away from hers. She stared into his chocolate-brown eyes and saw a subtle shift. He was looking at her with a strange awareness, as if really seeing her for the first time, as if he liked what he saw.

He actually licked his lips. His right hand slipped around her waist. First Vargas. Now Blake. What was going on here? Was she exuding some kind of irresistible pheromone?

She could have moved away, could have resisted.

But when he pulled her close, she melted into his embrace.

Never before had she been kissed like this. Though she was a virgin, she had enough experience to know what it meant to be aroused. Her blood rushed. Her pulse rate accelerated. Goose bumps shivered up and down her arms and thighs.

Blake held her tight, tilting her so her back arched slightly. His hand cupped her bottom and merged her loins with his. When she rubbed against him, the friction generated waves of heat that spread like an atomic reaction and exploded, not with a bang but a whoosh, like a prolonged sigh.

His other arm angled around her upper body and pulled

her tighter, so tight that her breasts crushed against his hard, muscled chest.

His mouth tasted of whiskey, an exotic flavor that she usually didn't care for. This taste was different, and she loved the sharp tang, couldn't get enough. Hungrily, she parted her lips and drew his tongue into her mouth.

Her senses heightened. She ran her fingers through his hair and reveled in the exquisite texture. His mysterious, utterly masculine aroma tantalized her nostrils. Her ears rang with precisely tuned chimes. Each note vibrated through her.

When her eyelids opened, she was dazzled by his perfect features. She inhaled his breath, drew it deep inside her lungs. She was meant to be joined with Blake. He was the man she'd been waiting for.

His grasp loosened.

She stepped backward. Still caught up in the pure pleasure of his kiss, she was unable to function normally. She couldn't speak, couldn't think. Her mind—usually sharp and clear—blurred in wonderful confusion.

Struggling to regain her equilibrium, she tried to choke out a coherent sentence. "We should, um, do something. I think. Do you?"

"Absolutely," he said.

She could tell by the flush of color on his cheeks and his grin that he'd been similarly affected by their kiss. But Blake had an excuse. He was half-drunk.

"Coffee," she said, grasping at the threads of reality.

Before she could float from the room, he grounded her with a statement of fact. "I talked to the homicide detective looking into my father's murder."

The importance of their investigation paled when compared to that incredible kiss. "Uh-huh."

"He's going to your house in Boulder. The crime scene investigators will look for forensic evidence."

The facts pierced her romantic haze like darts into a balloon. Her sensual epiphany began to deflate. "They won't find fingerprints. The men were wearing gloves."

"There might be a hair. A footprint." His gaze turned toward his father's desk. "They didn't find anything useful in here."

Back to earth, she realized that they were standing in the middle of a crime scene. The other time she'd been in his father's office she hadn't been paying attention. Her thoughts had been too distracted by finding out she was pregnant. "What were you doing in this room?"

"For one thing," he said, "my aunt refuses to come in here."

"Cut her some slack. Aunt Jean is a nice woman."

"I know. And I'm glad she's praying for me."

He didn't look glad. His features had become as rigid as Mount Rushmore. In less than a minute, he'd gone from "at ease" to strict "attention." His chin pulled back. His spine was ramrod stiff. It didn't seem possible for him to erase the passion they'd shared so quickly. "Was there another reason you came in here?"

"The whiskey bottle in the lower desk drawer," he admitted. "And I wanted to visualize what happened. Recreate the scene."

"Like we did at my house." She moved toward the windows, giving herself a wider perspective. *Don't think about sex. It's not appropriate.* "Tell me about the forensic evidence."

"As if you were my partner."

"Exactly."

Grudgingly, he said, "My father was seated behind the

desk. Shot three times in the chest. He had a gun in his hand."

"Was his gun fired?"

"Four times."

Blake pointed out the bullet holes in the wall. The pitted marks, circled in black to facilitate forensic photos, were above the framed photographs on the wall. Almost at the ceiling. Either Dr. Ray was a terrible marksman or he hadn't been trying to hit his target.

She asked, "Signs of a struggle?"

"None."

"Do you have a theory about what happened?"

He stepped away from the sofa and stood beside her. When his arm came close to hers, he leaned away, almost as if he wanted to avoid touching.

"Shortly before he was murdered, Dad sent me an e-mail, which explains why he was at the desk. The person who broke in bypassed the alarm system."

"Suggesting a professional burglar." She glanced at the wall safe behind the desk. The heavy door stood ajar. "What happened to the contents of the safe?"

"Gone."

Eve understood why the police suspected a burglary gone wrong. The evidence indicated that an armed intruder had disabled the security to enter the house and proceeded to the office with the intention of robbing the safe. "Did he keep valuables in there?"

"Not to my knowledge," he said. "The safe was for important documents, like deeds and investment information. Since all his information on the Prentice study is missing, I suspect those papers were in the safe."

That was why he'd said his father's research was stolen. "Was anything else taken?"

"His laptop."

Seeking a different visual angle, she went behind the desk. In spite of the clutter, she discerned an order. Unopened mail and magazines were on the left side. The file folders and papers on the right showed signs of use. A framed photograph of Blake and his mother leaned against those piles.

Blood stained the leather chair and the worn Persian carpet. Splatters dotted the desktop clutter in an irregular pattern. "Some of these files have been moved."

"I've shuffled through these papers. Nothing of interest. Mostly, it's outdated correspondence and notes from conferences. No patient files."

"Where did he keep his patient files?"

"At his office downtown. He shares space with a couple of other shrinks. I've already been there to search for the Prentice-Jantzen research."

"What about patient confidentiality? I'm surprised they'd let you go through the files."

"They didn't," he said. "But I stood over the secretary's shoulder as she flipped through documents and scanned the computer."

She noticed that the center area of the desk was cleared; that must have been where Dr. Ray placed his laptop. Without touching, she leaned down to examine the surface which was dotted with blood. "Apparently, he moved his laptop before he was shot."

"Why do you think so?"

"If the laptop had been on the desk, there would have been a blank space in the spatters."

"Good observation."

"Suppose he put the laptop in the safe," she said, "because he knew it contained valuable information—data that he didn't want to fall into the wrong hands."

"Which meant that he knew someone was after it." His

voice took on an edge of enthusiasm. "My dad was aware of the threat. He knew they were coming for him."

Now they were getting somewhere. "What else can you tell me about the forensic evidence?"

"He was shot in the heart. His death was almost instantaneous. Which means he wouldn't have had time to retaliate with four shots."

She drew the logical conclusion. "Dr. Ray fired first. Before he was hit."

"And he aimed high."

The logical action when being attacked would have been to shoot directly at your assailant. "What might cause your father to sit at his desk and fire four shots toward the ceiling?"

"Maybe he heard the intruder in the hallway and fired his gun to warn him off. Before he was hit, he had enough time to punch the speed dial and alert the security company."

Without sitting in the bloodstained desk chair, she pantomimed those actions. First, she pretended to hit the button on the phone, then she cocked her finger like a gun. "Like this. Bang, bang, bang, bang."

Blake moved to the doorway, playing the role of the assassin. "The killer steps inside and shoots."

"But if your father knew he was being attacked, he would have ducked behind the desk for cover."

"Unless he recognized his attacker. That might have caused him to pause for a fatal few seconds."

Their logic was beginning to create a complete picture. "He hides his laptop in the safe. Then, he hears an intruder, calls security and fires warning shots. Then he stops himself from shooting when he sees someone he knows. The killer wasn't an anonymous intruder or a burglar or even a hitman. This was someone he recognized. A coworker. Or a patient."

"Or someone he'd known from birth," Blake said darkly. "One of the subjects from the study."

Someone like them. A highly intelligent individual bent on murder.

Chapter Seven

In the kitchen, Blake leaned against the oak cabinets and watched as Eve precisely measured coffee grounds and poured them into the basket of the coffeemaker. She'd taken off her shoes, revealing slender, well-shaped feet. He had to wonder what the rest of her body looked like under the shapeless Trekkie T-shirt and loose-fitting denim slacks.

She sure as hell didn't work at being attractive. Hers was an unintentional beauty. Potent, nonetheless. Damn it, he shouldn't have kissed her. That was just plain wrong.

"Do you think half a pot is enough?" she asked.

"Doesn't matter." He wished that she'd stop treating him like a drunk. It took more than a couple of shots to affect him. "Coffee doesn't really sober you up."

"Is that the voice of experience talking?"

"The only real effect of caffeine on alcohol is to make you a more wide-awake drunk."

"I'll settle for wide-awake." She turned on the coffee-maker and faced him. "Are there any security measures we should be taking?"

"I turned on the burglar alarm."

"The same system that the killer disconnected before?"

"This is an upgrade." The security company had been

apologetic about the failure of their equipment and had installed a state-of-the-art digital system that supposedly couldn't be breached without setting off buzzers. Still, she had a point. Blake knew better than to trust everything to technology. "Plus, you've got me as a bodyguard."

Her wide mouth stretched in a grin. "Is that supposed to be reassuring?"

"Seriously, Eve. I can protect you."

"Seriously? You're not armed."

Actually, that wasn't true. He'd borrowed a handgun from the general, which he'd hidden under the pillows in his bedroom. He didn't need an arsenal to protect her, and she needed to understand that. "I always carry a knife."

She challenged him, "Are you any good with it?"

He whirled, grasped the handle of a butcher knife in a block on the counter, pulled it and threw. The blade stuck in the oak door frame, exactly where he'd been aiming. "How's that?"

"You made your point." She shrugged. "No pun intended."

Her nonchalance was annoying; he'd been going for shock and awe. "Come on, Eve. That was one hell of an impressive display. At least give me an 'atta boy.'"

"Can you show me how to do it?"

"Depends. How's your coordination?"

"Not bad." She padded across the tiled kitchen floor to the refrigerator. The shelves inside were packed with plastic containers of leftovers. In the crisper, she found a bag of oranges which she scattered on the countertop. Giving him a smirk, she started juggling a couple of them.

"Only two?"

"Getting warmed up."

She added a third orange. Her concentration was intense.

The tip of her tongue poked against her lower lip as she rotated the oranges in the air. Damn, she was cute.

"How about four?" he teased.

"Three's good." Her hips swayed in rhythm with the motion of her arms. "I only do prime numbers."

"Like five," he said.

"Think you can outdo me?"

She tossed the oranges to him, one at a time. Without missing a beat, he continued to juggle. Three were easy. When she flipped a fourth toward him, he worked it in.

"Atta boy," she said as she opened the refrigerator door again.

In his peripheral vision, he saw her take something else from the fridge. A small white oval. An egg.

Before she could throw it, he stopped juggling, allowing the oranges to thud to the floor. He stepped forward, took both her hands and squeezed them around the egg. The shell cracked but nothing oozed out.

"Hard-boiled," she said, looking up at him with mischief in her eyes. "I put them away when I was helping your aunt. Did you really think I'd pelt you with a raw egg?"

"The thought crossed my mind."

That wasn't the only thing he was thinking. Standing close to her, he remembered the way her body had molded against his. She'd felt too good in his arms; it couldn't happen again.

He forced himself to release her hands. Pacing across the floor, he yanked the blade from the door frame and returned it to the butcher block. "Since you're the target, it's probably best if we sleep in the same room."

Though her grin didn't slip, her eyes widened. He imagined that she was calculating her response. "What are you suggesting?"

"Sleep," he said. "Anything more would be wrong."

"Wrong?" Her smile vanished. "That seems like a strong word."

Their kiss in his father's office was a mistake. He hadn't considered the ramifications. Apparently, neither had she.

When he looked into her lovely, intelligent blue eyes, the heat in the kitchen shot up by several degrees. The delicious aroma of freshly brewing coffee swirled around them. If he reached out, he could touch her, pull her close against him. He was physically attracted to her. And he shouldn't be.

"Genetically," he said, "we might be brother and sister."

Her brother? Eve stared at him with a mixture of disbelief and disgust. Had she kissed her brother? And enjoyed it? "You're creeping me out, Blake."

"Think about it. Prentice drew from a limited number of volunteers. They had to meet certain requirements in terms of physical health, mental acuity and fertility. The testing wasn't all that easy. This was over twenty years ago when the IVF process was relatively experimental. Of course, lots of guys would be willing to participate—"

"But not so many women."

The procedure for harvesting eggs was more complicated than the male side of the fertilization equation. How had Prentice convinced these women to be involved? She tried to imagine how she'd react if approached by a scientist and asked to donate the most personal, most private part of herself.

"Eve? Are you all right?"

"I'm thinking." *Be logical.* If Prentice had asked her to volunteer to be pregnant, she would have certainly refused. Raising a child changed the entire focus of her life and involved a great deal more than mere biology. But giving up an egg? Or two? Or ten? "I would have done it. In the name of science and to help other women who were infertile, there's a more than sixty-six percent chance that I would have said yes."

"Like your biological mother."

Here was evidence: her values were similar to those of the nameless, faceless woman who had donated her egg. Eve wondered what other traits they shared. Had her mother been a scientist? More important, was she also Blake's mother? There had to be a way to calculate the odds.

She remembered an earlier conversation. "There were twenty-four superbabies in the study."

"How do you know that?"

"Vargas told me."

At the mention of Vargas's name, Blake scowled. "Keep in mind that he might also be your brother."

"Whatever." She wasn't attracted to Vargas, certainly not in the same way she was drawn to Blake. "It does seem likely that there were fewer female volunteers—each being given a drug that caused them to produce several eggs per cycle. The question is—how many? Four? Fourteen?"

"Without the documentation, there's no way of knowing."

She hated the uncertainty, hated the possibility that she and Blake could be genetically related. Finally, she'd found a man who rang her chimes, and he might be her brother.

"It can't be," she said emphatically. "We don't look anything alike. Don't have the same coloring. My eyes are blue. Yours are brown."

"That's not proof."

Reaching up, she pushed back the hair on his forehead.

"Ha! You don't have a widow's peak, but I do. That's a dominant characteristic." She grabbed his chin and turned his head. "Oh, no, we both have detached ear lobes."

He shoved her hands away. "Stop groping me."

"I'm not." If he was her brother, groping would be sick. "I need to develop a probability model for you and me utilizing secondary physical traits."

"Face it," he said. "Until we have access to information about our biological parents, we won't know for sure."

"DNA," she said triumphantly. "All we have to do is compare our DNA."

"The testing could take a while."

"I've already had my DNA profiled." She'd volunteered for a study in grad school. "It'll take some digging, but I can get the results. How about you?"

"The army requires that you give blood for DNA testing, and I know my sample has been processed."

He raised his coffee mug to his lips, trying to hide the tension in his mouth. Again, she marveled at how easily she could read his expressions. She knew, without asking, that the processing of his DNA was related to an unfortunate event, probably to get positive identification for a soldier killed in action. "I'm sorry," she said.

"Sarge was a good man. He gave his life to save the rest of the platoon. We were forced into hiding for ten days."

During which time, the army must have compared his remains with the DNA of the other missing soldiers. Her heart ached for Blake's sadness and his sorrow. The empathy she felt was painful, as if they were truly close. As close as a sister?

"We need to get those DNA results," she said. "And we need to move our investigation forward. I don't want to hear any more grumbling about how you always work alone. We're in this together."

"Got it, sis."

"Don't," she snapped. "Don't joke about it."

He finished his coffee and rinsed the cup in the sink. "Where do we start? You said you had a lead."

"Dr. Trevor Latimer." She went to the kitchen table, flipped open the condolence book and ran her finger down the page until she was pointing to the name. "Not only was he at the funeral, but I recognized his name from the clinic where Prentice met me for my supposed examination. Do you know him?"

"We probably shook hands at the funeral. I don't remember."

"He knew your father. And he knows Prentice. I say we start with him. Maybe your father had an address book."

Blake gave a quick nod. "I've got a better idea. Follow me."

She trailed him down the hallway toward his father's office. When she found herself checking out his broad shoulders and tight butt, she groaned and looked away. Sisters do *not* notice if their brothers have cute bottoms.

He opened a door halfway down the hall, and she followed him into his bedroom. As soon as she looked at the queen-size bed with the navy-blue comforter, her imagination flashed an image of Blake sprawled out on that bed. *Wrong!* She turned toward the wall and faced an array of framed photos. The tidy grouping made her think this was his mother's decorating work.

In a group picture of men in army fatigues, Blake stood with his buddies. All were shirtless. She couldn't take her eyes off Blake's muscular chest and six-pack abs. He had an incredible body. *Wrong!*

Standing at the desk, he powered up his laptop. "Let's check out our suspect."

His bedroom was fairly small. Apart from the chair

behind the desk, there was nowhere to sit except for the bed, and she decided against lounging there. She fidgeted. "You said something about sleeping in the same room. That's not going to work for me."

"Not in here," he agreed. "The guest bedroom next door has two single beds."

"Terrific," she muttered. They'd be separated by probably four or five feet of wide-open space. No temptation at all? Ha! "Anything on Latimer?"

He read from the computer screen. "He's an M.D., an OB-GYN who specializes in treating infertility. That explains how he'd know Prentice."

When Latimer allowed Prentice to use the facilities at his clinic, he might just have been doing a favor. "Any indication of how he knew your father?"

"I'm looking at Latimer's photo. He wears glasses. Looks young."

She moved toward the computer so she could see the picture, which meant she was also closer to Blake. Carefully keeping a space between them, she read the biography of Trevor Latimer. "He's twenty-five years old, born in New Mexico."

"Like us. And Vargas."

Latimer had the smarts to be a superbaby. A doctor with his own clinic at age twenty-five had to be a genius. "I guess that answers the question of how he knew your father. He was part of the study."

"We should pay him a visit."

"Now?"

When Blake stood up, his arm accidentally brushed against hers, and they both took a step backward. He checked his G-Shock wristwatch which was typical wear for Special Forces. "It's not even nine o'clock."

It felt much later. This day had been packed with

revelations—emotional highs and lows and everything in between. She knew that from this day forward, her life was changed. "I'm ready if you are."

He strode to his bed, reached under the pillow and pulled out an automatic pistol. "Ready."

Chapter Eight

Blake wasn't drunk, not even close, but he left the driving to Eve and rode shotgun in the passenger seat of his dad's station wagon. As she drove, he scanned the streets, looking for any anomaly that might turn into a threat: a person in a parked car, headlights following them, a loiterer with a cell phone.

Nothing he saw set off alarm bells.

Eve merged smoothly onto the highway leading toward downtown Denver. "How am I doing?" she asked.

"Smooth and steady."

"I'm a good driver," she said. "And an excellent partner."

To tell the truth, he was glad to have her working with him. During the past several days since he had returned to town, he'd been butting his head against stone walls. The homicide detectives and their forensic teams responded quickly to his questions and had given priority to the autopsy so the body could be released for burial. But they'd been convinced from the start that his dad was the victim of a burglary gone wrong. Their investigation was cursory at best.

Likewise, the family attorney wasn't much help. His focus was on putting his dad's affairs in order.

His aunt Jean had advised him to accept his dad's passing and move on with his life.

Until he hooked up with Eve, his investigation had gone nowhere. Together, they were taking action. It felt good.

He leaned back in the passenger seat and considered Trevor Latimer as a suspect. If his dad was killed to suppress information about the study, there had to be something in those stolen documents that threatened Dr. Latimer. Or maybe the young OB-GYN was a loyal protégé of Prentice, willing to kill to protect his mentor from embarrassing, possible actionable revelations. Why did Latimer come to the funeral? Revisiting the scene of his crime?

In central Denver, Eve parked at the curb outside an impressive two-story, white stucco house with a cupola on top of the red-tiled roof. She gave a low whistle. "Looks like Dr. Latimer has done pretty well for himself."

"Like Vargas," Blake said. "How come I didn't get biological parents with the millionaire gene?"

"Me, neither."

"Does that mean we're kind of alike?"

She punched his arm. "I'm not your sister."

Her voice was angry, frustrated. He could tell that she was a lot more shaken up by their possible genetic relationship than he was. To be sure, a brother and sister shouldn't be hot for each other. He shouldn't be yearning to touch her, shouldn't be turned on by her scent or the way her mouth twisted when she was thinking. But this wasn't the first time in his life that he had to stifle his sexual appetite. He could cope.

Together they proceeded along the curved sidewalk leading to the front door. The meticulous landscaping, groomed flower beds and artistically pruned shrubs were well-lit. A wrought-iron railing marked one edge of the path.

A golden light shone from the left side of the house. Through the polished glass of the bay window, he saw a tall, thin man with glasses playing a violin. The bluesy, mellow tones of "Harlem Nocturne" were audible. A piano accompanied.

Eve paused to listen. "Beautiful."

And sexy. The music made him think of summer nights and sultry, forbidden desires. It made him think of Eve in stilettos and a black silk slip. He blinked to erase that inappropriate and totally unrealistic image. She probably didn't own a pair of high heels.

At the carved, double door, he rang the bell. The music continued as the door was opened by a stocky, balding man in a button-down blue shirt and dress slacks. A five-o'clock shadow darkened his jowls. "May I help you?"

"We're here to see Dr. Latimer. He was at my father's funeral today. I'm Blake Jantzen."

"Yes, I recognize you."

"Were you at the funeral?"

"I'm Dr. Latimer's driver. Please come in. I'll see if he's available."

He and Eve waited in the tiled entryway. The design of the house reminded him of a soft-serve, vanilla ice-cream cone—all rounded edges and curved archways. From where they stood, they could see through the front room to a series of French doors that opened onto a garden, also well-lit. When the music stopped, the resulting silence felt ominous. He thought of Nero fiddling while Rome burned.

Blake unbuttoned his blazer, giving him access to the holster he wore on his hip. He counted the seconds. Latimer was obviously here; they'd seen him through the window. If he refused to meet with them, it could only be because he had something to hide.

The driver returned and beckoned to them. "This way."

The study with the bay window was furnished in earthy southwestern tones. The gracious proportions of the room and the floor-to-ceiling bookcase gave the impression of solidity, as if this home had been here for a hundred years.

The tall, blond man he'd seen through the window tilted his head and looked down his nose through his glasses. He held his violin in his left hand and extended his right. "I'm surprised to see you, Blake. Again, my deepest condolences for your loss."

His linen shirtsleeves had been rolled up to the elbow, revealing thin forearms and long, skeletal fingers. Nonetheless, his grip was strong.

Standing behind a portable keyboard was someone else who had attended the funeral. His name was Peter Gregory. Blake had known him since they were teenagers but hadn't seen him for a couple of years. Peter's style had changed. He wore about four pounds of silver jewelry in rings, cuff bracelets, neck chains, earrings and a nose ring. Everything else was black and tight. His black hair stuck out in spikes. Eyeliner circled his pale gray eyes.

Blake introduced him to Eve. "Peter Gregory. His dad shares an office with mine."

When he bumped fists with Eve, she said, "Your father is a psychiatrist. That must be interesting."

"Not the word I'd use for daddy dearest."

When she shook hands with Latimer, he noticed that the doctor didn't move from where he stood. People came to him, not the other way around. He held on to her hand and leaned closer to her, squinting behind his thick glasses.

His lips thinned in a smile. "Are congratulations in order, Ms. Weathers?"

Eve snatched her hand away. "How did you know?"

"I'm an OB-GYN, specializing in infertility. I've come to recognize the glow that comes when a woman is pregnant."

"Do you know Dr. Edgar Prentice?" she asked.

"Oh, yes. For a long time."

When he reached back and felt the arm of the chair before sitting, Blake understood Latimer's aloof manner. He was visually impaired. That explained the bright lights and the railing by the path.

What Blake didn't readily comprehend was the connection with Lou Gregory's son. The aristocratic Latimer and the leather-clad, obviously antisocial Goth guy were a mismatch. "How do you two know each other?"

"We met at the cemetery," Latimer said. "After we talked, we discovered we were both part of an IVF study that your father did with Prentice."

His dad's funeral had pulled in the superbabies like a magnet. Not an unexpected result. Each of these subjects had communicated with his father once a year for the survey; he had been part of their lives.

"Us, too," Eve said as she pointed to herself and to him. "We were part of the study."

Blake watched both men for their reactions. Peter shrugged as if he couldn't care less, while Latimer seemed mildly interested.

"I must admit," Latimer said, "I never understood the purpose of the study, other than tracking a group of subjects born at about the same time. But I did enjoy my talks with your father. Dr. Ray employed techniques for the treatment of post-traumatic stress disorder to help me cope with my recent disability."

Eve settled at the end of the sofa nearest him. "Were you injured?"

"My, you're direct." He turned his head toward her. "What's your profession? Scientist?"

"Mathematician," she said. "I didn't mean to be pushy about your injury."

"Just curious," he said. "I understand. Three years ago in Indonesia, I was infected by a virus that caused nerve damage and degeneration of my vision. I'm legally blind."

She reached out and touched his hand. "Will you recover?"

"I like to believe there's a possibility."

"Hope is good."

Her smile was bright and friendly. Though Blake wouldn't have chosen such a straightforward approach, he thought she was doing a good job getting Latimer to open up.

Peter Gregory was another story. He'd gone behind his keyboard. His fingers floated above the keys as if playing a silent melody.

The stocky driver stepped into the room. "Can I bring anyone a drink?"

Though Eve looked as if she was going to say yes, Blake quickly refused for both of them.

"Nothing for me," Peter said. "It's time for me to hit the road."

"So soon?" Latimer's disappointment was evident in his voice. "Please come back any time. I very much enjoyed sharing my music with you."

Peter came out from behind the keyboard and approached Latimer. "Before I go, may I? One more time?"

"Of course." Latimer handed over the finely grained rosewood violin. To Eve, he explained, "This rare instrument was crafted by Scolari of Cremona. When Peter and I talked, he couldn't wait to see the Scolari."

With the violin settled under his chin, Peter flexed his ringed fingers and drew the bow across the strings. The resulting sound had a deep, incredible resonance. Peter closed his eyes and played. Each note trembled with distinct clarity. Blake recognized the piece as a concerto his mother had played on the piano, but the music truly came to life on the violin. Peter was brilliant. Like Vargas. And Latimer. It couldn't be coincidence that three of the superbabies were gifted musicians.

As the last notes faded, Eve exhaled a deep, appreciative sigh. "Amazing. You've got to be a professional."

"That's right." He carefully placed the violin on its stand and faced them. "I'm Pyro."

"Wow, I've heard of you," Eve said. "One of the guys I work with is a big fan. You do techno-metal rock, right?"

"I'm not into labels." He sneered. "If I was, I'd call our music post-apocalyptic punk with a metal edge."

"I know one of your songs. 'Eat the Beast.' Right?"

He gave a short laugh as he went back to his keyboard. "It's 'Beat the Beast,' baby."

He slammed out a series of chords and let out an unintelligible wail that set Blake's teeth on edge. Why would somebody who played Mozart like an angel assault the ear drums with this crap? When he made eye contact with Peter/Pyro, he saw a reflection of darkness and rage. "Did you ever play for my dad?"

"Dr. Ray wasn't into my original compositions."

Because he had taste. Of the three superbabies they'd met, Pyro was the most likely to have had more than a superficial relationship with his father. Their families knew each other. "What about your dad? Does he like—"

"We don't talk."

The edge of hostility between them grew wider and

deeper. Blake's instincts told him that Pyro was an enemy.

Eve bounced to her feet. "I like your stuff. If you're playing around here, I'd love to get tickets. For my friend."

"Tomorrow night. At Bowman Hall on Colfax. It's going to be my last show for a while." He started packing up his keyboard. "I'll leave backstage passes at the box office."

"Thanks." She beamed. "It's been great meeting you both. Dr. Latimer, you have a beautiful home."

"Thank you, but this house belongs to my parents. After my father left the military, he established a successful import/export business which he insists on running day to day, even though he's in his seventies."

"What's the name of his business?" Blake asked.

"Latimer and Son." A frown pulled at the corners of his mouth. "His dynastic ambitions were thwarted when I went into medicine. My mother, rest her soul, encouraged me to be a doctor. Specifically, an obstetrician. She called Dr. Prentice a miracle worker. She was forty-four when I was born. She and my father had given up hope of having a child when Prentice approached them."

"They could have adopted," Eve said.

"I agree," he said quickly. "But not my father. He wanted his bloodline to continue."

"So, he was happy when you came along."

"My birth changed his life."

A snapshot of Dr. Latimer's history began to form in Blake's mind. He'd been a late-in-life baby, much like Blake. After his son's birth, his father quit the military and founded a business, something he could leave to his only child.

Latimer cleared his throat. "Though I'm glad to be better acquainted with you both, I can't help wondering why you've come here tonight."

"The study," Pyro grumbled. "That's what this is about."

Blithely ignoring his hostility, Eve said, "Actually, we were trying to reach Dr. Prentice. Do either of you know where we could find him?"

"At his clinic in Aspen," Latimer said.

"He's on vacation," Eve said. "Since you both have the same specialty, I thought you might have some idea where he'd vacation."

He gestured toward the doorway where his driver stood silently. "Randall, would you please find the phone numbers for Dr. Prentice?"

Eve continued to press. "Have you ever consulted with Prentice?"

"Occasionally," he said.

"I suppose that when he's in town, he visits your clinic. Maybe even sees patients there."

"He's used my facilities." Latimer steepled his long, slender fingers. "Frankly, my research has taken a far more experimental direction. Genetics is a vital, aggressive field, and Prentice hasn't kept up with the times."

"Whatever," Pyro said. "I'm outta here."

"Wait." Blake wanted to see their reactions when he told them about the study. "There's something you need to know."

Pyro looked bored, shifting his weight from foot to foot. "Spit it out."

"Dr. Latimer, you asked why my dad would want to monitor the babies born in the study. It's because we shared more than in vitro conception. The embryos were genetically engineered, using the sperm and egg of highly intelligent, physically healthy donors."

Latimer paled. "Are you saying that my mother and father aren't my biological parents?"

"They didn't know," Blake said. "They weren't told."

Pyro threw back his head and laughed. "I knew it. I knew that old fart wasn't really my father."

In contrast, Latimer appeared to be devastated. He sank lower in his chair. "I don't believe you. Dr. Prentice would never do anything so unethical."

Eve moved toward him. "This must be a shock."

He waved her away with an elegant flip of his wrist. "Please leave."

"I'm so sorry." She shot Blake an angry glance. "We should have been careful in the way we told you."

"Leave," Latimer said. "I wish to be alone."

Blake guided her toward the door. Before they left, Randall handed him a note with phone numbers. In a low voice, he asked, "Is it true?"

"Afraid so."

"Dr. Latimer won't be happy." His heavy brows pulled into a scowl. "He's had a rough few years. You should have known him before the illness. He was a different man."

"Randall!" Latimer called from the study.

The stocky driver opened the door and ushered them out.

Pyro dashed outside ahead of them. He danced on the lawn, still laughing. "I'm reborn, man. This is the best day. Ever."

Blake glanced back toward the house. "Not for everyone."

Chapter Nine

Because she hated unquantifiable variables, Eve thought their conversation with Latimer had been unsatisfactory. Though he accused her of being too direct, he'd been far too vague. Was he closely in contact with Prentice? Close enough to kill for him? She tossed the car keys to Blake and slipped into the passenger seat.

Before he started the car, he handed her the note from Randall. "Nothing new here. You already had these phone numbers for Prentice."

"We did learn one important clue."

"What's that?"

"Latimer talked to Prentice today. That's the only way he'd know I'm pregnant."

"What about the glow?"

"Oh, please. That's an old wives' tale."

On the street in front of them, Pyro loaded his keyboard into a van parked under the streetlight. He wouldn't be hard to trace; his vanity license plate proudly repeated his name: PYRO. Turning to face them, he snapped both hands open. A flame exploded from his fingers.

"Wow!" She applauded. "Very cool."

"Lighter fluid," Blake muttered. "Cheap trick."

Pyro bowed before he jumped into the driver's seat and took off.

"He seems awfully happy to have different parents." She was a little bit fascinated by this techno-punk rocker who played classical violin, but she didn't trust him. "Do you think he's faking?"

"Hard to tell. He's a performer."

"I've heard that when a person lies, there are measurable physical reactions. Dilated pupils. Sudden hand gestures. Licking of lips."

"Handy information if you're questioning a suspect in a laboratory," Blake said as he drove to the corner and turned.

"Do you have experience in that field?" As soon as she spoke, she realized her question was obvious. He was Special Forces. "Of course, you've done interrogations."

"Let's just say that I've dealt with my share of informants and rats. When it comes to lying and liars, I usually go with my gut reaction."

"What does your gut tell you?"

"Both these guys have something to hide."

She'd been watching Latimer when Blake had revealed that he was not, in fact, genetically related to the parents who had raised him. Though she hadn't been able to see the doctor's eyes clearly behind his thick glasses, his fingers had tensed. He'd inhaled a quick, sharp gasp. Obvious reactions.

"From what Latimer said about his father," she said, "the genetic truth could create problems."

"Oh, yeah. Old man Latimer sounds like a 'blood is thicker than water' type. He wants an heir, a son to carry on his family name and business." Abruptly, Blake pulled over to the curb. "That's what I call a motive."

"Why are you parking?"

"I want to see what Latimer does next." He opened his car door. "Coming?"

"Are you suggesting that we spy on him?"

"That's the plan."

She hesitated for half a second to consider the ethics of their actions. Spying was sneaky. But they were looking for a murderer, which justified a certain amount of devious behavior. She hopped from the car and followed him as he dashed across the wide lawns in this upscale neighborhood. Though the city streetlights provided clear illumination, the tall trees and ample shrubbery created shadows.

When they rounded the corner, she saw headlights on the street. Blake pulled her close and ducked behind a shrub. He crouched close behind her. She heard his breathing, felt the warmth of his body. The physical attraction she'd managed to put on hold rose up again.

She tried to funnel her thinking in a different direction. "What did you mean when you mentioned motive?"

"Suppose that Dr. Latimer's father found out about the genetics. He'd be ticked off, might even disinherit his son. The good doctor would lose his cushy lifestyle."

His logic made sense to her. "So if Dr. Ray threatened to reveal the information in the study, Latimer had a motive to kill him."

"Yep."

"One thing he's not faking is his blindness," she said. "I noticed a couple of books in Braille on the shelves."

The headlights passed, and Blake guided her closer to Latimer's white stucco mansion. Instead of peeking in the front bay window, they crept around to the side of the house. Blake peeked at the edge of a window and whispered, "He's on the phone. Looks pissed off."

"Can you hear what he's saying?"

"Not really." He leaned closer, nearly pressing his cheek against the glass. "Now, he's talking to Randall. I think he said something about the car."

"Are they going somewhere?"

"That would be my guess," he said. "They left the room."

From far inside the house, she heard a door slam.

"Let's go," Blake said. "We need to follow them."

Abandoning subtlety, they raced across the grassy lawns toward the corner where the vehicle was parked. The short sprint got her blood pumping. When she dove into the passenger seat and closed the door, she felt exhilarated.

"Down!" Blake pushed her forward so her head was on her knees. "There's a car coming out of the alley."

When the headlights passed, she popped up. "Was it them?"

"I saw Randall in the driver's seat." He fired up the engine. "Fasten your seat belt."

As she buckled up, he maneuvered the station wagon around and whipped toward the main road. His driving was pure Indy 500. "You're going too fast. You'll attract attention."

"I need to see which way they turn at the stoplight."

She peered through the windshield. "Is that the car? The one with the rhomboid taillights?"

"If rhomboid means wraparound, yes."

On the main boulevard, she focused on the taillights as Blake dodged through traffic, keeping a distance from the car Randall was driving. When a truck pulled between them, she buzzed down the window and stuck her head out. She still couldn't see the rhomboid lights. "The next time we stop, I can jump out and see where they are."

"Stay in the car."

Their pursuit of the other vehicle was turning out to be fun. Who knew investigating could be such a kick?

When Randall headed northwest, she recognized the

route. "They're going to Dr. Latimer's clinic. I'm sure of it."

"How far is it? Can we get ahead of them?"

"With the way you drive, yes." She glanced up at the street sign and read the number. "Go straight. I'll tell you when to turn."

Using three lanes of traffic as cover, he zipped through a yellow light, leaving Randall behind. "We'll get there first and be out of the car before they arrive."

He parked on the far side of the square three-story building and flung open his door. She leaped from the car and followed him. They hid in the shadows at the edge of the building just as Randall drove toward the front entrance.

Jiggling a set of keys in his hand, Latimer's driver left the car and approached the building.

"Where's Latimer?" she whispered.

"Still in the car."

"How can you tell?"

"Randall left the engine running." Blake leaned his back against the wall. "Latimer has a clear view of the entrance, so we can't follow Randall inside."

"But Latimer's vision isn't good."

"Even if he can't identify us, he'll sure as hell notice two figures breaking into his building."

Two floors above them, office lights went on. She tilted her head back as if she could see through the glass and stone. "Randall is looking for something. Your father's missing documents?"

"I'd like to think you're right, but Latimer's no fool. He wouldn't keep anything incriminating in his office."

She stood beside him. Shoulder to shoulder, but not touching. "Were you really going to break in?"

"Maybe not. There's probably a surveillance camera

pointed at the entrance, and I wouldn't want you to get arrested."

"I could handle it."

She gazed up at his perfect profile, and he smiled down at her. They were well and truly partners. Hard to believe. When she'd gotten out of bed this morning and dressed in black for the funeral, she never dreamed her life would be so radically altered by nightfall. She'd started the day as a solitary mathematician. Now she was pregnant, and she'd met a man who was…someone special.

The lights above them went out.

She peeked around the edge of the building, waiting until Randall emerged. He went to the car and opened the door. Very clearly, she heard him say, "It's safe."

They drove away.

AFTER RETURNING TO HIS father's house, Eve went to the guest bedroom with the matching twin beds and got settled. She shoved her suitcase out of the way in the closet and unzipped the top. Since she'd been at the end of her laundry cycle, her choice in nightwear had been severely limited. Not that she owned any silky lingerie, but this outfit was super geeky: blue flannel pajama bottoms with images of Wonder Woman and an oversize T-shirt in faded red with the Hogwarts coat of arms.

In the adjoining bathroom, she washed her face, brushed her teeth and changed into her dorky nightclothes, telling herself that looking good didn't matter. She didn't want to be desirable. Nothing was going to happen between her and Blake. At least not until after they compared their DNA and knew for sure that they weren't related.

Though there was a desk in the pastel-green bedroom, she took her laptop to bed, where she sat cross-legged in the middle of the green-and-brown plaid bedspread.

Powered up, she began to search for her old friend Hugo, who had used her DNA results for an experimental profile of humans and orangutans. Since she hadn't contacted Hugo in three years, she suspected his old e-mail name—MonkeyMan—was incorrect. Sure enough, her message bounced back in seconds. But she knew his interests—primatology, Indiana Jones movies and saving the rainforest. He wouldn't be hard to locate.

She heard a tap on the door and called out, "Come in."

Like her, Blake had changed into sleep clothes. Even though he was carrying her purse, his army-green T-shirt and black sweatpants looked sexy. She noticed the lower edge of a tattoo peeking out from the sleeve on his left arm.

"All right," she said, "show it to me."

His eyebrows lifted. "What exactly did you want to see?"

She felt herself blushing. "Your tattoo, of course."

He rolled up his sleeve to reveal a winged man. "Icarus," he said. "From the ancient Greek story about the danger of flying too close to the sun. All the men in my platoon got this tat to honor Sarge. His name was Isaacs, and he hated the nickname Icky. Still, I like to think of him flying high."

She'd been ready to give him a hard time about creepy body art, but his tattoo had deep significance—a very valid reason for a tat. "I have one, too."

"Where?"

She pulled down the collar of her Hogwarts T-shirt to show him the one-inch long tattoo. "The symbol of pi. I got it to celebrate my master's degree."

After a quick glance, he looked away as though embarrassed. Him? A great big macho Special Forces guy? Did the top of her left breast intimidate him?

He dropped the purse on her bed. "Check the messages on your cell phone. You had a call from Vargas."

"You looked at my cell phone? I never gave you permission to pry into—"

"Hey, I didn't listen to your messages." He flopped onto the bed beside hers. "Let's hear what the billionaire has to say."

She took out her cell phone, noting that she'd received several calls from the guys at the lab and one from her neighbor. Setting the phone to be on speaker, she played back the Vargas call.

"Hi, Eve. It's David Vargas. I'd like to meet you for lunch tomorrow. One o'clock at the Gilpin Grill in Cherry Creek. This isn't strictly pleasure. I have some business to discuss—an idea that might benefit the research you're doing at Sun Wave."

"Clever," Blake said. "He's trying to hook you with a business proposition."

Or maybe he was actually attracted to her. Was that so hard to believe? "What should I say?"

"Meet him." He rolled onto his back.

"Are you coming with me?"

"Don't tell Vargas that I am. But, yeah. I'm your bodyguard. I go where you go."

First, she called her neighbor and made arrangements for the feral cats. Then, she texted an acceptance to Vargas. The callbacks to coworkers would wait until tomorrow. She looked over at the other bed where he had burrowed under the plaid comforter. Sleeping? Though it was almost midnight, she was wide awake. "Blake?"

"What?"

"When Randall said, 'It's safe,' he might have been talking about security."

"Didn't we already discuss this?"

"Yes, but we were trying to think of an object. Like your father's documents. Or Latimer's DNA test results. A photo. Some kind of proof. What if Randall meant that the whole office was safe."

"Tomorrow. We'll think about it tomorrow."

As she gazed at his lumpy form, she found herself wishing he'd stay up and talk to her, maybe even give her a good-night kiss. Even if it was wrong? Even if he was her brother? With a renewed sense of purpose, she returned to her computer search.

After a few minutes, he growled, "When are you going to turn off the light?"

"As soon as I locate MonkeyMan."

"Is that a porno site or your boyfriend?"

"Neither. MonkeyMan was the e-mail name for Hugo Resnick, a primatologist. He's the guy who did my DNA. Shouldn't you be looking for your own DNA results?"

"Tomorrow, we're going to a clinic at Fitzsimons," he said. "I figure General Walsh will be able to access my results a lot easier than I can."

"Why Fitzsimons? I thought the veteran hospital was closed."

"My dad worked there part-time at the PTSD clinic. It's a place he might have kept copies of his documents. Plus, I need equipment to continue with this investigation."

"Like what?"

"Another weapon, ammo, bugging devices, infrared goggles and a vehicle. My dad's old station wagon is fine for trips to the grocery store. But I need a car with more horses."

He was such a typical male. "It's all about the hardware."

"You guessed it."

Within fifteen minutes, she'd located Hugo the MonkeyMan and sent him an e-mail. Hopefully, he wasn't in Borneo doing research. With luck, she'd have a reply from him tomorrow.

She turned off the bedside lamp and got under the covers. "Good night, Blake."

"Night."

She'd barely gotten settled when she heard a loud buzzing noise. The house alarm had been activated.

Chapter Ten

At the sound of the alarm, Blake was awake. Alert. Ready.

The Sig Sauer that had been on the bedside table was in his hand. Safety off, he aimed two-handed at the closed bedroom door. He reversed position, pointed the barrel at the thin light filtering through the plaid curtains on the windows. No immediate threat was visible.

He scissored his legs free from the comforter, leaped across the narrow space between the twin beds and covered Eve with his body. He'd wanted to touch her. But not like this, damn it.

No time to explain. He pulled her off the bed.

In a few steps, they were inside the adjoining bathroom where the only window was high off the floor. Unfortunately, there wasn't a bathtub where she could take cover.

He felt her standing close behind him. No whimpering. No complaining. Like a good soldier, she was waiting for him to tell her what to do. *A damn good question.*

They could hunker down and wait for the security company to respond in ten, maybe fifteen minutes. With the bathroom door ajar and his Sig Sauer aimed at the closed door leading into the bedroom, Blake was confident that he could hold off the threat until help arrived, but it went against his grain to sit back and wait. He wanted to nab this son of a bitch.

As if she'd read his mind, Eve said, "You want to go after him."

"I can't leave you unguarded."

"They won't hurt me." She spoke loudly enough to be heard over the alarm. "The only reason they're after me is the baby. They want to monitor my pregnancy, make sure I don't give the baby up for adoption."

"Your logic is solid." *As always.*

"You're the one in danger, Blake."

She was right. Her baby was the prize, and he fell into the category of collateral damage. They'd shoot him to reach her, but he was willing to take that chance.

From the instant he heard the alarm until now couldn't have been more than four minutes. He eased open the bathroom door and took a step. "Stay here."

"While you risk your life?" She latched on to his arm, preventing him from leaving. "No."

He peered through the dim light from the window at her upturned face. He could have given her a long-winded rationale, citing his experience and the need for action, could have told her that victory never went to the faint-hearted. But only one fact was important. "They killed my father."

She winced. Her hand dropped from his arm. "Be careful."

He appreciated her sensibility. She'd been raised on military bases and knew what it meant to be a warrior.

He slipped through the bathroom door. The most likely place for an ambush was the hallway outside the bedroom door. He had to move fast. Stay low.

Opening the bedroom door, he poked his head into the hallway and withdrew. The wood on the doorframe splintered, but he heard nothing but the blaring alarm. The shooter must have been using a silencer.

His instincts and training told him to attack. Dive into the hallway and roll, come up with his gun blazing.

He felt Eve's touch on his shoulder. What the hell? She should have stayed in the bathroom.

"The window," she said. "You can catch up to him outside when he tries to escape."

Smart. "Open the window and take a look. If you don't see anybody, jump out."

While she did as he said, he fired into the hallway, engaging the shooter.

When he saw Eve slide through the window, he ran across the bedroom and followed. His chest scraped against the narrow casement frame, but he was outside in a moment.

He could already hear the approaching sirens. The shooter inside the house would be making his escape. From the front or the back? He scanned the cars parked on the cul-de-sac.

Beside him, Eve said, "I don't see the SUV that was outside my house."

The back of his father's house opened onto a yard with a fence. Beyond was a strip of forest with pines and cottonwoods that separated this property from the neighboring development. If Blake had broken into this house, he would have chosen that route.

He looked down at Eve. "I can't drag you into the forest. Too risky."

"The sirens are close. As soon as they're here—"

"That's when I'll go."

The streetlight slanted a dramatic shadow across her

face. She reached up and placed her hand on his cheek. "Please don't get yourself killed."

"I never do."

She kissed him. Her lips pressed hard against his, taking his breath away. It felt too good to be wrong.

When the security vehicle came into sight, she ran toward it. He took off in the opposite direction, circling the house. The porch light over the back door was off, and the lights from the street didn't reach this far.

He crept through the moonlight, hiding in shadow and cursing himself for being barefoot. He kept in constant motion, knowing that to stand in one place meant he'd be an easy target. He employed every caution but felt no fear. This was his element. He'd been trained in armed pursuit and capture.

At the fence, he peered into the trees. A night wind rustled the branches. The alarm and the noise from the security team arriving at the front of the house masked the sounds of the intruder retreating.

To his far left, he saw movement. He squeezed off a couple of shots and ducked. He saw the flash of gunfire. The intruder had gone this way.

He jumped the fence and ran toward the place where he'd seen gunfire, dodging behind trees and taking shots when he could. Though he hadn't been counting, he knew he was almost out of bullets.

The pine needles, twigs and cones tore at the soles of his feet, but he was narrowing the gap, closing in on his quarry. A burst of loud gunfire told him that the man with the silencer had been joined by another shooter.

There were at least two of them and one of him. They were armed. He was almost out of ammo. And barefoot.

But he had backup. He heard the security guards rushing into the backyard behind him.

Firing his last bullets, Blake charged forward.

He emerged from the trees onto a paved street with modern, two-story houses and tidy lawns.

The taillights of an SUV raced away. From this distance, he couldn't tell if it was the same vehicle he'd seen at Eve's house in Boulder.

They turned the corner and were gone.

AFTER THE SECURITY company personnel repaired the lock on the back door and the uniformed police officers left, Blake sat across the kitchen table from the homicide detective who had investigated his father's murder. Detective Joseph Gable propped his chin in his hand as though his neck was too tired to hold up his head. His tan suit was rumpled and had a grease stain on the left lapel. His eyelids drooped. The worry lines across his forehead had deepened to furrows. It was almost two o'clock in the morning. Homicide was a rough beat.

Eve placed two mugs on the table: coffee for Detective Gable and some kind of herbal tea for him. She'd made a fuss over the scratches on his feet. Even though none of his injuries were deep enough to require stitches, she'd cleaned his feet, applied antiseptic and bandages. He didn't need pampering but didn't mind having her play nurse.

She spoke to the detective. "Would you like anything to eat? I can zap some leftovers."

"I'd like some answers." He turned toward Blake. "Where did you get the Sig?"

"General Stephen Walsh," he replied. "After Eve was attacked at her house, I though I might need firepower."

"Do you have other weapons?"

Blake didn't think the homicide detective would be

amused by his display of knife skills or any reference to the fact that he knew thirty-seven ways of killing a man with his bare hands. "I'll be seeing the general tomorrow, after which I expect to be fully armed."

"And dangerous," the detective said. "It's not your job to go after the bad guys. That little shoot-out of yours could have resulted in tragedy."

Eve stepped up to defend him. "We were attacked. Not the other way around."

The detective held up his hand to forestall further comment. "Tell me what you know. I'll take it from here."

As far as Blake was concerned, the police had already had their chance to investigate, and they had failed. He wasn't about to stand down. "Did you find evidence at Eve's house?"

"We got fingerprints. Yours. Eve's, of course. And—"

"Wait a minute," she interrupted. "I didn't give you my fingerprints. Why am I on file?"

Blake grinned. "Something you're not telling me? Are you in ViCAP? Or CODIS?"

"Explain what those letters stand for, and I'll tell you."

"Violent Criminal Apprehension Program is a databank that includes fingerprints. CODIS stands for Combined DNA Index System."

"A list of DNA for criminals," she said thoughtfully.

"It was started to track sex offenders," Gable said, "but it's a much wider scope. Don't worry, you're not in either of those databases. We had a match for your prints because of your work at Sun Wave, handling government contracts in sensitive locations."

"Any other prints at my house?"

"Two other people you work with." His bloodshot

eyes glared in her direction. "We found no sign of a break-in."

"Which I already explained," she said. "I was feeding the alley cats and left the door open. It wasn't smart, but I really didn't expect to be attacked."

"Can you tell me why these guys came after you? And how do they connect to the murder of Ray Jantzen?"

She leaned against the counter. Though she was still wearing her Wonder Woman pajama bottoms, she'd covered her Harry Potter T-shirt with a gray hoodie. With her face washed clean of makeup and her blond hair tousled, she looked younger than twenty-five. "I'm sure Blake has already mentioned the Prentice-Jantzen study."

The detective nodded. "Go on."

"Well, that's the connection," she said. "Have you spoken to Dr. Prentice? What did he tell you?"

"Why do you think he's after you?"

Blake suppressed a grin. Answering a question with another question might throw off the average witness, but Gable didn't know Eve. She had a mathematician's logic and focus.

"Ask Dr. Prentice," she said. "You need to look at his phone records to see who he's contacted, and you should check his bank accounts for large deposits to known criminals. Like hitmen."

"Give me a reason," the detective said. "And I'll get a warrant."

Blake saw the reluctance in her eyes. She didn't want to explain the strange circumstances of her pregnancy, and he didn't blame her. Not only was her story unbelievable, but it violated her privacy.

"Believe me," she said. "If there was anything I could say to help you find the murderer, I'd tell you in a heartbeat."

"I'm listening," he said. "Start at the beginning. What happened at the funeral?"

She shook her head and shrugged.

Detective Gable sipped his coffee, licked his lips and waited for them to speak—standard cop procedure for getting witnesses and suspects to open up.

Blake wasn't interested in wasting time with a staredown. "Here's the deal. If we discover information you can act on, we'll be in touch."

"I advise against pursuing your own investigation."

"There's no law against asking questions." He held his mug to his lips and inhaled the sweet, minty fragrance. The tea didn't live up to the aroma; it tasted like tree bark.

"I know your reputation, Blake. You're Special Forces. You've got dozens of citations for valor and two Purple Hearts. You're a hero, a man of action. But this is suburban Denver, and we're not at war."

His father had been murdered. He couldn't think of a more compelling reason for him to use his Special Forces training.

"I'm warning you," the detective continued. "No violence. Don't go Rambo on me."

"I understand."

The detective took a final sip of coffee and stood. "You should be safe tonight. The security company left a car and two guards out front."

A service that Blake was paying extra for. He didn't begrudge the money. It was worth it to get a good night's sleep. "We'll be fine."

Detective Gable looked toward Eve. "I can't offer you protection in a safe house, but I would strongly advise you to leave town until this is over."

She nodded. "I appreciate your concern."

On this point, Blake agreed with Detective Gable.

Though he valued Eve's intelligence and enthusiasm, he didn't want to put her in danger.

After he showed the detective to the door and reset the alarm, he turned toward her. "Gable is right."

"About what?"

He hobbled down the hallway. "You should leave town."

In the guest bedroom, he stretched out on the twin bed nearest the door. As soon as he was prone, his injuries caught up with him. The soles of his feet prickled. The scrape on his rib cage where he'd gone through the narrow casement window ached. Running through the forest, he'd gotten a couple of other scratches on his arm. No big deal. Nothing serious. Leaning back against the pillows, he pulled up the covers.

To his surprise, she sat on the edge of the bed beside him, closer than necessary.

"I already considered going somewhere else," she said. "It's not feasible. For the next seven months while I'm pregnant, I'm in jeopardy. And what happens after I give birth? Prentice might come after my child. I can't spend the rest of my life on the run."

The lamplight shone on her cheekbones and chin. He studied her face—her wide, expressive mouth and the cute little bump on her nose. Messy wisps of wheat-blond hair fell across her rosy cheeks. Her lightly tanned complexion highlighted the startling blue of her eyes. All together, she was a fine-looking woman.

"Latimer was right," he said. "You're glowing."

"That's an old wives' tale. Not grounded in science."

He took her hand, laced his fingers with hers. Sister or not, he wanted to kiss her. "You're beautiful, Eve. Golden and warm."

She gave a tug on his hand but didn't pull away. "There's something about me that you should know."

"You can tell me anything."

She turned her head away as though she couldn't bear to look him in the eye. "I'm a virgin."

Oh, hell.

Chapter Eleven

The next morning at Fitzsimons, Eve fidgeted in an uncomfortable chair along the wall in General Walsh's outer
office. Her gaze went to a clock on the secretary's desk,
watching as the minutes ticked by. She crossed her legs
and swung her ankle in tight circles.

"Nervous?" Blake asked.

"I'm fine."

After last night when she'd told him she was a virgin,
he'd been more cautious around her, treating her like a
fragile piece of glass. But she'd wanted him to know because they kept bumping into each other…with their lips.
It seemed impossible to avoid his embrace. Inevitable that
they would soon make love.

All night long, she'd dreamed of him. On some level,
she'd known that she wasn't actually on a tropical beach
with palm trees and a tranquil azure sea. She hadn't really
been watching Blake rise from the waves, shake the water
from his hair and come toward her. In dreams, her senses
had been fooled. She had smelled the salty tang of the surf.
Her toes had dug into warm sand. When dream Blake had
yanked her into his arms, her lips had tingled and she had
tasted his kisses. With her willing hands, she had sculpted
his taut biceps, his chest, his abdomen and his thighs. The

springy black hair on his chest had tickled her nose as she had trailed kisses down to his belly button.

Her subconscious mind had been sending her a message, telling her loud and clear that Blake was the man she'd been waiting for. She was meant to be with him. Finally, to make love. No longer to be a virgin.

Sitting next to him in this bland office was pure torture. She folded her arms below her breasts to avoid accidentally touching him. When she suddenly gasped, she realized that she hadn't been breathing. To keep from inhaling his scent?

If the general's civilian secretary hadn't been sitting behind her desk and tapping away on her computer, Eve might have given in to her desires and thrown herself on Blake.

"What's wrong?" he asked.

"Nothing," she lied.

"Worried about your lunch with Vargas?"

That thought hadn't crossed her mind. "Maybe I'm a little bit tense."

"Yeah," he said. "Your arms are wrapped tight. Looks like you're wearing an invisible straitjacket."

"You think I'm crazy?"

"A little bit."

She turned her head and dared to look at him. He wasn't wearing camouflage battle fatigues but might as well have been. His cargo pants covered his ankle holster, and she was pretty sure he had other weapons stashed in the pockets. A white T-shirt molded to his chest, and his loose, untucked, black-and-gray patterned shirt hid the knife sheath on his belt.

Her gaze lifted to his perfect face and sank into his dark, chocolate eyes. Purely delicious! Did it really matter if their DNA matched?

She looked away. They'd find out soon. This morning, before she had brushed her teeth or took a shower, she'd powered up her computer to see if MonkeyMan had responded. There was his e-mail with her DNA profile attached. All they needed now was Blake's record.

When the general opened the door to his office, she bounded to her feet so abruptly that she almost stumbled. "Good morning, sir."

"No need for formality." He gestured to his casual slacks and collared golf shirt with a Torrey Pines logo. "Today, I'm just another old duffer. Do either of you golf?"

"Not for a while," Blake said as he shook the white-haired man's hand. "There's a hell of a fine course in Dubai, but most of the Middle East is a giant sand trap."

"Your dad was lousy off the tee but made up for it on the greens. He could sink a sixty-foot putt. No sweat. He used to say that golf was half skill and half psychology."

"And what do you say?" Blake asked.

"It's all about the objective. Get the ball in the hole."

Their small talk was driving Eve crazy. She understood that a certain amount of chat was needed to build trust, and men liked to bond over sports, but she was burning with anxiety. "Speaking of objectives," she said. "Were you able to access Blake's DNA records?"

While the general conferred with his secretary, Blake nudged her shoulder. "Calm down."

Don't tell me to calm down, Mr. Perfect. Dream Blake would have understood her urgency. He would have been as desperate as she was to get those records.

"Not yet," the general said. "My request has been initiated. It'll take a while to get results."

She forced a smile. "Would it help if you said it was a matter of life and death?"

"Not at all, kiddo. This is the army."

"In the meantime," Blake said, "I'd like to see the clinic where my dad worked."

"Sure thing."

The general escorted them into the hallway and down the corridor. As soon as they stepped outside, he said, "I put together the equipment you requested, Blake. And I managed to wrangle up a vehicle worthy of a superspy."

"Thank you, sir."

The general paused, looked up at the blue Colorado sky and ran his hand over his close-cropped white hair. "I promised not to ask questions. To tell the truth, I don't really want to know what you're up to. But I'm not a complete lamebrain."

"No, sir," Blake said.

"Here's what I think. You don't believe the police theory that your father was killed by a burglar. You think his murder was premeditated, and you're going after the man who did it." The general shot him a glare. "Don't answer that."

Eve watched as Blake listened without moving a muscle. Though she'd spent most of her childhood on and around army bases, she'd never been this close to a mission getting under way. Her dad had never shared the details of his assignments with her or Mom, and she hadn't considered his clerical work as an information analyst to be very interesting. Certainly not dangerous.

Now she had to wonder if he'd been privy to the details of espionage. Not all the heroes in the military were Special Forces like Blake.

"I have one concern," the general said. "If you discover that your father was killed by a veteran, leave his punishment to me."

"Yes, sir," Blake said.

She really didn't think Dr. Ray had been killed by one

of his veteran patients, unless one of those men was connected to the Prentice-Jantzen study. She asked, "General, how much do you know about Dr. Edgar Prentice?"

His steely blue eyes connected with hers. His face was expressionless; she couldn't tell if her question had irritated him or aroused his curiosity.

He said, "I know Prentice worked with Blake's dad."

"Twenty-six years ago," she said, "the army funded a study for Prentice and Dr. Ray. On in vitro fertilization."

"Babies aren't my field of expertise. My wife thinks I volunteered for overseas duty to avoid changing diapers."

"How many children do you have?" she asked.

"Five. All girls." A warm grin cracked his stony façade. "And I have three grandbabies. Two boys and another beautiful baby girl."

He started walking again, and she fell into step. Their conversation had given her something to think about other than her outrageously inappropriate lust, and she was glad to find that her brain was capable of normal functioning.

Dr. Ray shared space in a small office with four desks. The only person in the room was a slight, thin man with wire-framed glasses. Though his identification badge identified him as Dr. Puller, he seemed too young to be a counselor. Another superbaby?

Dr. Puller was quick to shake Blake's hand and offer his condolences. "We already packed up your father's belongings," he said. "I thought Connie, our unit secretary, delivered them to your house."

"You're correct," Blake said. "She also delivered a pecan pie, and I owe her a thank-you."

The thin man adjusted his glasses. "Was there something else?"

"A list of his patients," Blake said.

"Those files are confidential. But Connie could check the records if you know who you're looking for. I don't think Dr. Ray was seeing anyone outside his regular group sessions. He only worked here one afternoon a week."

Eve asked, "Did you ever sit in on his groups?"

"As often as I could. Dr. Ray brought more than skill to his sessions. A wisdom." He shoved his hands into the pockets of his sweater vest. "I learned by observing him."

His obvious respect for Dr. Ray made her think of the superbabies again. "Dr. Puller, how old are you?"

"Thirty-two."

"You look younger," she said.

"I know." He gave a sheepish grin. "That's why I wear the glasses. My wife says they make me look mature."

She was relieved to know that he wasn't one of the subjects of the study. They already had too many suspicious people to keep track of.

"We're looking for a specific individual," she said. "He might have been one of Dr. Ray's patients. He'd be in his mid-twenties, born in New Mexico. We can't give you a physical description, but he's highly intelligent, gifted."

Puller thought for a moment and shook his head. "Sorry. No one comes to mind."

He took them to the main reception area and introduced them to Connie, who was clearly the brains of this particular unit. While Blake arranged for the secretary to send his father's patient list to his computer, Eve considered the possibility that Dr. Ray had been murdered by a patient.

She didn't have training in psychology, but it seemed logical that a murderer would have an abnormal personality and would, therefore, be seeking psychiatric help.

But Blake's father hadn't been attacked in a fit of homicidal rage. The crime had been premeditated; his records had been stolen. The murderer wanted to suppress the information in those files—a secret that was important enough to kill for.

BLAKE COULDN'T HAVE ASKED for a better vehicle.

In the officer's parking lot, General Walsh glided his hand along the sleek lines of a midnight-blue Mercedes Benz sedan as he detailed the specifications. "She's fully loaded with a V-8 engine and heavy-duty shocks. There's a self-contained, untraceable GPS system and satellite phone. A steel-reinforced frame with an armored roof, floor and side panels. Bulletproof glass, of course, and a ballistic, self-sealing gas tank. You can drive this baby through a war zone and come out the other side without a scratch."

The armored Mercedes was one hell of an upgrade from his dad's serviceable, old station wagon. Blake approached the car with reverence. "I think I'm in love."

"She's a couple years old," the general said, "but still a beauty."

Eve asked, "How many miles per gallon?"

"Irrelevant," Blake said.

"You know I drive a hybrid, and I work at a company developing solar energy systems. It's important to be green."

Not taking his eyes off the Mercedes, he replied, "Would you throw out the Mona Lisa because the paint wasn't water soluble?"

"Your argument is illogical," she said. "You're justifying a questionable ecological decision based on aesthetics."

"You're saying that we should all drive ugly cars."

"If it saves the planet, yes. There should never be a rationale for wasting our precious resources."

He threw out an example he knew she'd understand.

"Like all those resources wasted on the Hubble telescope? Do we really need a better photo of the Horse Nebula?"

"Oh." She went silent.

The general circled around to the trunk and popped it open. "Back here, I stashed the equipment you requested."

Blake checked out the extra guns, ammo, surveillance devices and infrared goggles—all useful tools that would help in investigating. But the Mercedes? It was beyond anything he ever expected. "I don't know how to thank you, sir."

"Your father was a good man. He helped a lot of soldiers. Now, it's my turn to help you."

"Excuse me." Eve popped up beside him. "What is this sort of vehicle used for?"

"Secure protection. A couple of years ago, the Democratic National Convention was held in Denver. There were a lot of high-ranking individuals in town—men and women who were targets for terrorists."

"And you used this vehicle to drive them around."

"We had a whole fleet. This one, we kept." He clapped Blake on the shoulder. "Do the right thing."

Blake was so excited to get behind the wheel that he barely noticed Eve sliding into the passenger seat. He ogled the dashboard. There were as many dials as a cockpit but tastefully displayed in Mercedes Benz style.

When he turned the key in the ignition, the Mercedes hummed at a perfect pitch. Grinning like a lunatic, he glanced at Eve. "You might want to buckle up."

"Why? Is this gas-guzzler going to sprout wings and fly?"

"I wouldn't be surprised."

Driving from the parking lot was like riding on a swift and powerful wind. The smooth leather seats cushioned his butt. The steering handled like a dream. He wanted to take this baby out on the open road. For the first time since he was told of his father's murder, he felt something akin to pure joy.

"Well?" she asked. "Does the car live up to your expectations?"

"She's amazing." He glided to a stop at a light and turned his head toward her. "You look good in a Mercedes."

"Uh-huh. You'd think a brain-sucking zombie looked good in this car."

"I mean it." Nestled in fawn-colored leather, her T-shirt and denim jacket could pass for casual elegance. Her tousled blond hair almost appeared to have style. Most important, she was relaxed. The nervous intensity that plagued her this morning was gone.

When he turned right, she looked up. "This isn't the most direct route to downtown."

"I'm taking the highway," he said. "Because I feel the need."

"The need for speed," she completed the quote. "*Top Gun*. My dad loves that movie."

"Aviators can be a pain in the butt. But they are cool."

She picked up the satellite phone. "I should try calling Prentice on this phone. He wouldn't recognize the number."

"Give it a shot."

She plugged in the number and waited for an answer. "He's not answering."

"Right," he mumbled. "That would be too easy."

"Tell me about the doodads in the trunk."

"High-tech surveillance equipment and weaponry. You're going to like this stuff."

"I'm not interested in guns, Blake. I'd rather have you show me how to defend myself without killing anybody."

Avoiding serious harm to your opponent ran counter to his training. Not that he always fought to the death. But he never held back, no matter what the consequences.

Chapter Twelve

Eve had to admit that the tiny communication device fitted into her ear was a very cool gadget. She heard Blake clearly, even though he'd taken a position down the block from the restaurant where she was supposed to meet David Vargas.

In addition, she wore a microphone pin so Blake could hear what she said. The secret communication made her feel like a superspy. As she entered the Gilpin Grill in Cherry Creek North, she whispered, "I'm going inside."

In her ear, Blake responded, "I know. I can see you. You don't have to tell me everything."

At the door, she was met by a host who whisked her to the leather-padded booth where Vargas awaited. He slid out from behind the table and greeted her with a kiss on both cheeks, which was not the way she usually said hello. Her typical lunch with the Sun Wave crew tended to be pizza or fast food. Not linen tablecloths and heavy silverware. Though many of the restaurant patrons, including Vargas, wore suits, she didn't feel out of place in her denim jacket. This was casual Colorado where millionaires sometimes dressed in beat-up jeans and scruffy boots.

Vargas loosened his necktie, pulled it off and stuffed it into his pocket. "Excuse the corporate uniform. I had a meeting with attorneys this morning."

"Tell me about your business."

"Investments and properties, cashing in and cashing out. Not all that interesting."

He gave her a warm, somehow charismatic smile. His features weren't as perfectly symmetrical as Blake's. His wide-spaced eyes and narrow chin made his face into an inverted triangle, like a cat. The streak of white in his black hair also seemed animalistic.

She noticed his widow's peak—a genetic trait that she shared. Smiling back at him, she said, "It sounds like you work with numbers. That's my field."

"Right. You're a math genius."

"I wouldn't say genius."

"Don't be modest." He signaled to the waitress. "I looked you up. You're well-respected in your field."

She ordered water and checked out the pricey menu. While Vargas discussed wine with the waitress, she heard Blake in her ear. "Get him to talk about the study. He's known for years about his genetic parents."

Having him inside her head was disconcerting. He'd already penetrated her imagination. Images of his face, his arms, his chest and all the other parts played on a continuous loop.

Vargas leaned toward her. "Are you sure you don't want to sample the wine?"

He wouldn't be asking if he knew she was pregnant, which seemed to indicate that he wasn't aware of her condition. On the other hand, he might be testing her. "Water's fine. And I think I'll have the free-range chicken salad."

"I recommend the hamburger. It's Kobe beef." He pulled on his earlobe—a detached earlobe like hers and Blake's.

"Chicken's fine." As far as she was concerned, the time

for small talk was over. "Do you think we're genetically related? You know, brother and sister?"

"You like to get right to the meat," he said.

"Even if it's not Kobe beef."

His voice lowered to a confidential tone. "In the study, Dr. Prentice had a limited number of subjects to use as sperm and egg donors."

He ran through the same logic that she and Blake had already figured out. She asked, "When you found out about the study, did you try to find your genetic parents?"

"Neither Dr. Ray nor Prentice would share that information. Their volunteers were promised that their identities would never be known. Safeguards were taken."

Those volunteers probably never knew what happened after their initial contact with Prentice. Twenty-six years ago, the world was a very different place, with limited Internet access and information sharing. Less technology meant more privacy. More secrets.

In her ear, Blake said, "How does he know safeguards were taken? He's holding something back."

She should have caught that slip from Vargas. "How do you know? About the safeguards?"

His gray eyes widened slightly—only a millimeter, but it was enough to tell her that he was aware that he'd taken a misstep. "Numerical codes were used instead of names."

"And you know this because…"

"I've seen the records."

"You hacked into Prentice's computer files," she said. An excellent idea. "What did you find?"

"There were no names," he said. "Not for the donors and not for the babies. Each individual was assigned a random number. After I had my own DNA run, I could compare. My biological parents are 73 and 15."

The waitress brought his wine to the table, and he went

through the ritual of swirling, sniffing and tasting. His attitude betrayed no sign of nervousness. He seemed to be in absolute control, leading her toward whatever conclusion suited his purposes.

She knew that his hacked data would provide a great more information than random numbers. Having Prentice's files was how Vargas knew there were twenty-four babies. The DNA profiles would indicate gender, and he'd told her that there were only two females. Therefore, he had a fifty percent chance of knowing her relationship to him.

After the waitress left with their order, she rephrased her initial question. "Am I your sister?"

"Half sister." He raised his wineglass to her in a toast. "We share the same mother."

Apparently, she'd misread him from the start. Vargas hadn't been flirting with her. He'd been…establishing a brotherly connection? Somehow, that didn't seem right.

Family was important to her. And by family, she meant the mother and father who had raised her, the grandparents who had spoiled her, the aunts and uncles and cousins who had exchanged birthday cards. Vargas was nothing to her. And yet, he was genetically closer to her than any of those other people.

In her ear, Blake said, "I'll be damned."

"Just what I was thinking," she responded.

"What?" Vargas asked.

"Nothing." She pulled her thoughts together. "Knowing that you're my half brother is disconcerting. It shouldn't make a difference. Our relationship is nothing more than biology."

"I feel something, too. When I saw you at the funeral and figured out who you were, I felt…" He rested his hand on his heart. "An inner warmth. I was happy that I'd found you."

"Wait a minute, how do you know it's me? The other female in the study could be the other woman."

"You both have the same mother. Different fathers, though."

Which meant that Eve had a half sister. If she hadn't been pregnant, she would have drained his wineglass and asked for more. A gallon more. "Where is she?"

"I don't know her name," he said. "The parents who raised us were all in the military, which meant they moved around a lot. And women are harder to trace than men. They get married and change their names."

"Have you located other men who were in the study?"

"I guessed about Blake. And there were a couple of guys at the funeral. Dr. Trevor Latimer?"

In her ear, Blake said, "Don't confirm."

She knew that. *Loose lips sink ships.* "What made you think he was one of us?"

"He's our age and already an OB-GYN with a thriving practice, which indicates high intelligence. Here's an odd coincidence. I'm a part-owner of the building where he has his offices."

"You've met him before."

"No. First time I saw him was the funeral."

She didn't believe in coincidence. It seemed far more likely that Vargas knew about his relationship to Latimer and solidified the connection by being his landlord. "Do you own many buildings like his?"

"I'm part of an investment group that owns forty-seven commercial properties in and around Denver," he said. "Which leads me to a proposition I wanted to discuss with you."

"Proposition?"

In her ear, Blake said, "Don't let him get you off track. Bring him back to the study."

There might have been a clever way to navigate these waters and lead the conversation back to the study, but she lacked that skill, especially when facing somebody like Vargas. With his business talent, he must have been a genius when it came to negotiations.

Her only ploy was being direct. "No proposition. Not now. I want to talk more about the study."

His smile was pure charm. "Whatever you want. Ask your questions."

"About Prentice's data," she said. "I'd like to take a look at the DNA profiles."

"Give me your e-mail, and I'll send a copy as soon as I get back to my office."

It occurred to her that he'd hacked into Prentice's files and was likely to do the same to hers. Not that she had any deep, dark secrets in her personal files. But the loss of privacy concerned her.

Still, she wrote down her e-mail address and passed it across the white linen tablecloth toward him. When he took it, their fingers touched and a spark raced up her arm. This wasn't sexual energy like she had with Blake. Vargas felt dangerous, as though their shared DNA gave him too much access to her inner thoughts. Of course, that was untrue. He couldn't know what she was thinking or feeling, unless…unless he'd also taken a look at the psychological information obtained by Blake's father during their annual interview. He must have done so; he wouldn't leave that stone unturned.

She asked, "What did you find when you hacked into Dr. Ray's records?"

"Very little." He didn't bother denying her implied accusation. "Blake's father wasn't a high-tech person. He didn't keep information on his computer."

But he'd used a laptop which had been stolen from

his office, indicating that the killer thought it had value. "Maybe you didn't look in the right files."

"Not a chance. I'm thorough," he said. "Think about it, Eve. When you did interviews with him, he made notes on a yellow legal pad. Right?"

"That's true. And the annual surveys we filled out were always in printed form."

She leaned back in her chair as their meal arrived. Her chicken salad was excellent.

In her ear, Blake said, "I hear you crunching. You're eating, aren't you? Damn, I'm hungry."

She made yummy sounds to tease him. "Mmm. This is the best chicken I've ever had."

Blake moaned. "You're killing me."

"Perfectly seasoned." She smacked her lips. "Tasty."

With a puzzled expression, Vargas studied her. "It's nice to see a woman who enjoys her food."

"I bet you date a lot of skinny supermodel types who don't eat at all."

"Good bet," he said.

In her ear, Blake muttered, "Get back to the topic."

Purely to annoy him, she said, "I could eat all day. I could order some dessert, maybe cheesecake or chocolate brownies or everything on the menu."

"Whatever you want," Vargas said.

Looking across the table at him, she gestured with her fork. "You said there wasn't much on Dr. Ray's computer. Tell me what you found."

"A statistical abstract with all the areas of study encoded. Without the key, all I could discern was that Dr. Ray discovered some correlations between DNA and certain behaviors."

"Like what?"

"Psychological traits, like introversion or extroversion. Or skill sets, such as our shared proclivity for numbers."

"Or talents," she said, thinking of the musical abilities displayed by Vargas, Latimer and Pyro. "But these traits weren't labeled?"

"If you like, I can send you the abstract."

"Great." Once she had these numerical samplings, she might be able to learn more about the study results. She was good at cracking codes. "I'd like to see Dr. Ray's personal analysis. To see what my behaviors said about me."

"I'm surprised that you trust psychology. Genetics is more scientific."

"True enough, but I believe that we make our own decisions. Genetics might have given me an ability in math, but I chose to study it."

"Our lives start with DNA. It's the most important factor in determining our course."

"I can't blame genetics for my personal choices, which happened to include watching every single episode of *Star Trek: The Next Generation*. I had a huge crush on Commander Data."

"The android who longed to have human feelings," he said. "An interesting choice."

"I wanted to help him. To be the woman who made him smile and laugh and fall in love."

"You're a romantic," he said. "Looking for a soul mate."

Before she met Blake, she would have scoffed at the idea of soul mates. Now, she wasn't so sure. The way she responded to him didn't make logical sense. "With all the possible mating combinations, it's statistically unlikely that one particular man and one particular woman are destined to be together."

"What about you and Blake?" he asked.

Am I that obvious? "What about us?"

"Genetically, it seems likely that you'd be well-matched."

His questions and perceptions were throwing her way off balance. In her ear, Blake warned, "Don't respond. Keep the focus on him. And the study."

"Enough about me," she said. "What about your secrets? What did you tell Dr. Ray?"

"I always felt different," he said. "Which was fine with me. I expect others to come up to my standards."

"If they don't?"

He didn't answer her question. Instead, he sipped his wine and changed the subject. "Now that I've found you, Eve, I want to spend more time together. I want to know you."

"And if I don't measure up to your standards?"

"You will," he said.

If she'd set out to choose a half brother, she would have looked for someone more empathetic and forthcoming. Vargas drew her toward him with his natural magnetism, but he was the opposite of warm and cuddly. If she wasn't worthy of his standards, she had no doubt that he'd throw her under the bus.

"How's your relationship with your parents?" she asked. "By parents, I mean the people who raised you."

"Positive. As you know, I've been financially successful. I've taken care of Mom and Dad, bought them a house in Florida."

"What about your genetic parents," she asked, returning to another topic he'd skillfully sidestepped. "Have you made a search for them?"

"How could I? All I have is their DNA."

She didn't believe him. Vargas believed that genetics

determined behavior and achievement. He would have desperately wanted to find his biological parents, would have spared no expense in hiring experts and hackers. "Did you look into the DNA databases?" she asked. "The military has pretty extensive records. Or CODIS."

"I hired a researcher. He didn't find anything." Dismissively, he brushed away that topic. "Are you ready to hear my proposal?"

"Sure."

"Like you, I support ecological causes, and I appreciate the work you're doing at Sun Wave on alternative energy sources." When he grinned, she noticed that he had a dimple in his right cheek. Just as she did. "Being green might be a family trait."

"Most intelligent people realize the importance of saving the planet."

"True," he said. "I'd like to offer several of my properties to be used as Sun Wave alternate energy prototypes. And I'll cover the cost for the installations."

"That's very generous."

"And not a bad tax write-off." He raised his glass to her. "Here's to working together."

Though she felt as though he was manipulating her, she couldn't refuse. At Sun Wave, they'd run into obstacles when it came to setting up prototypes for solar energy. She raised her water glass and clinked her rim with his. "I can't say no."

"We're partners," he said. "Brother and sister."

He seemed to be claiming her as a possession. Her shoulders tensed. Vargas might be involved in Dr. Ray's murder. He might even have pulled the trigger himself. She had to get out of there before she blurted an accusation. "Much as I'd like dessert, I have somewhere else I need to be. As I'm sure you do."

When she rose to say goodbye, he hugged her. "We're family, Eve. If there's anything you want, anything at all, call me."

Outside, the bright afternoon sun warmed her face and thawed her tension. She felt like a fly that had escaped the spider's web. Vargas might be her half brother, but he wasn't necessarily her friend.

She looked down the two-lane street with cars parked on both sides. An hour ago, she'd left Blake outside a specialty tea shop. He was nowhere in sight. "Blake? Where are you?"

In her ear, he responded. "Turn left and keep walking. Don't worry. I'm nearby."

"Where?"

"Play along with him," Blake instructed.

"Who?"

"Just do it."

Why was he so cryptic? Just once, she'd appreciate an explanation from him instead of a terse command. *Just do it?* She pivoted, went to her left as he'd ordered and walked. There wasn't much of a crowd on the sidewalk—a couple of business types, shoppers who were visiting the boutiques, tourists—nobody who appeared to be dangerous.

She'd only gone a couple of steps when Latimer's driver, Randall, stepped out of a doorway and blocked her path.

Chapter Thirteen

Blake had been aware of Randall's presence for the past half hour. He'd been watching from the opposite side of the street when the stocky, balding man had come around the corner, stopped at the entrance to the Gilpin Grill and peeked inside. After speaking on a cell phone, Randall had gone to a stone bench beside a planter filled with orange and yellow geraniums where he'd sat, waiting and making no attempt to hide.

Blake had concluded that Randall was the messenger. But what the hell was the message? Obviously, Latimer's driver had come to the Gilpin Grill to see Eve. How did he know where to find her? Had Vargas tipped him off to the location? The idea of Vargas and Latimer working together worried him.

Instead of a direct confrontation, Blake had decided to hold off and see what unfolded. As he had listened to Eve's conversation with Vargas through his earpiece, he had stayed out of Randall's sightlines. His military experience had schooled him in methods to make himself invisible. Less than a month ago, he'd led a covert rescue operation in a Pakistani city. Dodging through those narrow streets had been easier than blending into this upscale warren of shops and restaurants.

He had maneuvered into a position where he could study

Latimer's chauffeur. Randall was heavy but not flabby. His broad shoulders and upper arms stretched the seams on his lightweight sports jacket. When he had turned his face upward to catch the sun, Blake had noticed his misshapen nose, a couple of scars and a cauliflower ear. At one time in his life, Randall might have been a boxer, and he would have been the kind of fighter who put his head down and came at you like a tank—unstoppable, capable of taking punishment and of dishing it out.

When Eve had come out of the restaurant and followed his directions, she was face-to face-with Randall. She smiled and said, "This is a coincidence."

Blake was close enough that the sound of her normal voice harmonized with the tinny echo from his earpiece.

"Good afternoon," Randall said. "Will you come with me, please? Dr. Latimer is waiting."

They crossed the street at the four-way stop sign and walked north. They made an odd couple. Beauty and the beast, Blake thought as he watched the sway of her hips. Eve seemed to get prettier every time he saw her; she was definitely growing on him. His desires were complicated by her admission that she was a virgin. If they made love, he'd be damn sure that was what she wanted.

Within a block, the shops had faded into an expensive residential area with massive private homes and classy town houses. Through the earpiece, Blake warned her, "Whatever you do, don't get in the car."

Still on the opposite side of the street, he narrowed the physical distance between them.

Through Eve's listening device, he heard Randall ask, "Do you know where Blake is?"

"I can honestly say that I don't." Eve sounded annoyed. "Do you mind telling me what we're doing?"

"Dr. Latimer would have come by himself, but he's having a bad day."

Blake wasn't surprised. After they had left his house last night, Latimer had seemed panicky. The stress couldn't be good for his illness.

Randall approached the heavy bronze Cadillac that they'd seen him driving last night and opened the door.

From this angle, Blake couldn't see the interior of the car. He watched as Eve braced her arm against the roof and peered inside. "Hello, Dr. Latimer. What's this about?"

Latimer responded, "Please get in."

She stood up straight. "It's such a lovely day. Why don't you step out here and we can talk."

"I need to conserve my strength."

Blake saw Randall move into position. One shove from him and Eve would be in the car. He had to prevent that action. Stepping into the open, he shouted, "There you are."

He jogged across the street.

Quietly, Randall stepped back. For a husky man, he was talented at fading into his surroundings. Blake reminded himself that silent threats were often the most deadly.

He approached Eve and gave her a little hug, subtly removing her earpiece. "I thought you were going to wait for me outside the Grill."

"Well, I ran into Randall."

Blake leaned down and greeted Latimer. "Nice to see you."

"Please," he said, "get in the car. Both of you."

Latimer looked like hell. Behind his thick glasses, his eyes were sunken. Greasy strands of blond hair plastered across his forehead.

Blake nodded to Eve. "You sit back here. I'll stay up front with Randall."

If the driver tried anything, Blake would be ready for him. Once situated in the passenger seat, he turned and looked into the back.

Though the weather was pleasantly warm, Latimer shuddered inside a shawl-like sweater. His lips barely parted as he spoke. "Finding out about my biological parents was difficult for me. Devastating." He drew a ragged breath. "My father—the man who raised me—provided me with a very good life. When I chose medicine instead of the family business, he encouraged my dream, sent me to the best schools, arranged for mentors. He's a good man. The best."

"I understand," Blake said. "Ray Jantzen is the only father I've ever known, the only man I want to be my father."

"My work with infertility involves genetics," Latimer said. "In a way, that makes it harder for me to accept that the man who raised me isn't my father."

"Sure he is," Eve said. "Real parenting involves nurturing. Laughter and squabbles. Pain and happiness. That's what makes a parent. Love is more important than biology."

He couldn't believe the supremely practical Eve would be touting the value of relationships and love. This was a woman who relied on facts, not emotions. If his dad had been able to hear her talking about relationships and nurturing, he would have been proud.

"I know," Latimer said, "that you're trying to locate the list of genetic parents."

"The information is pertinent to my dad's murder," Blake said.

Latimer stared at him. "My father must never know that we're not of the same blood."

"I don't see a problem," Eve said. "There's no reason why he should be informed."

Blake knew the decision wasn't theirs to make. By not informing the parents, Prentice had committed fraud. A crime. A prosecutable offense. There was an obligation to bring the truth to light. "If the police are involved, we can't control the outcome."

"I've already spoken to Pyro," Latimer said. "Though he appears to be delighted that his father isn't really his father, he promised me that my family wouldn't be brought into it. Can you do the same? Continue your search, but erase my name from the list."

Which would be committing yet another fraud. "I can't make that promise."

"What if I made it worth your while?" Latimer shifted in the backseat. The slight movement caused him to wince as though his bones were sore. "I can arrange for you to meet with Prentice."

A tempting offer. But as soon as Latimer spoke, Blake knew he was dealing with a liar. Last night, Latimer had claimed that he didn't know the whereabouts of Prentice. Dealing with all these superbabies was like playing chess with several genius partners. Latimer had his agenda. Vargas had another plan. Every move had a countermove until the final checkmate. "How well do you know David Vargas?"

"I don't."

Blake looked toward Randall. "If Vargas didn't tell you, how did you know that Eve would be at the Gilpin Grill?"

Randall stared through the windshield. His meaty hands rested on the steering wheel as though he was driving. "I dropped a GPS tracking device in her purse."

"What?" Eve erupted from the backseat. "Why do people keep bugging me?"

With a shrug, Randall said, "I thought it might be useful to know your movements."

"We weren't spying on you," Latimer assured her. "We didn't even turn it on until after I'd talked to Prentice this morning."

Her blue eyes narrowed in an angry glare. For a woman who claimed to be logical, she had a lot of passion seething under the surface. She snarled, "I must have called Prentice a dozen times and he won't pick up. Why did he take your call?"

"I don't know," Latimer said.

"I don't believe it. And I don't believe that you aren't in touch with Vargas. He's part-owner of the building where you have your offices."

Latimer seemed to retreat deeper into his illness. "My office lease is handled by a Realtor. I've never met this person you're talking about."

Eve seemed to assess his response and find it rational. She still wasn't letting Latimer off the hook. "Where's Prentice? Where is he taking this supposed vacation?"

"He's not vacationing," Latimer said. "He's in hiding."

"From what?"

"Isn't it obvious?" Latimer said. "He's been threatened."

"Who's after him?"

"He didn't give me a name." With an effort, Latimer straightened his shoulders. "Will you work with me? Do everything you can to delete my name from the list?"

"I'll try," Blake said. "Tell me more about Prentice."

"He didn't go into great detail, but he told me that he'd performed an IVF procedure for a great deal of money.

Though he successfully implanted the embryo, the father turned on him."

It didn't take much to read between the lines. Prentice was talking about Eve's pregnancy. "Who's the father?"

"I don't have a name." Latimer turned to Eve. "I assume you're the mother. Do you know the father of your baby?"

She waved her hands in front of her face, erasing his question. "Prentice did this to me for money?"

"A great deal of money," Latimer said. "His clinic in Aspen has an extremely high overhead. These are difficult financial times for everyone."

Eve's anger went out of her. She slouched back against the car seat. "Why?"

"You can ask Prentice yourself," Latimer said. "Tomorrow night at my office. Eight o'clock. That's all I can tell you. Now, I need to go home."

So did Blake. He needed time to think. Prentice wasn't involved in a scheme to develop a race of superbabies. He'd implanted Eve for a cash settlement. Money. The oldest motive in the book.

LEAVING LATIMER BEHIND, Eve shuffled along the sidewalk beside Blake. She was frustrated and mad as hell. She couldn't believe how much had been thrown at her. Everything—lock, stock and…baby.

Because of factors beyond her control, she was a pregnant virgin. An unwilling pregnant virgin. An unwilling pregnant virgin who was attracted to a man who might be her brother. Worst of all, the unknown father of her baby was a crazy person, possibly homicidal.

The only way her life could get worse was if armed thugs were after her. Oh, wait! They were.

She grumbled, "I want a weapon."

"I thought you wanted to learn hand-to-hand combat."

"I do. And I also want a gun."

"Feeling like shooting somebody?"

"Several somebodies," she said, "starting with Prentice. Can you believe he messed up my life for a paycheck?"

"A really big paycheck," Blake said.

"I don't care if it was a million dollars. He had no right to violate me. This sounds crazy, but I would have felt better if my pregnancy was part of an experiment. You know, creating the next generation of superbabies."

"Maybe it is. We don't know the motives for your baby daddy."

They approached the supersleek Mercedes, and he gallantly opened the door for her.

She eyed him suspiciously. "Why so gentlemanly?"

"After your fancy lunch with Vargas, I figured I better step up my game."

"Vargas? Sure, he's got money and class and isn't bad to look at, but you're…" Teasing, she patted Blake's clean-shaven cheek. "You're you."

"What's that mean?"

"Don't go fishing for compliments, Mr. Perfect."

While she nestled into the soft leather seats, he went around to the trunk where he kept his arsenal. When he got into the car, he handed her a plastic device that was about the size of a remote control with two pincers on the end.

"Stun gun," he said. "Flip this switch to activate, press the business end against your attacker and pull the trigger. Nobody gets killed, but it stops an assailant in their tracks."

"I like it." She squeezed the plastic handle. "Like *Star Trek* when you set your phaser to stun."

"Don't set it off by accident. That's several hundred thousand volts, and it really hurts."

When she went to stash her weapon in her purse, she remembered that Randall had dropped a GPS tracker in her shoulder bag. As Blake eased away from the curb, she dumped the contents onto the floor in front of her. Hunched over, she shifted through her wallet, sunglasses, various receipts, an emery board, cell phone, lipstick and various other detritus until she found the small round disc. "Aha!"

"Do I want to know what you're doing?"

"Making sure Latimer doesn't know where we are." She lowered the window and tossed it into the street, hoping that it would be picked up by a squirrel and hidden away forever. "Okay, where do we go from here?"

"I was hoping for an excuse to drive this fine vehicle to Aspen, but Prentice is coming to us. No need to track him down."

"Unless Latimer pulls a double cross." She didn't think he'd take that chance. Hiding his genetic secret from his parents seemed important to him. "He really looked miserable."

"Don't let sympathy cloud your thinking," Blake warned.

"I won't." She pushed aside her emotional reaction. "Just the facts. Latimer has a tenuous connection to Vargas through the lease on his building. And he knows Pyro. And he lied to us about not being able to reach Prentice. However, he seemed truly shocked when we told him about his genetic parents."

"Or was he shocked that we knew?"

"A possibility," she conceded.

"We can't trust him. When we go to his office, we'll be prepared for an ambush."

He stopped short to avoid a careless driver, then reached out and patted the dashboard. He murmured, "That's okay, Ms. Mercedes. I won't let anything happen to you."

He wasn't trying to charm her, not like Vargas, but Blake drew her like a magnet. She wanted to ruffle his hair or give him a little kiss on the cheek. "You still haven't told me our plan for this afternoon."

"First, I want to go back to the house and find the box of stuff from the clinic at Fitzsimons. It sounded like Dr. Puller and Connie cleared off his desk pretty quickly. There might be a clue."

"We have lots of other research to do. Vargas promised to send me the results of his hacking into Prentice's and your dad's computer."

Blake reminded her, "He also said there were no names attached."

"I'm good at breaking codes."

She flipped open her cell phone to check her e-mail messages. Nothing from Vargas. But there was a message from General Walsh. It had to be Blake's DNA results.

Her fingers trembled above the keys. Finally, she'd have her answer. She'd know if she and Blake were brother and sister.

Chapter Fourteen

At the house, Eve set up her computer at the desk in Blake's bedroom where she could use his printer. After these anxious hours of wondering, she was almost afraid to compare their DNA profiles.

Before Blake barged into her life, she hadn't felt like she was missing anything by not having a relationship. Her work was enough. She was happy as a single person. Not lonely, not really. But now she was different. Irrational, crazy emotions intruded into her life equation. She wanted to be with him, and she knew he felt the same way about her. If it turned out that they were genetically related, they had a problem.

With a few clicks on the keyboard, she opened the e-mail from General Walsh's secretary. When the DNA chart appeared, she sat and stared blankly.

Blake hovered at her shoulder. "What are you waiting for?"

"Does it really matter what it says? It's only genetics. Even if it turns out wrong…"

"Damn it, Eve. Read the charts."

She printed out his DNA results to compare with her own. "These profiles aren't detailed or conclusive. They couldn't be used in court to determine paternity."

"But they're close enough to tell if we're related. Right?"

"I'm not a genetics expert. I'm remembering information that my friend, Hugo the MonkeyMan, explained to me when I helped him coordinate his study." Sometimes her eidetic memory came in handy. "These charts will show thirteen core STR loci and their chromosomal positions as well as twenty-five alleles."

"In English," he said.

"It's like a fingerprint. With the exception of identical twins, nobody has the same DNA. However, family relationships can be determined through comparison of the—"

"Just do it."

She placed the two sheets of paper side by side. There were zero matches and few similarities. Yes! There was no genetic reason to keep them apart. "I'm not your sister. Not your half sister. We're not related."

He pulled her out of the chair and into his arms. "Then it's okay if I do this."

His mouth pressed hard against hers. At first, she was surprised by the intensity of his kiss. She'd never been ravaged before but suspected that this was what it felt like. Exciting. Confusing.

Her heartbeat accelerated, and her blood rushed. She could almost hear the surging as a fierce energy swept through her. She clung to him, pressing herself so tightly against his chest that she felt as if they were merging into one being.

They toppled backward onto his queen-size bed, and the air left her lungs. She was breathless, literally gasping.

He rose above her, and she looked up into his coffee brown eyes, perfectly spaced. His lips parted, not smiling but inviting her.

She flung her arms around his neck and dragged him down on top of her, welcoming the crush of his full weight.

He rolled to his side, still holding her. "Gently," he said. "I want this to last."

Why should they go slow? Her heart was racing, and her decision was made. Blake was the man who would take her virginity. "Am I doing something wrong?"

He traced the line of her jaw. "Usually, it's the guy who wants to go fast."

"Like I told you, I'm not exactly what you'd call experienced."

"Virgin territory." He smiled. "Are you sure you're ready?"

"Why not? I'm already pregnant."

His eyes darkened. "What Prentice did to you is unthinkable. I'm sorry you have to go through this."

It didn't seem as bad when she was with him. "The worst part is that I have no frame of reference. I don't know how to be pregnant. There must be vitamins I should take. Should I go to a doctor to make sure everything is all right?"

"Whatever you need, I'll support you."

She believed him. "Thanks."

"The last thing I want is to hurt you. Are you sure about making love?"

He cradled her in his arms, comforting her with surprising gentleness and kindness. Blake was a man's man, an alpha male who naturally took charge. This empathy showed another side of him. Not only did he care about her, but he actually seemed to understand how she felt.

A tear spilled down her cheek. There hadn't been time for her to cry, and she didn't want to start weeping now.

She wiped it away. "I want to make love. I want to know what it's like."

As he stroked her shoulders and tenderly rocked her in his arms, she let go of the anger and emotional pain she'd been holding in check. Prentice had stolen a precious part of her life—the natural progression of courtship and love that resulted in creating a baby. A heavy sob tore from her gut, and her tears flowed. More emotion than she'd felt in her entire life broke free in a torrent.

Blake absorbed her outburst. He murmured while she sobbed and cursed. He held her and waited until the storm abated to a whimper and she subsided into a quiet aftermath.

She sighed. "I didn't know that was in me."

"It's okay."

When he smiled at her, she turned her face away. "I must be a mess."

"You look good to me."

Yeah, sure. She knew her eyes were red. Her face, blotchy. "I'd like to wash up."

He rose from the bed and pulled her to her feet. Then he took her arm as though he was escorting her to a grand ball instead of to the bathroom down the hall. As she walked beside him, her step was light, buoyant. Her tears had washed away the anxiety that weighed upon her.

In the bathroom, he lifted her and sat her on the countertop beside the sink. She should have told him that she was facing the wrong way and needed the mirror to clean up, but she was curious about what he intended to do.

He turned on the faucet and dampened a washcloth. "Close your eyes, Eve."

The warm cloth stroked her forehead and cheeks. He lightly kissed her lips, washed again and patted her face dry.

She felt his hands glide down her black denim pants to her feet. When he removed her shoes and socks, her toes curled. "What are you doing?"

"I always feel clean after my feet are washed."

When he stroked her instep, a shiver raced up her legs. She opened her eyes and looked down at him, kneeling before her like the prince with Cinderella. This wasn't how she thought making love would be, but she liked it.

The warm washcloth caressed her toes. She closed her eyes again and leaned back, enjoying the sensations that raced through her. Though he touched only her feet, a tingling started in the pit of her stomach. She was aroused, very definitely aroused.

"You have pretty feet," he said as he dried her feet. "Pink, little toes."

She truly wished that she'd had a pedicure. "You've seen my feet before. When I was wearing my sandals."

"Now they're naked."

Which was exactly what she wanted to be. Completely naked. When he stood, she looked him straight in the face. "I should take off my T-shirt so you can wash my chest."

He pulled the T-shirt over her head. His eyes warmed as he gazed down at her. She loved the way he was looking at her, with relish and approval.

His thumb touched the pi tattoo above her left breast. "I like it."

"On second thought," she said, "I should wash you, too."

With quick dexterity, she unbuttoned his shirt and pushed it off his shoulder. His T-shirt came next. His muscular chest with a light sprinkle of hair was, of course, perfect. On his flexed bicep the tattoo of Icarus looked like fine art.

"Another thought." Her voice had taken on a husky tone. "Forget the washcloth and kiss me."

He parted her thighs and stepped between them. It felt natural to wrap her legs around him and to embrace him as they kissed. His flesh was warm, and the friction of their bodies generated even more heat. In a matter of minutes, she'd gone from weeping to an amazing excitement with too many sensations to count.

Her primal brain—the hypothalamus—took over, and instinct ruled her behavior. Every touch, every sense and taste had a distinct clarity. Though unaware of why she was doing what she was doing, she knew that he liked to be touched in the crook of his elbow and kissed on his earlobe.

He unfastened her bra to fondle her breasts. When he flicked her nipple with his thumb, a hum of pleasure purred through her. Contented but greedy, she wanted more.

With her legs still wrapped around him, he lifted her off the countertop and carried her down the hall to the bedroom, where they stretched out on the bed.

Though she wanted to take mental snapshots of every second, she couldn't concentrate when he rained kisses over her eager body. Before she realized what was happening, their clothes were gone and they were under the sheets.

Boldly, she grasped his hot erection. When she tugged, he shuddered.

"Slow down, Eve."

"Why do you keep saying that?"

"Because I want this to be good for you. I want you to be ready for me."

She really didn't know how she could be more ready. Sensations zinged through her, and she could feel them building to a crescendo. Still, she lay back on the sheets.

"I guess I should ask about condoms. I'm already pregnant, but—"

"I've been tested recently. I'm clean. You?"

"Um, virgin."

"Right. No condom required."

As he held her gaze, his hand slipped down her body to the juncture of her thighs. When he parted the sensitive folds, she gasped. *Oh, my God, this is really happening.* His finger entered her, and she thought she was going to burst.

"Slowly," he whispered.

The only way she could keep from exploding was by reciting prime numbers in her head. She only got to twenty-three. "Now, Blake. I want you inside me. Now."

He poised above her. Then, with a thrust, he filled her. She arched to meet him, and their passion took on a fierce rhythm, driving toward an ecstasy she'd never felt before. A final thrust and then all the clichés were true. The fireworks. The perfect harmony. The incredible release.

Blake shuddered above her. He fell onto the sheets beside her. When she looked at him, he was beaming.

A residual tremor rippled through her and she reveled in the sensations.

When her breathing returned to something like normal, Blake was watching her. His dark, sexy eyes glittered as he asked, "How was it?"

She stroked his tat. "I have no basis for comparison."

"How did you feel?"

"Like every cell in my body was about to explode, and then I had what I'd identify as an orgasm. Maybe more than one. Is that right?"

"That's correct." He ran his thumb across her lips. "You must be happy. You're smiling."

"Must be." She couldn't help teasing him. "It could have been better. Everything improves with practice."

"Don't worry, Eve. We'll be doing this again." He kissed her. "And again."

She snuggled into his arms. Beyond his shoulder, she saw daylight streaking through the drawn blinds in his bedroom. "It's not even five o'clock. We still have things to do today."

"No rush."

They were meeting Prentice tomorrow night at Latimer's office, and she wanted to be prepared. "We came here to look for the box of your father's things that Connie brought over from Fitzsimons."

"You're right."

He kissed her forehead and rose from the bed. For a moment, she lay back and simply stared at his well-proportioned body. The ratio of his shoulders to his lean hips amazed her. Even though she wasn't an artist, she appreciated the strength and sheer beauty of the male form. She would never forget this moment, this perfect moment.

"Your dad was right," she said.

"About what?"

"He kept encouraging me to open up and have relationships. He said I'd enjoy them." She remembered Dr. Ray's kind smile as he listened to her compare herself to a prime number that didn't need anyone else. "Do you think if we'd met earlier, you and I would have been attracted?"

"I don't look back and think of what might have been." He pulled on his cargo pants. "Always move forward."

"Spoken like a trooper," she said.

Though she agreed that the present was the only firm basis for understanding, she couldn't help speculating. What would happen to her precious new relationship with

Blake when they found his father's murderer? A quick
analysis of probability told her that they would part and
go their separate ways. She doubted that he'd quit the
Special Forces to stay with her, especially since she was
pregnant.

When she was dressed, she followed him into the attached double garage where the Mercedes filled the space
left by his dad's station wagon. Blake caressed the roof
as he circled around the car. "I don't have high hopes for
finding useful evidence in this stuff. Dad only spent one
afternoon a week at Fitzsimons."

"But he knew that people were after information about
the study. He might have chosen the most unlikely place
to hide it."

"I think I put the box back here, under the workbench."

"Did your dad do building projects?"

"He tried. But he wasn't much good as a handyman."

She remembered that Vargas had pointed out Dr. Ray's
reluctance to use new technology. "And he didn't particularly like computers."

"He was an old-fashioned guy."

Blake lifted a box onto the workbench and started taking
things out: a cactus, a wide assortment of pens, a calcula-
tor with extra-large numerals and a misshapen ceramic
bowl.

Eve picked up the vase. "Did you make this?"

"A second-grade project. Art isn't one of my talents.
Nor is music. Nor making money like Vargas." He turned
toward her. "Are we sure that my genetic parents were
outstanding individuals?"

She nodded. "Your gifts are physical. You excelled in
sports. You're in the Special Forces. And you can throw a
knife with pinpoint accuracy."

"Ha! I knew you were impressed when I did that."

She glided her hand down his back and patted his butt. "Not to mention your skill in making love."

"That's genetic?"

"You inherited your physical attributes and your stamina," she said. "But there's an emotional component. I'm not sure what Dr. Ray would call it."

"Empathy." From the box, he took out a framed photograph that was a duplicate of the one in his office. "Me and Mom. Dad loved this picture. I never knew why he didn't update it. He always said this photo was the key to his happiness."

An interesting phrase. "The key?"

Blake glanced up sharply. "He said it several times."

"Take it out of the frame."

Blake unfastened the backing on the frame. Written on the flip side of the photograph were twenty-four names and twenty-four corresponding numbers.

Chapter Fifteen

Blake turned the photograph over in his hands, impressed by his dad's cleverness and irritated at himself for not figuring out the clue sooner. "He gave me the answer. The key."

Eve nodded. "Dr. Ray must have known for a long time that the information generated by the study was dangerous."

"He should have told me." Though Blake didn't claim genius status when it came to intellectual stuff, he was damned good in a fight. "Why the hell didn't he call on me for help?"

"Because this was his battle."

She was blunt but accurate. Blake nodded. "He thought he could handle it by himself."

"Also, he didn't want to tell you about your genetic parents."

"Why? It wouldn't have changed the way I felt about him."

Her clear blue eyes softened. "I'm the wrong person to ask when it comes to motives, but I'd guess that your dad's rationale for keeping this secret had something to do with his love for you."

He wished he could go back in time to when his father was alive and tell him how much he loved him and respected him. Ray Jantzen was the best father any man could have.

He handed the photo to her. "Now what?"

"We check my computer to see if Vargas fulfilled his promise and sent the DNA charts and your dad's statistical abstracts."

He followed her into the house. The twenty-four names they had just discovered were a list of suspects—people who would kill to keep the information contained in the Prentice-Jantzen study a secret. But Blake had the feeling they'd already encountered the man who murdered his father. Trevor Latimer. David Vargas. Or Pyro.

In his bedroom, Eve pounced on the laptop computer. Her slender fingers skipped across the keyboard as she pulled up e-mails. "Oh, good. Here's the stuff from Vargas."

While she opened the file and studied what looked like an incomprehensible array of data, he sprawled on the bed. The linens were disheveled from their lovemaking, and it seemed like a waste of time to straighten the sheets. He fully intended to mess them up again.

With Eve, once was definitely not enough. She sure as hell didn't make love with the shyness of a virgin. She was demanding in a good way, curious and sexy and passionate.

She hunched over the computer. Deciphering the data was her bailiwick. There was nothing he could do right now, except wait.

"Vargas sent the charts." She spun around in the swivel chair. "Dr. Ray's key gives us names for the subjects. That's the good news."

"And the bad?"

"Number one—there are no names for the genetic parents. Number two—your father's data can't be interpreted without knowing what he was testing for."

"Behavior." Seemed obvious to Blake. "Dad used his annual questionnaire to assess behavior."

"All those questions." She rolled her eyes. "Do you prefer a party or a quiet evening alone? Do you work better on your own or when being given clear direction? How many times do you have sex in a week?"

"I never answered that one," he said.

"Awkward for you." She started the printer. "I really hated the 'on a scale of one to ten' section. Are you a happy person? A self-starter? Fearful?"

When he was a child, filling out the annual questionnaire had been a game. The older he got, the more he had resented the questions. Still, the results interested him. "Are you sure you can't read the data?"

"It's a statistical analysis on a graph. All numbers."

"Which you love."

"I do, indeed." Her smile was cute and sexy at the same time. "Unfortunately, words are sometimes necessary. It appears that your father rated thirty-two behaviors for each subject. But he didn't label the behaviors."

"Come again?"

"We need another key."

Each layer of complication piled on top of the one before. If Eve hadn't been helping him, he'd have gone berserk by now. "I guess that means I need to search. What am I looking for?"

"A list of behavioral characteristics. You know, like introversion and extroversion. Or depression. Stuff like that. There are thirty-two."

He rolled off the bed and stretched his arms over his head. Impatience built inside him. He longed for action. "I'll start in Dad's office."

First, he went to the kitchen and opened the fridge. All he'd had to eat since breakfast was gelato, but the array of plastic containers filled with funeral casseroles was downright depressing. He threw together a sandwich from cold cuts and devoured it as he walked down the hallway.

In the doorway, he stopped. Entering the room where his father had been killed shouldn't have bothered him. He'd been in and out of here dozens of times. This moment was different because he'd been thinking about Dad, feeling the ache of losing him.

His sandwich tasted like dust in his mouth. He tossed half of it into the trash can. His dad and mom had loved this house, and he had good memories of family time together. A sense of bittersweet nostalgia enveloped him.

He needed to make this right. No matter how impossible it seemed, he would find the killer. When he did, he'd gut this room and start over. Nope, that wasn't enough. The hell with redecorating; he'd sell the house. With both parents gone, there was no reason to stay in Denver. Except for Eve. He wanted to spend more time with her, and it didn't seem right to abandon her while she was pregnant.

Thinking of her grounded him. She'd given him a job to do: find the key.

He pawed the stuff on his dad's desk. The obvious hiding place was the photograph of him and his mom—an exact duplicate of the one he'd had at his office.

Blake detached the backing and found nothing but a photo. He ran his finger around the edge of the frame, feeling for an encoded chip or microdot. As if his dad, who could barely handle e-mail, would use such a sophisticated device.

To find the answer, he had to think of Ray Jantzen, the man who had raised him. Blake whispered, "Where is it, Dad?"

He could almost hear a reply. *Think, Blake. Don't rush. Take your time.*

Though the desk was cluttered, his dad's thinking followed methodical patterns that made it harder than hell to put anything over on him. Blake clearly recalled one of his father's interrogations after he'd stayed out past curfew. The questions went from how he'd lost track of time to how much he'd been drinking. Their final discussion always seemed to circle back to Blake's tendency to take risks. *Look before you leap.* How many times had his dad said that? "Excessive Risk-Taking" was probably one of the personality behaviors on his chart.

He started opening file folders and thumbing through the contents. His dad's words jumped out at him. An intellectual tone, sometimes stuffy, was apparent in the typed pages of articles he prepared for publication and speeches for presentation at conferences. More revealing were the doodles and scribbled notes in the margins that ranged from "boring" to a row of exclamation points.

In one paper, "Correlation of High Intelligence and Anti-Social Personality Disorder," his father had jotted the initials *P.G.* in the margin. Peter Gregory? The coauthor was listed as Ryan Puller.

Might be useful to give that shrink a call.

As Eve pored over the genetic charts, relationships became clear. Her own DNA profile showed that she didn't have any matches for both mother and father, but she shared a mother with Vargas, the other female and two other people whose names she didn't recognize from the Condolence Book. Blake's genetic mother also provided eggs for four other subjects.

To clarify the interrelationships of the genetic fathers, she laid out graphs and variation equations. Vargas appeared to be the only subject who had a singular genetic father.

Then she turned to Dr. Ray's charts of behaviors rated between one and ten. In her psychological profile, most rankings ranged between three and five, which appeared to be in the normal range. One spiked to an eight. Because she was an introvert? Or had ability in math?

Two names had an unusual number of eights and nines, probably indicating extreme behavior. One was Vargas, who probably considered the high numbers to be a mark of achievement. The other was Pyro. Despite their similar behavior patterns, they didn't share genetic traits. Interesting. These statistics might be proof of Dr. Ray's theory that upbringing was more important in personality development than DNA. As she'd told Vargas, it was all about choices.

Blake's profile had an eight and a couple of sixes. She traced her finger down the list of his characteristics. For the first time in her life, she wished for words instead of numbers. She wanted to know what he was thinking *and feeling*. He'd made love to her with such incredible gentleness. How much did he really care about her? As much as she cared about him?

She frowned at the charts in her hand as she swiveled back and forth in the desk chair. Spending time with Blake had been fun. Making love had been amazing. But relationships had a downside. There would come a moment when they said goodbye. And she'd miss him.

"Ha!" He charged into the room. Energy sparked around him like lightning bolts. Whatever he'd found in his father's office must have been significant.

"I really hope," she said, "that you've got solid information for me."

"I just got off the phone with Dr. Puller. He and my

dad collaborated on a thesis about high intelligence and antisocial personality disorder. Bottom line—smart people make good sociopaths."

"Define sociopath."

"Criminal mastermind."

"Now you're getting into my territory." She grinned. "Criminal masterminds are necessary for epic fantasy battles between the forces of good and evil. But I'm guessing that you're not talking about alien geniuses who want to rule the universe."

"Not really."

"Then you'll have to be more specific."

"Think of somebody ruthless and glib. He'd have a lack of empathy and an inability to tell right from wrong." He pointed at the list of names. "Reminds me of Vargas."

"That's unfair. Vargas hasn't been ruthless or evil. He's been cooperative in sharing his data."

"Which he stole by hacking into my dad's computer. Come on, Eve. He's trying to manipulate you."

"How?"

"Feeding you a fancy lunch and offering those buildings for Sun Wave experiments. He's leading you on with all that talk about how you're his sister and you can ask him for anything."

"Actually, he is my half brother. According to the DNA records, we have the same mother."

"You're defending him."

"I'm focusing on the facts."

In her talks with Vargas, he'd been charming, even charismatic. She wondered if that was a behavior measured by Dr. Ray. "Did your father's paper say anything about sociopaths and charisma?"

Blake nodded. "Puller said that they were the kind of salesmen who'd promise anything to close a deal."

"That fits. Vargas knows how to say all the right words. I'm sensing that he has a hidden agenda, which is odd because I don't usually pick up on things like that. You know, motives."

He spun her around in the swivel chair and pulled her closer to the bed. "I like the way you reason things through."

"You're just pleased because I think Vargas is a jerk."

"That, too."

He slid his hands along the outside of her thighs and scooted her closer for a kiss. The light pressure of his mouth on hers was a powerful distraction, especially when he was sitting on the bed they'd torn apart.

She opened her eyes and stared at him. Looking at that perfect face would never grow tiresome.

"What do you think of my information?" he asked.

"Finding the key to interpret Dr. Ray's list of behaviors would have been more useful."

"I've got Dr. Puller working on it. The number thirty-two was familiar to him. He's checking into psychological profiling tools used by the military."

"When you talked to him about the sociopath study, did Puller say that Dr. Ray mentioned any names?"

"My dad was too discreet for that. He referred to Subject X and Subject Y. No names." With the back of his hand, he stroked her cheek. "Why do you ask?"

"Two subjects show indications of extreme behavior. One is Vargas."

"And the other is Peter Gregory," he said. "My dad wrote his initials in the margin. What else have you figured out?"

"Mostly, I've been checking the DNA evidence and trying to figure out relationships." With a sigh, she turned away from him and dragged her attention back to the facts.

"It's a patchwork family tree with five mothers and eleven fathers."

Blake picked up the pages she'd scribbled on. "Somewhere in this is a motive."

"It'd help to know the identities of the sperm and egg donors," she said.

"How would that be useful?"

"More data could flesh out the picture." And there was another reason, one she hadn't really acknowledged until she said it out loud. "And I'm curious."

She couldn't help wondering about her biological parents. Who were they? What had they done with their intelligence?

She loved the parents who raised her, and she knew they'd accept her no matter what. Mom and Dad weren't going to be thrilled when she told them she was pregnant and unmarried and didn't know the father of her child. But they wouldn't turn their backs on her.

She thought of the tiny being growing within her. This was her baby. The people she'd always called Mom and Dad were the baby's grandparents. But she couldn't help wondering.

"I'm curious, too," he said.

"I thought of checking the military database. But this was twenty-six years ago. There probably wouldn't be any results."

"And a lot of paperwork."

"We could try CODIS."

"Might as well." He took out his cell phone and paced across the bedroom to the window. "Let's give Detective Gable something to do."

She left her chair and followed him. Outside, daylight was waning, and she had a pretty good idea about how she wanted to spend the rest of the afternoon and night. She wrapped her arms around him and leaned against his back, listening to his voice as he spoke to the police detective.

Though it seemed like a contradiction, she felt comfy and excited at the same time. There was so much to learn about the emotional side of life and relationships.

Blake completed his call with a promise to send the DNA charts via e-mail to be run through CODIS.

When he turned to face her, she read passion in his smile. His dark eyes warmed her blood and sent a zing of anticipation through her body. Making love this time should be even better; she wasn't a virgin anymore.

"I think we have time." He ducked his head and kissed her quickly. "We'll make time."

She pressed against him. "Are we going somewhere?"

"We need to check out Peter Gregory." He kissed her more deeply. "Tonight is Pyro's concert."

Chapter Sixteen

Heading toward downtown Denver in the sleek armored Mercedes, Blake glanced over at Eve in the passenger seat. They'd been in the car for less than eight minutes, and she was already asleep. She'd told him that she was going to nap, tilted the seat back and...zap!

Even in repose, she was vibrant. The light from the dashboard caught on the wisps of hair that fell across her forehead. Her nose twitched. Her lips were bruised from a thousand kisses, but she was smiling like a woman who had been well satisfied from an afternoon of loving.

Blake considered himself a very lucky man to be with her.

Doubling back through traffic, he watched headlights and looked for other signs that they were being followed. No need to worry about bugs or GPS devices. Not in this car. A built-in scrambler made their movements untraceable.

He merged onto the highway and checked his G-Shock wristwatch. The Pyro concert started at ten, which gave him enough time to get there.

It was hard for him to think of Peter Gregory/Pyro as a rock star. Or a criminal mastermind. In Blake's mind, Peter had always been a brat—the only son of Lou Gregory who was a friend and coworker of his dad.

They had first met ten years ago, just after Blake's dad

had joined the group practice. The office staff, their families and friends had gathered at the Gregory home for Lou's fiftieth birthday party.

Both Blake and Peter had been fifteen, and their parents had expected them to hang out together—an intention that went bad when Peter threw a hissy fit and locked himself in his bedroom, refusing to come out. Blake remembered feeling relieved; he wasn't interested in getting friendly with a scrawny, pale-skinned, spoiled whiner who couldn't get over himself long enough to sing "Happy Birthday" to his own father.

Over the years, he and Peter had bumped into each other a half-dozen times at various family and office get-togethers. Their standard practice was to give each other a nod and find somebody else to talk with.

Blake should have looked closer at Pyro, should have recognized him as a threat.

Eve exhaled a soft little sigh and shifted position to get more comfortable in the soft leather upholstery. She'd been as surprised as he had been when they had looked up Pyro online and sampled his post-apocalyptic, techno-metal rock. His sound wasn't unusual—a hard-driving beat with a discordant keyboard refrain. The lyrics were the revelation.

His latest featured song was about "The Twenty-Four." They would rise up together, these powerful yet unknown heroes with superpowers, and they would conquer the world. All would bow before them. *Twenty-four.* No co-incidence that it was the same number as the subjects in the Prentice-Jantzen study.

At Latimer's house, when they had told him about his genetic parents, Pyro had claimed to be happily astonished. *Liar!* Not only was he aware of the study but he'd given considerable thought to their supposed genetic superiority. Hell, he'd written a damn ballad to sing their praises.

Additionally, he had access to the office where Blake's father might have kept his notes. Pyro could easily have stolen the research notes or made copies.

But why would he care? As a supposed rock star, it was to his advantage to claim a weird parentage. If Pyro's psychological profile showed a tendency toward antisocial personality disorder, he'd wear that label like a badge of honor.

Exiting the highway, Blake negotiated the stop-and-go city traffic on the route to Bowman Hall on Colfax Avenue, an old redstone building that had been through many transformations since its early days as an opera house. The marquee announced, "Tonight Only. Pyro." The doors had opened, and a grungy crowd jostled each other on the sidewalk to get inside.

With a little effort, Blake figured that he and Eve could fit in with the rest of the audience. True, he had a military haircut, but he hadn't shaved in two days. Nor would Eve stand out. She was, as usual, wearing a weird T-shirt with a winged monster and the word *Jabberwocky* in Gothic script. She claimed the shirt was a tribute to Lewis Carroll, a mathematician. Oh, yeah, she'd blend right in.

But he didn't want to risk taking her into a crowd. There were too many distractions, too many chances for someone to grab her.

As he parallel-parked on a neighboring street where the old mansions had been converted to offices, she wakened. When she stretched and yawned, her arms fully extended over the dashboard. Her fingers opened wide and curled shut. She hunched her shoulders, then relaxed. When she looked at him, her eyes were bright and alert. "I'm ready."

"That was a speedy wake-up."

"Da Vinci said sleep is a waste of time. All our bodies only need a twenty-minute nap every four or five hours to stay refreshed. To tell the truth, I prefer the Einstein plan."

"What's that?"

"Eight to ten hours a night." She tugged on his sleeve. "Let's pick up our backstage passes at the box office and watch the concert."

"Not necessary." After the short online sampling, he really didn't want to subject his ears to Pyro's techno-rock wailing. "Our goal is to get Pyro alone after the show and ask him a couple of questions."

She shrugged. "If he's guilty, why would he talk to us?"

"Ego."

Surrounded by his groupies, Pyro wouldn't want to look weak by avoiding them. "In that 'Twenty-Four' song, he planned to lead the rest of us into a brilliant future. You and me? He sees us as his followers."

"Not likely."

"Maybe you're his queen."

"Even worse." She rested her hand on her belly. "What if this is Pyro's baby? Do you think it was him? That he paid Prentice to do the IVF procedure on me?"

"Doesn't fit his persona," he said. "Pyro thinks he's all-powerful and irresistible. He'd try to seduce you."

But Pyro hadn't contacted them. They'd found him. What was he up to? The rocker was playing a game, but the end goal remained a mystery. The only course of action that made sense to Blake was face-to-face confrontation.

"When we see him," Eve said, "what should we do?"

"I could beat a confession out of him."

"Seriously, Blake."

"He already lied once, pretending that he didn't know about the study. I want to know why. What else is he hiding?" He checked his watch. "Let's give him a half hour or so to get the concert rolling."

She unfastened her seat belt and leaned toward him. "Do you think Ms. Mercedes would be jealous if I kissed you?"

"This is a very sexy vehicle." He shot his seat back and pulled her onto his lap. "But you have special features that the car can't match."

As they kissed, he told himself that an effective bodyguard wouldn't allow himself to be preoccupied with romance. But he just couldn't keep his hands off his beautiful, willing partner.

THOUGH THEY STOPPED short of having sex in a car parked on a city street, the windows of the Mercedes were steamed up when Eve got out. Not exactly classy, but she felt too good to care.

Blake strode around the hood to join her on the sidewalk. In an attempt to disguise his military bearing and look like a Pyro fan, he'd allowed her to line his eyes with kohl. He'd stripped off his button-down shirt, which he tied around his waist to hide his holster. His sleeveless white T-shirt showed off his tattoo and his muscular arms. In her opinion, he was so outrageously masculine that nobody would dare question his right to be anywhere he chose.

Her Pyro fan disguise was to mess up her hair and tie a knot in her Jabberwocky shirt to make it tight across her breasts. Blake had convinced her to leave her purse in the car, but she stowed her cell phone and the stun gun in her pockets.

As they strolled along the street in the warm June night, she realized this was the closest they'd come to a date. With all the passion they'd shared, he hadn't even taken her out to dinner. "When this is over, we should go out."

"Out where?"

Apparently, the eyeliner had lowered his IQ by a solid fifty points. "To dinner and a movie. A moonlit carriage ride though the city. Dancing might be involved."

"A date." He took her hand. "I wish we had more time. I've only got a couple more weeks on leave."

After his leave was up, he'd be gone. Back to the Middle East or wherever. She didn't want to think about how sad she'd be when he left.

As they approached the box office, she noticed clumps of people standing around near the entrance. Some were smoking. Several wore black shirts with red letters that identified them as Pyro staff. How many people were needed to put on a concert like this? From the clip they'd watched online, she knew that Pyro used a lot of fireworks in his act, including an effect called the "Wall of Flame."

While Blake picked up their backstage passes, she focused on two of the Pyro staff who wore dark glasses even though it was night. The taller guy had a gold pinkie ring with an amber stone. Cleft chin. Small ears. His companion had a pug nose, big ears and a paunch around his middle.

Her eidetic memory kicked in. She knew them. They were the two men in business suits who had broken into her house. They turned away from her and went through the glass doors that led into the theater lobby. As she watched, they went through a door at the far left. It almost seemed as if they wanted her to see them.

Blake joined her and slipped her backstage pass around her neck. She looked up at him. "I saw the guys who tried to grab me at my house."

His pretense at being a laid-back Pyro fan transformed. His body tensed, ready for action. The liner around his dark eyes made him look fierce. "Where are they?"

She pointed to the interior of the lobby. "They went through that door. To the left."

"Stay with me, Eve. Behind me."

Though she hadn't noticed him pulling his weapon, the Sig Sauer was in his hand. Keeping the gun close to his side so it wasn't obvious, he moved quickly into the lobby.

At one time, this theatre might have been a rococo jewel box. Not anymore. The floor was dirty brown tile. The fancy moldings and the walls were painted black. Two sets of double doors led into the auditorium. From inside, she heard crashing drums and a wailing keyboard solo.

Nobody else was in the lobby. Apprehensive, she glanced to the left and the right. "It seemed like they wanted me to see them. This could be a trap."

When he opened the door, sound erupted. The place was packed. People were waving their arms, cheering and dancing in front of their seats and in the aisles. There was a sense of the music building toward a screaming crescendo.

Blake closed the door and stepped back. "Were they wearing staff shirts?"

"Yes."

"You might be right about a trap. We'll take a different route. They probably went backstage."

Outside, they ran around the side of the building toward the rear. At the stage door, a husky man in a Pyro staff shirt stood guard. The door was open, and an undercurrent of noise pulsated into the night.

Blake paused. He took out his cell phone. "I'm calling Detective Gable. We need backup."

Good plan. Her heart hammered inside her rib cage.

Peering toward the street, she saw a threat in every shadow. They should go back to the car, lock the doors and wait for the police to arrive.

Blake snapped his phone closed. "Gable's on the way. Should be here in fifteen minutes."

"And we'll wait for him," she said hopefully.

"These guys have gotten away from me twice. It's not going to happen again. I'll take you to the car. You can wait there."

Alone and unprotected? Even though the Mercedes had reinforced armored siding and bulletproof glass, she felt safer with him. "I'll stay with you."

"Is that a logical decision?"

Nothing she felt about him was rational, but she knew that if something bad happened to him while she was hiding in the car, she'd never forgive herself. "Let's go."

At the stage door, Blake concealed his gun and flashed their passes. They entered the backstage area.

The brilliant stage lights focused on Pyro. In the wings, it was dark. There was a lot of clutter from cables and ropes and a lot of space, both horizontal and vertical. Heavy curtains rose two stories high. Above them were catwalks. The backstage crew gathered near the curtains as though preparing to do…something important, maybe the "Wall of Flame" effect. Was Pyro reaching his finale?

Blake kept his back to the wall. "Do you see them?"

The music was so loud, she could barely hear him. "They vanished."

"We can go behind the back curtain to the other side."

"Wait."

With Blake close beside her, she went over to a guy with shoulder-length dreadlocks and showed him her backstage pass. Leaning close so he could hear her over the music, she said, "I'm looking for two guys on your staff. They always wear dark glasses."

When he nodded, his dreads bounced. He pointed toward a doorway without a door. A dim light shone from within, showing a stairwell leading down.

Blake guided her toward that light. There was nothing sexual about the way his hand rested on her waist. He was directing her. "As a general rule," he said, "it's not a good idea to ask the enemy for directions."

"At least we have a direction."

"Or we're being pointed toward an ambush."

It stood to reason that these men had also been the ones who had attacked at Blake's house with guns blazing. They were dangerous. The sensible thing was to turn back, but Blake didn't hesitate.

As they descended to the basement, she reached into her pocket and took out the stun gun. How did this thing work? She opened the safety and squeezed. Electricity arced between the two prongs on the end. It seemed too small to do serious damage.

On the bottom stair, he paused. As soon as they stepped into the open, they'd be an easy target. The music throbbed above them—not as loud down here. The beat was an echo, reminding her of the danger, heightening her fear.

Blake poked his head outside the stairwell and drew back quickly. "There's a hallway with a door."

"Okay." Why was he telling her?

"Ready?"

She repeated, "Okay."

Blake slung his arm around her waist and pulled her across the hallway at the foot of the stairs in a swift move. He twisted the handle on the door. Locked! Using his shoulder, he crashed through. They were inside a dark room.

The first thing she did was hit the light switch.

A single bare bulb illuminated a storage room, packed with boxes, old props and dusty costumes. The smell of grit and filth disgusted her.

Blake pulled her close. "I didn't get a real good look out there. Beyond this hallway, there's an open space—a big room. Not many lights. Theater junk scattered around."

"They could be hiding anywhere." Ready to pop out and open fire. "I say we wait for the police."

"We could use the backup," he agreed. "I'm guessing that this basement extends all the way under the stage to the opposite side. There must be several exits. They could escape before Gable gets here."

And he wanted to apprehend them in the worst way. She understood. These men were his best lead to finding his father's murderer. "What do we do?"

"Make them reveal their position. Draw their fire."

Her heart thudded. "You want them to shoot at us?"

"Not exactly."

Literally trusting him with her life, she said, "Tell me what to do."

Chapter Seventeen

Blake based his attack on two factors: these two hired guns weren't experienced in combat, and they were cowards. Twice before, they'd run from him. More difficult was the problem of engaging in a firefight while keeping Eve safe. He couldn't leave her in this room where she could be easily captured.

He told her to stay low, to find a hiding place in the larger room outside the hallway and to use her stun gun if anyone approached her. Any minute, Detective Gable would be here.

"Why not wait for him?" she asked.

"Gable's smart," he said. "He'll block the backstage exits. But he won't have the manpower to monitor the audience. The Pyro staff can use the crowd to escape."

"The whole staff? Do you think they're all involved?"

"Don't know. All I'm worried about right now is apprehending these two."

Grabbing junk from the prop room, he threw together a dummy target that would go ahead of them. He had to move fast, to provoke gunfire before they knew what they were shooting at.

He turned to her. "Ready?"

She nodded mutely. Her eyes were wide but not fearful.

Her bravery touched him. He would die to protect this woman.

While the music throbbed from overhead, he dashed from the hallway into the larger room. In the dim light, he saw open space, junk and shadows. With one hand, he thrust the makeshift dummy in front of them. The other hand held his gun.

A flash of gunfire showed the position of his adversaries. Straight ahead and to the left.

Blake threw the dummy to the right and ducked behind a crate. They were only ten feet from the gunmen. "Stay here," he told Eve.

He moved away from her, drawing their fire. He was close enough that he could see them when they peeked out to shoot. He returned fire. Even louder than the music, he heard a shout. One of them had been hit.

The other man took off running. The son of a bitch was going to get away. Again.

Blake couldn't pursue until he knew the first gunman was no longer a threat. He approached the place where he'd seen gunfire. The man was down. Bleeding. Unconscious.

Blake took his gun and ran across the basement. He was just in time to see the second man, the taller one, dive into the stairwell.

He followed. A narrow flight of stairs led straight up to an open doorway. He aimed both handguns in front of him, ready to blast anyone stupid enough to get in his way.

Without firing a shot, he emerged in the backstage area. Under normal circumstances, his two-gun entrance would have attracted attention. But the backstage area was busy with what had to be the climax to the concert. The lights onstage flashed and flared. Smoke machines blew a heavy mist across the floor. He caught a glimpse of Pyro breathing fire.

In an old building like this, there would be strict regulations about setting off fireworks, but the Pyro staff had come up with their spectacular special effect—the so-called wall of flame.

Blake had seen it online, but the real thing was more impressive. A shimmering, translucent curtain of red, orange and yellow strips rose slowly from the back of the stage. Lights flashed against it. A wind machine rippled the fabric. From the audience, it would look as if a wall of flames consuming the theater.

Behind his keyboard, Pyro screamed about how "The Twenty-Four" would take over the world. Blake caught sight of his quarry.

He pursued, jumping over cables on the floor and shoving people out of his way. Smoke billowed around his feet.

The area behind the scrim with rising flames allowed light to bleed through. Blake spotted the other man. Diving, he tackled his adversary, knocked him to the floor, flat on his belly. He shoved his guns into his belt and disarmed the other man. Finally, he had this guy. Finally, he'd get some answers.

The music stopped. The stage went black.

From the auditorium, the audience screamed for more.

Backstage, dim safety lights cast minimal illumination. Blake heard voices around him, felt hands pulling him off their friend. Instead of fighting one man, he was battling a mob.

He heard a shout from his left. "Police. Freeze."

A hand grasped his shoulder and pulled him back.

Blake wrenched free before he lost his grip on the gunman, but the guy had seen his chance. He struggled, put up a hell of a fight. "Back off," Blake yelled. "I'm with the cops."

His words had no effect. The rest of Pyro's staff swarmed him, dragged him off the man he had pinned on the floor. It was tempting to use the gun to clear the area, but these others might be innocent.

On his feet, Blake reacted by instinct. Using the butt of the gun, he whacked one guy in the head. Another doubled over in pain when he unleashed a hard jab to the gut.

In the shadows, he saw somebody moving to help him, pulling the attackers away from him. There wasn't enough light to see who was on his side, and Blake's only concern was to catch the gunman who attacked in the basement, to prevent him from fleeing.

The lights came back up. He saw the man fighting on his side. Vargas. His nemesis. What the hell?

Blake pointed to the gunman who was escaping. "Stop him."

And there was Eve. She jabbed her stun gun into the man's side, and he went down.

AN HOUR LATER, Eve sat on the edge of the stage with her feet dangling. She'd always prided herself on being observant, but she hadn't been able to produce much in the way of useful information when questioned by Detective Gable. Too much had happened too fast. The shooting. The music. The chase. The wall of flame.

Her brain was still sorting through the details.

The aftermath was equally confusing. An ambulance raced in and picked up the man who Blake shot in the basement. He was expected to survive, thank goodness. Other paramedics treated the various people injured in the backstage brawl.

The other man—the guy Blake risked his life in

pursuing—was in custody, not talking and demanding a lawyer. Who was he? The rest of Pyro's staff claimed they didn't know. According to them, these two jerks in sunglasses had joined their crew a few hours ago. Were they all lying? Gable and the other police were still sorting out witness accounts, taking names and checking identifications.

She exhaled a sigh, and her shoulders slumped. Close to midnight, her energy was running low, and she wished she could take another Da Vinci–style power nap.

Vargas came up behind her. "Mind if I join you?"

"Suit yourself."

He sat on the edge of the stage beside her. In his jeans and denim shirt, he looked casual but still expensive. His left hand was wrapped in a bandage. "Are you all right, Eve?"

"I wasn't injured."

"You handled yourself well."

Though raised on military bases, she tended to be more of a pacifist. Not a fighter. She hadn't expected to enjoy using the stun gun, but when she had zapped the bad guy and he had gone down, she'd felt a kind of thrill.

That exhilaration was long gone, replaced by the frustrating awareness that they still had too many unanswered questions. She wanted answers, starting with Vargas. "Why are you here? At lunch, you told me that you didn't know any of the others, including Pyro."

"I saw him at the funeral. Thought I might take advantage of the concert to meet him. It was a bad idea."

She'd seen him join in the fight when Blake was struggling with the gunman. Vargas had taken his side, which meant he was an ally. Or was he? She knew better than to trust her genetic half brother. "A bad idea? Why?"

"Because Pyro has left the building." He shrugged.

"According to his staff, he always ends his concerts the same way. The big finale with smoke and flames. Then, he's gone."

"I doubt he vanished into thin air."

"The police can't reach him on the phone. Supposedly, he goes underground after a big performance. They might not hear from him for days."

In her opinion, Pyro's convenient disappearance meant he was fleeing the scene. Coupled with his connection to the two thugs who broke into her house, Pyro was beginning to look a lot like the person who had killed Blake's father. Unfortunately, circumstantial conjecture wasn't proof.

Vargas cleared his throat. "Did you get the information I e-mailed to you?"

"Yes, thank you." Her guard went up. She needed to be careful about how much she revealed. "It's difficult to decipher, but I saw that you and I share the same mother. Your father, however, is unique."

"I noticed that, too. I was the only child from that sperm donor."

An observation wasn't an answer. Tomorrow night when she finally talked to Dr. Prentice, she'd get closer to the truth. "In the psychological profile, you showed several extreme behaviors."

"My ratings were high."

So were Pyro's. "Do you have any idea what behaviors were being measured?"

"I'm aggressive," he readily admitted. "And I'd rate high in organization. I'm an effective public speaker. Also, I have musical talent and an exceptional ability with numbers."

"I wouldn't give you high marks for modesty."

"I'm confident with good reason." He grinned. "I get results."

She thought of the traits for antisocial personality disorder. "Would you call yourself ruthless?"

"I wouldn't. Others would." He reached over and patted her hand—an uninvited attention that made her want to pull away from him. "Before my twentieth birthday, I was a millionaire. What does that say about me?"

"That you're not a pussycat?"

"God, I hope not."

Blake joined them, taking a seat on her other side. Stage dirt smeared his sleeveless white T-shirt, and she noticed a couple of bruises on his bare arms. The eyeliner had left dark smudges on his face. He reminded her of a warrior, embattled and heroic.

Leaning around her, he spoke to Vargas. "I haven't had a chance to thank you. I appreciated your help."

"The least I could do," he said. "Eve was the one who really saved the day."

When they both looked at her, she was embarrassed. "Shucks, boys. It was nothing."

Vargas asked, "What have the police found out?"

"They have basic identification," Blake said. "The two thugs are from San Francisco. No current warrants, but they've both got criminal records."

"How did they get backstage?"

"The stage manager said they told him they were pyrotechnic specialists, studying the act to come up with new special effects. They flashed a bogus contract."

With his right hand, Vargas smoothed the white streak in his black hair—an unnecessary gesture because his hair wasn't out of place. She wondered what it would take to shatter his smooth façade. An accusation?

"Statistically," she said, "Dr. Ray's psychological profiles show that you and Pyro had much in common."

"Not surprising," Vargas said. "Even if we don't share the same DNA, we were designed to be high-functioning."

"Designed," Blake said with disgust. "I hate that idea."

Simultaneously, she and Vargas asked, "Why?"

She glanced over her shoulder at her genetic half brother. Knowing that she was speaking for both of them, she said, "There's nothing wrong with scientific experimentation."

"I've got nothing against science," Blake said. "But I'm not an experiment. My life is a hell of a lot more than a sperm and egg that got mixed together in a petri dish."

"That's your father's thesis," Vargas said. "He always said that upbringing and environment are more important in psychological development than genetics."

"My dad didn't get involved in this study for science. He did it for love."

She marveled at the beautiful simplicity of his reasoning. "Dr. Ray loved his wife and wanted to give her a child, even if it meant dealing with Prentice. When you were born, he loved you, too."

In his way, Dr. Ray had loved all of them, all the subjects in the study. He followed their development—year by year—with an interest that was more than statistical.

And one of them had killed him.

She turned to Vargas, determined to shake his overwhelming confidence. "You and Pyro have other similarities. You're both musically talented, both successful in your field."

"Stop right there." Vargas gestured to the auditorium that lay before them. The lights were up, showing the litter on the floor, the dirty walls and the rows of beat-up seats. "I wouldn't call a performance in this third-rate venue an example of success."

"Pyro has a following," she said. "All those screaming fans think he's a star."

Vargas scoffed. "He's a prancing moron leading others of his ilk."

"And you have something else in common," she said. "Both you and Pyro knew about the study. That's why he sings that song about the twenty-four—the superheroes who are going to take over the world. How did he find out? Do you know?"

"I don't," Vargas said. "It could be that Pyro and I are flip sides of the same coin."

Or maybe, just maybe, Vargas was lying. What was that description of sociopathic behavior? They could look you in the eye and tell you what you wanted to hear. Their idea of truth was defined by whatever was best for them.

"Here's the good news," Blake said. "Detective Gable says we're free to go."

He rose to his feet, grasped her hand and pulled her upright. Standing, she realized that her legs were a bit wobbly. In some ways, this had been the best day in her life—the day when she finally lost her virginity. In others, this twenty-four-hour period had been exhausting.

Blake smiled down at her. "Tired?"

"Oh, yeah."

"Get some rest," Vargas said. "A woman in your condition needs plenty of sleep. Don't hesitate to call me if you need anything. That goes for both of you."

Blake shook his hand. "Thanks, again."

As Vargas strode off the stage, she snuggled against Blake's chest. "Sleep sounds really good to me."

"I don't want to drive all the way back to the burbs," he said. "We'll stay in a downtown hotel tonight."

She thought of crisp sheets and chocolate mints on the pillow. "Wonderful."

Halfway down the street to the car, she was hit by an insight. "Vargas is up to something."

"I'd agree," Blake said. "Even though he took my side, I don't trust—"

"He said that a woman in my condition needed sleep."

"And?"

"I never told him I was pregnant."

Chapter Eighteen

Spray from the steaming hot shower pelted Blake's shoulders and ran down his back, soothing the minor bruises from his brawl at the theater. Staying in a downtown hotel had been the right decision; he was so tired that he might have fallen asleep at the wheel driving back to his dad's house, and it would have been a shame to wreck that beautiful Mercedes.

Random thoughts popped inside his brain. Vargas knew more than he was telling. Having him show up at the concert where the two thugs made their final play had been more than coincidence. If anyone was clever enough to be a criminal mastermind, it had to be Vargas.

But Pyro had fled the scene. A classic admission of guilt?

And what about Latimer? His contact with Prentice was damned suspicious, and he had a strong motive to suppress the information in the Prentice-Jantzen study.

One of those men had killed his father. If Blake hadn't been so tired, he might have reached out and grasped the solution.

Getting out of the shower, he dried himself off and wrapped a towel around his waist.

In the bedroom, the lights were on, and the flat-screen television showed a late-night talk show. Apparently, Eve had been trying to stay awake. Swaddled in a terry-cloth robe, she sat on top of the quilted bedspread. In her limp hand, she held the TV remote, but her eyes were closed, and her head drooped forward. She reminded him of a kid, struggling to stay up past bedtime. "Oh, Eve," he murmured, "what am I going to do about you?"

The connection between them grew deeper with every moment he spent in her presence. Truly, he thought of her as a partner. She was brave, smart and damn good-looking. Her hair, still damp from the shower, fell in blond tendrils to frame her lovely face. Gently, he kissed her forehead and took the remote from her hand.

He turned off the television. Silence filled the room. They would be safe tonight.

When he repositioned her under the covers, she murmured but didn't waken. He threw off his towel and slipped into bed beside her. Still asleep, she snuggled into his arms.

Being with Eve felt right. If she'd been awake, she would have pointed out the logical objections to why they couldn't be together. His work in Special Forces required him to travel all over the globe. She was pregnant, and the father of her baby might be the man who had killed his dad. If awake, she'd tell him that they'd only been together a couple of days and he'd get over her.

Blake knew better. He trusted his feelings more than the facts. His heart told him that Eve was the woman he wanted. She was his destiny.

He dropped into a deep, peaceful sleep.

Later that night, still in a dream state, he felt her supple, naked body resting in his arms. He caressed the curve of her slender waist, marveling at the satin texture of her skin. When he stroked the flare of her hips, she moved closer to him.

Stretching, she molded her body to his. She planted a moist kiss in the hollow of his throat. Unsure of whether he was awake or asleep, he accepted the fantasy. In the sweet, silent darkness, he made love to her.

IN THE MORNING, Blake awakened gradually, aware that he was sleeping in a strange and luxurious bed. He reached across the sheets, expecting to find Eve. She was gone.

His eyelids popped open. Where was she? Had she vanished like a dream? An irrational sense of bereavement shot through him. He didn't want to lose her, didn't want to be apart, not even for a minute.

Leaving the bed, he went to the closed bathroom door and pressed his ear against it, listening. He didn't hear water running. "Eve?"

"Oh, good. You're up. Come on in."

He pushed open the door and saw her, fully dressed and alert. She sat cross-legged on the bathroom floor with her laptop open in front of her.

He asked, "What are you doing?"

"I didn't want to turn on a light and wake you." She beamed a smile. "I was wide-awake and figured I could use this time to update a project at Sun Wave."

"You've been working?"

"Sure. With my cell phone and my computer, I can do most of my work from any location."

"Anywhere?" he asked. "Even on the other side of the planet?"

"Or from outer space." She closed her laptop and stood. "But if we're going that far, I'd like to get breakfast first."

Aware that he was naked, he retreated into the bedroom and gathered up his clothes. The glimmer of a plan took root in his mind. If all she needed for work was a computer, there was no reason why she couldn't come with him when he returned to the Middle East. Of course, he wouldn't take her into an active combat zone. But there were safe places.

While he showered again and dressed, he came up with a plan for the day. First, breakfast. Then, shopping. His clothes from last night were filthy with backstage dirt, and Eve probably felt the same way about her clothes. Maybe he could convince her to buy something more attractive than a T-shirt.

He came out of the bathroom into the large bedroom where the curtain was open. Sunlight poured through the window; it was after ten o'clock in the morning.

Eve sat at the cherrywood desk with her laptop open in front of her. He came up behind her, rested his hands on her shoulders and peeked at the computer screen, expecting to see an indecipherable array of equations. Instead, he saw typed paragraphs.

Leaning down, he kissed her cheek. "What are you working on?"

She turned her head and kissed him back. "We got a reply from Dr. Puller. He found a statistical key to decipher your dad's information. It was an old form used by the military to measure personality traits."

"This should be interesting." In the course of his military service, Blake had undergone a vast number of surveys and tests for both physical and mental ability. The results were usually annoying. He stood at the window and looked out. They were on the tenth floor and would have had a nice view of the mountains if there hadn't been another tall building in the way.

"Dr. Puller interpreted the numerical codes. He wanted to be sure we understood that this kind of statistical survey isn't an exact science. The traits indicate potential behavior rather than fact. For example, a person might have a leaning toward creativity but it doesn't mean they'll become an artist."

"What does it say about you?"

"Puller didn't know my name, of course. He only had the random numbers for identification."

He sensed that she was dancing around instead of giving him the answer. "Let's hear it, Eve. Are you a potential…" he tried to think of what would be the most incongruous fate for her—something illogical and nonscientific "…poet?"

"I wouldn't mind that at all. Poetry requires an understanding of stanza and tempo. Numbers."

"Maybe you're a potential palm reader."

"Yuck. No."

He teased, "A stripper?"

"You wish." She left the desk and joined him at the window. "I'm an introvert. No surprise there. I'm also logical and judgmental with a strong sense of right and wrong."

It didn't take a psychological profile to make that analysis. Two minutes of conversation with her would lead to the same result. "What else?"

Her wide mouth pulled into a frown. "I'm patient, nurturing and empathetic. Apparently, I have all the traits of a good mother."

She looked so disappointed that he almost laughed. "Is that a problem?"

"Well, it's convenient since I'm pregnant. But I never thought of myself that way. Me? A mom?"

He pulled her into his arms and kissed the top of her head. Puller's conclusion didn't shock him in the least. From the time he'd seen her caring for the feral cats in her alley, he'd known that she had a nurturing personality. "It's not so bad. Madame Curie was a mother."

"When I was growing up and all the other girls played with baby dolls, I never had an interest. My favorite toys were geometric. Like building blocks."

"No reason why you can't do both. Play with babies and build skyscrapers with solar panels."

She tilted her head up and grinned at him. "Now let's talk about you."

"Let me guess." He remembered all his dad's lectures. "I'm too reckless."

"Correct," she said. "You're also decisive and goal-oriented. According to Puller, once you set your mind to something, you won't rest until you've achieved it. You deal well with trauma, which is lucky considering your line of work."

He was waiting for the downside. "What else?"

"A lot of your decisions are based on emotion. As much as you're a fighter, you're a lover, too."

As soon as she spoke, he recognized an important part of himself. "That's my dad's influence."

Throughout Blake's life, his dad had shown him—through words and by example—that emotion was important. No matter what course had been charted by his genetics, his upbringing taught him to care about other people and made him a better man.

Eve rested her head on his chest. "We were lucky, you and me. We had good parents."

"What about the other subjects?"

"Problems. Nasty problems." She stepped away from his embrace and returned to the computer screen. "Latimer is selfish and demanding with a huge ego."

"What about Pyro and Vargas?"

She winced. "Both show sociopathic tendencies."

"Meaning?"

"High potential for violence."

EVE WASN'T SURE IF breakfast in the hotel coffee shop counted as a first date. Blake had invited her, chosen the place and he paid for the food. But the meal was more about expedience than enjoying each other's company.

The shopping trip that followed breakfast definitely wasn't a date. They'd gone to a trendy little boutique in Larimer Square—not the kind of place she usually shopped. Blake kept pushing her toward sexy satin things and plunging necklines. She settled on a formfitting black cashmere sweater with short sleeves. It wasn't her first choice, but she liked the way he looked at her when she was wearing it. He insisted on buying the long, belted sweater that went with it because it might get chilly later, and they didn't have time to go back to the house.

Their visit to the police station definitely wasn't a date. Nor was it useful. Detective Gable informed them that the two men in custody had lawyers and refused to say who had hired them. When it came to investigating Vargas, Gable's hands were tied. Vargas might be a raging psycho, but he was also a wealthy and powerful member of the community. Gable needed more than a psychological profile to get a warrant. Pyro was another story. The police were on the lookout for him, but he hadn't surfaced.

At six o'clock—two hours before they were scheduled to meet Prentice—Blake took her to a Mexican restaurant in west Denver. He chose the place because he thought she'd like it. And there was candlelight. When they were shown to their table, he held her chair as she sat.

"This is a date," she said.

"If you say so."

"Have you brought other women here?"

"Once or twice." He sat across the table. "None of them were as beautiful as you."

"Thank you." She'd been trained to politely accept compliments, even if they were blatant exaggerations.

"I mean it. That black cashmere sweater makes your skin glisten like a pearl."

His flattery reinforced her sense of being on a date. "Why this restaurant?"

"I know the family who owns the place. The food's great. Later on, there's a mariachi band."

"The possibility of dancing," she said. "That seals the deal. This is definitely a date."

"Courtship rituals aren't important. You know how I feel about you, Eve."

In point of fact, she didn't know. He hadn't actually stated his feelings. Though they'd made love four times, including that dreamy passion in the hotel last night, there had been no declarations. "I like going out, being wined and dined—visiting different places, seeing different views, tasting different foods."

"Do you take many vacations?"

"Not really." Usually, she used her time off to visit family. "I enjoy traveling, but making all the arrangements isn't my thing."

"I'd take care of the arrangements."

She wasn't sure what he was getting at. "It almost sounds like you're offering to sweep me away to some exotic locale."

"Have you ever wanted to see the pyramids? I know a guy who charters boat trips on the Nile."

"I'll bet you do." When they'd walked through the door of the restaurant, he was greeted like a long lost son. Blake was the kind of guy who made friends easily.

"The Middle East is incredible. Have you been there?"

"No." Her dad had been stationed in Germany when she was very young, but his other postings had been stateside.

"When my leave is up, I want to take you back with me."

That was a bit more of a date than she'd been hoping for. "You want to take me where?"

"To wherever I'm posted." He reached across the table and took her hand. His manner was calm, as though he was suggesting a walk about the park instead of a trip to the other side of the world.

She shook her head. "I can't."

"This morning, you told me that you could do your work anywhere. All you need is a computer and a cell phone."

That was true. There was a strong likelihood that she could arrange a consulting position with Sun Wave that didn't require her to be in the office. She could communicate via video feed and… Her imaginings came to an abrupt halt. *What am I thinking? I can't run off to faraway places with Blake.* She hardly knew him. "Have you forgotten that I'm pregnant?"

"Medical care isn't a problem. Some of the best hospitals in the world—"

"It's not that," she said. "When I have my baby, I want to be with family, with my mother."

"You'd be with me," he said.

Her gaze met his, and her resistance faded. Every beat of her heart said, *Go with him. Follow this perfect man to the ends of the earth.*

This isn't happening! Every decision she'd ever made was based on logic. She needed to make charts and graphs and figure the statistical probability of forming a successful relationship under these circumstances.

His cell phone rang. Without releasing her hand, he took it from his pocket and checked the screen. "It's Gable. I need to answer."

Leaning back in her chair, she stared at the flickering candle on the table, not knowing whether to laugh or cry. Nothing made sense. And yet, everything was clear.

He ended his call. "Gable finished running the DNA from all the biological parents through CODIS. He got a hit."

A momentary panic rushed through her. What if the hit was one of her parents? What if the criminal database showed that her DNA came from a felon? "Who was it?"

"Pyro." His jaw tightened. "Pyro's biological father is a convicted serial killer."

Chapter Nineteen

The match from CODIS sapped Blake's appetite. His *carne asada* burrito was made the way he liked it with the chili hot and the cheese smooth, but he could barely make a dent in his extra-large portion.

Eve had looked up information on Pyro's father using a phone app. It had taken the FBI twelve years to track this bastard down. With over forty kills in seven different states attributed to him, he was a Ted Bundy–type serial killer—charming, intelligent and grotesque in his cruelty. And they were dealing with his son.

"Just because Pyro shares his DNA," Eve said, "it doesn't mean he'll turn out the same way."

"What about the psychological profile?"

"It's not proof." Her voice was firm. "Detective Gable told you that he had no evidence against Pyro."

"Until now, he hasn't been looking. That's changed. Gable is checking Pyro's schedule for his on-the-road concerts to see if it coincides with any unsolved murders in those towns."

"It isn't right to condemn him because of his DNA." She bit into her fish taco, chewed and swallowed. Apparently, a dinner-table chat about a serial killer didn't turn her stomach. "If we start making judgments because of genetics, then—"

"We aren't talking about a scientific theory, Eve. Pyro could have killed my father. Possibly others. When he does his disappearing act after his concerts, where does he go? What does he do?"

She leaned across the table and stared into his eyes. "He's not a case study. He's Peter Gregory, and you've known him since you both were teenagers. Your father has been observing him since he was born. Do you really think Dr. Ray would have misdiagnosed a serial killer?"

She had a point. If his father thought there was a possibility of Peter doing violence to himself or anyone else, he would have contacted the police. "Do you think Prentice knew?"

"We'll find out tonight." She checked her wristwatch. "In less than an hour."

He forced himself to eat. Eve was correct. Making assumptions about Pyro based on his DNA was ignorant; it went against everything his father believed. A person's fate wasn't predestined by their genetics.

"If Pyro is the murderer," Eve said, "what's his motive?"

"If my dad's research became public, a lot of people would condemn him."

"Not his fans. He breathes fire onstage. The extra element of danger would be a plus for Pyro's concerts."

Earlier, he'd drawn much the same conclusion. The negative publicity related to having a serial killer for a father would be a problem for their other two suspects, Vargas and Latimer. Pyro wouldn't give a damn.

"Okay, let's look at his onstage performance. In his song 'The Twenty-Four,' he talks about building a heritage from the original subjects of the study. That gives him a reason to want you to be pregnant."

"Yuck. As if I'm some kind of breeder?"

"You tell me. You're the science-fiction expert."

Her brow pulled into a scowl. "It fits with the whole 'take over the world' mentality."

"The threats to you started when you suggested that you might give the baby up for adoption. Pyro might lose track of the child."

"But I only talked to Prentice."

"Who must have communicated with the murderer." Dr. Prentice had a great deal to answer for. Blake couldn't wait to get his hands on that old coward.

She finished off her food and dabbed at her lips with the corner of her napkin. "I wish we'd had time for you to give me self-defense lessons."

"You did okay with your stun gun. All you have to remember is to go for the vulnerable spots."

"Like what?"

"Eyes, nose, gut, groin, knees. And you have to hit hard. Don't hold back."

This meal—their first real date, according to Eve—had started well. When he proposed taking her with him, she'd warmed to the idea. Though she'd objected, he'd seen acceptance in her eyes, and he'd allowed himself to imagine a future with her. For a moment, he'd managed to push the tragedy of his father's murder from his mind.

The call from Gable re-tuned his focus. Mentally, he dedicated himself to finding the killer and bringing him to justice.

DURING THE DRIVE to Latimer's office, Eve couldn't stop thinking about floating down the Nile with Blake, sharing his life in exotic places. She'd been tempted to take that leap, to throw away her life as a singular individual and join him.

In the lights from the dashboard, she studied his profile.

His straight nose was so perfect that he should have been on a coin. Was it possible that a man like Blake wanted to live with her? In a few short days, how could he care so much? The word *love* hadn't passed his lips. Nor had she made that declaration.

Though inexperienced in matters of the heart, she figured there should be a commitment before she abandoned her life in Boulder and followed him to the ends of the earth. Did he love her?

She had to know.

"Earlier tonight," she said, "you told me that you wanted me to come along when you returned to active duty."

"That's right." He braked for a stoplight and turned toward her. "We'll talk later. I need to maintain focus on the task at hand."

"I just have one question."

And she knew the answer she needed to hear: *Because I love you.* That was all he had to say. If he loved her, she could acknowledge all the strange and wonderful feelings that stirred when she looked at him or thought of him or heard his voice. She needed to know if he loved her.

"Okay," he said. "Shoot."

"Why? What is the single most important reason you want to take me with you?"

"I told you before," he said. "My dad's last wish was that I take care of you."

Of all the things he could have said, that might have been the most insulting. He made it sound as if she was an obligation, a burden. The hell with him. "You're officially off the hook, Blake. I can take care of myself."

"We'll talk about this later."

There were so many other things he could have said. He could have told her that he wanted her with him because she was sexy. Or because she was different from the other women he'd known. He could have told her that he couldn't live without her.

But his offer didn't have anything to do with her. Being her bodyguard was a job. "There's no need for discussion."

Her mind was made up. Thank God, she hadn't started packing her bags and making plans. She hadn't made a complete fool of herself.

"Eve, please—"

"No talking." She held up her hand. "Let's just get this over with."

The Mercedes glided into the parking lot outside Latimer's three-story office building. The last crimson rays of sunset reflected in the rows of windows and gave the square building a more interesting appearance than when they'd been here at night. Vargas's building, she remembered. Would he designate this structure as one that could be converted to solar energy? She looked away, not really caring. Her future felt bleak. She'd be alone. Pregnant. *At least, I'm not a virgin anymore.*

Blake parked beside the Cadillac sedan that Randall used to chauffeur his boss. He peered through the windshield. "Where's Prentice's car?"

"He could be running late."

"I don't like the way this looks," he said. "Call Latimer. Find out where Prentice is."

"Yes, sir." She snapped a sarcastic salute. He was always giving orders, making demands. Why had she vaguely considered living with him? Her call to Latimer went straight to voice mail. "He's not answering."

He pulled his gun. "Let's check it out."

Remembering what she'd done at the theater, she left her purse behind, slipping her cell phone in one pocket and the stun gun in another.

As they approached the glass doors at the front of the building, she reminded him, "Latimer's office is on the third floor."

"I know. I was here with you the other night."

"Just trying to be helpful."

She couldn't wait until this so-called investigation was finished. They'd talk to Prentice, find out the name of the murderer and call Detective Gable to make the arrest. Then she could say goodbye to Blake. He'd stride off into his perfectly handsome world, and she'd go back to...being herself.

Her fingers stroked the edge of the long cashmere sweater he had insisted on buying for her. She wasn't meant to wear clothes like this. A Trekkie T-shirt suited her just fine—an extra-large to fit her when she was in the last stages of pregnancy.

The doors at the front pushed open. In a small office building like this, there was no guard at a front desk. The polished floors at the front led to two elevators.

She heard the pop of gunfire. "Damn."

Blake pulled her into the stairwell. "Stay with me. Just like you did at the theater."

Assuming there was some tactical reason why they couldn't use the elevator, she followed him up three flights of stairs. The gunfire continued in sporadic bursts.

When they reached the third floor, Blake positioned her behind the door. Breathing hard, she pressed her back against the concrete wall. Before he could deliver his order, she said, "I know. I should stay. Right here."

He whipped open the door and dashed through.

Trembling, she waited, holding her stun gun. Fear built up inside her. The internal pressure was unbearable. To calm herself, she counted prime numbers. Her brain stumbled and stuck on twenty-five. *Not a prime.* Why was she thinking of twenty-five? It was her age. Blake's age. They should have more years. Together? *No, we won't be together.*

Her usually organized mind bounced wildly from one thought to the next. She was confused, horribly confused. Her hands rose to her temples as though she could control her brain by holding the sides of her head. If she stood here by herself, she'd surely go mad.

With her stun gun in hand, she opened the door and peeked into the well-lit hallway. The elevators stood in the center of the third floor. At either end the hallways took a ninety-degree turn, creating a square within the square building. The hall was clean and plain with one exception: blood stained the carpet and splattered on the clean white walls.

A single shot rang out. She didn't see the gunman. Or Blake. Or anyone else. Only the blood.

She went around the corner to the left. The door to Latimer's office stood open.

She glanced over her shoulder toward the stairwell. If she went back, she'd be safe from stray bullets. But safety was relative. If someone attacked her in the stairwell, she couldn't escape. In the theater when Blake had taken off in pursuit of the bad guy, she'd made a reasoned decision to follow him. The safest place she could be was close to him.

Ducking low, she darted toward the open door. Blake was inside, crouched behind the receptionist's desk in the waiting room where a row of slate-blue chairs lined the walls and magazines rested on a coffee table. Smears of blood marked the floor, leaving a trail.

Blake called out, "Damn it, Latimer. Put down the gun."

"Stay back." Latimer's voice was high and scared. "You can't take this from me. I won't let you."

In the narrow corridor that led to the examination rooms, she caught a glimpse of Latimer. He lurched forward, fired wildly and stumbled back. He wasn't wearing his glasses, which meant he was nearly blind. And armed.

She scooted across the floor to Blake's side. He pulled her close. "I was starting to worry about you. I'm glad you're here."

An unwanted thrill went through her. She nodded toward the hallway. "What's happening?"

"As near as I can figure, Latimer has lost his damn mind. He thinks I'm after him."

"The blood?"

"I don't know. I haven't seen anybody else."

From down the hall came another desperate shout. "I know you're there. Don't come any closer."

She looked to Blake. "Have you tried getting closer?"

"I don't have a death wish," he said. "And I don't want to shoot him."

"Maybe you could throw something. You were pretty accurate with that knife in the kitchen."

Latimer fired another wild shot.

"The problem," Blake said, "is that I can't stand up and take aim."

"Maybe I should try talking to him."

"Go for it. A woman's voice might reassure him."

She faced the narrow hallway but stayed behind the desk. "Dr. Latimer? Trevor Latimer? It's me, Eve Weathers."

"Eve?"

"That's right." Her mouth felt dry. She licked her lips and forced herself to swallow. "I'm here with Blake, and we're not going to hurt you."

"Show yourself."

Before she could stand up, Blake caught her arm. "Keep him talking. Get him to disarm himself."

"Trevor," she said, "you invited me here. Remember? You said you were setting up a meeting with Dr. Prentice. Do you remember that?"

"Of course, I remember."

"I want to help you. But you have to put the gun down first. Toss it into the hallway."

"Then I'd be helpless. No."

"Please, Trevor. We're on your side. Please trust me."

"No," he shouted. "Where the hell is Randall?"

She'd forgotten all about Latimer's chauffeur and body-guard. To Blake, she whispered, "Have you seen him?"

"When I came onto the floor, I made a circuit of the hall-ways, but that doesn't mean he's not hiding out there."

She eyed the blood. "Or he was shot."

Calling out to Latimer, she said, "When did you last see Randall?"

"He came with me into the building. While I was in my office, I heard shooting. Got my gun from the safe. And the ammo. Then I stumbled. Lost my glasses." His voice was growing weaker. "They can't have it. They can't take it from me."

"Take what?" she asked. What was so important that he'd protect it with his life?

"Can't take it." He fired another shot.

Unreasonable and panicked, he was hanging on to his sanity by a thin strand. Somehow, she had to get through to him. "There's a lot of blood out here. Somebody has been wounded, seriously wounded. And you're a doctor. You can help them."

"Is it Randall? Is he hurt?"

"Throw down your gun, and we'll look for Randall. We need your help."

There was silence, and she hoped that she'd reached him.

In a dull voice, Latimer said, "All right, I'll help in any way that I can."

Both she and Blake peered over the edge of the desktop as Latimer stepped into the narrow hallway and dropped his weapon.

Blake hurried to pick up the gun. She went to Latimer. She would have embraced him, but he was holding a metal container that looked like a big thermos in front of him.

Gently, she patted his arm. "What's in there?"

"Frozen sperm. Mine. It's my only chance of having a child." He exhaled a ragged breath and sagged against the wall as though he wasn't strong enough to stand on his own. "My illness left me sterile."

"I'm so sorry."

"If it weren't for Dr. Prentice, I wouldn't even have this small amount of viable sperm."

"What do you mean?" she asked.

"He took a sperm sample from me as a part of the Prentice-Jantzen study. I assume he did the same with all the subjects."

"All of you?" Even Blake? She'd have to ask him about Prentice's physical exams.

"Eight months ago, I was fine. And now…"

She couldn't help feeling empathy for this man, her own age, who had suffered the terrible ravages of disease. At the same time, her rational mind told her that his sterility was an obvious reason he might have wanted to impregnate her. He knew how such things worked; he was a fertility specialist. The most damning evidence of all: Latimer was in touch with Prentice.

"Was it you?" she asked. "Am I carrying your baby?"

"What?" He squinted, trying to see her. "What are you talking about?"

"The first time you saw me, you knew I was pregnant."

"I made an educated guess. This is what I do for a living, Eve. I help women get pregnant. I know the signs."

"Like glowing? You don't really expect me to believe that." She leaned closer, hoping that he could see her anger.

"All right," he said angrily. "Dr. Prentice mentioned that a woman close to Blake was pregnant. And you walked into my house with your hand resting on your belly."

"You'd been talking to Prentice."

"Occasionally."

"Where is he? You promised that he'd be here."

He drew away from her. "I was supposed to call him after you arrived. If you want to talk to him, use the cell phone on my desk."

Blake turned on the light in one of the examination rooms and cursed. "Over here, Latimer."

Collapsed on the floor beside the padded examination table with stirrups was Randall. His chest was covered with blood.

Chapter Twenty

While Blake and Latimer worked on Randall, Eve slipped out of the examination room. They'd called 911. Soon the parking lot outside would be filled with ambulances and police cruisers. The office would be crawling with cops.

Before she'd gotten involved with Blake, her only contact with the police was the occasional speeding ticket. Now, she knew the drill. There would be questions, confusion and a total lack of privacy.

Latimer had told her that the cell phone on his desk would connect with Prentice. She needed to make that call before the chaos descended.

Blake poked his head out of the exam room. "Eve, go out to the hallway so you can direct the paramedics. Randall needs a hospital. Every minute counts."

"I'm on it."

Before she went to the outer door, she dashed into Latimer's private office and grabbed the cell phone.

In the bloodstained hallway, she paced in front of the elevators. Prentice had the answer to her burning question: who was her baby's father?

Though she wanted to scream at him and make demands, she knew better. Prentice wouldn't respond to threats—not from her, anyway. If ever in her life she needed to be calm and rational, this was the moment. She had to convince him to tell her the truth.

She scrolled through the list of Latimer's contacts until she found the number, and she made the call.

Prentice grumbled, "It's about time, Latimer. I expected to hear from you ten minutes ago."

"It's Eve Weathers. Don't hang up."

Impatiently, he snapped, "What is it, Eve?"

"We obtained your initial research and Dr. Ray's analysis. I've deciphered most of the DNA database."

"Good for you."

His cold, sardonic tone irritated her. She lashed out. "You were careless, Doctor. You recruited a serial killer as one of the sperm donors."

"My selection process was based on IQ tests, accomplishments and health. Unfortunately, he qualified."

"Thank God, he was only the father of two subjects."

"Three," he corrected her.

"I read the DNA charts, Dr. Prentice. There was Pyro and one other man."

"You're not as clever as you think, Eve. From what source did you obtain these charts?"

"From Vargas." She had trusted the information from her genetic half brother. A mistake? "Vargas was the only subject with a unique sperm donor."

"Because he made it up," Prentice said. "David Vargas has the same genetic father as Pyro."

The serial killer. If that information was made public, Vargas would be profoundly embarrassed. In his business dealings, reputation was everything. He couldn't afford to be the son of an infamous serial killer.

Her mind took the next logical leap. "Please don't tell me that Vargas is the father of my baby."

"Certainly not. You share the same mother."

"But he's the one who paid you, isn't he? He wanted me to be pregnant."

"Because you share the same mother," Prentice said. "Vargas wanted a child that shared his DNA—the good DNA. You or your half sister could provide him with a legacy."

"That's crazy. Why wouldn't he use his own sperm? Or hire a surrogate mother to carry his baby?"

"He wanted to eliminate the DNA from his biological father, the serial killer. You share half his DNA—the good half. And he made a logical and compelling argument. You've met him, Eve. He's very convincing. I had assumed that once you knew you were pregnant, you'd come around. According to Dr. Ray's psychological analysis, you'll make an outstanding mother."

"But Dr. Ray wouldn't go along with the plan. Vargas had to kill him to keep him quiet."

Prentice rushed to say, "There's no evidence to that accusation."

"But we both know it's true. That's why you went into hiding, taking a supposed vacation. You're afraid of Vargas."

"I advise you to make the best of this situation. Think of the advantages. Vargas has enough money to provide your child with a top-notch lifestyle, an excellent education."

"It takes more than money to make a father. It takes love." She heard herself echoing Blake's words.

"We can work this out. We'll draw up contracts."

She couldn't believe he was advising her to work with the man who had probably killed Blake's father, the son of the most infamous serial killer since Jack the Ripper. "I'd rather sign a deal with the devil."

"Because you don't have all the data. There's one more important bit of—"

The cell phone was torn from her hand. She'd been so engrossed in her conversation that she hadn't heard anyone approach. He grabbed her around the torso. His other hand covered her mouth.

"Come quietly." She recognized Pyro's voice. "I won't kill you, Eve, but I can hurt you a lot."

He dragged her backward toward the stairwell. One arm was pinned to her side, but she struggled with the other. Kicked back with her legs.

"Fine," he muttered. "We'll do this your way."

He pressed a cloth over her mouth. The sharp tang of a chemical compound prickled her nostrils. She tried not to breathe but couldn't help inhaling.

The fight went out of her. Thought drained from her mind as she lost consciousness.

As soon as the paramedics arrived, Blake stepped out of the way. With Latimer's help, he'd done everything he could to keep Randall alive, from rudimentary first aid to starting an IV line. The chauffeur had lost a lot of blood, and there was internal damage, but he was still breathing.

In the front waiting room, Blake turned to Latimer. "Randall's going to make it. He's a fighter."

"Thanks to you. I mean that sincerely. Thank you."

"Hey, I just did what you told me. You're the doctor. You saved him."

Latimer straightened his spine. His eyelids tensed and twitched, but he appeared to have regained his self-control. "I apologize for what happened earlier. I haven't been myself. Not since you told me about my biological parents."

Two uniformed cops entered and rushed toward the examining room. Blake looked past them to the outer hallway. He didn't see Eve.

Latimer continued, "I've been so absorbed in my own problems that I forgot that I could help others. That's why I became a doctor. Working with you to save Randall showed me that I can still contribute. I'm not dead, yet."

"Good for you." This was an important moment for Latimer, and Blake would have paid more attention, but he was beginning to worry. "Do you know where Eve went?"

"The last time I saw her was when I told her that she could contact Prentice using my cell phone on my desk."

"Where's your office?"

"Straight back and to the right."

"Thanks." Blake clapped his shoulder and dodged past the two cops blocking the narrow hallway.

In Latimer's office, he searched for the cell phone. It was nowhere in sight. He saw no sign of Eve.

Had she gone down to the car? He looked out the window into the gray light of dusk. Two more police cars pulled into the parking lot with lights flashing. *Damn it, Eve. Where are you?* He knew she was angry; she'd made it crystal clear that he'd said the wrong thing. Instead of telling her that he cared about her, maybe even loved her, he'd talked about his duty to honor his father's last wish. Not the smartest comment he'd ever made, but he had had too much on his mind to be sensitive.

And she hadn't given him a chance, hadn't given him time to explain. Was she mad enough to go storming off by herself? He didn't think so. There was still a threat, and Eve knew to be careful. Where the hell was she?

Avoiding questions from the officers who wanted to take his statement, he made his way into the hallway outside Latimer's waiting room. He'd told her to come out here and direct traffic when the cops and paramedics started to show up. What if someone had been waiting? What if he'd directed her into an ambush?

Near the stairwell, he found the cell phone. By some miracle, it hadn't been trampled. He hit redial and held it to his ear.

A voice answered immediately, "Eve? What happened?"

"Who's this?" Blake asked.

"Dr. Edgar Prentice. To whom am I speaking?"

He wanted to crawl through the phone and strangle the old bastard. "This is Blake Jantzen."

"Are you with Eve? Is she all right?"

"Why wouldn't she be?"

"I'm not sure what happened," Prentice said. "We were having a conversation, and she was interrupted. It was sudden. I fear someone might have…taken her."

"Someone," he said coldly. "You know who it was. You've known all along who was after her."

"In point of fact, I can't be sure. I don't have actual physical evidence."

"Don't waste my time playing games, Prentice."

"This can't come back to me," he said nervously. "My practice is already on shaky ground and I—"

"Stop! No more excuses! You'll start cooperating now. You have no other choice."

"I don't?"

"If anything happens to Eve, if she's harmed in any way, you'll have a reason to be scared. Because I will hunt you down." He paused to let his threat sink in. "Where would they take her?"

There was a moment of silence. The paramedics came into the hallway with Randall on a collapsible gurney. Another set of cops emerged from the elevator.

Finally, Prentice said, "There's a private airstrip in the

mountains between Boulder and Nederland. I believe it's called V-Base."

"And the *V* stands for Vargas." Blake had known from the first time he met Vargas that he was trouble.

"Be careful when you're approaching. It's my understanding that Pyro likes to play with explosives."

Both Vargas and Pyro? And a minefield? Things just kept getting more and more complicated. "What else can you tell me?"

"There's one last thing you should know. It's extremely important."

Chapter Twenty-One

Slowly, painfully, Eve became conscious. The inside of her head felt as if it was going to explode. Her limbs were stiff and cold. Her mouth tasted as if she'd been sucking on cotton balls. She licked her lips. God, she was thirsty. She pried her eyelids open.

Her wrists and ankles were bound with rope. She was huddled on a couple of blankets inside what seemed to be a barn. The only light came from a couple of hanging bulbs. One wall was completely open. The air smelled of machinery and grease.

Looking through the door into the moonlit night, she saw a long, flat stretch of land that had been cleared except for occasional clumps of persistent weeds. An airstrip. This wasn't a barn; it was an empty hangar.

Ignoring the throbbing inside her head, she struggled to sit up. Since her hands were tied in front of her, she might be able to unfasten the ropes at her ankles. She bent her legs to the side and twisted around. With numb fingers, she attacked the knots.

Outside the open door, she saw the shadows of evergreens rising on hillsides, and she heard the silence of the mountains. How far had they gone? She turned her wrist and checked her watch. It was only ten o'clock—not enough time to make a long drive. They were still fairly close to Denver. As if that made a difference? Disappearing in the vastness of the mountains was easy, and she knew it'd take a miracle for Blake to find her. He was smart and clever and had access to sophisticated technology, but he wouldn't know where to look. She might never see him again. A sob climbed up her throat. With an effort, she suppressed the sound.

She couldn't rely on Blake to rescue her. She had to do it by herself.

Her shoulders ached from the uncomfortable stretch as she fought with the ropes, but it was worth it. The knots loosened. Pyro hadn't done a real good job of tying her legs. She'd been surprised to see him, especially after what Prentice had told her. Vargas was the real villain.

With a final kick, the ropes around her ankles came off. She struggled to her feet. Standing intensified her headache. What had she inhaled that made her pass out? Chloroform? When she turned her head, the world went spinning.

She had to escape. The airstrip meant a plane was coming. She could be flown to any location, locked up until she delivered the baby. Then what? After she gave birth to the Vargas heir, she was expendable.

Staggering a few steps, she stumbled and fell hard onto the packed earth floor. Her legs were so stiff that it felt as if her bones had cracked.

"Eve!" Pyro bellowed. "I see you, Eve."

She forced herself to her feet. She wanted to run but only managed a few clumsy strides before he caught hold of her arm. Weakly, she said, "Let me go."

"Can't do that. You could be hurt bad. Exploded into a million pieces."

A surge of anger gave her strength. "What the hell are you talking about?"

"Come along," he said. "I'll show you."

As he dragged her onto the airstrip, the chill night air hit her face, and she revived a bit more. Concentrating hard, she focused on Pyro. His spiked black hair contrasted with his pale, moonlit face. With all his piercings and silver jewelry, he looked like a combination rocker and vampire. If she could get a clear shot at him, she'd smash that nose ring all the way into the frontal lobe of his sick brain.

She stumbled along beside him. "Why are you doing this?"

"You said your friend was a fan. You know my music. I thought you'd understand 'The Twenty-Four.' We have a destiny. We're the future. Why don't you get it? Aren't you supposed to be smart?"

Way too smart to follow his delusional thinking, but she wanted him to keep talking until she figured out a way to break free. "When did you find out about your genetic background?"

"If you paid attention to my songs, you'd know. I gave the date, almost a year ago, when Vargas approached me." He yanked her along with him. They were almost in the middle of the airstrip. "It's a revelation. A revolution."

"What does Vargas want you to do?"

"I'm a rock star. That makes me the front man. I'll draw people to our cause, build an army."

"And Vargas foots the bill."

"Oh, yeah, he's the money man. He's setting up record deals, hired a publicist."

"And the two guys who came after me at my house? Did Vargas hire them, too?"

"Yeah, I guess. The Big V works in mysterious ways."

She knew that Pyro had been duped, blinded by the promise of fame. He saw himself as a noble warrior, a leader. And he didn't recognize the downside. "Did Vargas tell you the identity of your biological father?"

Pyro threw back his head and laughed. Though he wasn't a big man, his gestures were larger than life. "I know he's a genius. Outsmarted the FBI for years."

"He's a serial killer."

"I've been working on a song about him. One of those 'sins of the father' things. When I start doing interviews, my DNA is going to make me special."

The idea of using a serial killer father as a publicity ruse disgusted her. Did he really believe he'd get away with this? Though they were the same age, he seemed a lot younger. Like a kid caught up in a dark fantasy game, he couldn't see reality. "Are you like your father? Have you committed murder?"

"You're talking about Dr. Ray's murder." He scowled as dramatically as a mask of tragedy. "I wouldn't hurt him. I liked him. He used to let me play his piano."

Though he'd lied to her before, she wanted to believe that he wasn't all bad. There might still be a spark of humanity in him. "What about the shoot-out at Latimer's office?"

"I was there."

But did he shoot Randall? Was he too disconnected to understand what she was asking?

He shook his head. "Too bad about Latimer. He's sick, real sick." In his right hand, Pyro held a small plastic device. "Watch this."

He pointed and pressed a button.

At the edge of the airstrip, an explosion erupted. Dirt, rocks and weeds spewed into the air in a burst of orange flame.

Stunned, she stared as the flame quickly died, leaving a smoke trail. Her ears rang with the noise.

Pointing with both fingers, Pyro turned in a circle. "I've got bombs all around. I can detonate using a remote. And they're motion-sensitive. Step on one and you're dead."

"Why?" she asked.

"Go ahead and run, Eve. If you're feeling lucky."

"Why the hell would you do this?"

"It's Pyro's wall of flame. For real." His hands rose above his head as though he'd reached the climax in one of his concerts. Then, his arms dropped.

He shrugged and gave her a boyish grin. He almost looked innocent. "I like things that go boom. Always have. Good old Dr. Ray used to worry about me setting fires."

Dr. Ray had been right to worry.

BLAKE WATCHED THE LAST wisp of smoke from the explosion curl above the treetops and disappear into the night sky. During his tours of duty, he'd had enough experience with improvised explosive devices to know they were, above all, unpredictable. He might choose a safe approach to the airstrip or, just as likely, he'd step on a trigger that would detonate another bomb.

He had to believe that Pyro brought Eve here to wait for Vargas, who would probably arrive in a small plane. Blake wouldn't let her be taken away from him. Eve was the woman he loved. And the mother of his child.

Prentice had been smug when he had told Blake that Vargas selected him as the sperm donor to be matched with her egg. His rationale was that Eve had the brains, and Blake had the brawn. They'd make a perfect match for the next generation.

Though he didn't agree with their logic or their procedure, he was overwhelmed by an amazing sense of fulfillment. This was his destiny. To be a father. Even better, Eve was the mother of his child.

He'd never believed in fate, but his love for her seemed preordained. They were meant to be together, to raise a family together. He couldn't wait to see her face when he told her, which meant he'd better get his butt in gear.

Using the GPS in his Mercedes, he'd found this location. For the past ten minutes, he'd been scouting the perimeter, keeping an eye on Pyro. For a while, he considered using a sniper rifle from his arsenal in the trunk to take Pyro out. If this had been a hostage situation in a war zone, that was how he'd handle the situation. But Blake didn't know if Pyro was guilty, and he didn't have the right to play executioner.

If he wounded Pyro from a distance, he wouldn't be close enough to prevent the rocker from taking revenge on Eve. Blake needed to get onto that airstrip.

Moving silently through the forest, he returned to the one-lane dirt road where he'd parked the Mercedes. Wistfully, he patted the sleek midnight-blue fender of the armored car. "I'm sorry, baby. You have to make the ultimate sacrifice."

Behind his back, Pyro had turned on the lights to illuminate the field. It was a short runway. Vargas must be flying a single-engine prop plane. As if to confirm that conclusion, he heard the hum of an approaching aircraft.

Blake armed himself. He kept the Sig Sauer as a handgun, clipped another holster to his belt, slung an M16 across his shoulders and moved his knife sheath to the back of his belt for easy access. Then he started the car.

It seriously pained him to damage this fine vehicle, but heading straight down the dirt road was the fastest approach.

He saw the single-engine Cessna touch down.

Pyro, holding Eve's arm, walked toward the plane.

There wasn't a minute to spare.

Still hidden in the trees, Blake gunned the engine. The road sloped down to the airstrip, and he hoped there would be enough momentum to carry the car forward. He pointed the car straight down and took off. As soon as he was out of the trees, he jumped from the driver's seat.

The Mercedes rolled down the hill, unscathed for several yards. At the edge of the airfield, the Mercedes hit the IED. The explosion was strong enough to stop the vehicle and tear off the front fender. If Blake had stepped on that bomb, he would have been toast. But the armored car weighed thousands of pounds, enough to keep her from flipping onto her side.

Though Blake had intended to run down the path cleared by the car, he saw a better way. Keeping his footprints in the tire tracks to avoid any other bombs, he got behind the wheel. He turned the key. The Mercedes started. Damn, this was one hell of a fine car.

He drove onto the airstrip.

As soon as Eve saw the Mercedes, she took heart. Blake was coming for her.

Taking advantage of Pyro's momentary astonishment as he stared at the approaching vehicle, she drew back with both hands—still tied together at the wrist—and swung as hard as she could.

When she hit him directly on the nose, he let out a scream and fell to his knees. Remembering Blake's quick lesson on self-defense, she kicked him in the crotch.

Pyro keeled over backward, curled into a ball.

She aimed another hard kick at his lower back, then another to his head. He was unconscious. She took the gun from his hand, but she couldn't hold on. Her fingers wouldn't grip.

Looking up, she saw Blake leap from the Mercedes.

Vargas was faster. She hadn't seen him emerge from the plane, but he was beside her. He pulled her in front of himself, using her as a shield. His gun pressed against the side of her head.

He yelled to Blake, "Not another step. This is a hair trigger."

She saw Blake halt. He was fifteen feet away, close enough that she could see the strength and determination on his face but too far for him to attack. He held the Sig in both hands, ready to shoot.

In a low, dangerous voice, he said, "You won't kill her. You want her baby."

"I'll make that sacrifice. Throw down your weapons."

Vargas held her so tightly that she couldn't struggle, could barely breathe.

Blake took a step closer.

The muzzle of the gun pressed harder against her skull. She didn't want to die.

"Here's my deal," Vargas said. "Throw down your weapons, and Eve will live. I'll take care of her and the baby."

All she could hear was the unspoken conclusion. If Blake disarmed himself, he'd be killed before her eyes. "Don't do it," she shouted. "Shoot him."

"He won't risk your life," Vargas said. "Blake's a hero. An honorable man. He wouldn't be able to live with the guilt if he was responsible for your death. Isn't that right, Blake?"

Without a word, Blake unfastened the holster on his belt. He reached over his shoulder and divested himself of the M16 rifle. Holding out his hand, he dropped the Sig Sauer.

Vargas shoved her to the ground. He raised his gun and pointed it at Blake. "I win."

"You won't get away with this," Blake said.

"I knew you were weak. Like your father. He died holding a photo of you and your mother."

Blake moved so fast that she couldn't describe his motions. She only saw the aftermath. His knife was buried to the hilt in Vargas's chest. He gasped. A look of horror and shock distorted his features. Still, he tried to aim his gun.

She saw Blake running toward them, but she was closer. She lunged, hit Vargas on the shoulder. He went down.

Blake grabbed his weapon. He leaned over Vargas, felt for a pulse, then shook his head. "He's dead."

She'd never seen a man die before, but all she felt was relief. They were safe. Finally, safe.

Blake knelt beside her and unfastened the ropes on her hands. "Are you all right?"

"I've been better."

Gently, he surrounded her with a warm embrace. Her arms were too weak to do more than drape around him, but she returned his kiss.

"I have something to tell you." He looked around the airstrip with the battered Mercedes at one side and the Cessna on the other. Vargas lay dead. Pyro hadn't recovered consciousness. "This doesn't seem like the right place."

"Seems to me that you'd be comfortable on a battlefield."

"I talked to Prentice, and he told me the name of your baby's father."

She braced herself for bad news. "Tell me."

A wide grin spread across his face.

"You?" She couldn't have been more shocked.

"My sperm. Your egg. We're going to have a kid."

Never again would she be a singular person, and the change in her life was more wonderful than she ever could have imagined. She and Blake would be parents. "For the next kid, let's do it the old-fashioned way."

He hugged her hard, making her a part of him. Then he lifted her to her feet. His gaze rested lightly upon her as he brushed the dirt from her shoulder. "You pretty much destroyed that nice sweater."

"Some women aren't meant to wear cashmere." She pressed against him. "Some women are meant to float down the Nile on a chartered boat."

"Does that mean you're coming with me?"

"Because I love you," she said.

"And I love you, Eve. With all my heart."

* * * * *

HOOK, LINE AND SHOTGUN BRIDE

BY

CASSIE MILES

First published in Great Britain 2011
by Mills & Boon, an imprint of Harlequin (UK) Limited,
Eton House, 18-24 Paradise Road, Richmond, Surrey TW9 1SR

© Kay Bergstrom 2010

ISBN: 978 0 263 88518 7

46-0411

Harlequin (UK) policy is to use papers that are natural, renewable and
recyclable products and made from wood grown in sustainable forests. The
logging and manufacturing processes conform to the legal environmental
regulations of the country of origin.

Printed and bound in Spain
by Blackprint CPI, Barcelona

Chapter One

A flat tire.

Tom Hawthorne slammed the door to his Toyota SUV, slammed it hard. Why the hell had he decided to take a shortcut instead of staying on the highway? It was the middle of the night, and he was stuck on this winding gravel road in a mountain valley. No other cars. Not a cabin in sight. Only the stars bore witness to his rage. "Son of a bitch."

Lately, things had been going wrong more often than right. He would have felt cursed if it wasn't for Angela.

The thought of her cooled his temper. He carried her image with him always, through the hell of the battlefield and the horror of working triage as a Marine Corps medic. Angela's sweet love made everything bearable.

As he opened the rear of the SUV, he took out his cell phone. Surprise, surprise, he actually got a signal.

She answered right away, as though she'd been waiting for his name to pop up on her caller ID. "Good evening, Mr. Hawthorne."

"Hello, Mrs. Hawthorne." Though they'd been married eight months, he still enjoyed claiming her as his wife. "I'm going to be later than I thought. I got a flat."

"Bummer. How was your night out with the boys?"

Boring as hell. "I'd rather be with you."

"But it's traditional for a Marine to blow off steam while he's home on leave."

One-handed, he hauled out the spare tire and the jack. If he'd still been a drinker, he might have had more fun on his night out with old buddies at a bar. The only alcohol Tom had consumed in the past year was a glass of champagne at their wedding. "The hour-and-a-half drive to the mountains was too long. And I lost twenty-seven bucks at pool. But you could make me feel a whole lot better, baby. What are you wearing?"

"Flannel pajamas." She laughed. "Are you fixing that tire or what?"

"Give me some incentive," he murmured. "Tell me about your sexy nightgown."

This was a game they'd played for years, and she was good at it. Her voice lowered to a purr. "I'm standing in front of the fireplace, and I'm warm all over. I have on a black, see-through nightie. It's short—so short that it doesn't even cover my bum if I bend over."

He closed his eyes, relishing a mental picture of Angela's slender waist and round butt. "Your hair?"

"Loose and tangled all the way down my back. Oh, and I have those highlights I've been wanting to get to perk up the brown."

"What kind of shoes?"

"High heels, of course. And silky black stockings. And a lacy garter belt."

"Baby, I can't wait to get home."

"Can't wait for you to be here." Her voice returned to a normal tone. "How long do you think it'll take?"

"It's after ten now. I'd say eleven-thirty." He set down the jack beside the flat.

"How's your buddy Max doing?" she asked. "Does he like being a daddy?"

"Looking at pictures of his baby was the best part of the night. I'm ready to start a family of our own." He looked up and saw headlights approaching. "Hey, there's somebody else on this godforsaken road."

"Maybe they can help you," she said.

"It's just a flat tire. I don't need help."

The other vehicle—a truck—jostled around a curve at an unsafe speed. He was an accident waiting to happen. Luckily, Tom had managed to pull onto the shoulder and had left his lights on. The other driver should be able to see him.

"When you get home," Angela said, "I'll make you some hot chocolate with whipped cream."

"Sounds nice." Damn, that truck was moving fast.

"I love you, honey."

The headlights blinded him. The truck was headed directly at him. What the hell?

The impact crushed him against the side of his SUV. His legs collapsed and he hit the gravel. The truck backed up. The engine revved. He was coming again. This was no accident.

Tom was a dead man. He knew it. He spoke his last words, "Love you, too."

ANGELA HAWTHORNE lay on her comforter, fully dressed, staring at the digital bedside clock as it clicked to that fateful time: 10:23.

A little over five years ago, her husband had been killed by a hit-and-run driver at exactly that moment. She'd heard the crash, heard his last words and then her phone went dead.

One-zero-two-three.

Her world stopped. Her breath caught in her throat. *Oh, Tom. I miss you so much.* She was poised at the edge of an abyss, wishing she could leap into ultimate forgetfulness and knowing that she never would lose her memories.

The moment passed.

A gust of wind splashed rain against the windowpanes. This was one of those summer electrical storms that started in the mountains and swept down to attack Denver with a fury. The distant thunder even sounded like artillery.

When she rose from the bed, she felt light-headed. She shook herself. Her eyes took a moment to focus as though she'd had too much to drink.

She slipped her feet into a pair of well-worn loafers and shuffled down the hall to her son's room. Benjamin Thomas Hawthorne, almost four years old, was her miracle baby.

After Tom's first tour of duty, he'd insisted that they create a stockpile of frozen embryos in case anything happened to him. She'd objected, mostly because she didn't want to acknowledge the possibility of her husband being wounded or, God forbid, killed. He'd soothed her fears and promised to come back to her, but his work as a medic meant he came into contact with a lot of disease. He hadn't wanted to take a chance on having his DNA damaged or becoming sterile.

Every single day, she was grateful for Tom's foresight. Less than a year after his death, she'd undergone the in vitro fertilization process. Nine months later, she gave birth to Tom's son.

As she opened the door to Benjy's room, the light from the hallway slanted across the foot of the big boy bed that had replaced his crib. He'd kicked off his covers and sprawled on his back on top of his dinosaur-patterned sheets. His honey-brown hair, a bit lighter than hers, curled around his ears.

His curtains—also dinosaurs—fluttered. His window was partially open, and the rain spattered across the sill.

She thought she'd closed all the windows when the rain started but she must have missed this one. As she pulled the window down and locked it, she noticed that the screen was loose. Something she'd have to repair in the morning.

After she tucked the comforter up to Benjy's chin, she kissed his forehead. He was an amazing kid, full of energy and incredibly bright. Everyone told her that she should start looking into preschools for gifted children.

Her fiancé was especially adamant on the subject of Benjy's education. She exhaled a sigh, wondering for the hundredth time if she was making a mistake by remarrying. No doubt, Dr. Neil Revere was a catch. At age thirty-six, he was ten years older than she was and well-established in his career as a virologist and professor at University Medical. He was wealthy, handsome, kindhearted and he loved Benjy. What more could she possibly want?

As she left Benjy's room and stepped into the hall, another bout of dizziness sapped her strength. She leaned against the wall. These nervous jitters had to stop. It was far too late for her to be having second thoughts about Neil. The wedding was Saturday. Three days from now.

When the phone rang, she jumped. Was she imagining this call in the night? Reliving the past?

She dashed into the front room and grabbed the phone, half expecting to hear Tom's voice. "Hello?"

"It's me, Shane. I wanted you to know that I'm running late."

Please don't tell me that you have a flat tire. "That's okay. I'm awake."

"No need for you to stay up. I'll get a motel room tonight and come over in the morning."

"You're staying here," she said firmly. Shane Gibson was Tom's cousin—the only family member who'd be attending her wedding. "I have the extra bedroom ready, and I made some of those macadamia nut cookies you like so much."

"You talked me into it," he said. "I won't be much longer. I can already see the lights of Denver."

When she set the phone on the coffee table, her heart was beating too fast. The erratic thump echoed inside her rib cage like a snare drum. She sank onto the sofa and concentrated on breathing slowly, in and out. Slowly, slowly. Her skin prickled with tension. A heat wave rose from her belly to her breasts to her throat to the top of her head. God, she was burning up. Sweating.

She'd felt this way before. Always at night. Always at the same time.

When she'd told Neil, he said her symptoms sounded like she was having a panic attack. He wanted her to see a psychiatrist, but she refused. She'd gone to a shrink after Tom's death and hated the process of talking and talking and never finding answers. As a mom and the half owner of a breakfast restaurant, she didn't have time to wallow in the past. Instead, she'd taken the mild sedative Neil prescribed for her. The pills usually worked. But not tonight.

Gradually, her pulse returned to normal. Leaning back against the sofa, she wiped the sheen of sweat from her forehead with the back of her hand. *I'm fine. I've got to be fine.* There were dozens of details she needed to handle before the wedding. Though it started as an intimate ceremony, the guest list had somehow expanded to nearly 150.

She'd be glad to have Shane here to help take care of Benjy. Shane and her husband had grown up together in a small town in Clear Creek County. Shane still lived in Silver Plume, where he was a deputy sheriff. Of all Tom's friends, Shane had been the most understanding. His was the shoulder she cried on.

And she had a secret agenda for Shane while he was in town. Eyes still closed, Angela smiled to herself. She planned to fix him up with the French woman who provided pastries for her restaurant. They were both tall with black hair and blue eyes. Obviously, made for each other.

Happy thoughts of matchmaking filled her mind, and she breathed more easily. *Everything's going to be just fine.* She dozed for a moment before a loud clap of thunder roused her. *No sleeping allowed.* She'd promised Shane that she'd be awake when he arrived.

Her legs were steady when she rose from the sofa, and she was pleased that her bout of nerves had passed. In the entry to the kitchen, her hand paused above the light switch. She saw a reflection in the window above the sink. A light? But that didn't make sense. That window faced the backyard. She squinted hard and focused on the dark beyond the glass panes.

She saw two lights, side by side. As she watched, they grew larger. Like the headlights on a truck. A ghostly truck. The lights bore down on her. Closer and closer. Coming right at her. They were going to crash through the window.

Reflexively, she threw up her hands.

When she looked again, the lights were gone.

A hallucination? No, it was too real. She knew what she'd seen. Without turning on the overhead light, she crept across the tile floor, leaned over the kitchen sink and peered into the yard. A flash of lightning illuminated the shrubs, the flowers and the peach tree. No headlights. No truck.

It must have been some kind of optical illusion—a trick of the light and rain.

She filled a plastic cup with water from the sink and took a sip.

A loud crash came from the hallway.

The cup fell from her hands and splashed water on the kitchen floor. The noise came from the direction of Benjy's bedroom. She remembered his open window with the loose screen. Someone could have climbed inside through that window.

She grabbed a butcher knife from the drawer by the sink, dashed down the hallway and flung open the door to her son's room. With no thought for her own safety, she charged inside. He wasn't in the bed. Frantic, she turned on the light. He was gone. *Oh, God, no.*

"Benjy?" Her voice quavered. "Where are you?"

Her heart thumped hard and heavy. She ran to his window. It was closed, exactly the way she'd left it.

The door to his closet was slightly ajar. Holding the knife in her right hand, she grasped the door handle with the left and pulled the door open.

With a huge grin, Benjy greeted her. "Mommy."

She placed the knife on his dresser and gathered him into her arms. She held him tightly against her breast—relieved that he was all right and terrified of the unknown danger that might still be in her house. *Something had made that crash.* She couldn't let down her guard, couldn't pretend that nothing had happened. "Why were you in the closet?"

"I don't know."

He didn't seem frightened. Wide awake and alert, but not scared. "Were you hiding?"

"I couldn't find my stegosaurus. I want him to sleep with me."

"Benjy, this is important. Was anyone in your room?"

"Mommy, what's wrong?"

She struggled to keep the tremor from her voice. "Everything's fine. We're going to be fine."

The doorbell rang. It had to be Shane. *Please let it be Shane.*

Benjy wriggled free from her grasp. She tried to grab him, but he dashed from his room and down the hall. Directly into danger? What if it wasn't Shane at the door?

She grabbed the knife and ran to the door behind her son. Loudly, she shouted, "Who's there?"

"It's Shane. I'm getting wet out here."

"Shane's here!" Benjy cried delightedly.

She flipped the lock and opened the door for the big, tall mountain man in his cowboy hat. She'd never been so glad to see anyone in her entire life.

Chapter Two

After years as a deputy sheriff, Shane was accustomed to dealing with crises. He read terror in Angela's eyes. Something had thrown her into a panic, and she wasn't a woman who scared easily.

He ruffled Benjy's hair and pulled Angela into a one-armed hug. "What's the problem?"

Trembling, she whispered, "I think someone broke into the house."

"Did you see him?"

"No."

"Do you think he's still here?"

Her voice cracked at the edge of a sob. "I don't know."

With a small child in the mix, this wasn't the time for a showdown with an intruder. He separated from Angela. *Was that a knife in her hand?* What the hell was she thinking? He scooped her son off the floor and said, "Let's go for a drive."

"You're wet," Benjy said.

"Rain will do that." He dug his cell from his jacket pocket and handed it to Angela. "Make the call to 911."

She stared at the phone as though it might grow fangs and bite her. "I don't want to contact the *C-O-P-S*. I might be imagining things. Could you just take a look around?"

He'd never been able to say no to Angela. From the first

time Tom introduced her as his fiancée, she'd been able to twist Shane around her little finger. Not that she asked for much or tried to manipulate him. Angela didn't have a devious bone in her body. She faced the world with a straightforward determination. A flame burned within her. Sometimes she was bright as a torch. Other times, like now, she was a flickering candle. He'd do anything to nurture her delicate fire.

"You said you might be imagining things," he said. "Why?"

"I heard a crash. Down the hall."

"Toward your bedroom?"

"Yes." Her lips were tight. Beneath the sweep of her long brown hair, her forehead pinched. She was desperate, stressed to the breaking point.

"I'll take care of this," he said.

He was pretty sure they weren't dealing with a drug-crazed psycho, mainly because they hadn't been attacked while standing here talking. But he intended to take her supposed imagining seriously. Until he knew better, he would assume there was an intruder.

From where Shane stood, he could see that the small living room and the L-shaped dining area were clear. The kitchen was straight ahead and the lights were on. If someone was hiding in the house, he was down the hall to the left.

"Here's what we're going to do," he said as lowered the boy to the floor. "Benjy, I want you and your mom to stand here, right by the door. If I yell, you run outside as fast as you can. Understand?"

"Yes." He held up his arms. "Can I hold your hat?"

"You can wear it."

When he placed his hat on the boy's head, Benjy giggled. "Look, Mommy. I'm a cowboy."

"You sure are." Protectively, she placed her hand on her son's thin shoulder.

"Why do we run outside?"

"It's a game," she said.

Suitcase in hand, Shane went toward the hallway. As soon as he was out of Benjy's sight, he unzipped his bag and took out his Sig Sauer. He almost hadn't brought his weapon. Firearms generally weren't needed at a wedding.

Moving fast, he entered the first bedroom, the guestroom that usually served as a home office for Angela. He looked into the closet and under the bed. Found nothing.

In the bathroom, he yanked aside the shower curtain. Nobody here.

As he approached Benjy's bedroom, he could hear Angela reassuring her son, telling him that Shane would be right back and everything was okay. He hoped she was right.

Except for the messed-up covers on the bed, Benjy's room was exceptionally neat. The closet was almost empty.

The last room to search was Angela's—the bedroom she'd once shared with his cousin. In a glance, Shane scanned the cream-colored walls and dark wood furniture. After he checked the small adjoining bathroom and the closet, he lowered his gun and returned to her room. A lilac scent perfumed the air; it was Angela's special fragrance. He never smelled lilacs without thinking of her.

Though he could tell that she'd been clearing out her things in preparation for the move to her new home, there were mementos scattered around the room. A tortoiseshell hairbrush set that belonged to her grandmother. A plate with Benjy's baby handprints. A handmade quilt Shane had bought for her at a firemen's bazaar in the mountains. Lots of photographs decorated the walls, including a formal wedding portrait of her and Tom. He wondered if she'd take that picture when she moved in with her new husband.

Finding no intruder, he closed the open window in her bedroom. He noticed that a framed watercolor of yellow roses had fallen from the wall, probably blown down by a gust through the window. The glass in the frame was cracked.

In the guestroom, he slipped his gun under the pillow, then returned to the front door, pushed the door closed and locked it. "No problem."

A nervous smile touched her full lips. "Thanks, Shane."

"I think I might have found what spooked you." He held up the eight-by-ten watercolor. "This picture fell off the wall."

"Ha! I knew I heard a crash."

When Benjy tilted his head to look up, Shane's hat fell to the floor. The boy scrambled to pick it up and returned it to his head. "Did you ride your horse?"

Shane crouched down to his level. "You know I'm not really a cowboy. I'm a deputy."

Benjy gave him a stubborn scowl. "A depitty cowboy."

"And you're a kid who needs to go back to bed. I'll see you tomorrow."

While Angela escorted her son back to his bedroom, Shane went into the kitchen. He'd visited this house often enough to know where everything was. Usually, the countertops were covered with fancy little appliances. Not tonight. Like the rest of the house, the kitchen sparkled. Except for a plastic cup on the floor and a water spill near the sink. Using paper towels, he mopped up.

All this cleanliness must be due to the Realtor's "For Sale" sign in the front yard. The house had to be kept spiffy for showings.

He found a plate of macadamia nut cookies on the small kitchen table and poured himself a glass of milk. This was a nice little ranch-style house in a good neighborhood. It ought to sell fast, and Shane told himself that he was glad to see Angela moving on with her life. When Tom and Angela bought this place a couple of months before their wedding, he'd helped them paint and move in the few sticks of furniture they'd owned. He remembered their high hopes for the future. After Tom finished his time in the military, he'd planned to go to med school and become a doctor.

He munched his way through three cookies while he thought of the good times and the bad. Angela was about to take another big step forward, and so was he.

She joined him. After getting Benjy back to sleep, she'd taken a moment to comb her wavy hair and pull it back in a ponytail. Though she was more composed than when she'd answered the door, he saw tension in the set of her jaw. Her cheeks were flushed. She'd lost weight.

"Thanks for checking out the house, looking for the bogeyman." She sat opposite him at the small table. "I guess I've got a bad case of prewedding jitters."

"I'm no expert," he said, "but most brides tend to get fussy about bouquets and cakes and seating arrangements. They don't go running around their house with a butcher knife."

"After I heard that crash, I went to Benjy's room. He wasn't in the bed. I was terrified."

"Where was he?"

"Hiding in the closet. I don't know why." She rested both elbows on the table and propped her chin on her fists. "I've been edgy, not sleeping well. You know how I can get. Not that I'm comparing a case of nerves to how I felt after Tom died."

He remembered. She'd been overcome with grief, and

he'd stayed with her nearly the whole time, except when he went back up to the mountains to follow up on the investigation into the hit-and-run accident that had killed his cousin. The detectives on the case had been competent, but they'd never apprehended the driver of the vehicle that ran him down.

He studied the woman sitting opposite him. A few days before getting married, she should have been excited and happy. "What's making you feel this way?"

"The wedding has gotten out of hand. I didn't think it would. Neil has a small family. Since both my parents are dead, I don't really have anybody."

"You've got me," he said. "And I'm honored to be walking you down the aisle."

"Tom would have wanted it that way. It's symbolic that you're giving me away."

He didn't like the way that sounded. He wanted to hold on to their friendship. "I'm not leaving your life. Or Benjy's. Like it or not, I'm always going to be hanging around."

"I like it."

She had the warmest smile. When she relaxed, he saw that candle flame inside her grow steady and strong. He reached across the table and took her hand. "Your wedding shouldn't be a burden."

"I've missed you." She gazed into his eyes. "It's been over a month since I've seen you."

"Anytime you need me, I'm just a phone call away." He looked into her eyes. The color of her irises had always fascinated him—a greenish-gray that seemed to change with her mood and the clothes she wore. Right now, they were more green, matching the cardigan she'd thrown over her white V-neck shirt. "Tell me how your quiet little ceremony turned into a monster."

"Everybody means well." She gave his hand a squeeze,

rose from the table and went to the sink to get a glass of water. "At first, I only wanted to invite my partner at the restaurant and the main chef. When the other employees heard, they wanted to come, and I couldn't say no."

Her south Denver restaurant—Waffles—was only open for breakfast and lunch. "Your staff isn't too large."

"Right, and I figured we'd have the reception at Waffles in the evening so catering wouldn't be a problem. Just a casual dinner. Then Neil's friends and coworkers wanted invitations. Doctors and nurses from the hospital. And professors from the university. Important people." She took a sip of her water. "Not that the woman who's working on a cure for malaria is more important than one of my busboys, but I want to put my best foot forward."

"I understand."

"Before I knew what was happening, I was arranging for tons of flowers and a DJ and imported champagne and a fancy cake." Her eyes flashed. "That reminds me. I hope you're not dating anybody special right now because I've got someone I want you to meet. She's French."

"Ooh-la-la." He hated being fixed up but didn't want to burst her bubble.

"On top of everything else," she said, "I'm selling the house, and it has to look great."

"Is that why you're still living here instead of at Neil's house? For showings?"

"For convenience," she said. "My house is five minutes away from the restaurant and from Benjy's babysitter. It's easier to stay here while I handle the wedding preparations. Neil lives on the outskirts of Boulder. It's a forty-five-minute drive, longer if I run into traffic."

It seemed to him that a couple in love would want to be together no matter how problematic. If he'd been getting married to Angela, he would have turned his life upside down to be with her.

"I'm here now," Shane said. "Tell me what you need, and you can consider it done."

She gave him a quick hug. "I'm glad you're here. When I heard that crash in the bedroom, I was imagining the worst."

"And it was nothing serious," he said. "The wind must have knocked the painting off the wall."

She looked puzzled. "What do you mean?"

"Your bedroom window was open."

Her eyes widened, and she gasped. "It was closed. I'm sure it was closed. I remember the rain splattering against the panes."

If that was true, someone had opened the window. She was right about the intruder. "Are you sure?"

"Oh, God, I don't know." Her hand rose to cover her mouth. "I think so. Is there a way to prove someone was inside?"

"I doubt anyone was inside. With all this rain, they would have left wet footprints, and I didn't see anything."

She shuddered. "What if they were standing outside and peeking in?"

He thought of his gun under the pillow in the extra bedroom. If somebody was sneaking around the house, he needed to secure his weapon. "Stay here."

He retrieved his gun and checked the window in the guestroom. It was locked. Moving fast, he surveyed the other windows and made sure they were all fastened.

When he returned to the kitchen, she was pacing. Her moment of calm had been replaced by renewed panic.

"Angela, listen to me."

"How could I be so careless? I know I should keep the windows locked, but I have them open during the day. When

I checked on Benjy earlier tonight, his window was open and the screen was loose. Somebody could have slipped inside. Into my son's room!"

"The window is locked now. I checked."

"I don't understand. Why would anyone want to rob me?"

He fastened his holster on his hip and put the gun away. Holding her by both shoulders, he stared into her eyes. "This isn't a typical break-in. Nothing was stolen."

"What are you saying?"

"This is personal." Somebody wanted to hurt her, to frighten her.

"How do you know?"

"I'm not a big-city cop, but I've seen my share of trouble-makers and stalkers."

"A stalker? Oh, damn. What am I going to do?"

"You and Benjy need to move out of this house as soon as possible. Tonight. Maybe you can stay at Neil's house."

"I can't. I don't want him to think I'm crazy. Or helpless."

"He's going to be your husband. If you can't share your fears with someone you love, who can you tell?"

"Not tonight." In spite of her raging fear, her voice was determined. "I won't wake Benjy again. I'm putting him through too many changes. A new house. A new daddy. A new babysitter. I can't tell him that mommy has a stalker. I don't want to scare him."

"I understand." And he figured he could handle just about any threat. "We'll stay here. I'll make sure we're safe."

"Thank you, Shane." She flung her arms around his neck and held on tight. Her slender body pressed against him, and he tried to ignore his natural response to having a beautiful woman in his arms. This was Angela, after all.

She'd been Tom's wife, then his widow. Now she was engaged to another man. Shane had no right to feel anything more than friendship.

But she was so warm. He closed his eyes for a moment as he embraced her. Quietly, he said, "I won't let anybody hurt you."

He heard the front door open. Still holding her, he drew his gun.

Dr. Neil Revere strode into the kitchen. "What the hell is going on?"

Chapter Three

Shane considered himself to be an honorable man. As such, he'd never seduce a woman who was about to get married to another man. Unfortunately, Neil didn't know him well enough to understand that finding Angela in his embrace was purely innocent, and there wasn't a real good way to explain what he thought he saw.

Angela left his arms and went toward her fiancé. She kissed his cheek. "I didn't expect to see you tonight."

"I told you I'd be stopping by after my meeting. You must have forgotten." He peeled off his wet trenchcoat and tossed it over one of the chairs by the kitchen table. As he tugged at his necktie to loosen the knot, he said, "You're forgetting a lot of things lately."

Though Shane didn't like the way Neil snapped at her, he cut the doctor some slack. Finding his bride-to-be in the arms of another man was damn awkward.

Ignoring her fiancé's rebuke, Angela forced a smile. "Neil, you remember Shane Gibson."

"Of course." He glared at Shane as though he were a virus that needed to be stamped out. "You'll be giving Angela away at the wedding."

Shane holstered his gun and shook hands. "I haven't had a chance to congratulate you. You're a lucky man to be marrying Angela."

Warily, the two men sized each other up. Physically, Shane had the edge. At six foot two, he was a couple of inches taller. He was probably five years younger and certainly in better shape, since being a deputy in a mountain community meant he sometimes had to go on rescue missions and sometimes had to break up bar fights.

Neil managed to smile without showing a bit of friendliness, which was okay with Shane. He didn't have to like this well-dressed doctor with the dark, serious eyes. The only thing that mattered was for Neil to be a good husband to Angela.

"Tell me, Shane. Is there a reason why you had your gun drawn?"

"Angela had an intruder. Somebody creeping around the house."

"My God." To his credit, Neil's hostility shifted to concern. He stroked Angela's cheek. "Are you all right? And Benjy? Is he okay?"

"Yes and yes," she said. "I didn't actually see the intruder, but the window in my bedroom was opened. And in Benjy's room, too."

"Are you sure you didn't just leave the windows open by mistake?" His voice was skeptical. "Absolutely sure?"

"What are you insinuating?" she asked. "I'm not making this up."

"It's okay, honey. I know you've been upset, having trouble sleeping." He seemed to be examining her as though she were a patient. What was wrong with this guy? He ought to be comforting her.

Neil continued, "Getting married can be very stressful, and I know change is difficult for you. If you're having panic attacks, there's nothing wrong with that. I'd like for you to get help with—"

"I'm fine." Angela's voice was strong. "If you don't

believe me about the intruder, talk to Shane. He's in law enforcement, and he believes me. When you came in, we were discussing what to do next."

"Is that so?" Neil wheeled around to face him. "It didn't look like you were talking."

Shane replied in a cool, professional tone. "In my opinion, there was an intruder, possibly preparing to enter. It's unlikely that the motive was robbery. Burglars don't break into a house when the owner is awake and walking around."

"What was he after?"

"Being apprehended wasn't the intruder's primary concern. He wanted to frighten Angela. He might be a stalker. Or somebody who has a personal grudge." He turned to Angela. "Have you received threats?"

She shook her head. "Not that I recall."

"Maybe from a disgruntled employee," he suggested. "Or someone associated with the restaurant. A supplier. Even an angry customer. Take your time. Think about it."

She sank into a chair beside the table. Her shoulders slumped. A moment ago, he'd been critical of Neil for treating her like a patient. Now, he was interrogating her like a victim.

As her friend, he knew what she needed. He'd seen Angela through the worst time in her life—after her husband was killed. She needed his support. Even though her fiancé was standing right there, Shane sat in the chair next to her and gave her a hug. "If you don't want to deal with this now, it's okay. We can wait until—"

"I want to get it over with," she said. "I'm thinking. But I can't come up with anybody who wants to hurt me. A couple of months ago, I fired a waitress, but she got another job."

Gently, he said, "Have you noticed anything unusual? Maybe had the feeling you were being watched?"

"I've been kind of spooked. Nervous, you know. Especially at night."

He considered the possibility of a peeper. Not usually a violent criminal. But this guy had opened windows. He seemed to be planning something more than just watching. "Earlier, we talked about moving you and Benjy to Neil's house."

"It's the obvious solution," Neil said. "I suggest that we get everything packed up and make that move right now."

She stood and confronted them both. "I don't want to frighten Benjy. We're staying here tonight, and that's final."

A muscle in Neil's jaw twitched, but he conceded. "All right, Angela. We'll do this your way. Have you at least called the police?"

"I don't want to," she said stubbornly. "There's nothing the police can do."

"You're being unreasonable."

Shane wouldn't have been so blunt, but he agreed with Neil on this point. "The police can dust for fingerprints, look for trace evidence and talk to your neighbors."

"I don't want any more investigating. Not now. Not ever again." Her eyes flashed with anger. "The police did plenty of investigating when Tom died. To what end? They still didn't find his killer. All their poking around was a waste of time. If you gentlemen will please excuse me, I'm going to bed."

She turned on her heel and left the room.

Shane's natural instinct was to follow her, to soothe her worries and offer comfort. But that wasn't his job. He looked toward Neil, expecting him to follow his fiancé and make sure she was all right.

Instead, Neil checked his wristwatch. "This is a waste of time. I have a lot going on with work, especially since I'll be gone for a couple of weeks on honeymoon. Coming here tonight was incredibly inconvenient." He glared at Shane. "And I didn't expect to find you."

Shane offered no excuses for his presence. Though he'd been planning to stay at a motel, he'd responded to the urgency in Angela's voice when she invited him.

"I suppose," Neil said, "that you'll be staying the night."

"I'm not going to leave her and Benjy unprotected."

"Fine. I'd stay myself but I'm in the midst of some very important meetings."

What could be more important than the safety of his bride and her son? Shane kept that opinion to himself.

"Tomorrow, we'll get them moved," Neil said. "I have plenty of room at my house. You're welcome to stay there until the wedding."

Considering what had happened tonight, it was generous for him to offer. "I appreciate your hospitality."

"It's no trouble. My housekeeper hired people to help out until after the wedding, and I have other houseguests. I believe you know one of them—Dr. Edgar Prentice from Aspen."

"We've met."

"He's a fertility specialist and an ob-gyn. Your cousin Tom sought my uncle out when he decided that he and Angela should go through the process of creating frozen embryos."

"I know."

"In a way, Uncle Edgar was Angela's midwife, even

though he didn't deliver Benjy. Ironic. Now, I'll be Benjy's father."

"Stepfather," Shane corrected. Nobody but Tom should be recognized as the father of Angela's child.

"I'll see to Angela now."

As he watched Neil stride toward Angela's bedroom, Shane wanted to stop him. Neil wasn't the right man for her. He was cold and arrogant and sure as hell didn't put Angela first. *None of my business.* Shane didn't have the right to tell her who to marry or what to do with her life.

He sat at the kitchen table, took the last macadamia nut cookie from the plate and bit into it.

When Angela lashed out against law enforcement, he hadn't been surprised. Shane had listened to hours of her complaints about how the Park County Sheriff's Department had failed to bring her husband's murderer to justice. She'd gotten to the point where she refused to even talk to them.

That had been his job.

The investigators had compiled quite a bit of evidence. The flat tire was caused by three nails that could have been picked up from any number of construction sites in the mountains. The indentations in Tom's SUV indicated that he'd been hit by a truck, and the crime scene investigators found bits of black paint. From the tire tracks, they could tell that after Tom was hit, the truck backed up and hit him again.

The police theory was that the driver of the truck was drunk or otherwise incapacitated. After he hit Tom, he backed up to see if he could help and accidentally ran into Tom a second time. The driver had gotten out of his car and had left a fingerprint in Tom's blood on the Toyota.

The print matched nothing in the database, and the cops had other factors working against them: It had taken over two hours to locate Tom's body. There were no witnesses. They'd never been able to locate the black truck.

The final conclusion from the Park County Sheriff's Department was vehicular homicide. The driver of the black truck was never found.

Shane understood Angela's pain and frustration, but he knew the investigators had done their best to solve the case. A hit-and-run accident was cold-blooded—the kind of case that would haunt the investigative team almost as much as it troubled Shane.

His instincts told him that Tom's death wasn't an accident. He was targeted, mowed down on purpose. Shane believed that Tom's death was premeditated murder.

THE NEXT MORNING, Angela felt like a new woman. Her usual schedule meant jumping out of bed at four in the morning and dashing like mad to have Waffles ready for business at six-thirty. Not this week. While planning the last details of the wedding, she had enough on her plate, so to speak. Though she might stop by the restaurant and help out, they weren't expecting her.

With no need to rush, she took a long, luxurious shower. When she meandered into kitchen after eight o'clock, Shane had already made coffee and fed Benjy. He greeted her with a grin and a joke about sleeping late. What an amazing friend! He made her laugh, always made her feel comfortable.

And he wasn't bad to look at in his jeans and cowboy boots. His black hair was in need of a trim before the wedding. Not that any of the women in attendance would notice. They'd be too busy swooning over his sky-blue eyes and rugged masculine features. It was hard to believe Shane was still single. There had been a couple of live-in girlfriends over the years, but he'd never once walked down the aisle.

After they dropped off Benjy at the babysitter, she slipped behind the steering wheel of her van and turned to Shane. "Before I stop by Waffles, I have to pop into the dress shop for a final fitting on the wedding gown. You don't mind, do you?"

"Bring on the ruffles and lace," he said. "I told you I'd do anything to help, and I meant it."

"Oh, good." The very idea of super-macho Shane in a dress shop amused her. "After the gown, we can go to the florist, then stop by the lingerie store."

He groaned. "As long as I don't have to have my toenails painted pink. Isn't the maid of honor supposed to do this stuff?"

"Yvonne's busy running Waffles. But don't worry. I'm sure I can come up with some manly, testosterone-driven tasks for you, too."

"Like moving you and Benjy to Neil's house?"

She hadn't planned on making that move until she and Neil got back from their two-week honeymoon in Baja. Even then, it would be difficult. His house was far from her work, her favorite market and everything she was familiar with. "It's so inconvenient."

"But safe," he said.

It hadn't escaped her notice that he was wearing his holster under a lightweight summer blazer. Shane definitely took her intruder seriously.

Not like Neil. She didn't like the way he'd reacted last night. In his opinion, she was having panic attacks, and he wasn't going to change his mind. Though she admired her fiancé for his decisiveness, she wished that he'd listen to her side of the story.

"After you're married," he said, "how are you planning

to run Waffles? You're at the south end of the metro area in Littleton and Neil's almost in Boulder."

"Neil wants me to quit."

"But you don't want to."

"I don't know." She'd given the issue so much thought that her head ached. "It's a bridge I'll cross when I come to it."

She turned off the main road into the four-block area known as Old South Clarkson Street. With several boutiques and restaurants, it was a pleasant, neighborhood place for specialty shopping. On weekends, traffic closed down in the morning for a farmers' market.

She drove past Waffles, pleased to see that the tables they set up on the sidewalk for summer were all filled. Around back in the alley, she pulled into her parking space.

"Why are we stopping here?" Shane asked. "I thought we were going to look at a dress."

"It's only four stores down."

She hopped out of the car and started down the alley. Though Shane's legs were a mile longer than hers, they walked at the same relaxed pace. When they were together, life seemed to take on a more natural tempo, almost as though he carried the easygoing mountain lifestyle with him.

"There's something I've been meaning to tell you," he said. "You're not the only one who's making changes."

He was always steady and predictable, someone she could count on. "What are you up to?"

"I'm moving to Denver."

"Leaving the mountains? You?"

"I'm turning thirty this year, and I looked around and saw that I was doing the same thing every day. Arresting the same drunks on the weekend. Driving the same roads. Living in the same house I was born in."

"Is this because your parents aren't in Silver Plume anymore?"

"Maybe so." He shrugged. "Mom and Dad moved to Phoenix two years ago. And my sister's in New York City. But this really isn't about family. It's about me."

"And you want to try something different."

"I'm taking a job with a Denver-based security firm. At first, I'll be doing bodyguard work, but there's training available. I want to get into computers. And I've been learning to fly a helicopter. Man, there is nothing like being up in the sky."

When she looked up at him, she saw a spark of excitement in his blue eyes. "I'm happy for you, Shane."

"Time goes fast. I didn't want to turn around and find myself turning into a sixty-year-old man who never left Silver Plume."

She opened the rear door to Linda's Dress Shoppe and went inside. There was nobody in the storeroom, which was typical. She called out, "Anybody home?"

Linda, the proprietor, stuck her head into the back room. "Hi, Angela. I'm busy out here. You go ahead and put on the gown. I'll be with you in a minute."

There was an informal sewing area in the corner with tables for cutting fabric, a couple of armless dress forms and a rack of clothes zipped into black garment bags with Linda's logo emblazoned on the front. A hot pink label stuck to one of the bags had Angela's name.

Since she hadn't wanted a fancy gown for her second marriage, she'd picked out a strapless dress with a bit of lace and a matching jacket to cover her shoulders when it got colder at night.

Shane stood beside a sewing table. "This is strange."

"What?"

"Right here, next to the scissors and spools, there's a kitchen knife."

When she took a closer look, anxiety shot through her. "It's a boning knife. And it's mine."

"How do you know?"

"The red dot on the handle." No one was allowed to touch her chef knives. When she wasn't using them, she kept them tucked away in a locker in the restaurant office.

She unzipped the garment bag, pushed the plastic aside and stared in shock. Her wedding gown had been slashed to ribbons.

Chapter Four

Unable to believe what she was seeing, Angela tugged the ragged edge of the ripped white fabric. The skirt had been sliced multiple times. Bits of lace hung like entrails around the bodice. The gown was ruined beyond repair.

Scared and confused, she turned away. On the table was the boning knife—her knife! Was it possible that she had done this? She couldn't remember. Had she suffered a blackout?

The thought terrified her. True, she hadn't been in her right mind lately. The lack of sleep and stress had taken their toll. Last night, she'd imagined headlights crashing through her kitchen window. But she hadn't gone completely insane. Not yet, anyway.

Shane touched her shoulder. In a low voice, he asked, "What do you want to do?"

For one thing, she didn't want Linda to see this disaster. The owner of the dress shop would have too many questions, and Angela didn't have answers. "Get me out of here."

"Done."

He tossed the knife into the garment bag with the dress and zipped it up just as Linda bustled into the back room with her long, silk scarf flowing behind her.

"Sorry to keep you waiting," she said. "I had a mixup

with the register. Thought I'd lost a hundred and fifty bucks. Then I remembered that I went to the bank last night."

Linda was a lovable scatterbrain. But not crazy. *Not like me*. She thought of Neil's diagnosis that she needed to see a psychologist. He might be right.

While Shane introduced himself, she gathered her wits, hoping to appear normal. Not that she needed to worry. When she was with Shane, other women hardly noticed her existence. Even without his hat, he was one hundred percent sexy cowboy.

He beamed a slow smile at Linda and said, "Angela is having second thoughts about the dress. She wants to take it home and decide if this is actually what she wants to wear."

"Brides are all the same." Linda grinned up at him. "Always fussing about the details. When I got married, I was as nervous as a squirrel on a highway, jumping from one median to another."

When Angela forced herself to speak, her voice seemed to be detached from her body. "Remember that white suit I tried on before?"

"Indeed, I do. To tell the truth, I liked you better in that outfit than in the gown. The suit seemed more…" Linda flipped the end of her scarf and chuckled. "More suitable."

"We'll take both of them with us," Shane said. "Then, Angela can make her decision later."

"Fine with me," Linda said. "But you still need alterations on the gown, Angela. You've been losing weight, and a strapless bodice needs to fit like a second skin."

While Shane went to the front of the store with Linda to make arrangements, Angela let down her guard. She sank onto a stool beside the cutting table and stared, unfocused. What was wrong with her? The inside of her head whirled like a blender. The shelves and boxes in the storeroom seemed to be closing in on her. She was suffocating.

She didn't remember taking the knife from the restaurant, and she sure as hell didn't recall attacking her dress. Was she sleepwalking? Had she done this in a blackout? *It didn't happen. Dammit, I'm not crazy.*

But if she hadn't done this, that meant someone else had. Everybody who worked in this area knew that Linda often neglected to lock the back door, and Angela's dress had been sitting here for several days, unguarded.

She stared at the garment bag. Who could have done this? Why did they want to sabotage her wedding?

SHANE ESCORTED HER through the alley. Though his hands were occupied with holding both dress bags, he was prepared to toss them aside if he saw an approaching threat. Last night, Angela had an intruder. This morning, her gown was attacked. Clearly, someone wanted to hurt her—or at the very least, terrorize her.

Adrenaline pumped through his veins, making him hypervigilant. Ironically, he realized that he was acting as her bodyguard. In a few weeks, that would be his regular job at PRESS—Premier Executive Security Systems. No longer a small-town deputy sheriff, he was already stepping into the world of big-city dangers.

When she clicked the lock to open her van, he placed the garment bags in the back and turned to her. "We can't ignore what happened."

"We can try." Avoiding eye contact, she opened the driver's-side door. "I still need to check with the florist and make sure the bouquets are—"

"The daisies will wait." He caught hold of her arm, stopping her before she shot off in a different direction. "We need to figure out who did this."

"How did you know about the daisies?"

"They're your favorite flower. White daisies." When she married Tom, it was winter and she settled for white roses. Now daisies were in season.

"I got my daisies," she said, "even though Neil wanted orchids."

That made sense. Orchids were hothouse flowers, expensive and delicate. Angela was a daisy person—cheerful and bright.

"You got me off the subject," he said. "We need to investigate, starting here at Waffles."

"Are you kidding? I'm not going to go marching into the restaurant and accuse my friends. These are people I work with, people I trust and care about."

"They're also the most likely suspects. They have access to your knives. They know—as you do—that it's easy to slip in and out of the dress shop through the back entrance."

She shook her head. "Nobody I know would be so mean."

"Let's think this through." He gently took the car keys from her hand. "When was the last time you used your knives?"

When she shook her head, her high ponytail bounced. Sunlight picked out strands of gold in her soft brown hair. "I don't remember."

"Think about it. Were you at Waffles yesterday?"

"I came in early to help with the breakfast rush, but I didn't unpack my knives. One of the waitresses was sick, and I filled in for her."

"And the day before?"

He could see her calming down as she considered the facts. "I put in almost a full day, and I was in the kitchen. So I must have used my knives. Believe me, I would have noticed if one was missing. I've had that set for seven years."

Seven years ago was before they met, before she'd married his cousin. He'd never really thought about that time in her life. Her youth. Her childhood. "How old were you?"

"Eighteen. I'd just graduated from the Cordon Bleu culinary school in London, and the knives were a present to myself—symbolic of my new career as a chef."

Shane wasn't a gourmet, but he'd heard of Cordon Bleu. "How come I didn't know you had such a fancy background? And how did you wind up in London?"

"When I was growing up, I spent a lot of time overseas. My dad was stationed in Germany."

He'd known that. "And your father passed away when you were just a kid."

"Not much older than Benjy," she said. "I barely remember him. My mom struggled for a couple of years before she remarried, and she worked in restaurants. That's where I got my love of flavor and texture." A tiny, nostalgic smile touched her mouth, and he was glad to see her calming down. "She died when I was a senior in high school. I had the choice of college or Cordon Bleu, and I wanted to cook."

"You were looking for something," he said.

"A taste." Her finger traced her lower lip. "You know what it's like when you bite into something really good? It's pure joy. I love seeing other people experience that sensation when they're eating something I created. Their eyes close. And they hum. Mmm."

He liked seeing her with a smile on her face, but he couldn't ignore the threats. "We're way off track."

"I know. And I'd rather not think about any of this. All I want is to get through the next couple of days."

"Whoever slashed your wedding gown is sending you a

message, and it's not a love note. I hate to say this, Angela, but you're in danger."

She turned away from him, stared across the alley at a six-foot-tall redwood fence. Her slender arms wrapped protectively around her midsection as though she were physically holding herself together. "What if it was me?"

He didn't understand what she was saying. "Explain."

"I might have imagined the intruder last night. There's really no proof that anyone was outside the house."

Earlier this morning, he'd inspected the ground outside the windows and found no footprints. The only possible bit of evidence was that the screen on Benjy's window was missing a couple of screws.

"What about the dress?" he said. "I'd call that proof."

"Not if I did it myself." Though the morning was warm, she shivered. "I've been an emotional basket case lately, and don't ask me why because I don't know."

"Something to do with getting married," he said.

When she looked at him, he saw a painful vulnerability in her eyes. Her mouth quivered. "I'm scared, Shane."

"It's okay." He pulled her close, offering his shoulder to cry on. "Talk to me."

"Being married to Tom was the best thing that ever happened to me, but it was a bumpy road. Right from the start."

Shane knew his cousin's flaws better than anyone. After his first tour of duty, Tom had a pretty serious case of post-traumatic stress disorder. And he was a recovering alcoholic. Before he and Angela got married, he quit drinking. She'd been good for him, helped him straighten out. "Tom wasn't perfect. Nobody is."

"This isn't about Tom. It's about me." Her body tensed. "Maybe I'm not cut out to be married."

"I don't believe that. You're a warm, loving woman. Look at what a great job you've done with Benjy."

Without thinking, he dipped his head and gave her a quick kiss on the forehead. Her hair smelled of lilacs. When she smiled up at him, the gray-green of her eyes seemed as deep as a mountain glen. Holding her felt so damn good; he didn't want to let her go. But Angela wasn't his woman. She was about to be married to another man.

"Thanks, Shane. You always know what to say."

He stepped away from her. "Let me do my job as an almost former deputy and investigate. I want to figure out who messed up your dress, and I'm starting here. At Waffles. Take me inside, and show me where you keep your knives."

Her eyes narrowed suspiciously. "Do you promise not to interrogate anybody?"

"Not unless they come at me with a loaded gun."

He strode to the rear door of the restaurant and pulled it open. Inside, the warmth of the kitchen flowed around him in a wave of breakfast aromas—bacon, coffee and freshly baked muffins. The back door opened into a hallway between the walk-in refrigeration unit and the office, which was their first stop. The office space had two small desks—one for Angela and one for Yvonne Brighton, her partner. Two tall, metal file cabinets stood beside two lockers.

Angela opened the locker nearest the door.

"You don't keep anything locked," he said.

"Sometimes I do. At the end of the day."

She removed a black cutlery bag from the lower shelf. When she opened it on the desk, he could see the empty slot where the boning knife should have fit with the rest of the set. Angela touched the space and looked up at him. "Now we know for sure. It's my knife."

It would have been simple for someone to slip inside

the office and steal her knife. The friendly atmosphere of Old South Clarkson Street made for lousy investigating. "I might be able to get fingerprints off the handle."

"Most people aren't that dumb," she said. "We keep a stock of throwaway gloves in the kitchen."

Though he nodded in agreement, he figured he could stop by the PRESS offices later if he wanted to check for fingerprints. They had a forensics department and computer access that rivaled that of the Denver PD.

Angela's partner popped into the office. Yvonne Brighton was a tall, big-boned woman who did a killer Julia Child impersonation. A lopsided navy-blue chef hat covered most of her curly brown hair. She gave them a toothy grin. "I thought I heard someone back here."

She charged at Shane and enveloped him in a giant bear hug which he happily reciprocated. He liked Yvonne. She was funny and smart—too smart to put anything over on. Before she stepped away from him, she patted his shoulder holster and said, "Expecting trouble?"

"Shane has a new job." Angela rushed to explain. "He's working for a bodyguard company."

His new employer was far more complex, but he didn't correct her. "I'm moving to Denver."

"Terrific!" Yvonne wiggled her eyebrows. "Or should I say *très magnifique!* Angela and I have somebody you really need to meet."

"The French woman." He gritted his teeth. What was it about a single man that turned women into matchmakers?

"Marie Devereaux. Very pretty. And an excellent baker. She's doing the wedding cake, which means it'll be beautiful and taste good, too. You'll like her."

"If you say so."

"I most certainly do."

Yvonne wasn't shy about giving orders. When it came to managing the restaurant, she and Angela complemented each other perfectly. Angela provided the empathetic voice of reason, and Yvonne made sure things got done.

She sat in the swivel chair behind her desk. To Angela, she said, "I'm glad you're here. I need a break. Could you take care of the kitchen for a couple of minutes while I chat with the mountain man?"

"No problem." Angela grabbed her knives and went toward the office door. "I feel guilty about not being here more often this week."

When she left the office, Shane positioned himself in the doorway so he could keep an eye on her. Despite the cozy atmosphere of Waffles, he hadn't forgotten the danger.

"We need to talk." When Yvonne pulled off her chef's hat and ruffled her hair, he noticed a few more strands of gray. He didn't know Yvonne's age, but she had two grown daughters. She exhaled a sigh. "I'm worried about Angela."

"I'm listening."

"She's been dragging in here like she's half-dead. Dark circles under her eyes. Hair hanging limp. I've seen her hands trembling. And she must have lost ten pounds in the last two weeks." Yvonne scowled. "It reminds me of how she fell apart after Tom's death."

"I remember." Though Angela and Yvonne weren't in business together five years ago, they'd been friends. "You and your husband helped her through that tragedy."

"And you. In spite of the grief you were carrying, you were one hundred percent there for our girl."

In the kitchen, he saw Angela step up to the grill. Her hands moved nimbly as she poured batter and flipped pancakes. She sprinkled powdered sugar on one order, dropped a dollop of sour cream topped with three blueberries on another. Graceful and fast, never missing a beat, her food preparation was a virtuoso performance.

Shane turned his attention toward Yvonne. Her concern was obvious and sincere, and she knew Angela better than almost anyone else. "Why do you think she's upset?"

"It's almost like she's haunted."

"Nervous about getting married again," he suggested.

"Oh, I don't think marriage bothers her."

"Then what?"

"It's Neil," she said. "He thinks running Waffles is beneath her. His wife should stay at home and tend to his needs. Can you see Angela doing that? Within a month, she'd be climbing the walls."

"If Neil gets his way and Angela quits, what happens to Waffles?"

"I'd sell the place," she said without hesitation. "We've had offers."

Yvonne's theory didn't tell him much about possible intruders or the person who slashed the wedding gown. Instead, it pointed back to Angela herself. Her fear of getting married—to Neil or anyone else—was eating at her, making it hard for her to sleep.

Still, he found it hard to believe that she'd destroyed her wedding dress in the throes of a blackout. Whether awake or asleep, Angela wasn't the type of person who committed outright vandalism.

He turned to Yvonne. "You seem pretty sure about Neil."

"I am." For emphasis, she slammed the flat of her hand on the desktop. "She shouldn't marry him, and I'll do just about anything to stop her."

Chapter Five

From his car seat in the back of the van, Benjy chanted in a singsong voice, "George Washington, John Adams, Thomas Jefferson."

Angela asked, "And who is president number thirteen?"

"Easy," Benjy said. "Millard Fillmore. And twenty-three is Benjy Harrison. He's the best. He's got my name."

Her son had an uncanny gift for memorization. He could repeat an entire book back to her after she read it aloud just once. He rattled off the multisyllable names of dinosaurs without a glitch. And he loved lists, like the presidents.

From the driver's seat, Shane said, "What number is Teddy Roosevelt?"

"You mean *Theodore* Roosevelt," Benjy said. "Twenty-six."

"*Theodore* used to visit Colorado a lot," Shane said. "The next time I take you up to the mountains, I'll show you a hunting lodge where he stayed."

"Mommy, I want to go to the mountains. Now."

"Soon," Angela promised. To Shane she said, "Turn left at the next stop sign."

Nervously, she checked her wristwatch. They were running late.

After Shane convinced her that it wasn't smart to stay

at her house, she'd packed up a few essentials and some of Benjy's toys. Neil's house was safer. Not that it was a fortress, but he had a top-notch security system.

When she'd called Neil and told him their plan, he sounded pleased, which didn't surprise her a bit. Neil liked to have things under control—his control.

They'd made arrangements to meet at his house at one o'clock sharp for lunch. It was past that time now. Angela fidgeted in the passenger seat, knowing that Neil's housekeeper, Wilma, would be annoyed. Her thin mouth would pull down in a disapproving frown, and her eyes would fill with judgment.

At the stop sign before they entered Neil's cul-de-sac, a black truck crossed in front of them. Thousands of similar vehicles cruised the streets of Denver, but every time she saw one, she was reminded of the hit-and-run driver who killed Tom. The black truck was a bad omen.

"Straight ahead." She pointed. "Pull into the driveway."

Shane gave a low whistle. "Wow. That's a whole lot of house."

Three stories in English Tudor style, Neil's seven-bedroom house took up the end of a cul-de-sac that bordered on forested land. His perfectly manicured lawn stretched like a green carpet to the double-wide oak doors beneath the porch. Summer flowers and cultivated rosebushes, which were tended twice a week by gardeners, made brilliant splashes of crimson, yellow and purple.

Every time she beheld this magnificent house, Angela wondered how she'd handle the responsibility of caring for the property. Being mistress of the manor didn't come naturally to her. With the gardeners and the housekeeper and the people who came to clean, she felt as if she was moving into a hotel instead of a home that was truly her own.

As soon as they parked, Benjy threw off his seat belt and scrambled free from the car seat. "Open the door, Mommy."

To Shane, she said, "We can leave the suitcases here for now. We're already eight minutes late for lunch."

"Is that a problem?"

She didn't want to admit that she was worried about the housekeeper's opinion and trying her best to live up to everybody's expectations. "I like to be on time."

As soon as she opened the van door for Benjy, he jumped out. With his backpack tucked under his arm, he bounced along the sidewalk to the porch.

Neil opened the door and stood there, framed by his grand and beautiful home. In his white shirt with the open collar and his gray linen slacks, he looked elegant. Lean and healthy, he had a summer tan from playing golf and tennis. His sandy-blond hair curled above his forehead. His best features, as far as she was concerned, were his dark eyes. There was a fierceness in those eyes, an indication of passions that ran deeper than his sophisticated outer veneer.

When he lifted Benjy in his arms and gave the boy a hug, her tension eased a bit. She could see that Neil cared about her son. Marrying him wasn't a mistake.

As she and Shane approached the porch, Neil said, "I have a surprise. My dad just arrived from Virginia."

She stiffened her spine. Only once before had she met Roger Revere, retired general and former JAG lawyer. He'd made it very clear that she needed to shape up if she truly wanted to be a member of their family. He would certainly disapprove of her disheveled hair, the smear of cooking grease on her chinos and her well-worn sneakers.

"You boys go ahead to lunch," she said. "Start without me. I need to freshen up."

"Take your time," Neil said as he carried Benjy through the foyer to the dining room.

Shane hung back. He touched her arm. "Are you okay?"

Not okay. I'm a wreck. She felt like a big, fat mess—confused and borderline nuts. "I'll make it."

"Whatever you need, I'm here for you."

His offer of unconditional support touched her. Everybody else in her life made demands and passed judgment. Not Shane. He'd seen her at her worst, and he was still her friend.

Forcing a grin, she turned away from him. "Start without me. I'll be there in a jiffy."

She darted up the stairs to the second-floor master bedroom she would be sharing with Neil, probably from this day forward. The black-and-white décor felt sterile and cold. The only pictures on the walls were black-and-white photographs of landscapes—places she'd never been. In the adjoining bathroom, she closed the door and leaned against it.

The tension she'd been holding at bay coiled tightly around her, squeezing her lungs and making her heart beat too fast. No matter how fiercely she denied the threat, she felt danger all around. Either she was going insane or someone was after her. *I've got to calm down.*

She dug into her purse and took out the amber vial of the prescription sedatives Neil had given her. She was only supposed to take one at night before bed, but she needed to quell her rising fears. Even if she fell asleep this af-

ternoon, that was better than running through the house
screaming.

Popping off the cap, she tapped a light blue pill into her
hand and swallowed it dry. Soon, she'd be more relaxed.

In the mirror over the sink, she confronted her reflection and groaned. Making herself presentable was going to
take more than a fresh coat of lipstick. This would require
a major repair job.

FOLLOWING NEIL, SHANE entered the spacious living room
with a fireplace at the south end. When they were outside the house, he'd noticed two chimneys rising above
the gables. As he'd said to Angela, this was a whole lot of
house—big and classy with Persian rugs, heavy furniture
and framed oil paintings. Two older gentlemen sat opposite
each other in oxblood leather chairs.

One of them he recognized as Dr. Edgar Prentice. Prentice was the doctor Tom had used for the frozen embryo
procedure, and Shane vaguely recalled some kind of recent
scandal involving Prentice's fertility clinic in Aspen.

Slowly, Prentice unfolded himself from the chair. He
moved with hesitation as though he suffered from arthritis.
Even stooped, he was nearly as tall as Shane—taller if
Shane counted the thatch of thick white hair.

"We've met before," he said.

"Tom Hawthorne was my cousin. I came to your office
with him."

"And you've remained in contact with his wife for all
these years. An admirable display of loyalty."

His comment made Shane's relationship with Angela
sound like an obligation. Nothing could be further from
the truth. "I'm privileged to call Angela my friend."

The old man's eyes lit up behind his glasses as he focused on Benjy. "This must be the young man I've heard so much about."

"I'm not a man," Benjy said. "I'm a kid."

"Of course. And what's in your backpack?"

"Stegosaurus, T-Rex, Triceratops. Want to see?"

The boy plopped down on the carpet. With much straining, Prentice bent lower, listening intently as Benjy unpacked his plastic dinosaurs and talked about the Mesozoic era.

Neil introduced him. "Shane Gibson, I'd like you to meet my father, Roger Revere."

In contrast to Prentice, the stocky, red-faced man sprang from his chair with impressive vigor. Shane braced himself for a power handshake; he wasn't surprised when Roger glared into his eyes and squeezed hard.

Though Shane wasn't a fan of macho games, he matched the older man's grip. It went without saying that Shane was stronger; he was probably thirty years younger than Neil's father. If he'd been feeling gracious, he would have let Roger win this little battle. But he sensed the importance of establishing dominance.

Smiling through gritted teeth, Roger continued to apply pressure. "I hear you're a sheriff in the mountains."

"I was," Shane drawled. "A deputy sheriff in Clear Creek County. But I'll be moving to Denver soon."

Neil arrowed a sharp glance at him. "Angela never mentioned anything about your move."

"Because I just told her this morning." With a flick of his wrist, Shane broke free from the prolonged handshake. "I'm taking a job with Premiere Executive Security Systems."

"Impressive," Neil said. "They're one of the best in town."

"I met the owner last year during a mountain rescue situation." The search for a missing client had been a harrowing few days, fortunately with a happy ending. "We have a lot in common."

Roger stuck out his square jaw. "I suppose that means you'll be seeing more of Angela."

"And Benjy," Shane said. "I sure hope so."

"Maybe you can convince her to cut down on her hours at the pancake house," Roger said gruffly. "The only person she needs to be cooking for is my son."

Though he didn't agree that Angela should quit her job and become a full-time wife unless that was what she wanted, Shane sidestepped the issue. "She works hard."

"Nothing wrong with dedication," Roger said, "as long as you've dedicated yourself to a worthy goal. As you know, my son has an acclaimed reputation as a virologist. He cures illness. He's saving the world, dammit. His wife should be something more than a cook."

Shane couldn't let Roger's idiotic statement go unchallenged. "She's a chef. Not a cook."

"What's the difference?"

Roger had stuffed his right hand into his jacket pocket, and Shane hoped that his muscular handshake had cracked a couple of bones. "It's hard to explain unless you've tasted her food. There's a damn good reason why her restaurant always has a line. She's an artist." He remembered a description Yvonne had once given. "A culinary artist."

"It's true," Prentice said as he straightened his posture. "Angela concocts recipes with the skill of a chemist. She trained at Cordon Bleu in London."

A tall woman with thinning black hair stepped into the room. Her long, skinny fingers twisted in a knot. "Gentlemen, it's time for lunch. Please come to the table before the soup gets cold."

Shane was hungry but didn't really want to sit down to a meal with these guys. He reconsidered his plan to stay in one of the guestrooms at Neil's house. Though he wanted to be close to Angela in case she needed protecting, he didn't like the Revere family—father or son.

"Before I sit down," Shane said, "I should see what's keeping Angela."

"You go ahead and relax," said Dr. Prentice. "I'll check on her."

As Prentice left the room and crossed the entryway to the staircase, Shane noticed that his arthritic shuffle changed into a confident stride. He was much stronger than he had appeared when he rose hesitantly from his chair.

Why had Prentice tried to create the impression of being a tired, elderly man? As a lawman, Shane knew that a man who lied about one thing will lie about another. He needed to check out Dr. Edgar Prentice and find out what else he was hiding.

SINCE SHE'D ALREADY moved many of her clothes to Neil's house, Angela had a lot of options. She'd chosen a cotton dress in conservative navy blue with white trim because it seemed least likely to provoke a response from Neil's father. As she finished brushing her hair, she heard a knock on the bedroom door.

Her first instinct was to lock the door until the little blue pill worked its magic and numbed her nerves, but she wasn't a coward. Slipping into a pair of navy flats, she marched to the door and opened it. "Dr. Prentice?"

"Angela, you look lovely—glowing like a new bride. I hope you don't mind if I take a few minutes alone with you."

He didn't wait for her answer. Instead, he entered the huge bedroom and closed the door behind himself. Though he didn't flip the lock, she felt trapped. "What did you want to talk about?"

In spite of his smile, his expression was serious, reminding her of the way a doctor looked before he delivered bad news. "Perhaps you should sit down," he said. "It's a medical issue."

Taking her arm, he guided her across the huge bedroom to a black chaise near the window. She really didn't know Prentice well at all. The process of creating the embryos took a couple of months, but she had only a half a dozen appointments at his office in Aspen. For the in vitro procedure, she had used a doctor in Denver.

She perched on the edge of the chaise. Her mind raced with dire possibilities. Was there something he'd discovered in her DNA? Some horrible genetic disease? Something that might affect her son? "This isn't about Benjy, is it?"

"Your son appears to be a remarkable child. Very bright. And healthy." He paced away from her. "It's best if I start at the beginning."

Suspiciously, she said, "All right."

"Twenty-six years ago, in the early days of in vitro fertilization, I was involved in a study on a military base in New Mexico. The Prentice-Jantzen study was designed to monitor children born in vitro throughout their lives."

She was the right age and born in New Mexico. "Was I one of those children?"

"Your parents were having difficulty conceiving. I was happy to help. I performed the IVF procedure."

She had never known. Her mother never told her. It was a decidedly odd coincidence. Both she and her mother had in vitro babies. Both times, Prentice was involved.

He continued, "Unfortunately for our study, your father received an overseas assignment, and I lost track of you. When you and Tom showed up in my offices and I ran your DNA, I identified you."

"Why didn't you say anything then?"

"It didn't seem necessary. You had your life in order, and it wasn't my place to complicate it."

She was beginning to have a creepy feeling about this conversation. "Why are you telling me this now?"

"Two reasons," he said. "The first is that you're getting married and should know the truth. And the second…" He paused. "Certain individuals have made allegations about the Prentice-Jantzen study. I want you to understand the situation from my perspective."

"Allegations?"

"I've always done what I thought was best for both the parents and the children. There are those who have accused me of withholding vital information."

Though he looked like an eccentric grandfather with his shock of white hair and thick glasses, he had the intensity of a much younger man. She shouldn't underestimate him. "What kind of vital information?"

"There were medical reasons why your parents couldn't conceive. There's no need for me to go into detail. The bottom line was that they would never have a child. The embryo I implanted in your mother was not her own. And not your father's, either."

It took a moment for Angela to fully comprehend. "The embryo," she said. "That was me. Right?"

"Correct."

"Are you saying that my parents weren't my biological mother and father?"

"Correct again. Using what was cutting-edge technology twenty-six years ago, I successfully created and implanted twenty-four embryos using the sperm and egg from highly intelligent, physically outstanding individuals."

She shook her head, trying to wrap her mind around what he had just told her. Her upbringing hadn't been ideal, but she had loved her mom and dad. They weren't her parents? "I can't believe it. This is impossible."

"It's merely science," he said.

"Why didn't Mom tell me?"

"She never knew."

Angela was shocked. Though Prentice had admitted that he'd withheld vital information, this was fraud. "How could you do this to them? To me?"

"I never set out to hurt anyone," he said. "When your parents signed on for the study, they desperately wanted a baby, You can understand that, can't you?"

"Yes."

Her desire to have a baby had been a visceral need. In the days following the IVF procedure, every waking moment centered on her ability to conceive. When she knew she was pregnant, her heart nearly exploded with joy. Had her mom felt the same way? Were they alike in spite of genetics?

"I gave your parents a precious gift," Prentice said. "I gave them you—a bright, beautiful, healthy infant. Do you think they would have loved you less because you didn't share DNA?"

"If they had known—"

"But they didn't. As far as they were concerned, you were their child."

And they had loved her and cared for her to the best of their ability. "I must be crazy because this is beginning to make sense to me."

"I expected as much. You're a practical woman."

"My biological parents," she said. "Who are they?"

"I can give you their DNA profiles, but not their names. The participants in the study—sperm and egg donors— were anonymous."

Prentice had offered a glimpse of a family she never

knew, and she wanted a wider view. "What about the other subjects in the study? I'd like to meet them."

"I advise against such a meeting. None of the others are your biological brothers or sisters. You, Angela, are the unique product of genetic engineering."

Was that good news? Or another reason for concern?

Chapter Six

The bedroom door swung open, and Benjy dashed across the snowy-white carpet with his little arms and legs churning. He jumped onto her lap. "It's time to eat, Mommy. Wilma said so."

Snuggling him close, she kissed his forehead. If it weren't for Prentice and for Tom's foresight, she never would have conceived her wonderful son. Life without Benjy would have been dark and grim. Unimaginable.

She stood, holding Benjy on her hip. He was getting too heavy to carry, but she was willing to strain her muscles to maintain the physical connection between them.

Looking beyond her son's angelic face, she caught Prentice's eye. "I have absolutely no problem with anything you've done, Doctor. I'm grateful."

With a kind smile, he reached toward her, linking himself with her and with Benjy. "So glad we had this little talk."

Neil had followed Benjy into the bedroom. He stepped up beside her. "That's a lovely dress, Angela."

"Thank you."

In spite of his compliment, she couldn't quite bring herself to meet Neil's gaze. Her talk with Prentice brought Tom to the forefront of her mind. Tom had been so insistent about the frozen embryos. She missed her darling husband who had died too young.

But she knew beyond a shadow of a doubt that Tom would want her to move on. He'd told her so. Because he was a soldier in harm's way, he'd insisted on discussing what would happen if he were killed in battle. Time and again, he'd said that he didn't want her to crawl into the grave beside him. If he died, he wished for her to honor his memory by living her life to the fullest. That wish was one of the main reasons she'd decided to have Benjy.

Moving on, dammit. She would be married, again. She would open a new chapter in her life. As they left the bedroom, she looked up at her husband-to-be. Even though she didn't always feel a zing when he touched her, Neil was a good man, dedicated to curing disease. "Dr. Prentice has been telling me some very interesting things."

"I know all about it," he said. "As a doctor and a scientist, I'm intrigued by your unusual conception."

"You knew?"

"You're a very special woman, Angela."

Genetically engineered, whatever that means.

At the top of the staircase, she paused. When she looked down, the angle of descent appeared to be as steep as a precipice. Her feet rooted to the landing. Though the sedative had surely taken effect, a wave of heat washed through her.

"Are you all right?" Neil asked.

She wanted to tell him but sensed that this was the wrong time to show signs of weakness. His father and his housekeeper would look upon her with scorn. Neil shouldn't have to make excuses for her; he should be proud of her.

Carefully, she lowered Benjy to the floor. "I don't think I'm strong enough to carry this big boy."

"It's okay, Mommy. I can go down all by myself."

While Benjy and Prentice went down the staircase, she clamped her hand onto the banister and took the first step. If she didn't look down, this wasn't so bad. Fighting vertigo, she took the next step.

When Neil touched her shoulder, it felt as if he was shoving her down the stairs. "You go on ahead," he said. "There's something I need in the bedroom."

Before she could object, he deserted her. She stood alone on the second stair from the top. It felt as if she was onboard a ship in the midst of a storm, and the deck was rolling wildly. It was all she could do not to grab onto the banister with both hands and weep.

Benjy had already reached the bottom. "See? I made it."

"That's good, honey."

At the bottom of the staircase, Shane appeared. Without hesitation, he climbed the stairs and took her hand. "You look good."

Her fingers latched on to his hand. *Please don't let go.*

He tucked her arm into his. "Here's a chance for us to practice for the wedding ceremony when I give you away."

Humming the "Here Comes the Bride" tune, he anchored her as she descended. His support reassured her. Without asking, he'd seen her distress and come to her rescue. He was the best friend she'd ever had.

At the dining-room table, she was seated between Neil, who sat at the head, and his father, Roger. Directly across from her was Shane. Beside him, Benjy and Dr. Prentice carried on a conversation about presidents and dinosaurs.

While she sipped the bland cream of tomato soup that Wilma had prepared, Angela had the sense that she was outside her body, floating over the polished oak table and looking down. She saw hostility between Shane and Roger as a streak of fiery red. In contrast, Prentice and Benjy had a mellow glow; they seemed to be bonding. Neil—the conductor of this weird color symphony—skillfully blended conversations and comments.

The meal progressed through salad and a particularly heavy casserole with predominant flavors of cheese and salt. If Wilma had been the least bit open, Angela could have improved her cooking skills a hundred fold. But that wasn't going to happen. The housekeeper had her own way, and she wasn't going to change. The running of the kitchen would have to be decided after the wedding.

After the store-bought cherry pie dessert, Neil turned to her and asked, "What else needs to be done for the wedding?"

"I have a list," Angela said. "At this point, it's just a matter of double-checking the details."

Neil touched her hand and smiled. "I suppose you have your gown all fitted."

Her heart sank as she remembered the tattered white fabric. "It's taken care of."

"And the reception?"

"Since we changed the venue for the reception dinner to the country club, there's no need to worry about the food. I know the chef, and she's good."

"Mommy is a chef," Benjy announced.

"And a very good one," Shane was quick to add.

Neil lifted her hand to his lips and lightly kissed her knuckles. "Is there anything I can do to help? You've been so busy, and I think the stress is wearing you down."

"That's true," Wilma said as she cleared plates. "She's losing weight."

"I'm fine," Angela said. And she meant it. The colors had receded. The vertigo had passed. Actually, she felt pretty good. "It's all under control."

"Glad to hear it." Roger pushed back from the table. "This might be a good time to deal with the business aspect of the marriage."

What was he talking about? "Business?"

"Pre-nup," he said with a scowl.

She and Neil had already discussed the need for a pre-nuptial agreement. They would both keep the assets they brought into the marriage. That part was simple. After that, the finances got complicated, and she'd left the details to her accountant and Neil's attorney, who also handled his finances.

While Prentice and Benjy went outside to play, Neil and his father escorted her toward the den which served as a home office for Neil. The floor-to-ceiling bookshelves held row upon row of medical and virology texts, including a book that Neil had coauthored and was being used in his classes. Afternoon light slanted through multipaned windows and shone on Neil's antique mahogany desk. The den always intimidated her, reminding her of how very little she knew about Neil's area of expertise.

She was glad that Shane had ambled along beside her— not insisting that he be a part of this proceeding but there to support her just the same.

Roger stood at the door. "This is a private matter, Shane."

Instead of leaving, Shane lowered himself onto the long sofa behind the coffee table. He rested his ankle on his knee, and leaned back. "I won't be a bother. Don't mind me."

"I most certainly do mind." Roger's jaw tensed. His dislike for Shane was obvious. And unreasonable, in her opinion. Neil's father was as slimy as a toad. He sputtered, "My son's finances are none of your concern."

"I want him here." Angela surprised herself by speaking

up. "Shane is one of my dearest friends. I have no secrets from him."

"It's all right, Dad." Neil stepped behind his desk and opened the top drawer. "This should only take a minute."

Grumbling, Roger seated himself on a chair near the window. His crossed leg mimicked Shane's pose.

Neil centered a stack of legal-size documents on the desk and turned them toward her. "The attorney marked all the places we need to sign and initial. Then dad will witness, and we're done."

She picked up the closely typed sheets. "There must be thirty pages here."

"More or less." He handed her a pen. "Some pages are nothing more than listings of property. The attorney thought it was wise to make everything crystal-clear. To avoid misunderstandings."

When she sat in the armless chair on the opposite side of his impressive desk, she felt more like an applicant for a loan than a bride-to-be. As she looked down at the pre-nup, the legal language swam before her eyes in an array of "whereases" and "heretofores." She flipped through a couple of pages. "Can you give me a summary?"

"What's mine stays mine. What's yours stays yours. And there's a whole other category of what becomes ours after the wedding."

Though she didn't want to make a fuss, some of these details might be important. "I really should read this."

"By all means," Roger said. He bolted from his chair and hovered beside her. "If there's anything you don't understand, ask me."

"Angela," Neil said, "look at me."

His voice compelled her. She stared across the desk. This was the man she intended to marry and spend the rest of her life with. "I'm sorry to be so difficult."

Neil's dark gaze linked with hers. "You trust me, don't you?"

"Of course I do." Trust was the most important part of any relationship.

"Just sign the papers. Then we can spend the rest of the day relaxing. It's a sunny afternoon. Not too hot for August. We can sit in the backyard and watch Benjy play." His voice lowered to an intimate level. "Maybe go to bed early."

It had been weeks since they made love. "What about your colleagues in town? I thought you'd have to go back to the virology lab."

"You're more important. Our marriage is more important."

Somewhat reassured, she looked down at the pre-nup. Reading through these clauses was a daunting task, but she was a businesswoman, and she knew better than to put her signature on anything without knowing what it said. "I could have my attorney check it over."

"You could ask him," Neil said. "But there isn't much time. The wedding is the day after tomorrow."

Roger snatched the papers from the desktop. "I'd be happy to help you. We can go real slow, page by page, so you can understand every comma."

She reckoned that he was trying to be kind, but she despised the note of condescension in his voice. She wasn't a complete idiot, after all.

"Excuse me," Shane said as he left the sofa and approached the desk.

Angela compared the three men standing around her. Roger was a former general and JAG lawyer, certainly a powerful man. Neil's standing in the international medical community gave him an aura of gravitas. But Shane was a lawman, accustomed to taking charge of uncomfortable situations. Though his manner was easygoing, he easily dominated the other two.

"Seems to me," he said, "that Angela needs her own legal representative to review the documents."

Roger bristled. "Are you questioning my competence?"

"Not a bit. But you're Neil's dad, which puts you in his camp. She needs somebody who's on her side."

"Don't be an ass," Neil said. "There's nothing contentious in these papers."

"Fine," Shane said. "Then there shouldn't be a problem. I'll take Angela to see her attorney and—"

"I've had it with you." Neil came around his desk to confront Shane directly. "Last night, I found you with my fiancée in your arms. Now you're stirring up trouble over a simple signature. Who the hell do you think you are?"

"Angela's friend."

Those two simple words rang with truth. Shane cared for her. He'd stood by her.

"Friends come and go," Neil said. "In less than forty-eight hours, I'll be her husband."

"Maybe so," Shane drawled. "Right now, you're just a guy with a pen and a stack of unsigned documents."

Neil took a step closer to Shane. His fingers tightened into fists. The tendons on his throat stood out. "She doesn't need friends like you—an ignorant, low-born cowboy who doesn't have two nickels to rub together."

Angela surged to her feet. "That's enough, Neil."

"Oh, please. You're not taking his side, are you?"

"Shane is my friend," she said. "Nobody—not even you—talks to my friends like that."

"His behavior is intrusive and unwanted. This agreement is between you and me."

"Then why is *your* father here?" she demanded. "Why

did *your* attorney draw up these papers? Don't I have a say?"

"Of course." He gave her a hard, cold stare. His eyes were as black as a starless night. "You didn't have a problem with these arrangements before."

"I never thought the pre-nup would be so complicated."

"Dammit, look around you. The artwork in this house is worth more than you'll earn in a lifetime. Did you think I wouldn't protect my investments?"

"I have something to protect as well," she said.

"What?"

"My self-respect." She took the documents from Roger's hands. "My attorney will be advising me on whether or not to sign the pre-nup."

"Wait," Neil said harshly. "You're not leaving. You wouldn't dare."

The hell I wouldn't. "Watch me."

Chapter Seven

Shane was glad to see Neil's house in the rearview mirror. If he had his way, he'd never return to that oversize mansion with the two chimneys and the perfect lawn. But that choice wasn't his to make. Unless Angela said goodbye to Neil, Shane had to figure out how to face her fiancé without tearing his head off.

Kneeling on the passenger seat, she was turned around, tending to Benjy in the back. The kid was having a minor meltdown.

"Not tired," he shouted. "Wanna play."

The plan had been to leave Benjy at Neil's while Shane took Angela to her attorney's office. But her son had a different idea. As soon as his mom stepped into the backyard, he'd run toward her. "Home," he'd shouted. "I wanna go to my house. Wanna play with friends."

Prentice, who had been babysitting, had gestured helplessly and said, "I don't know what's got into him. We were playing catch, talking and laughing."

Shane knew. Benjy was a smart little guy, sensitive as all hell. The boy must have sensed that his mom was upset. And he reacted.

Right now, Angela was doing her best not to show emotion as she talked to her son. "Were you and Dr. Prentice playing?"

"He's old."

"Yes, he is. What kind of games did you play?"

"I wanna go to Lisa's house." Lisa was the four-year-old daughter of his babysitter. "Lisa. Lisa. Lisa."

Angela prepared a juice box with a straw for him. "Do you like Dr. Prentice?"

"Mommy," he whined, "didn't you hear me? He's very old."

"But nice. Right?"

Shane figured that she was trying to find out if Prentice had done something to set off this tantrum, and he was pretty sure that she wouldn't succeed. Getting a coherent answer from a grumpy three-year-old was like asking a trout to sing.

She handed Benjy his juice, turned around in her seat and buckled herself in. Her gaze focused straight ahead, through the windshield. Her nostrils flared. Breathing heavily, her breasts rose and fell.

She looked as if she was on the verge of her own tantrum, and he would have been glad to see her express her anger. She had every right to kick and scream. "Where are we headed?"

"I should call my attorney before we go to his office," she said. "Get on the highway and head south."

He didn't know his way around Denver too well, and her van lacked a GPS directional system, but he didn't mind driving aimlessly if it meant putting distance between her and Neil. The disrespectful way he treated her was just plain wrong. When Neil talked about the pre-nup, he made it sound as if he was an aristocrat who had to protect himself and all his possessions from a gold digger. What a crock!

Though Shane didn't know the details of Angela's finances, she owned her home and her restaurant was successful. She wasn't rich, but she was doing well. Not that dollars and cents mattered to her. She was less interested in accumulating wealth and more focused on bringing joy to the people around her.

She finished her phone call and groaned. "This is one of those days when everything goes wrong."

"Your attorney?"

"He's in court today and tomorrow. And his associates are a married couple who are on vacation until next week. One of the paralegals in his office could read the pre-nup, but if there's a need to negotiate, I feel like I should have somebody with legal weight on my side."

Or she could postpone the wedding. That was Shane's honest opinion, but he didn't want to add to her burden of stress by pointing out that Neil had ambushed her. "Why did Neil wait until the last minute to give you the pre-nup?"

"Well, it took a long time to inventory his various hold-ings. And he wanted his father's advice." She didn't sound convinced by those reasons. "This has turned into such a mess."

He glanced over his shoulder into the backseat. "On the plus side, Benjy's already asleep."

She reached back and took the juice box from her son's limp fingers. "He was tired. That's why he was so cranky."

"You seemed to think that Prentice got him riled up."

"Which is ridiculous," she said. "Dr. Prentice is a nice, grandfatherly person."

Shane wasn't so sure. "What's his relationship to Neil?"

"He's a close friend of the family." She rubbed at the parallel worry lines between her eyebrows. "Prentice told me something that it's going to take a while to understand. It's not necessarily a bad thing. But unexpected."

"Do you want to talk about it?"

"Absolutely. But not right now."

He reminded himself to check out Dr. Edgar Prentice's background and current problems. "I have a solution for your lawyer problem. Earlier today, I talked to my new boss at PRESS."

"PRESS?"

"Premier Executive Security Systems," he said. "The head of the company, Josh LaMotta, has a law degree. He's not currently practicing, but I'm guessing that he's a heavy-duty negotiator—a five-hundred-pound legal gorilla."

"Let's go see him."

He merged onto the highway. The PRESS offices were at the south end of town in the Tech Center near Centennial Airport, where they kept the company helicopter. Shane made a quick call on his hands-free cell phone to confirm that Josh was in.

After driving a few minutes in silence, he became aware that she was watching him. "Something on your mind?"

"You must get tired of always having to ride to my rescue."

"Much as I'd like to take credit for being a hero, it's not true. You're too strong and capable to be a damsel in distress. You do a fine job of taking care of yourself and Benjy."

"It feels like I'm falling apart. I had a physical not too long ago, and there's nothing wrong with me. But I've been having these dizzy spells."

"Is that what happened to you on the staircase?"

"Could you tell?"

Standing on the second step from the upstairs landing,

she'd been hanging on to the banister with a white-knuckle grip. "You looked like hell."

"Thanks a lot."

"Your eyeballs were rolling around in your head. Your knees were knocking. I thought you might just crumple up and fall over."

"It wasn't that bad," she said.

"Seriously, Angela, how often do you have these spells?"

"Usually at night when I can't sleep. I get hot, then cold. The room starts spinning around." She fidgeted in the passenger seat. "Here's the weird part. I'll look at the clock and see that it's ten twenty-three."

"The time when Tom died."

With only two days before she remarried, she must be thinking about him, remembering what it had been like the first time she walked down the aisle. She was taking a big step in her life; a certain amount of tension seemed natural.

He changed lanes. At three o'clock in the afternoon, it was close enough to rush hour that all four lanes on the highway were clogged.

She leaned forward to adjust the air-conditioning. "Neil gave me a prescription sedative to help me sleep. Sometimes, it works."

He was drugging her. "What kind of pill?"

"I don't know. It's robin's-egg blue."

"Did you take one this afternoon?"

She nodded. "It didn't help."

As a general rule, Shane was opposed to taking any kind of medication that wasn't strictly necessary. "Your dizzy spells might be a side effect."

"I already talked to Neil about that. He didn't think it was likely. These pills are supposed to calm me down, and my symptoms are the opposite of that. My pulse starts racing, and I get burning hot." A sigh puffed through her lips. "I'm just stressed out."

Still, he wanted to find out what was in those pills. PRESS had a forensics department, and they might be able to give him a quick answer. The problem would be to get his hands on the prescription without telling her that he was suspicious of Neil. Why would he drug her? It didn't make sense for him to give her something that made her agitated. It was to his benefit to have a smiling, agreeable bride.

She heaved another sigh. "I can't believe I blew up at Neil like that."

"He deserved it."

"You don't like him, do you?"

Not one bit. But he didn't want to make her life more difficult by criticizing her fiancé. "My only concern is that he's a good husband for you and a good stepfather for Benjy."

"He adores Benjy."

From what Shane had seen, that was true. Neil doted on the kid. "But you're not too happy about the way he treats you."

"Today wasn't a good example. He's usually calm and understanding. When we go out in public, he treats me like a princess. A couple of months ago, we went to a black-tie fundraiser for the hospital, and he rented an emerald and diamond necklace for me. I looked at the receipt, and that jewelry was worth more than my house. Neil thought I needed something to jazz up my plain black dress."

"You must have been real pretty."

"I guess." She gave a little laugh. "But it's not me. Not my style. It felt like I was playing dress-up at this big, sparkly, gala event. I would have been more comfortable in the kitchen with the caterers."

He'd always thought she was at her best when cooking. Whether stirring a fancy cream sauce on a burner or frying up freshly caught trout on a campfire in the mountains, she took on a glow of happiness. Humming to herself, she'd lift a tasting spoon to her lips and give a smile of pure pleasure. Emeralds and diamonds weren't needed to make her beautiful.

He wanted to believe that Neil appreciated her, that he knew what an amazing woman she was. "Have you done much cooking for Neil?"

"He's a big fan of my strawberry salad. He's conscientious about his weight, so he can't really appreciate French cuisine. Most of the recipes start with a pound of butter and heavy cream."

Shane's mouth began to water. "He doesn't know what he's missing."

"Neil is a man who knows what he likes. And I respect that. Also, he was telling the truth when he said that we discussed the pre-nup." Leaning over, she dug into her shoulder bag on the floor between her legs and took out the stack of documents that were held together by a metallic clip in the top left corner. "I might as well start looking through this stuff."

Traffic in their lane had slowed to a crawl, and he maneuvered to the left. At this rate, they wouldn't make it to PRESS for another half hour.

While she read, Angela hemmed and hawed. Her long hair fell forward in a shining brown curtain. She flipped from the first page to the next and the next without removing the clip.

Finally, he asked, "What does it say?"

"It's all about who owns what. There's a section about how Neil has no say whatsoever in Waffles."

"That should make Yvonne happy."

She thumbed through three pages. "There are a bunch of stipulations about if the marriage is annulled, if it ends in divorce after one year or five years or ten."

The whole idea of a pre-nup didn't make sense to him. Maybe he was old-fashioned, but he thought marriage should be about love and partnership and spending your life together. He supposed premarital agreements were prudent, like looking for the emergency exits when you got on a plane. Not that the escape route mattered if you were going down in flames.

She stopped rifling through the pages. Deliberately, she unfastened the metallic clip and removed two sheets from the center of the stack. "Dammit."

He looked toward her. "What's wrong?"

"More than I can say."

Her eyes narrowed to slits. He could tell that she was clenching her jaw. Though she didn't say another word, he could tell that she was furious.

ADOPTION PAPERS! Angela paced the length of the empty conference room beside Josh LaMotta's office. Neil had slipped an adoption agreement into the middle of their pre-nup. Did he really think that she was too stressed to notice?

Yes, they'd talked about the possibility. But they'd decided to wait before making a decision. The present and future custody of her child was of the utmost importance to her—not to be handled as a side issue in a pre-nup, as though her son were just another possession that needed to be declared and labeled.

The west-facing wall of the third-floor PRESS conference room was windows—all bulletproof glass—with a panoramic view of the Rockies. She stared at distant peaks as the sun dipped lower in the sky, wishing that the solar heat could burn away her anger.

At least, she was clearheaded. The moment she realized that she was looking at adoption papers, she'd decided that she wouldn't discuss custody in front of Benjy. Though he probably wouldn't understand, he'd surprised her on more than one occasion with his ability to comprehend. She didn't want him to think—not for one single moment—that his mommy wouldn't be with him for the rest of his life.

A half hour ago, when they arrived at PRESS, Shane introduced her to Josh LaMotta. Then he took Benjy to explore. Apparently, Premier Executive Security Systems was equipped with a great deal of computer equipment, a gym with a full basketball court and a forensics lab. Her only stipulation was that Shane avoid the shooting range in the basement. Benjy already showed far too much interest in guns.

She paced the length of the conference room again, pivoted and went back the other way. She hoped that she was overreacting, that the adoption papers had been included in the pre-nup by mistake. After she and Neil returned from their honeymoon and got settled into his house, they would discuss custody of Benjy. There were other legal documents that needed to be reviewed and revised as well—life insurance policies and wills.

She pulled out the chair at the end of the table and sat. In her will, custody of Benjy went to Shane, his godfather. Tom would have wanted Shane to raise his son. *And so do I.* She didn't want to change Benjy's last name; he was Tom's legacy.

But Neil would be raising her son, providing a home for him, going to his parent-teacher conferences, taking him to Little League games. Sooner or later, Benjy would start calling him "Daddy." A shiver ripped down her spine. Tom was his daddy, his only daddy.

When she heard the door to the conference room open, she bolted to her feet. Josh LaMotta had a serious expression on his face. She was afraid of what he might tell her.

Chapter Eight

While Benjy played with Josh in his office, Shane joined Angela in the conference room. Her jaw was tense. Her lips, tight. When she looked up at him, the color of her eyes betrayed her mood—dark gray and hard as steel. Nobody was going to push this lady around, and he was glad to see her determination. He wanted her to stand up to Neil.

On the long table, she'd made three stacks of documents. She rested her hand on the first pile. "These are conditions I can agree to without hesitation. The middle stack is 'maybe.' And the ones on the end are problematic."

"Tell me about the problems."

"Neil wants to adopt Benjy. These papers are the first step in that process."

On the surface, Neil's intention seemed perfectly natural. Her fiancé was a single man, and she was a mother with a child he loved. It seemed that Neil was doing the right thing, making sure that Benjy was taken care of. "I'm guessing that you've talked about custody before now."

"Well, yes. And we agreed to make those decisions later."

Her reluctance to assign custody said more about her state of mind than Neil's. She was willing to marry the man and have him raise Benjy, but she didn't want to think about giving up her child. Shane had a pretty good idea why she was disturbed. "This is about Tom."

"Benjy is his son. Benjamin Thomas Hawthorne. I don't want to change his name to Revere. He needs to know who his father was."

"I couldn't agree more." Shane wanted to preserve his memory as much as she did. "I won't let him forget, and neither will you. But Benjy might benefit from having a flesh-and-blood father."

"What do you mean?"

"You know what I'm talking about."

She turned her back and stalked away from him. At the far end of the conference table, she whipped around. "I know it's important for Benjy to have a positive male role model while he's growing up. And I know Tom would want his son to have a full life."

"You don't have to convince me."

"Here's something you need to understand." She came back toward him, one deliberate step at a time. "You saw me at the worst time in my life. You stood by me, and I'll never forget your support and your kindness. But I'm different now. I don't spend every waking moment thinking of Tom. Not anymore. I have Waffles. I have friends. My life is full, and Benjy is thriving."

Though she was looking straight at him, she sounded more like she was trying to convince herself. He said, "I'm proud of you. The way you've grown."

"I'll always be Tom's widow. But I'm about to become Neil's wife. I'm ready to turn that page."

And he wanted to be happy for her. Her life hadn't been easy; she'd lost both parents and a husband. But was Neil the right man?

He looked down on the three stacks of papers. "Did Josh have any advice?"

"He told me not to sign anything that made me uncomfortable."

"Hell, I could have told you that much."

"He's really glad that you're coming to work for him. He told me about how you met." She reached out, touched his shoulder and gave a light squeeze. "I'm not the only person who thinks you're a hero. Josh credits you with saving the lives of his three clients."

"Just doing my job." Mountain rescues could be a tricky business, and Shane had a lot of experience both in tracking and in pulling people out of dangerous spots.

"He says you're the best hire he's ever made."

"That remains to be seen." He had a lot to learn about personal security, especially when it came to the electronics. "Can we get back to Josh's legal advice?"

"The middle pile is about the possible dissolution of the marriage. Josh said it was one-sided."

"How so?"

"There were a lot of ways I could screw up and cause a divorce. But not so many for Neil."

From what he'd seen of her fiancé, that didn't surprise him. Neil wouldn't admit to any flaws. "What about the adoption papers?"

"I'm having a hard time dealing with the fact that Neil tried to sneak this past me. I've already made provisions for what happens to Benjy if I up and die."

"He comes to live with me." He reckoned that Neil hated the current setup. It might be one of the reasons he was so hell-bent on getting the adoption under way.

"You're his godfather." Her wistful smile contradicted the fire in her eyes, reminding him of her gentleness. "You'll always be in Benjy's life."

Not if Neil had anything to say about it. Shane was beginning to object to the adoption from his own standpoint. "Did Josh point out any legal problems?"

"There was a section defining what happens if either Neil or I become incapacitated."

"Incapacitated?"

"It's designed to cover dire circumstances. For example, if I go into a coma, Neil has full custody and makes decisions for Benjy."

"A coma? That's dire, all right." Legal documents seldom dealt with the good times. "But it makes sense. What bothered Josh?"

"The language was too broad. This clause says that Neil has immediate custody if I'm incapable in any way or manner—physically, mentally or emotionally—to care for my son."

"Does that mean Benjy could be taken away from you?"

"If I can't take proper care of him, yes." She glanced down at the papers. "I'm sure Neil is just trying to make sure my son is protected."

"From you?"

"Stop it, Shane. Don't make it sound worse than it is."

He couldn't ignore the threat. Being physically incapacitated fit her earlier example of prolonged hospitalization with a coma. But mentally? Emotionally? According to those vaguely defined terms, she could lose custody of her son if she had a nervous breakdown.

Her nighttime panic attacks took on darker implications. Had she imagined an intruder breaking into her house? Was she emotionally unbalanced enough to slash her own wedding dress? It wouldn't be hard for Neil to build a case against her, especially if she was living with him and taking medications he prescribed. He could make her look insane. He might already be laying the groundwork with his supposedly well-meaning suggestions that she should see a psychiatrist.

"The very same clause," she said, "applied to Neil. It's the same wording."

"But Neil hasn't been suffering from vertigo and panic."

"Usually, neither am I." Her lips pinched. "It's stress. After the wedding, I'll be fine."

"It wasn't stress that stole your knife and slashed your gown. You didn't imagine that. I was there. I saw the evidence. Someone carried out that act."

Her spine stiffened. "What are you suggesting?"

"Hell, I'll do more than suggest." He couldn't let her walk into this trap. "Neil is trying to make you look crazy."

"I can't believe that. He's a world-renowned virologist. There's no way he'd sneak through a back alley with my knife."

"He could hire someone to do it."

"But why?" Her voice trembled with anger. "To make me look insane and get custody of Benjy? Why would he want to do that?"

"I don't know his motive."

"Because there isn't one." Furious, she glared at him. "Whether you like him or not, Neil isn't a monster. He'd never do such things."

"Prove it," he said. "Give me one of those sedatives he prescribed for you and let me have the PRESS lab analyze it."

"Fine." She grabbed her shoulder bag from one of the chairs, dug inside and pulled out the vial. She tapped a pill into her hand and set it on the table. "Take it."

He slipped the light blue pill into his pocket. Tersely, he asked, "What do you want to do next?"

Moving stiffly but swiftly, she got right up in his face.

Her cheeks flamed. Her eyes shot daggers. Even her hair looked angry. "If you were anybody else, I'd tell you to go straight to hell. But we've been friends for a long time, and I know you think you're protecting me."

He *was* protecting her. Blinded by her imminent wedding, she couldn't see the danger coming at her like a freight train. "Correct."

"Let it go."

"Fine." Until he had proof, he'd step aside.

She tossed her head, and her long hair rippled. She flexed her slender shoulders, shaking off her anger. "Okay, then. All right. Can we pretend that we never had this conversation?"

"I doubt it." He wasn't letting go of his suspicions until he was proved wrong. "But we can call a truce."

"That'll have to be enough." She hoisted the strap of her purse onto her arm. "I need some time to cool down. I'd really like to go back to my house tonight if you think it won't be dangerous."

"I'll make it safe." *Safer than being with Neil.*

"As for the pre-nup," she said, "I don't know what to do. One thing is for sure. I hate the adoption and custody section."

He took those papers from the table and tore them in half. For emphasis, he tore the half into fourths.

Never before had he taken a strong position on what she ought to do with her life. His role had been to stand beside her and offer support. When she did well, he applauded. When she fell apart, he picked up the pieces. He never judged her.

As she looked at him, her eyes widened as though she were seeing him differently. "Well, I guess that decision is made."

"Damn right."

He didn't know why they were playing this game, but he'd make sure that Neil wouldn't win.

AT HER HOUSE, Angela stood on the front stoop while Shane checked the door to make sure the lock hadn't been tampered with. He bent down and focused the beam of a flashlight on the keyhole.

Benjy hovered close beside him. "What are you doing?"

"Making sure nobody messed with the door."

"It was locked," she said with some exasperation. Since the real estate agent hadn't scheduled a showing for today, she'd also fastened the dead bolt before they left. "And I have the key."

"Don't tell your mom, but you don't always need a key to open a lock."

"Really?" Benjy whispered back. "How does it work?"

"Magic," she said, hoping that Shane wouldn't insist on giving her son a lesson on how to pick locks. "Let's get inside."

Shane entered first and turned on the living-room light. He carried a large metal case imprinted with the PRESS logo. It contained the equipment for a top-of-the-line security system, which Josh LaMotta had been happy to provide free of charge with the stipulation that Shane do the installation as a training exercise. Though she was grateful to have the protection, she hated the necessity.

They'd already had dinner, but she went to the kitchen anyway. There was a lot on her mind, and cooking always helped her concentrate. As she washed her hands in the sink, she looked into her backyard, remembering her terror when she'd thought she saw approaching headlights through this window. Her panic was gone. With Shane in the house, she had no reason for fear.

He tromped into the kitchen with her son at his side and announced, "We're going to get started."

"Our house is going to be a fortress," Benjy said. He'd been excited and impressed with all the cool equipment he saw at PRESS. "With computers and valance cameras."

"Surveillance cameras," Shane corrected.

"Mommy, I want to be a bodyguard when I grow up."

"Not so fast," Shane said. "I thought you wanted to be president."

"I'll be both."

"Bedtime," she said sternly, "is in an hour."

Before they left the kitchen, Shane gave her a fond smile. Such a handsome man with his blue eyes and black hair, he truly was one of her best friends. It was impossible to stay mad at him, in spite of the terrible things he'd said about Neil.

She took a mixing bowl from the cabinet below the sink. Neil had left two apologetic messages on her cell phone, and she needed to call him back, but she wasn't sure exactly what she wanted to say. She was still angry about the way he'd dropped that pre-nup on her with his self-important father standing over her and looking down his nose.

She searched her cupboards. Since she'd been clearing things out, there wasn't much to choose from. But she could throw together a cinnamon and brown sugar coffee cake for tomorrow morning. As her hands busily sifted the flour and creamed the butter, her brain sorted out what she wanted to say to her fiancé.

There was no way she'd agree to the custody conditions of the pre-nup. On that point, she was firm. She'd refuse even if he insisted, even if he threatened to call off the wedding.

She groaned, thinking of the weeks of preparation that would go down the drain. She couldn't turn back now, she'd gone beyond the point of no return.

On the other hand, this marriage had turned her life upside down. She was selling this little house that she loved and moving far away from her business. Relocating Benjy presented another set of problems. Though she intended to keep him with the same babysitter when she came to work, she'd need backup nearer to Neil's house. He'd suggested a nanny, but she didn't want a full-time employee to take care of her son. Spending time with Benjy was the best part of her day. Why would she want to lose one minute of that precious time?

Neil really didn't understand what it was like to be a full-time parent. But he loved Benjy.

While she stirred the batter, she wondered. Did he love her? When she'd stormed out of his house this afternoon, he made very little effort to stop her. Not that it would have done any good. She wouldn't have listened. *How much do I love him?*

Her wooden spoon stilled. Planning the wedding had been so stressful that she'd forgotten the most important part. She and Neil hadn't been behaving like two people in love.

She spooned the batter into the greased pan and slid it into the oven. *Call him.* Back at the sink, she washed her hands again. From down the hall, she heard Benjy and Shane working on the security alarm project. Maybe she should go and watch them, make sure that Benjy was winding down for bedtime. *Call him.* She went to the fridge and looked inside. There were plenty of eggs and some wonderful baby Swiss cheese from the deli on Arapahoe. It might be handy to make a quiche. You could never go wrong with quiche.

Firmly she closed the refrigerator door, went to her purse and took out her cell phone. Neil would be her husband—the man she would share her life with.

She had to make this call.

Chapter Nine

After she'd gotten Benjy to bed, Angela opened a bottle of cabernet for her and Shane. Having a glass of wine at night was a simple ritual they'd started while she was struggling with the demands of being a new mother. While she was married to Tom, she'd never kept alcohol in the house, which was a huge sacrifice for a chef because wine was the perfect complement to so many foods. She didn't consider herself to be a wine connoisseur, but she had an excellent palate.

Sitting opposite each other at the kitchen table, they clinked glasses, and she offered a toast. *"A votre santé."* To your health.

"Cheers," he responded.

She took a sip of the full-bodied French wine, tasting a hint of mushroom and oak and enjoying the companionable moment. Spending time with Shane always seemed to put things into perspective.

"I called Neil and told him we'd be staying at my house tonight," she said. "He agreed to change the pre-nup. No problem. He'll take out the adoption section and the pages that pertained to cause for divorce."

"Leaving only the part about dividing up property."

"That's right." Neil's cooperation justified her trust in

him. On the phone, he'd been apologetic. "He's willing to bend over backward to make me happy."

"And get your signature." Though Shane restrained himself from scoffing, his gaze radiated pure cynicism. "I don't suppose he had an explanation for why he put in those clauses about being mentally or emotionally incapacitated."

"I didn't ask. I'm sure it was just some kind of lawyer language."

At least, that was what she told herself. She had to believe that her fiancé had no sinister ulterior motives. If Neil truly was trying to take Benjy away from her, she couldn't go through with the wedding. More than that, she had to run away from him—as far and as fast as she could.

Staring into the ruby wine, she said, "Tomorrow night is the rehearsal dinner. Neil asked if you'd be bringing a date and I told him you would."

"Great," he said with a grin. "I'll bring Josh."

"What?"

"It might be handy to have a negotiator on hand when you sign the pre-nup."

She hadn't thought that far ahead, but she wouldn't mind having backup when she faced Neil and his father. "That's okay with me, but what about Josh? He's already been incredibly helpful. I don't want to take advantage of your new boss."

"He won't mind," Shane said. "People like the Reveres and Dr. Prentice are his typical clients. An invite to the dinner and the wedding provides him with new contacts for PRESS."

"Okay, Josh is in. But I also want you to have a date—a real-live female date."

"You're talking about the French baker," he said. "The

way you're pushing her worries me. What's wrong with this woman?"

"Absolutely nothing. Marie has a sexy accent, a beautiful smile and great big blue eyes. She's tall and leggy and—"

"How tall?" he asked suspiciously. "Over eight feet? Does she have robins nesting in her hair?"

"Don't be a jerk."

"Does she even have hair?"

"Picky, picky, picky."

"Ha! I guessed it. You're trying to fix me up with a blue-eyed, bald giantess who bakes croissants."

She rolled her eyes. "No wonder you're still single."

"Nothing wrong with waiting for the right woman to come along." He sipped his wine and leaned back in his chair. "This is nice. You and me. Sitting here and relaxing."

"Very nice."

"I hate to bring up the stalker," he said.

"Then don't." She didn't want to face the possibility of a psycho stalker or the pre-nup or the endless details of her wedding. "Can't we just be normal people who chat about movies or books?"

"You're not normal, Angela. Like it or not, you're outstanding. Special."

His words tickled her memory. *She was special.* With all these other distractions, she'd almost forgotten about Dr. Prentice and his great big secret.

"Shane, do you remember when Tom first started talking about the frozen embryos?"

He arched an eyebrow. "What made you think of that?"

"Something Prentice said." Resting her elbows on the table, she leaned toward him. "I remember that Tom came home after a training session at the Army Medical Center, and he was all excited about having our embryos frozen."

"He'd heard a lecture from Prentice—something about biological warfare and the dangers of infection in the field. It scared the hell out of Tom. He was afraid he might come home sterile or put your future children in danger of some kind of genetic mutation."

"And he insisted on having the procedure done by Prentice even though the long trips to Aspen were inconvenient."

She'd been working as a sous-chef at an upscale French restaurant, and the head chef was a tyrant who complained about everything. Getting out from under his thumb wasn't easy, but she'd enjoyed the trips to Aspen, especially since they'd always stopped off to visit with Shane in Clear Creek County. After Tom deployed, Shane had actually taken her to the last appointment with Prentice.

"Anyway," she said, "Prentice ran my DNA. It seems that I was part of a study he did on an Army base in New Mexico. Twenty-six years ago, Prentice did the IVF procedure on several couples. Their children were supposed to be monitored throughout their lives, but my family dropped out."

"The Prentice-Jantzen study," Shane said. "You were one of those babies?"

"How do you know about it?"

"I ran a background check on Prentice while we were at PRESS. There was a recent murder related to the study, and some accusations of fraud. Prentice created embryos from high achievers. The babies were genetically engineered and didn't share the DNA of the mother and father who raised them." He drained the wine from his glass and poured more. "And you're a part of that study. Jeez, Angela, you're turning into some kind of trouble magnet."

"Neil thinks it makes me interesting," she said. "Plus, I have genius DNA. Maybe that's why Benjy is so bright."

"How does it make you feel? You weren't genetically related to your mother and father."

She shrugged. She might have been more disturbed if her father hadn't died when she was too young to know him. When her mother remarried, she had no genetic connection to her stepfather and hadn't bonded with him at all. They exchanged Christmas cards, but she hadn't seen him since her mother passed away eight years ago. When she wrote and told him she was getting married, he'd sent a congratulations card and fifty bucks. "My DNA doesn't seem all that important."

"Prentice lied to you." His voice deepened to a serious tone. Even though Shane was changing jobs, he had a lawman's stern morality. Lying was *always* wrong. "He didn't tell your parents that you weren't their biological child. And he never told you. That's fraud."

"It's not so black and white."

"You're defending him."

"I'm not saying what he did was right," she explained. "But my mother and father couldn't have a child, and Prentice made it possible. My mom carried me, gave birth to me and loved me as her only daughter. Who cares if our DNA didn't match?"

Though he sat motionless, she saw turmoil in his eyes as he tried to reconcile her opinion with the facts. In Shane's book, Prentice had committed a criminal act and deserved to be punished.

Usually, she trusted his opinion when it came to sorting out the good guys and bad guys. But how could she condemn Prentice? In a way, he was responsible for giving her Benjy.

"All the same," Shane said, "I'm keeping my eye on Prentice. I don't trust him."

"Once again, we'll agree to disagree. I think Prentice is a kindly old gent, and you think he's—"

"Up to no good." He pushed back from the table and stood. "Let's get back to the more immediate problem—namely, the stalker."

She rose to face him. "We seem to be jumping from one unpleasant situation to another. At least we see eye to eye on the stalker. He's definitely a bad guy."

"I can tell you that he's a lot more clever than I initially thought. And he's been here before."

A shiver trickled down her spine. "Watching me?"

"I don't want to speculate on what he's doing. It's easier if I show you."

The first stop was the guestroom where Shane would be sleeping tonight. He brought her inside and closed the door so their conversation wouldn't wake her sleeping child.

"First off," he said, "you need to remember that all the windows and doors are equipped with motion sensors. If you open one from the inside or the outside, an alarm goes off."

She'd heard the screaming banshee alarm when he and Benjy were installing the security system. "How do I turn it off?"

"There's a remote panel mounted by the front door. The code is Benjy's birthday."

"I can remember that."

"Over there is a monitor." He pointed to the dresser where a rectangular box with a screen sat amid a tangle of wires. "Go ahead and take a look."

On the split screen were black-and-white videos—a view of the front of her house and another that showed the back-yard. "You set up surveillance cameras."

"High-def cameras with infrared night vision that ensures we'll be able to identify anybody sneaking around. The equipment Josh uses is about a hundred times better than the Clear Creek County traffic cams. Benjy thinks it's pretty great."

"Me, too. It feels like I'm in a spy movie."

"It's supposed to make you feel safe."

She turned and faced him. Her big, broad-shouldered friend was a formidable man. There wasn't a stalker alive who'd want to mess with Shane. "The reason I feel safe is you."

"Aw, shucks, ma'am."

He grinned, and for a moment she felt a spark of attraction that was totally inappropriate for a woman who was about to be married to another. Quickly, she looked away. "What did you need to show me about the stalker?"

"After I set up the alarm system, I swept your whole house for bugs. In here, I found something."

He opened the kneehole drawer on the small desk under the window, reached inside and took out a small disc. "This bug does more than listen. It allows for two-way transmissions."

The disc—no bigger than a nickel—looked harmless but the implication horrified her. The stalker had been monitoring her, invading the privacy of her home. "Shouldn't we throw it away?"

"I've already disabled the device," he said. "It's nothing high-tech. You could probably pick it up online. I'm guessing that the effective range for this bug is only about a hundred yards. Your stalker could have been parked on the street, listening."

"What was he trying to hear?"

"He also planted one of these devices in your bedroom," Shane said, "but not in the kitchen or the front room. That makes me think that he wanted to hear your nighttime routine. He'd wait until after you put Benjy down for the night, after you took a shower and turned off the television. He'd know when you went to bed."

The hairs on the back of her neck prickled. She'd had no idea. When she read stories to Benjy or sang in the shower, when she curled up in bed and sighed, when she whispered to herself, he'd been listening.

Shane continued, "After you were asleep, he'd use the speaker function. He could make a loud noise from this room. Or he might use the speaker in your bedroom to talk to you."

"Why? What would he say?"

"It doesn't matter. The purpose was to keep you from getting a good night's rest."

She sank down on the twin bed in the guestroom. Though she couldn't exactly pinpoint the time when her edginess started, it was probably a couple of weeks ago when the wedding plans went into high gear. Being tired seemed normal; there was so much to do. But there were plenty of times she'd awakened in the night for no apparent reason. "I thought I was losing my mind."

"You were sleep-deprived. An effective torture technique."

"Shane, are you certain about this?"

"Come with me." He opened the door, and they tiptoed down the hallway to her bedroom where he again closed them in so Benjy wouldn't be disturbed. "Lie down on the bed."

She did as he said, watching as he reached up to the frame above the door. "What are you doing?"

"I'm operating this manually, but your stalker used a remote."

When he turned off the overhead light, she saw a flash

from above the doorframe. Like a flashlight beam, it aimed at her head on the pillow. She bolted from the bed. "Turn it off."

He flicked the overhead light switch. "If the noises didn't wake you up, he could activate this nasty little spotlight."

"And he could have timed it perfectly," she said. "Waking me up at ten twenty-three. I'd look at the clock. Think of Tom. My God, no wonder I thought I was going crazy."

"Seems to me," Shane said, "that the stalker's motive in doing all this was to terrorize you. He took pleasure in watching you fall apart. The slashed wedding gown should have been the last straw—the final act that sent you over the edge."

If Shane hadn't been with her when she saw that gown, she might have crashed and burned. She remembered the vertigo, the shortness of breath and the devastating fear that she'd destroyed the dress herself. "Who would do this to me? Why?"

"I don't have that answer," he said, "but I have a solution. Now that you know what's going on, you don't have to doubt yourself. There's not a damn thing wrong with you."

Except that a psycho stalker had targeted her. "What should I do?"

"Tonight, you get a solid eight hours of sleep. Tomorrow, you act with your usual confidence. Your stalker can't scare you anymore. He's lost. You've won."

This moment didn't feel like a victory. Someone hated her enough to rig up this elaborate scheme. He'd been lurking outside her house. Listening to her. Watching her stumble deeper into emotional distress.

"What do you think he'll do next? Am I in danger?" An even more terrible thought occurred to her. "Would he try to hurt Benjy?"

"I'll keep you safe. Both of you." Shane rested his large, reassuring hand on her shoulder. "Tonight, your job is to sleep. Since you know what's going on, you don't need a sedative. Right?"

She looked up at him. He hadn't directly accused Neil, but she knew what he was thinking. Shane had insisted that her prescription be analyzed.

"I won't take a pill tonight," she said. "But I want to be clear about one thing. Neil couldn't have done this. He's a busy man and wouldn't have had time to sneak around outside my house. Besides, stalking isn't the kind of thing he'd do."

"Because it's low class," Shane drawled. "Did you know that Jack the Ripper—a serial killer who disemboweled prostitutes on the streets of London—might have been related to the royal family? Evidence suggests he was a medical man."

"Seriously. You're not really comparing Neil to Jack the Ripper?"

"Until I know better, I suspect everybody," he said. "That includes your fiancé, his father and the housekeeper who made that pitiful lunch."

"Is there a way to narrow down that list?"

"With a stalker, it's difficult. He could be somebody who you don't even notice. Like a regular customer at Waffles or another shopkeeper or the guy who delivers packages. In his mind, he might have built up a fantasy relationship with you. An obsession."

"Why?"

"Some guys get crazy ideas in their heads," Shane said. "The important thing for you to know is that you didn't do anything to cause this. It's not your fault."

The idea of a stranger being obsessed with her was more frightening than if she knew who had set up this elaborate scheme. She was already regretting her promise not to take a sedative before bed. "How am I going to sleep?"

"There's nothing to be scared of," he said. "I'm here, and I'll keep you safe."

She believed him—believed *in* him.

Chapter Ten

The next day, all day, Shane acted as Angela's bodyguard. He wore his gun in a shoulder holster that was unnoticeable under his blazer and hid the tension in his gaze behind a pair of dark sunglasses. Though he didn't expect a straight-forward attack from her stalker, he was prepared.

Protecting her might have been easier if she hadn't gotten a decent rest the night before. Angela was operating at full throttle, fielding dozens of phone calls and finalizing wedding arrangements. With Shane driving her van, they went from Waffles to the florist shop to the bakery where he finally met Marie Devereaux, who was as pretty as Angela had promised. Her black hair and blue eyes almost matched his coloring, and her smokey voice, lightly tinged with a French accent, was sexy and charming. He should have been attracted to her, but he felt nothing when he shook her hand. No spark.

At four o'clock, they dropped Benjy off with the babysitter where he would spend the night, and they returned to her house so Angela could get ready for the rehearsal and the dinner at the private dining room in Neil's country club. Shane's preparations for the evening took only a couple of minutes. He changed from his plaid cotton shirt to a white one with a button-down collar and dusted off the toes of his boots. His jeans were okay for tonight; the dinner wasn't supposed to be formal.

Sitting in her living room, he waited. Josh LaMotta and the lovely Marie would meet them here, and they'd all drive north together.

Shane looked forward to the chance to talk with Josh and review the evidence. With insights from his new boss, he might be able to come up with answers; there had to be a better theory than what he was thinking now. But facts didn't lie and the pattern was obvious: Neil's custody demands in the pre-nup were designed to take Benjy away from his mother if she suffered a nervous breakdown, and her stalker used sleep deprivation to send her into a downward emotional spiral. The two events had to be connected.

Logic told him that Neil was behind the stalking, but he had no hard evidence. Not yet, anyway.

Angela emerged from her bedroom, checking her wristwatch and looking very nice in a gauzy light green dress with a thick belt that made her waist look tiny. Her thick brown hair was pulled back in a French braid that fell halfway down her back. Even though she was wearing platform sandals, she moved fast.

"We need to leave pretty soon," she said. "I don't want to be late to the chapel."

"Relax. They can't start without the bride."

"Are you sure Josh knows where I live?"

"He found his way down from Mount Elbert with nothing but a compass. I think he can make it from the Tech Center to your house." He stood and took her hand. All he really wanted was for her to be happy. If that meant marrying Neil, Shane would step aside like a gentleman. "You look great."

"Do you think I need more makeup?"

He hadn't noticed that she was wearing anything other than a bit of color on her lips. "You're perfect."

"And the dress? Not too plain, is it?"

In her eyes, he noticed a shadow, a hint that all was not right. "Something bothering you?"

"I don't know." Her slender shoulders rose and fell in a shrug. "I can't stop thinking about the pre-nup. And the stalker."

"Me, too."

"These things don't just happen. Somehow, I must have brought this on myself."

"You haven't done anything wrong." *Except getting involved with Neil.* He wanted to point the finger of suspicion, but the more he condemned her fiancé, the more she defended him.

"You always support me." Her pink lips curved in a grin. "I liked having you with me today."

"A free bodyguard. Not a bad deal."

The doorbell rang. Shane deactivated the alarm system, and opened the door for Josh and Marie, who had arrived simultaneously and were chatting. *In French.*

AT THE SMALL STONE CHAPEL in the foothills outside Golden, Shane positioned himself near the arched entryway and watched as the wedding party assembled on the grass. He was still wearing his sunglasses, still on alert.

After Josh seated Marie inside with the others, he took a position next to Shane. They were almost the same height, but Josh was as lean as a greyhound, which was ironic because he ate constantly—an appetite he blamed on his pasta-pushing Italian grandmother who made the best meatballs west of the Mississippi. He asked, "How was your day as a bodyguard?"

"Good practice." Not that he needed training. From his

years as a deputy, Shane had learned how to recognize trouble before it erupted. Being a bodyguard was second nature. "I couldn't ID anybody as the stalker."

"What were you looking for?"

There was a lot Josh could teach him in terms of technical skills and equipment, but Shane was confident in some abilities. He drawled, "I was kind of hoping for a name tag. You know, a badge that says, Hello, I'm a Psycho."

"Sarcasm?"

"This isn't my first ride on the merry-go-round. You know what I was looking for. Signals of lying. Furtive behavior. Inappropriate responses." All day, he'd been watching and analyzing. "Angela interacts with a lot of people. None came across as suspicious."

"And you got nothing from the security cams you set up at the house?"

"I checked the replay this morning. *Nada.*"

A portly little pastor bustled around, organizing the small procession. Neil would be waiting at the altar. Benjy, the ring bearer, and the daughter of the best man would come first. Since neither of the kids were here, Yvonne would be in charge of starting them down the aisle, after which she and the best man would enter. The bridal march would play and Angela would enter, escorted by Shane.

He didn't want to give her away. Tension clenched inside his chest. This wedding shouldn't be taking place.

"Can you take a bit of professional advice?" Josh asked.

"I guess."

"When you're working a small event like this, the client might want you to stand out so everybody knows there's a bodyguard present. Or they might want you to fit in. I'm guessing that Angela wants the latter."

"I'm fitting in."

"You're about as subtle as a fist. Quit flexing."

But Shane wanted Neil to know he was there, wanted to post a signpost that warned Neil, his father and Prentice that he was protecting Angela. "Since Angela is my client, I have an agenda of my own."

Josh nodded. "How long have you been in love with her?"

"We're friends. She was married to my cousin."

"Whatever you say." His dark eyes were far too perceptive. "In any case, I couldn't help but notice that you and Marie aren't exactly hitting it off."

"The mademoiselle is all yours."

"Merci beaucoup."

Shane scanned from the jagged foothills that rose behind them to the uncultivated acreage to the east. Though they'd had plenty of moisture this summer, the rolling hills had faded to a dull khaki with occasional green. He wasn't in love with Angela. Sure, he cared about her. And sometimes when he caught a sudden glimpse or her or saw her from far away, his chest got tight and he found it hard to breathe. Sure, he'd wondered what would have happened if he'd met Angela first, before his cousin. But it hadn't happened that way, and he'd be a fool to pine away with some kind of hopeless attraction to his cousin's widow.

His gaze focused on the group gathered in the small churchyard enclosed by a picket fence. Angela was talking to Yvonne, and their expressions were concerned. Probably talking about a problem at Waffles; Yvonne was going to have a rough time handling the restaurant on her own while Angela was on her two-week honeymoon in Baja.

Beyond the picket fence was a two-lane road. A line of traffic chugged past—two SUVs and a black truck. In the parking lot to the south, several vehicles were parked.

He looked toward Josh. "Now that you've met Neil, what's your read on him?"

"He's egotistical and self-important. His colleagues would say he has good cause. After all, he's a genius virologist who's saving the world from disease. Neil is the kind of man who needs to control everything. Hence, the custody section in the pre-nup. He's not somebody I'd choose to pal around with, but I'm trying to maintain a good opinion because Angela's marrying the guy and I like her."

"Do you think he's involved with the stalker?"

"He wouldn't do it himself," Josh said. "Wouldn't get his hands dirty."

"But he could hire someone."

"The big question is, Why? Even if Angela had signed the pre-nup, legal custody favors the natural mother. The court battles would go on for years."

So why did Neil want Benjy?

The pastor waved his hand, summoning Shane to take his position in the wedding procession. He came down the three wide stone steps and got into line.

Angela threaded her arm through his and shot him a grin. Under her breath, she said, "Were you paying attention?"

"Don't trip over my own feet. And don't walk too fast."

"Not complicated," she said.

The hard part would come after the ceremony started and the pastor asked if anyone objected to the marriage—the "Speak now or forever hold your peace" part. Shane objected. A lot.

IN THE PRIVATE DINING ROOM at Neil's country club, seventeen guests sat at two rectangular tables with white daisy centerpieces and brightly flickering candles. The French doors opened onto a deck with a view of a vast, green golf course.

Shane was seated at the head of the second table with Josh on one side and a plump, gray-haired woman who was an ob-gyn on the other. From his vantage point, he was able to observe most of the guests. In spite of his misgivings about the wedding, there was nothing sinister about this group that included a couple of employees from Waffles and colleagues who worked with Neil.

His gaze fixed on Angela. She was bright and vivacious, outshining Neil in every way. Her happy mood seemed to have started when they arrived at the country club and went into a private office where Josh read the revised prenup and she had written her signature with a flourish. As soon as she lifted the pen, a weight seemed to fall from her shoulders. By signing the prenuptial agreement, she was committed. There was no reason why the wedding shouldn't go forward.

Except for his suspicions.

He tried his best to put on a positive face. She was getting married. And he was supposed to be happy for her. Everybody else appeared to be having a good time. The meal started with a bite-size bit of pastry with blue cheese and an asparagus tip that Marie called an *amuse bouche.* "It's supposed to excite the palate," she said. "It gives the chef a way to show off."

The fancy tidbit made his stomach growl. The rest of the crowd tasted a red wine that was designed especially to complement the *bouche* thing, but he wasn't drinking. Not only was he driving home, but he wanted to keep his wits about him.

Leaning back in his chair, he tried not to scowl. There was nothing like being the only sober person in the room to make sure you had a dandy time.

Since Josh was occupied with chatting up the lovely Marie, Shane turned to the sweet-faced older woman beside him. "Dr. Davenport," he said, "how did you get to know Neil?"

"We met at the Army Medical Center. Actually, I'm much closer to Dr. Prentice," she said. "And please call me Emily."

"Okay, Emily." It occurred to him that instead of pretending to have fun, he could use this time to gather information. These rehearsal dinner guests could be suspects, after all. "Are you a fertility expert, like Prentice?"

"Heavens, no. Lab work isn't my thing. I'm a baby doc."

Her grandmotherly sweetness almost convinced him to stop his line of interrogation, but the clarity in her baby-blue eyes made him think that she might not view the world through rose-colored lenses. As a test, he offered a chance to gossip. "I understand that Dr. Prentice has had some legal troubles recently."

"He calls it genetic engineering, but I call it fraud." With an amiable smile, she added, "What the hell was he thinking?"

Apparently, this kindly, gray-haired lady had an edge. He leaned closer to her. "I don't know any of Neil's friends. Maybe you could fill me in."

According to Emily, the best man was on the same career track as Neil. Their supposed friendship was based on the theory of "Keep your enemies close." And the best man's wife—also a doctor—resented the time she took off from work to have her baby. "She's competitive. Little Benjy's intelligence threatens her, and she won't be friendly with Angela."

"Good to know," he said. "What about the young guy at the end of the table?"

"In spite of the baby face and the floppy brown hair, Jay Carlson isn't as young as he looks. Probably your age. Doesn't seem bright enough to have made it all the way through med school. Neil calls him a protégé, but uses him like a gofer. Carlson is the one who fetches the espresso drinks and tidies up the filing."

"He does Neil's dirty work," Shane said.

"Last summer, Carlson's main assignment was to build a gazebo in Neil's backyard."

"He has carpentry skills?"

"Which suit him a great deal better than the practice of medicine." Her deceptively sweet smile stayed in place. "The woman sitting opposite Carlson is a secretary at the med school. Blonde and bland and plain as mud. She has quite a crush on Neil."

The main course—beef Wellington—was served. While Shane was eating, he considered the protégé and the secretary. Either of them could have set out to terrorize Angela. The secretary might have been motivated by a desire to throw a wrench into the wedding. And Carlson could be doing more of Neil's dirty work.

Further chat with Emily revealed more of the harsh underbelly in Neil's supposedly idyllic world. It seemed that when these doctors weren't busy saving the world, they engaged in all kinds of nasty infighting. Every business had a dark side.

After their dinner plates were cleared and a custard dessert was passed around, he asked, "Tell me, Dr. Em, what do you like about your work?"

"I do it for the patients," she said simply. "Delivering babies makes me happy. I never set out to do research, but I stumbled over a genetic anomaly that gave me a big reputation."

"How big?"

She sipped her wine. "Enough that Neil and Prentice both want to be my best friend."

At the main table, Yvonne tapped her knife against her glass. "Attention, everybody."

Conversations stilled. The guests waited expectantly as Yvonne rose. In her high heels, she loomed over six feet tall. Her dress was an explosion of pink and purple. "After the wedding ceremony," she said, "it'll be time for toasts. But I thought it might be nice if we shared a few memories about the happy couple. I'll start."

Of course, her memory centered on Waffles. "The first time I met Neil, he showed up for breakfast. I knew he and Angela were dating so when he ordered an egg-white omelet, I ignored his request and brought him a praline waffle."

Yvonne nodded as everyone who had tasted Angela's finest recipe murmured with remembered bliss. She continued, "Neil ate the whole thing. I'm pretty sure that's when he fell in love."

Several other people offered comments. Neil's father blustered through a generic speech about gaining a daughter and a grandson. He never mentioned Neil's mother. Nobody talked about her, and the omission might be significant.

Dr. Prentice talked about Benjy and his dinosaurs.

Marie raised her wineglass and recited a love poem in French while Josh looked on adoringly.

Since Shane didn't really have any memories of Neil and Angela as a couple, he made a quick comment about how proud he was to be escorting the bride down the aisle.

Then, it was Emily's turn. "I remember," she said, "the first time Angela and Neil met. Six years ago. It was at the Army Medical Center where Angela volunteered and always brought the most delectable treats. She was in one of the common rooms, talking to injured soldiers. Most of the boys called her Angel."

Shane remembered how proud Tom had been of his wife and her volunteering. Everybody loved Angela.

Emily continued, "Neil passed by in the hallway. He came to a halt when he saw her. From the way he looked at her, I could tell that he wanted this lovely Angel for his own."

Even though she'd been married to another man. Shane swallowed his bitterness. From the start, Neil wanted to own her. Not to love her or cherish her. To him, Angela was just another possession.

Chapter Eleven

Today is my wedding day. Angela couldn't have asked for better weather—warm summer sunshine and clear, blue, Colorado skies. A good omen, she hoped.

In spite of the heavy meal last night, she got a solid eight hours' sleep, uninterrupted by the midnight whispers of her stalker, and she was absolutely bursting with energy. Rather than pace in circles for the next four hours before they needed to depart for the ceremony, she decided to get outside for a run. It was a perfect time; Benjy was with the babysitter.

Though she preferred jogging alone, Shane was still acting as her bodyguard and insisted on coming with. "Fine," she said, "as long as you don't bring your gun."

"No problem. I'll change."

Moments later, he emerged from the guest bedroom wearing a sleeveless T-shirt and baggy shorts. With his black hair uncombed and his jaw textured with stubble, he looked more like an urban guy who shot hoops than a deputy from Silver Plume.

She stared at his black running shoes. "I don't think I've ever seen you without your boots. You didn't used to work out."

"Nope."

"But now you do?"

He keyed the code numbers into the pad beside the front door and stepped outside. "There's a lot about me you don't know."

Since there wasn't much traffic, they jogged next to the cars parked at the curb. Her usual route—2.8 miles—looped through her neighborhood to a nearby park and back home again.

She set an easygoing pace. The steady rhythm felt good. She used to make this run every day after work as a way of winding down and shifting gears before she picked up her son, but her routine had been disrupted by the wedding preparations. She missed this physical activity. When her body was moving, her mind had a chance to reflect.

Today is my wedding day. From now on, this date would be circled on the calendar and celebrated in anniversaries. A special date. A date to be remembered.

She and Tom would have been married six years on the twelfth of November. It seemed so long ago. She'd been only twenty—young but not naive. She knew their marriage faced significant obstacles. His deployment into combat zones was one. His alcoholism, another. Though he'd stopped drinking, the issue was always present. They'd argued and struggled, but she had never, ever doubted their love.

She glanced over at Shane. "Tired?"

"Not me. You?"

"I feel great."

To prove it, she sprinted toward the corner house with the rows of yellow and purple pansies bordering the sidewalk. The garage door had been recently painted the same yellow as the cheerful flowers. On the next block, she saw two "For Sale" signs, like the one on her house. A pang of regret tightened her stride; she didn't want to leave. Her cozy neighborhood was nowhere near as upscale as Neil's, but she loved living here.

At the edge of the park, she slowed to a walk and caught her breath. The smell of freshly mown grass refreshed her senses. There were no children on the playground equipment surrounded by sand, so she went to one of the swings and sat. "I'm going to miss this."

"I'm sure Neil would buy you a jungle gym."

"Not the playground. This neighborhood. My house. All of this. My normal life."

He went behind her, hooked his hands through the chains and pulled her way back. When he gave a push, she went soaring. The toes of her running shoes pointed to the sky.

She kept her legs straight, and he pushed again. Her head tilted back; she was airborne.

Simple pleasures were the best. A run on a sunlit day. The sound of laughter. The aroma of a fresh-baked apple pie. Neil could give her emeralds and diamonds. He could send Benjy to the best schools and probably arrange for her son to go to Harvard. But would he play with her on a swing set?

It was an unfair question. She dragged her feet to stop. The love she felt for Neil wasn't like the fireworks with Tom or her friendship with Shane. Her relationship with Neil was mature and solid. Grounded.

Hopping off the swing, she turned toward Shane. She'd always been able to tell him anything, but talking about Neil was impossible. Shane hated her fiancé. He suspected him of being involved with the stalker and drugging her.

She launched into a different subject. "Looks like you're not going to have a date for the wedding reception. Marie was supposed to fall for you, but she and Josh hit it off."

He clutched his chest. "Shot down again."

"Oh, please." She'd seen how women reacted to this big, handsome mountain man and doubted that he got rejected often.

"For your information, I do have a date. Dr. Emily."

The sweet, little, gray-haired ob-gyn? "Huh? I never took her for a cougar."

"I like older women." He grinned. "The older, the better."

"Last night, when everybody was talking about their memories, I was surprised by what Emily had to say. Of course, I remember meeting Neil at the Army Medical Center, but I had no idea he'd seen me earlier and sought me out."

"Like a predator."

"Stop casting him in a bad light. Neil knew that I was married. He met Tom. They talked about anthrax." He hadn't chased her at all. Their relationship had developed gradually, over a period of years. "What else did Emily say?"

"She warned me about the best man and his wife. A super-competitive couple, they aren't going to be good friends, especially not if Benjy outshines their daughter."

Though Angela wasn't big on gossip, she knew that one of her wifely duties would be to attend events with Neil and entertain his colleagues. It was important to know what to expect. "Anything else?"

"Dr. Em doesn't like Carlson, Neil's protégé."

On this count, Angela agreed. "Neither do I. He's kind of creepy."

"Like a stalker?"

"I hope not." But Carlson sent out that kind of vibe. A couple of times, she'd caught him watching her with a little smirk on his face. "I don't think he'd do anything to jeopardize his mentor-student relationship. He worships Neil."

"And if Neil suggested the stalk—"

"We need to get back to the house." She wouldn't listen to another negative word about Neil. Turning away, she started jogging around the park.

Shane ran beside her. "You have to face the possibility."

"Can't hear you."

She picked up the pace, refusing to be drawn into vague speculation. Shane's dislike for Neil didn't translate into some kind of plot to drive her crazy and get custody of Benjy. Unless there was proof... Unless the tests on the sedatives he gave her showed something different...

All she wanted was to be married and happy. To make a good life for her son. To have some security.

Today is my wedding day.

THOUGH YVONNE CAME OVER to help Angela get ready for the wedding, there really wasn't much to do. The cream-colored silk suit fit perfectly, and she'd already decided to wear her long hair up. The only question was the pouffy net veil that would have been totally appropriate with the gown but looked silly with a suit. She pinned it on the top of her head. "I look like a cockatoo."

"I never got the point of wearing a veil," Yvonne said. "The groom already knows what the bride looks like so when he picks it up, there's no big shock. Unless you paint on a fake moustache."

"Or not." She tried the veil on the back of her head. "Maybe when I get to the chapel, I'll just stick a daisy from the bouquet into my hair."

Benjy came into her bedroom. In his little blue blazer

and necktie, he was utterly adorable. "Mommy, I don't want you to get married."

"And why is that?"

"You're going away with Neil."

"I'll be back before you know it." She didn't want to be apart from Benjy for two whole weeks, but taking a child on her honeymoon wasn't exactly key to a romantic relationship with her new husband.

"Hey, Benjy." When Yvonne squatted down to talk to him, the skirt of her forest-green sheath stretched tight across her bottom. "I'm going to miss your mom, too. But we'll have fun while she's gone. One day, I'll take you to the museum to see the dinosaur bones."

He held up two fingers. "Two times."

"Twice it is. And the zoo."

"We're going to the zoo," Benjy said. "I'm going to tell Shane. He can come with us."

As he ran from the room, Angela flung the veil onto her bed. A trip to the zoo with Shane and Benjy sounded like a hundred times more fun than the wedding ceremony. She looked into the mirror one last time and practiced her smile. She didn't look happy.

"You're gorgeous," Yvonne said. "A beautiful bride."

"I never wanted this big ceremony. It's too much."

Her friend shrugged. "You ought to make a good haul on wedding gifts."

"We already have too much stuff. Everything from my house will have to go into storage."

"You're not selling your things?"

"I probably should." The worn furniture she'd chosen with care would never look right in Neil's house.

Yvonne checked her wristwatch. "We're just about ready. Shane has everything packed. He shifted Benjy's car seat into the back of his Land Rover. And his bags. And your carry-on with the cosmetics."

Shane tapped on the open door before he entered. "Yvonne, would you watch Benjy? I need to talk to Angela alone."

"Sure thing, but we need to get moving." She tapped her wristwatch. "Ticktock."

As soon as she bustled out the door, he closed it. "I heard from the lab. They analyzed the pills Neil prescribed for you."

The air went out of her lungs. She sank down on the bed. "Tell me."

"Not sedatives," he said. "They're mild stimulants with hallucinogenic properties."

"What does that mean?" She had a pretty good idea, but didn't want to believe it. "When I took a pill, what would happen?"

"Your heart rate would accelerate. You sure as hell wouldn't be able to sleep. Your perceptions would be altered. The pills triggered your panic attacks."

"Are you sure?"

"I can show you the lab report." He knelt before her and took her hands. "I'm sorry, Angela."

Neil lied to her. All his supposedly considerate attention was a sham. How could he have done this to her? She'd thought she was losing her mind. She almost let him railroad her into seeing a psychiatrist.

Looking into Shane's gentle blue eyes, she saw pity. "Don't feel sorry for me. I got myself into this mess, and I'll get myself out."

"You're not alone," he said. "Whatever you decide, I'm here to help."

She pulled her hands away from his grasp and stood. Renewed energy coursed through her body. There was only one thing to do. In a tight voice, she said, "Excuse me, please. I need to make a phone call."

"I'll wait right outside the door."

She watched the door close, went to the dresser and picked up the outrageously expensive beaded white clutch purse that Neil had bought for her. Inside was a lipstick, a pocket holding her driver's license and ATM card, a comb and her cell phone. She dumped the contents into her usual shoulder bag that was full of the necessities of her life as a single mother and business owner. Her real identity didn't include fancy purses and big houses and oversize weddings. She should have known.

Neil's engagement ring glinted on her finger. She hardly ever wore it. The ring got in her way when she was cooking, and she was afraid of losing the pear-shaped diamond when she was chasing after Benjy. She never should have said yes to Neil's proposal.

She picked up the cell phone and hit speed dial.

Neil answered right away. "It's a beautiful day for a wedding," he said. "Are you on your way?"

"You drugged me."

"What are you talking about?"

"I had the blue pills analyzed. You wanted me to think I was having panic attacks."

"A misunderstanding." His voice turned cold. "We'll talk about it after the ceremony. The chapel is filled with daisies. It's magnificent."

"I won't marry you, Neil."

A silence widened the gulf between them. There was nothing he could say to change her mind. Not only had he attacked her sanity but his motives threatened her son. She'd never put Benjy in danger.

"Angela, be reasonable. Our guests are arriving. The

wedding gifts have been sent. Everything is ready and waiting for you."

A wave of anger washed over her. "Did you really think that I'd fall apart? That I'd ever be so far gone that I would give up my son? Leave him in your custody?"

"If you really cared about Benjy, you'd want him to have all the advantages I can provide."

You bastard! "The wedding is off."

"I'm warning you, Angela. I won't let you humiliate me like this."

"Goodbye, Neil."

She disconnected the call. It was over. In spite of twinges of guilt and shame, she felt an overwhelming sense of relief. Thanks to Shane's suspicions, she had avoided the worst mistake of her life.

And she knew exactly what she needed to do next. Flinging open the door, she faced Shane. "Benjy and I are coming to stay with you for a couple of weeks."

"You called off your wedding."

"In the nick of time."

He wrapped her in a hug, and she held on tight. Once again, he'd come riding to her rescue.

"You're doing the right thing," he assured her. "Throw some of your clothes and Benjy's into a bag, and we'll get the hell out of here."

With no time for careful packing, she threw clothes into big, black garbage bags.

Yvonne appeared to help. As she dumped the contents of Angela's underwear drawer into the bag, she said, "I couldn't say this before, but I never liked Neil. I'm glad you're not marrying him."

"Really?"

"He's the most condescending man I've ever seen. A lot of doctors are like that, but Neil is the worst." She slung the bag over her shoulder like Santa Claus. "Stay in touch, but don't worry about the restaurant. I've got it covered."

Within ten minutes of her phone call to Neil, they were packed and driving away from her house. From the back-seat, Benjy asked, "Where are we going?"

"To the mountains," Shane replied.

"Can I ride horses?"

"You bet."

When he pulled up at the stop sign on the corner, a silver SUV purposely drove in front of them and stopped, blocking their way. She should have known that Neil wouldn't let her go without a fight.

Chapter Twelve

Shane had expected trouble, but not so soon. They hadn't even gotten a block away from her house before facing a confrontation. Given a choice, Shane preferred to stand and fight. But not this time. First and foremost, he needed to get Angela and her son to a safe place.

From the backseat, Benjy piped up, "Why aren't we going?"

"This guy is a bad driver," Shane said. "It's no big deal. I'll talk to him. Maybe I should write him a ticket."

Benjy asked, "Can I come with you?"

In unison, he and Angela said, "No."

As he opened the car door, she shifted around in her seat to talk to her son. In her white suit with her hair all done up on top of her head, she looked formal and controlled. The only sign of tension was the flush of red that colored her slender throat and dotted her cheeks.

He strode toward the driver's side of the SUV. Though the window, he saw Carlson. Though Dr. Em had told him this guy was in his thirties, he looked like a rebellious teenager with his brown hair flopping over his forehead, hiding his eyes. His jaw nervously worked a piece of gum.

When Shane tapped on the glass, he buzzed it down. Through tight lips, Carlson said, "Neil wants me to drive Angela to the wedding."

"And you happen to be so close. It's almost like you've been spying on us."

His jaw stopped moving. "Why would I do that?"

"You like watching Angela." *Stalking her.* "Can't say as I blame you. She's a good-looking woman."

"Not my type." The words exploded from his mouth.

"Oh, I think she is. I think you've got a thing for her. And that could be a problem for you, Carlson. Neil wouldn't like it if you made a play for his bride. He might not want to be your mentor, and you could find yourself out of a job."

He chewed more vigorously as though he could draw strength from his gum. "That's not how it is. Neil wants me here, keeping an eye on things."

"You're just following orders."

"Damn right."

He sounded as if he was boasting. Dr. Em had been right in her assessment of Carlson's intelligence—not bright enough to be a doctor. He seemed barely clever enough to tie his own shoes. "Tell me, Carlson. Were you the one who planted the bugs in Angela's house? Or did Neil do that himself?"

"You don't know anything. You've got no evidence."

At the moment, he wasn't trying to build a legal case. His primary objective was to get Angela and Benjy out of town. "Here's one thing I know for certain. Neil is real fond of Benjy. That's true, isn't it?"

"Yeah," Carlson said suspiciously.

"He wouldn't want you to upset the kid. Right?"

He nodded.

Shane pulled his arm back, offering a clear view of his shoulder holster. He had no intention of using his gun, but he wanted Carlson to see the threat.

"Here's what's going to happen," Shane said. "I'll get back in my car and tell Benjy there's nothing wrong. Then

I'm going to drive away safely, following all the rules of the road."

"But they're supposed to ride with me."

"You can follow me. Drive safely. We don't want to put Benjy in a high-speed chase, do we?"

His gum chewing paused. He pursed his lips in a pouty expression that would have been unappealing on a woman. On a man, it was downright disgusting. "I guess not."

"We have an understanding." Shane patted the side of the car. "You pull out of my way, and we won't have any trouble."

As he stepped away from the SUV, he saw Carlson hold his cell phone to his ear. No doubt, he was getting his instructions from Neil.

Shane slid into the driver's seat of his Land Rover. If Carlson didn't move, he could drive down the block in reverse and make a clear getaway. But he preferred the simpler solution. He turned to Angela. "I think we have this straightened out."

"Should I call 911?"

"Nine-one-one," Benjy parroted. "911."

They were going to need backup, but Shane didn't want to bring in law enforcement. The police would be required to detain them and take statements, which meant that Neil would have time to get here. Angela's ex-fiancé would be a hell of a lot harder to deal with than his sidekick.

Carlson's SUV pulled forward, leaving their route unobstructed.

"We're just fine," he said. "Everybody buckled up?"

"I am," Benjy said cheerfully. "You know what? Mommy isn't taking a honeymoon. She's going to stay with me."

"In the mountains," Angela said.

Her gaze slid toward the sideview mirror. Though apprehensive, she didn't seem scared. Either she was putting on a brave face for Benjy or she was honestly unafraid. He hoped for the latter, hoped that she realized that calling off the wedding was the right move.

As he drove away from her neighborhood onto a main road, he glanced in the rearview mirror. Carlson's SUV hung on their tail, making no attempt to be subtle.

Shane had expected as much. He clipped his hands-free phone onto his ear and called Josh, who could provide all the backup he needed.

"Where are we headed?" Angela asked.

"The PRESS building."

"Yay," Benjy called out. "Can we go to the lab and look in the microscope?"

"Not today," Shane said.

"Neil has microscopes in his lab," Benjy said. "But he never lets me touch. Germs are very little. You can't see them unless you look real close."

"Not like dinosaurs."

"T-Rex is very big."

Shane used his signal lights and gave Carlson plenty of room to change lanes. His objective was to have the silver SUV trail him into the parking lot outside the PRESS building in the Tech Center. Following Josh's instructions, he drove around to the rear of the building where there was only one lane between the sidewalk and a row of parked cars.

He spotted Josh standing near the end of the sidewalk. Josh pointed, and Shane made a sudden sharp turn into a parking slot. Carlson stopped, not knowing which way to go.

At a signal from Josh, two PRESS vehicles moved into place—one at the front of the silver SUV and one behind. Carlson was trapped.

Josh jogged over to the Land Rover and looked in the

window. "It's a damn good thing I like you because you're turning into a major troublemaker."

Angela leaned over and said, "I'm so sorry for the inconvenience."

"Protecting you is good exercise." Josh grinned. "To tell you the truth, these guys are happy to have something to do other than desk work."

The "guys" Josh referred to included four of his employees who left their vehicles and took positions on both sides of the SUV. All wore dark glasses. Two wore dark blazers, and the other two had on knit golf shirts, also black, that showed off chiseled biceps when they folded their arms across their chests. These were men of action who worked out regularly in the PRESS gym. Not even Carlson was dumb enough to mess with them.

With obvious deference, he climbed out of the SUV and asked them to move their vehicles, please. When they didn't respond, he stared down at his toes and shuffled nervously.

Shane said to Josh, "I appreciate the backup."

"I aim to please."

"Give us fifteen minutes before you let him go."

"You got it."

Without warning, Angela flung open her door. Before Shane had a chance to object, she charged across the asphalt toward the silver SUV.

As soon as Carlson saw her, he darted toward her and waved. "Over here, Angela. You're supposed to come with me."

Carlson's "guys" stepped up to intervene, but Angela halted them with an upraised palm. "I can handle this."

From the backseat, Benjy asked, "What's Mommy doing?"

"Taking care of business," Shane said.

He watched as she and Carlson faced off. They stood about fifteen feet away from him. His hand rested on the door handle, ready to leap out if she required assistance.

"Hold out your hand," she said to Carlson. "Palm up."

"If you get in the car," he said, "we can still make it to the wedding on time. We can pretend this never hap—"

"Your hand," she snapped.

He did as she said.

She twisted the engagement ring off her finger and slapped it into his open palm. "Return this to Neil. I don't want to ever see it again."

He stared at the glittering diamond as though it was a scorpion. When he looked at her, anger twisted his features. "You ungrateful bitch, you can't treat Neil like this. Not after everything he's done for you."

"I don't owe him a thing." Though she kept her voice low, Shane heard every word. "Not after his lies. And the drugs. And the stalking. He tried to make me think I was insane."

"Didn't have to try too hard, did he?" Carlson sneered. "You're crazy. You can't call off the wedding."

"But I just did."

When she reached over and patted Carlson on the cheek, Shane swore he could see flames shooting from her eyes. Angela pivoted on the delicate heel of her white bridal shoe and stalked back to the car.

Carlson yelled at her departing back. "Neil is never going to let you go. Never."

Shane took the threat seriously. Neil and his minions had gone to a lot of trouble arranging this setup, and they wouldn't allow Angela to simply walk away.

ANGELA'S ANGER KEPT HER strong and focused as they drove into the mountains west of Denver. Neil's scheming had driven her to cancel her wedding moments before she was scheduled to say her vows. She was a runaway bride— the kind of low-class, ridiculous person who showed up on tawdry talk shows to jeer at the audience.

What kind of woman walked out on her own wedding?

She thought of the wilting floral decorations, the expensive invitations and the cake—Marie's spectacular five-tiered cake with alternating layers of lemon-vanilla and mocha-chocolate. Not to mention the gourmet menu for the reception dinner. All that food would go to waste. *How could I do this? I'm not this kind of person.*

She played by the rules, never cheated, tried to be kind and helpful. Everybody liked her, and she was glad for their approval. *Not anymore.* Imagining the faces of the wedding guests, she groaned inside. All those people must think the worst of her. Their sympathies would lie with Neil, of course. She'd be condemned as a heartless bitch who dumped her fiancé at the altar. Nobody would understand that she was the victim.

She corrected herself. *I'm not the victim. I escaped.* And she had absolutely nothing to feel guilty about. She'd rescued her son.

She glanced into the back, where Benjy had fallen asleep in his car seat. The late-afternoon sunlight warmed his face. His thick eyelashes formed perfect crescents on his cheeks. She would do anything and everything to protect him.

Her gaze swept from the backseat to the front and came to rest on Shane. They'd hardly spoken since they left the PRESS building. After he slipped a Johnny Cash CD into the dashboard player, he'd been talking on his hands-free phone, making arrangements. Now, he was as quiet as the surrounding forests that descended from jagged peaks to the edge of the winding two-lane road.

"I hope you know," she said, "that I trust you implicitly."

He nodded. "I get that a lot."

"I can't help noticing that we don't seem to be headed toward your house in Silver Plume."

"Because that's the first place Neil will look. Even that pea-brain Carlson would guess that location."

"Mind if I ask where we're going?"

"A little cabin that belongs to a guy I met a couple months ago. It's six miles down a dirt road into a canyon, the nearest neighbors are half a mile away and—here's the genius part—there's a high-tech alarm system."

"And your friend is okay with having us stay there?"

"I just talked to him. He's in California for the month doing some kind of consulting work for a software company. He's got some fancy computer equipment at the cabin. Benjy can probably figure out how it all works."

"Do you think these precautions are really necessary? Are we really in danger?"

"Yes."

She looked back at Benjy to make sure he was asleep and wouldn't overhear their conversation over the rumbling background music from Johnny Cash. "It's hard to imagine that Neil would threaten us. Not physically, anyway. He's a respected doctor."

"Who drugged you and arranged for a stalker and slashed your wedding gown."

Those were facts, indisputable. "How could I have been so wrong about him?"

"You're not to blame," Shane said. "Neil took a long time setting this trap. He laid the groundwork when you were still married to Tom."

And after Tom's death, Neil had really wanted her to have the IVF procedure. She remembered long, serious conversations with Neil holding her hand and telling her how much a baby would enrich her life. After Benjy was born, Neil had come to the hospital. He'd held the infant in his arms. "Maybe he thinks he has some kind of paternal connection to Benjy, that I never would have had the procedure if he hadn't encouraged me."

He shot her a stern glare. "You just can't help yourself, can you? You've got to see the best in everybody, even Neil."

"Am I that gullible?"

"You've got to take off the rose-colored glasses and see things the way they are. Neil is an arrogant son of a bitch who set out to hurt you and Benjy."

"You're right. I should forget about him and let it go. Getting married to Neil was a mistake that never happened."

"It won't be that easy," Shane warned. "There are too many unanswered questions."

She knew he was right. Neil wouldn't simply vanish into the night. Carlson had said it: Neil would never let her go. She had to be ready to stand up for herself. And for her son.

Chapter Thirteen

The first thing Angela did when they reached the cabin was to change into comfortable jeans and a T-shirt. She dashed into the bedroom and yanked off the suit. As she plucked the bobby pins from her hair, the super-hold hair spray she'd used to keep her up-do in place crackled and crunched. Too much in a hurry to look for a brush, she flipped her head upside down and dragged her fingers through the long strands until she had destroyed every trace of formality. She was free. Neil no longer controlled her life. No more pretending to enjoy dress-up receptions in borrowed jewels. Never again would she have to eat the swill prepared by his grumpy housekeeper.

Her lovely white wedding suit puddled on the hardwood floor. Her first impulse was to burn the damn thing, but she was far too practical to destroy an outfit she hadn't even worn once. She hung the suit in a closet that already held clothing belonging to Shane's friend.

While they stayed at the cabin, she and Benjy would be sharing the double bed in here. Since there was no other bedroom, Shane was stuck on the sofa.

With her long hair tumbling around her shoulders, she stepped into the open living room of the small cabin. To the right of the front door was a fireplace with the hide-a-bed sofa and two chairs that were homey but had definitely seen better days. The huge coffee table was a darker wood than the paneling on the walls. The kitchen screamed bachelor pad with a two-burner stove that was smaller than the microwave on the counter.

Shane's friend wouldn't win any housekeeping awards, but the cabin had a pleasantly rustic ambience—except for the office space to the left of the front door. An L-shaped desk held two computers and other high-tech equipment. The electronics didn't stop there. When they entered, Shane showed her how to deactivate the keypad alarm system, similar to the one he'd installed at her house.

While Shane put away the meager food supplies they'd picked up at a convenience store when he'd gassed up the Land Rover, Benjy charged toward her. He wrapped his arms around her legs and held on tight.

She scooped him up in her arms and kissed his pudgy cheeks. "How do you like the cabin?"

"Theodore Roosevelt did *not* live here."

"I don't suppose he did."

"There's no TV." His eyes strayed to the computer equipment. "Can I play with that?"

Now was as good a time as any to lay down some ground rules. The last thing she wanted was to ruin this valuable equipment. Inside the cabin, she ran through a list of things he could not touch without permission. Then, they stepped outside.

The log cabin perched on a wide ledge halfway up a steep road in a canyon. A log retaining wall kept the gravelly dirt from crumbling away beneath their feet. The covered porch stretched all the way across the front of the house. A hammock swung at one end, and there were two wooden rocking chairs.

Though many Colorado forests had been decimated by the pine beetles, the walls of this canyon above a trickling little creek were thick with Ponderosa pine and indigenous shrubs.

Benjy pointed at a chipmunk that scampered on the edge of the retaining wall. "Look."

Shane came onto the porch behind them. "Lots of critters live up here. Raccoons and skunks and squirrels. Plenty of deer and elk."

Benjy wiggled to get down. As soon as his toes touched the boards of the porch, he hopped down from the two-step stoop and ran toward the retaining wall where he'd seen the chipmunk.

"Be careful," she called after him.

There were dangers in the mountains. Her son could slip and tumble down the hillside. In addition to the friendly woodland creatures, she knew there were also bears and mountain lions. Even the plant life could be lethal. Though several species were edible, some of the brightest berries were poisonous.

As Benjy peered over the edge, she restrained herself from grabbing him and pulling him back. Though she would have liked to keep Benjy wrapped in a giant bubble of safety, she knew he had to explore and take risks.

"I have one rule," she said. "You don't go outside by yourself. One of us has to be with you."

"Okay, Mom."

The pristine front of his dress-up shirt was already smudged. "Let's go into the bedroom and get you into some better clothes for exploring."

He dashed for the door and she followed. Their rushed departure from her house meant that all Benjy's clothes had been flung into a black garbage bag. After a bit of digging, she found a long-sleeved T-shirt and a pair of jeans.

"You go now, Mommy. I can get dressed by myself."

She knew he could manage on his own, but she longed

for the days when he needed her to help him with snaps and buttons. Her little boy was growing up so fast.

As she left the room, she grabbed her shoulder bag. Then she joined Shane on the porch. "This place is terrific."

"The best part is that nobody knows about it. The guy who lives here keeps to himself. I'm probably the only visitor he's had since he moved up here."

Holding up her cell phone, she asked, "Can I turn it on?"

He warned, "There are ways of tracking the signal."

"But Neil is a doctor, not a superspy. Unless he hires somebody like PRESS to track me down, I don't think anybody will be triangulating my phone signal."

"You laid down the rules for Benjy," he said. "I'm going to do the same for you. No phone."

She clutched it to her breast. "Can I just check my messages?"

"Just this once. Then give it to me."

There were several calls from Neil which she skipped. She played back the message from Yvonne that was a simple, "You go, girl. Everything here is fine."

An unfamiliar number spiked her curiosity, and she played back the message. It was from Dr. Prentice.

"It's been a most unpleasant afternoon," he said solemnly, "filled with anger and speculation. I'm sure you believe you're doing the right thing, and I admire your fortitude. But I would very much like to talk. I might be able to give you some context for the present situation."

He suggested that they meet in person.

She turned off the phone and handed it to Shane. "Prentice wants to meet."

"Why?"

"He said something about giving context. Meeting him isn't a bad idea. He might have an explanation."

"Or he could be setting a trap."

Though she had no reason to suspect that Prentice had known about the plot to drive her crazy, the old doctor was clearly in Neil's camp. She couldn't trust him, but she desperately wanted answers. "I need to know why Neil did this. He didn't propose marriage because he loved me. That's for sure. But why? And why does he want custody of Benjy?"

"Tomorrow," Shane said. "We'll start investigating tomorrow."

She was anxious to get everything solved and neatly sorted out, but she trusted Shane. He'd been right about Neil. He was probably right about Prentice setting a trap.

Tomorrow would be soon enough.

THE NEXT DAY WAS TOO PERFECT. Angela had forgotten how much she loved being in the mountains. In the summer, the temperature was usually ten degrees cooler than in Denver. The air tasted fresh, and pure sunlight cleansed her senses. As she and Benjy strolled down the road to the creek running through the bottom of the canyon, the gravel crunched beneath her sneakers. She listened to the breeze as it ruffled the leaves of shrubs and whisked through pine needles. So peaceful. So beautiful. In the midst of all this natural beauty, she could almost forget that her life was in turmoil.

At the edge of the creek, Benjy got busy, throwing rocks into the cool, rippling water and poking into the dirt with a tangled stick. This was better than previous trips to the mountains; Benjy was the right age to enjoy the outdoors.

Her only complaint about the cabin was a lack of food supplies, and Shane had agreed. About an hour ago, he headed into town to shop. He'd told her to stay close to the cabin. If they heard a car coming, they should disappear.

Predictably, Benjy slipped on a rock and fell into the shallow creek. His whoops of laughter tickled her. Seeing him act like a regular kid gave her too much pleasure to scold him for not being careful. Kids were supposed to explore and get dirty.

As they climbed the road back to the cabin, Shane returned with the groceries. She'd given him a list of basics, but it was difficult to guess what they'd need. She didn't know whether they'd be staying here for a day or a week or a month.

He carried two huge cloth grocery bags into the kitchen and checked his wristwatch. "In eight minutes, I need to figure out how that computer works."

"Why eight minutes?"

"There's a satellite connection coming through."

"I'll help," Benjy said.

She took her son by the shoulders and pointed him toward the bedroom. "You need to change your clothes."

"Mom, I'm not cold."

"But you're wet. Go."

Grumbling, he dragged his feet as he left the room.

She stood behind Shane at the computer. "What's up?"

"I stopped by headquarters in the courthouse and did some research," he said as he followed a written list for various steps on the computer. "I wanted more information on how Prentice was involved in the murder of Dr. Raymond Jantzen."

She immediately remembered the study that dictated the circumstances of her birth. "Raymond Jantzen? Of the Prentice-Jantzen study?"

As he typed information into the computer, the screen

showed various menus. "I've set up a face-to-face talk with someone who was involved in the investigation. She was also one of the IVF babies in the study. Her name is Eve Weathers-Jantzen."

"Her name is Jantzen, too? What's her relationship to the man who was murdered?"

"Eve married Dr. Jantzen's son," Shane said. "He's stationed overseas, and she's accompanying him. Which is why you couldn't meet in person."

"Do we need the computer hookup? Can't you just tell me what she said?"

With a few more adjustments, he brought up a picture on the screen. The pixilated image showed a blue-eyed blonde woman wearing a green T-shirt that said, Geeks Rock.

Shane adjusted the audio. "Eve? Can you hear me?"

"Loud and clear. The satellite hookup is excellent."

Shane plunked her into the chair in front of the computer. "Eve, meet Angela Hawthorne."

Eve's mouth stretched in a gigantic smile, and she leaned forward as though she could come closer. "Wow, you're beautiful."

"Thank you." Angela returned the smile. "Where are you?"

"I could tell you, but I'd have to kill you." She laughed. "I've been waiting my whole life to say that. Sounds dramatic, doesn't it?"

Benjy rushed into the room. "I wanna see."

Angela popped him onto her lap and introduced him.

Though it didn't seem possible, Eve's smile got even wider. "Hey, Benjy."

"Do you know the thirteenth president?" he asked.

"Millard Fillmore." she said. "I always liked him because he ran for the Know Nothing Party."

Shane lifted Benjy off her lap. "We're going outside now. I saw some elk up on the ridge."

After they left, Eve said, "We don't have a lot of time on this connection. How much has Shane told you?"

"Nothing really. I know we were both part of the Prentice-Jantzen study, which means we're both twenty-six and born in New Mexico."

"And there are many more similarities." Eve's pixilated image on the screen cocked her head. "Would you mind pushing your hair back from your face?"

An odd request, but Angela complied.

"You have detached earlobes and a widow's peak. So do I." She ran her hands through her messy, shoulder-length blond hair. "These secondary genetic traits really don't prove much, but I have DNA analysis for every person involved in the study."

"Including me?"

"You and I were the only two females in a test field of twenty-four subjects. A statistical anomaly. There should have been more women, but the differential isn't necessarily outside the parameters of possibility. Since this study took place twenty-six years ago, I doubt that Dr. Prentice had the tools to manipulate the outcome."

Eve might look like a ditzy blonde, but her language showed a high level of education. "Are you a scientist?"

"Mathematician," she said. "And you?"

"I'm a chef."

"And I'll bet you're Cordon Bleu," Eve said. "Furthermore, I'd be willing to wager that you have exceptional comprehension skills. That's the plus side of Prentice's genetic engineering. We all have high IQs."

Neil had made a similar assumption, but Angela wasn't convinced. If she was so smart, why had she come within minutes of marrying a man who wanted to do her harm? "We should cut to the chase."

"Right," Eve said. "When Prentice set up his study, there were several sperm donors. Fewer women volunteered their eggs for harvesting. The in vitro process isn't a lot of fun."

"I've been through it," Angela said.

"Me, too."

Abruptly, the image on the screen shifted as Eve showed off her belly. "I'm five months' pregnant. Can you tell?"

Angela couldn't help grinning as she remembered her own excitement while she was carrying Benjy. "Bottom line, Eve."

Her face came back on the screen. "You and I have the same biological mother. We're half sisters."

Chapter Fourteen

Her sister? Angela felt her jaw drop. This couldn't be. *My
sister?* Those two words—words that other people took
for granted—were as incomprehensible to her as a foreign
language.

She'd never felt as if she was part of a real family. When
her father died, she was too young to remember him. There
were photographs and a stuffed bunny rabbit that he supposedly bought for her. But the warm place in her memory
where her father should have been was a blank.

Her mother had tried to make a life for them, but she
hadn't signed up to be a single mother, and Angela knew
that dragging a child from place to place was a burden.
She'd tried to be a good girl, tried to make herself useful.
But her mom seldom smiled.

After she got married again, Mom cheered up. At least,
she wasn't crying herself to sleep every night, and Angela
was glad for that, even though she felt like an outsider in
her stepfamily.

"I don't have any living relatives except for Benjy." She
drew back from the smiling blonde woman on the computer
screen. "My mother died when I was eighteen."

"I'm sorry," Eve said gently. "It must be tough."

"I do all right." Self-reliance was a huge part of her
character. There hadn't been a choice.

"The people who raised you, the people you called Mom and Dad, aren't your biological parents."

"I understand." Dr. Prentice had explained that part of the study.

"Then you know I'm not lying. Biologically, I'm your half sister," Eve said with absolute assurance. "That makes Benjy my nephew. And my baby will be his cousin."

Angela's doubts faded as she imagined the Thanksgiving dinners they could share, the homemade birthday presents she could fashion and the special dinners she could prepare. "What's your favorite food?"

"I'm developing a taste for hummus."

"I have a perfect recipe." But now probably wasn't the time to talk about food. "I want to meet you."

"As soon as I'm back in Denver," Eve promised. "In the meantime, Shane tells me that you've got a problem."

"The worst part is already over. I called off the wedding."

"Do you think your former fiancé is going to accept your decision and let you go?"

"Doubtful. And that's not because he loves me and can't live without me."

"Did you love him?" Eve asked.

"I must have. I agreed to marry him, but we didn't have a grand passion." She could have been talking to Yvonne or any of her other friends, but this conversation was different because Eve was her sister. Every word echoed with a deeper understanding. "We hadn't made love in weeks. Maybe a month."

"That sucks."

"Not too much. I've never been all that thrilled about what goes on in the bedroom. Not even with my first husband, and I definitely loved him." She couldn't believe she'd confided such a personal, intimate detail. "I've never told anyone that before."

"I'm no expert on sex," Eve said. "Until I met Blake, I was a virgin. But believe me, when it's done right, there's nothing better than sexual intercourse. And foreplay, of course. Lots of kissing and touching and—"

Her image on the screen was interrupted by static, reminding Angela that this satellite connection wouldn't last forever. She needed to focus. "Here's my problem. My ex-fiancé wants custody of my son. But I don't know why."

"If Prentice is involved, there's some kind of genetic connection. Do you have a DNA profile for Benjy?"

"I don't need one. After my husband was killed, I had the IVF procedure using a frozen embryo. My son's DNA is mine and my husband's."

Or was it? Her mind raced as she imagined alternate scenarios. She and Tom had gone to Dr. Prentice; they had trusted him. What if he had substituted a different embryo? She might be another unwitting participant in a genetic engineering experiment. Like her mother.

"All the same," Eve said, "run a check on Benjy's DNA. And anybody else you can think of. Your ex-fiancé. His family."

An impossible idea! "I can't ask them for DNA swabs."

The image jumped on the screen as Eve gestured emphatically. "Science might be the only way to get direct answers. Prentice likes to play God. Don't trust anything he says."

"Was he responsible for the murder of…" she paused for a moment while she thought of the proper relationship "…your father-in-law?"

"No," Eve said. "As far as I know, Prentice isn't a murderer. Just a scumbag."

"Do you think I should meet with him?"

"You might get answers, but I don't know if you want to get that close to him. Talk to Shane about it." Eve's wide mouth stretched in a toothy grin. "By the way, what's your relationship with him?"

"Shane is my best friend."

"Can I offer you some advice? Sisterly advice?"

Angela couldn't help smiling back at the image on the screen. "Can I stop you?"

"Probably not. Once I get started, I obsess on a subject until it's completely exhausted. Okay, here's my advice. Hang on to Shane. He's a good guy."

"Very good advice."

"I've got to go. We'll stay in touch via e-mail. And I'll send a copy of your DNA profile."

Angela reached out and touched the screen. "I always wanted a sister."

"Me, too." Eve was also touching the screen. "Give my nephew a big hug."

Static raced across the screen, and the picture dissolved.

For a moment, Angela sat back in the chair, trying to absorb what had just happened. Then she rushed for the door. She couldn't wait to tell Shane about her new family relationship.

Outside, he leaned against the porch railing, watching as Benjy scampered back and forth, gathering pinecones. Shane turned to look at her, tilted his cowboy hat back on his forehead and raised an eyebrow. "What's up? You look like you stuck your finger in a light socket."

"I have a sister." Though she wanted to shout the news, she whispered so Benjy wouldn't hear. "Half sister, actually. We have the same biological mother."

"You and Eve don't look much alike."

"Apparently, we share secondary genetic traits." She heard herself repeating Eve's language. "Whatever that means."

Her gaze settled on her son as he scurried toward her with two fistfuls of pinecones. When he got to the porch stoop, he hopped from one foot to the other. With each hop, he recited a U.S. president's name in a singsong cadence.

In a quiet voice, she asked Shane, "Should I tell him about his new aunt?"

"That's up to you."

Angela was certain that Eve and Benjy would love each other. Their coloring was similar—blondish hair and blue eyes, though Benjy's eyes were an unusual color of dark, stormy blue. Still, the genetic connection between Eve and Benjy was obvious in their intelligence. When it came to genius behavior, her son counted as a brilliant example of genetic engineering. *What if he isn't my biological child?*

If Prentice had created her son using some kind of superembryo, she could understand why Neil wanted custody so badly. Neil must have been watching Benjy grow, waiting until his intelligence could be confirmed.

She turned toward Shane. "I need to set up a meeting with Prentice."

THAT NIGHT AFTER BENJY was tucked into bed, Shane opened a bottle of merlot and poured a healthy dose into two mismatched water glasses. In the front room, he delivered one glass to Angela, who sat on the plaid sofa with her feet curled up underneath her. She smiled up at him. Her long hair curled around her cheeks and spilled down her back. Ever since she'd talked to her half sister, her mood had fluctuated between bubbly happiness and flat-out worry.

He sank into the chair beside the sofa, stretched out his legs, took a sip of wine and waited for her to confide in him.

"Nice wine," she said. "Can you do a DNA profile on Benjy?"

"Sure."

"How does it work?"

"I swab his cheek, seal it in a plastic bag and turn it in at the sheriff's office in Georgetown."

"How long will it take to get results?"

"If I mark it urgent, it ought to take only a couple of weeks."

She groaned. "That long? On TV, they get results in a couple of minutes."

"We don't exactly have a high-tech crime lab in Clear Creek County." Most of the local crime involved bar fights, domestic violence and vehicular issues. There were, however, exceptions. Two years ago, he'd investigated a rape case and wanted DNA results from semen in a hurry so he could put the offender behind bars. "I know somebody who can rush the results. It'll be only a couple of days."

"Eve suggested that I test Benjy. She said that if Prentice is involved, DNA is an issue."

The implication was clear. "She thinks Prentice might have substituted a different embryo for your in vitro procedure."

"Because of the Prentice-Jantzen study, I wasn't the biological child of my parents." Her eyebrows pulled into a scowl that caused parallel worry lines. "It's possible that Benjy isn't mine."

That suspicion had been dancing at the edge of his mind since he heard about Prentice's fraud in the study, but he hadn't voiced it. Angela had enough to worry about without second-guessing her child's biological heritage.

He drew up his legs, leaned forward in the chair and placed his glass of wine on the coffee table. His arms were open to comfort her and hold her. "Benjy will always be your son. His DNA doesn't matter."

She rubbed at her forehead to erase the worry lines. "When I first decided to have the IVF procedure, I wanted Tom's child. By having his baby, I thought I could keep a piece of him with me forever."

"I remember."

Tom's death had left her devastated. Even when she smiled, her eyes were a deep well of sorrow. A shadow of that sadness veiled her face.

"Sometimes," she said, "I still miss him."

"So do I."

"I'll always be his widow. I have my precious memories of Tom and of our time together. But I have my own life—the life I've built with Benjy. And with Waffles. Even with Neil." She gave an ironic laugh. "In a way, I should be grateful to him for helping me make a transition. By accepting his proposal, I realized that I could be married to another man."

"As long as it's the right man."

Her eyes brightened as she gazed at him over the rim of her glass. "Are you saying I should look for someone who's not trying to drive me insane?"

"Whatever floats your boat."

The stillness of the mountains wrapped comfortably around them. On quiet nights like this, he almost regretted his decision to move into town and work for Josh at PRESS. But that was because Angela was here. Her presence turned the solitude into peace. If he'd been alone in this cabin, he'd be itching to roam.

She shifted position on the sofa. "Eve also said I should

try to get DNA from everybody involved. Do you think there's any way to track down Neil's genetic profile?"

"I doubt that he's in the CODIS data bank of criminal DNA. I know the military has a lot of DNA records on file."

"Neil was never in the military, but his father was. Can we access that information?"

"Doubtful." An idea occurred to him. "What about Neil's mother? Nobody ever talks about her. She might be willing to provide a DNA sample."

"I don't know how to reach her."

Mentally, Shane put that research on his list of things to do: find Neil's mother. At this point, his to-do list was very short. Apart from keeping Angela and Benjy away from Neil, he didn't have a plan. "We need to come up with some kind of strategy."

"Starting with Prentice," she said. "Neil isn't going to stop coming after me until he knows for sure that there isn't a chance for him to get his hands on Benjy. I can negotiate, starting with Prentice."

"In a phone call."

"In person," she said firmly. "I want him to know I'm serious. To look him in the eye."

"Could be dangerous."

"Not if we meet in a public place. What's he going to do? Shoot me?"

The thought of Angela seeing anybody associated with Neil worried him. Whether or not she wanted to believe it, she was vulnerable. "I can set it up, and I'll make sure there's no chance for Neil to get anywhere near you."

"I need to find answers," she said. "After I talked to Eve, I started wondering when this plot to get custody of Benjy started. Prentice told me that he discovered I was part of the study when he ran my DNA for the embryo process."

"But he might have known earlier."

Prentice might have been targeting her all along. His lecture, which had so impressed Tom, might have been a setup. Neil might have been in on it from the start. "Do you remember what Dr. Em said? Neil purposely went after you when he saw you at the Army Medical Center. What if his good friend Dr. Prentice told him that you were special?"

"I was also married," she said. "Happily married."

Shane didn't think a woman's marital status would stop somebody like Neil—a guy with an ego as big as Mount Evans. "He might have thought he could steal you away."

"No way." She shook her head. "Neil and Tom met at the Army Medical Center. They weren't buddies or anything, but I remember that they talked about all the horrible diseases. The bird flu. And anthrax. And malaria. All of which might affect future children."

"Neil's conversation backed up Prentice's lecture." A sinister picture began to take shape in his mind. "They were working in tandem, warning him about exposures that could cause sterility or genetic problems for your kids."

If their plan had been to convince Tom that the only rational course was to create frozen embryos, it had worked. Tom had been adamant. He couldn't wait to get to Prentice and start the process.

"But why?" she asked.

"You said it yourself. You were biologically engineered. You have genius DNA."

"So what? What did Prentice hope to gain?"

"Your eggs."

Her eyes widened. "Okay, it sounds weird when you say that out loud."

But he was thinking darker thoughts. Prentice had needed Tom to convince her to undergo the process for creating their frozen embryos. Once her eggs had been harvested, there was no longer a need for her husband.

Tom's death in an unsolved hit-and-run accident seemed far too convenient.

Chapter Fifteen

The next morning, Angela went for a jog on the gravel road outside the cabin. First, she ran downhill toward the creek where the rushing water slipped like satin over the rocks, then she took a turn that went higher and higher. Jogging in mountain terrain was more of a cardio workout than she was accustomed to, and when she reached the top of the ridge, she stopped to catch her breath. On one side, the two-lane graded road dropped away, revealing a spectacular panorama of rugged foothills and jagged peaks. Hands on hips, she walked.

Physically, she felt better than she had in weeks. Maybe months. Her body had recovered from whatever was in those nasty blue pills Neil prescribed. Whenever she thought of what a chump she'd been, her anger exploded like a pressure cooker.

Neil had been clever. She had to give him points for sneakiness. She hadn't suspected his treachery until Shane opened her eyes. Now, her vision was 20/20, and she had to say that her future *without Neil* looked pretty good.

As soon as this was over, she'd go back to her regular life, taking care of Benjy and running Waffles. One of her regular patrons at the restaurant had been encouraging her to put together a book of her breakfast recipes. Maybe she'd take on that challenge.

And Shane would be living in Denver, working at PRESS. She hoped he'd stay at her house while he got settled. Having him around was no bother. The opposite, in fact. She'd enjoy making him dinner every night, going for walks in the evening, taking Benjy to the zoo on weekends. Maybe he'd stay with them for a long time.

She started jogging again.

In just a few hours, she was scheduled to meet with Prentice at a roadside café outside Silver Plume. Shane had laid out the strategy for this meeting with the foresight of a general.

The first thing to do was to drop off Benjy so he'd be safe. While she was meeting with Prentice, her son would be staying at a local horse ranch. The owner was a friend of Shane's family, and there would be other kids for Benjy to play with.

When they got to the café, Shane wouldn't accompany her inside. He had already arranged with the café owner to have her seated at a booth next to the front window where he could watch from the parking lot and be ready to intervene if Prentice tried anything.

As she jogged the last few yards to the cabin, her legs felt springy and strong. With any luck, she could get the answers she wanted from Prentice and negotiate an end to her unfortunate association with Neil Revere.

WHEN ANGELA DROVE Shane's Land Rover into the parking lot outside the Grizzly Bear Café, she understood why Shane had chosen this meeting place. The café sat at the far end of a wide clearing beside the road with nothing else around; it would be nearly impossible to stage an ambush here. Cars and trucks parked across the front and on either side of the large asphalt lot.

The restaurant was a dark wood structure about the

length of two trailers laid end to end. Above the entrance that bisected the front of the building was a faded picture of a grizzly, showing his claws. Windows stretched across either side. Though she knew Shane was already here, she didn't spot him in the parking lot.

Anticipation raised her pulse rate. She was excited to face Prentice and learn what was behind Neil's scheme.

When she entered and introduced herself to the man behind the cash register, he gave her a wink and escorted her to the window booth. After a quick glance at the menu, she ordered an orange soda and a buffalo burger. Not that she was hungry. But as a restaurant owner, she felt obliged to place an order if she was taking up space in a booth.

Before her food arrived, Dr. Prentice marched through the entrance as though he owned the place. Though his clinic was in the mountains, the exclusive Aspen lifestyle was a long way from Grizzly Bear Café. His jeans were tailored, and his fawn-colored leather vest had never been dirtied by an honest day's work.

He sat across from her with his shoulders straight and his chin tilted back. Adjusting his thick glasses, he looked down his long nose with an attitude of disdain. She remembered what Eve had said: this man liked to play God.

"Good afternoon, Angela."

His voice grated on her nerves. "Good afternoon."

"I must say, you surprised all of us when you called off the wedding. Many of the guests had already arrived, and there was no time to contact the others. We had to tell them all that you had a change of heart." A cruel smile touched his lips. "Some of them thought you were having a nervous breakdown."

Which was exactly what Neil wanted them to think. Had she unwittingly played into his hands? "I don't care what they thought."

"All those gifts will have to be returned."

"Neil should have considered the inconvenience before he drugged me."

"He was only trying to help you get over your insomnia. Is it possible that you overreacted?"

"Hardly." Though he ticked her off, she held her anger in check. "An overreaction would have been if I'd gone after Neil with a cleaver."

He signaled to the waitress. "I'd like a bottled water."

"I've spoken to Eve," she said.

His thick gray eyebrows rose above the rim of his glasses. "I thought she and her husband were out of the country."

"We talked via computer. She told me about the Prentice-Jantzen study. We're half sisters. Is that correct?"

"Yes, it is."

"Do I have any other genetic siblings?"

"I can't say. My part in the study didn't involve checking the DNA profiles for other matches. All I did was create twenty-four embryos from superior subjects. Many—like Eve—have established successful careers in complex, professional fields."

In spite of herself, she was curious. "And the others?"

"Those like yourself," he said. "You mustn't feel that your accomplishments are lesser than those of scientists or doctors, Angela. You're a creative person."

The way he said *creative* made it sound like something disgusting. "Are there other chefs?"

"There are musicians and an artist. All are high achievers, despite the fact that they were raised by average individuals. That was my thesis. Genetics trumps environment."

Though she could have argued the point, she hadn't arranged this meeting to discuss his crackpot theories. "When, exactly, did you know that I was one of your subjects?"

"As I told you, when you and your husband came to me."

That coincidence was just too handy to be believed. The odds against having her—out of all the people in the world—come to him must be astronomical. Eve, the mathematician, could probably give her a number.

Angela took a poke at his arrogance. "You must have felt like a complete fool when I showed up. There were only twenty-four subjects in the study. How could you lose track of me?"

He shrugged. "After your father died, your mother was in Europe. She didn't respond to any of our queries. After she remarried, she changed both of your names."

"All a matter of public record," Angela said. "We weren't in the witness protection program or anything. The Army was always able to keep track of her."

"For the purposes of our study, we needed consistent annual updates, which ceased when your father passed away. You were dropped from the list when you failed to comply."

"I was four years old."

"The failure," he said, "was your mother's."

Under the table, her hands drew into fists. Her mom wasn't the best parent in the world, but she didn't deserve to be called a failure. Angela swallowed the aggressive response that rose to her lips.

Talking to Prentice wasn't about getting even. She needed information. "Nevertheless," she said, "if you had wanted to find me, you could have done so."

"It's possible."

"Even after you supposedly figured out who I was, you avoided telling me the truth."

"It wasn't relevant."

The waitress arrived with his bottled water and her

buffalo burger with golden, crispy fries. Her gut clenched so tightly that she doubted she could stuff food down her throat.

But she lifted the burger and took a bite as if to prove that she wasn't rattled. She picked up a French fry and studied it with the kind of attention reserved for rare white truffles. She pointed the fry toward him. "Want a taste?"

Disregarding her offer, he sipped his water. "We need to talk about Neil. And I want to make this perfectly clear."

"Oh, please do," she said. "And speak in words of one syllable so I can understand."

"There's no need for sarcasm."

"Blame it on my creative side."

"Neil knew nothing about the stalking. It was all Carlson's idea. When Neil asked him to keep an eye on you, he got carried away."

She didn't buy one word of this explanation. "I wouldn't have thought Carlson was so clever."

"He has an unfortunate immaturity, but he's actually very bright. I referred him to Neil."

She filed that bit of information away for future reference. "Is Carlson from Aspen?"

"I met him there. At the time, he was a ski bum who dropped out of med school. You must believe me when I say that Carlson is terribly sorry for upsetting you."

Yeah, sure. "He sounded real apologetic when he was yelling at me in a parking lot outside the PRESS office."

"And, of course, Neil is devastated."

A twinge of guilt went through her, but she quickly banished any thought of sympathy. "He'll get over it."

"You and Neil are very well suited for each other. A good genetic match. You'd have remarkable offspring."

"Like Benjy?"

At the mention of her son's name, his cold attitude

thawed, and his smile turned sincere. Prentice morphed into the kindly grandfather she'd seen when they met at Neil's house. "Benjy is an exceptional child. So many people claim their children are gifted. So few truly are."

She hesitated before asking the question she desperately wanted answered: *Is Benjy mine?* No way would he give her an honest reply. He'd been content to deceive the twenty-four childless couples in the Prentice-Jantzen study.

Instead, she came at the issue from a different angle. "I'm having Benjy tested. I should have his DNA profile in just a few days."

The mask of kindness fell from his face. "Before you do anything rash, I want you to meet with Neil."

"I have nothing to say to him. I won't change my mind."

"It would be so simple. I have a cabin not far from here. I could take you there now."

She was immediately suspicious. "Is Neil at your cabin? Is he nearby?"

"Come with me," Prentice urged. "Just for an hour. Neil deserves that much. You humiliated him by calling off the wedding."

"I'm not the villain. Neil was trying to drive me insane. Did he tell you about slashing my wedding gown to shreds? Did he mention the hidden microphones designed to wake me each night at the moment when Tom died?"

"As I explained, Carlson was responsible for—"

"Carlson had nothing to do with that vile pre-nup," she said. "Carlson wasn't responsible for the carefully worded section in that document that gave Neil custody of my son. Why is he trying to take Benjy away from me?"

As soon as she blurted out those words, she knew she'd made a mistake. Her goal had been to cleverly trick Prentice into revealing some deeper truth, but she'd thrown her cards on the table and shown her hand. She'd let him see her greatest fear.

"You're being absurd," Prentice said.

"Am I? Isn't it true that Neil was only marrying me to get to my son?"

"My dear, I never realized you were so high-strung. You remind me of Neil's mother. Even at her best, she was a very high-maintenance woman."

She refused to let him sidestep the custody issue by changing the subject. "Answer my question, Doctor. Was Neil marrying me to gain access to Benjy?"

"I'm simply trying to help you understand—to gain a full picture. You can keep an open mind, can't you?"

"Not when it comes to my son."

"Such determination might be admirable if it weren't so misplaced. You need to know about Neil's mother."

"Why?"

"I'm not a psychologist, but my dear friend Ray Jantzen would say that men often choose wives who remind them of their mothers." He shrugged. "In this instance, the comparison could be significant. You see, Neil's mother has been hospitalized for years. She's a delusional schizophrenic. Tragic, really."

Was he accusing her of being psychotic? She sputtered, unable to find the words to respond to such an over-the-top allegation.

"Think about it," he said. "Neil's concern about your mental health—as evidenced in the pre-nup—could possibly derive from memories of his mother and what he went through with her."

She grabbed her shoulder bag and fished out her wallet to pay for the uneaten buffalo burger. "This conversation is over."

"Angela, Angela." He took off his glasses and rubbed the bridge of his nose. "Why won't you listen to reason?"

She took out a twenty—which provided a more than ample tip—and placed it on the table as she scooted out of the booth. "Don't contact me again. I'm done with Neil and with you."

Before she could run out the door, he grabbed her wrist. "You won't get rid of me that easily."

Anger surged through her veins. She glared into his face. Then, she gasped.

His eyes! Without his glasses, she could clearly see his eyes. They were the same unusual blue-gray as Benjy's.

Chapter Sixteen

Technically, Shane was on duty today. He'd given his two weeks' notice but was still a Park County deputy sheriff. In spite of his navy-blue uniform shirt and his badge, his heart wasn't in his work. He'd ignored two calls from the dispatcher regarding a speeder in nearby Georgetown. It went against his grain to do a half-assed job, but today the other deputies would have to pick up the slack. His only focus was on keeping Angela safe.

In the parking lot outside the Grizzly Bear Café, he'd changed positions several times, making certain that no one—neither Carlson nor Neil—was lurking in the nearby trees. He leaned against the side of the patrol vehicle where he had an unobstructed view through the front window of the restaurant. Even from a distance, he could tell that Angela was plenty angry.

On his walkie-talkie, he communicated with the other deputy he'd posted at the rear of the restaurant. "You see anything?"

"All clear. How much longer do we have to stay?"

Through the window, he saw Angela stand up. "Only a couple of minutes. It looks like she's leaving."

He kept his eye on Prentice as Angela headed toward the exit. The old man was using his cell phone, probably reporting back to Neil. Shane glanced toward the far edge of the lot where Prentice had parked his vehicle—a Cadillac Escalade SUV that he'd angled across two spaces to keep anyone from bumping the chrome.

When Angela emerged from the restaurant, Shane got into the patrol vehicle. Their plan was for her to drive a safe distance away from the café before they met up. Her high ponytail bounced as she stormed toward his Land Rover with car keys in hand. Her shoulders were tense. She looked as mad as the grizzly on the sign over the café entrance.

He spoke into the walkie-talkie. "We're done here. Come around front, and I'll buy you lunch."

"You owe me more than that, buddy. I want a full breakfast cooked by Angela with crepes and that egg thing she does."

"Frittata," he said with a grin. "You got it."

Two years ago, Angela and baby Benjy had visited him for a week. Though she was supposed to be relaxing, she'd put together a breakfast for everybody at the courthouse. Some of the deputies were still talking about the frittatas, and at least four of them had asked her to marry them after tasting her cooking. He leaned forward to slip his key into the ignition.

He heard the squeal of tires, looked up and saw a black sedan swerve into the parking lot. The driver's-side door flew open. Neil jumped out.

"Son of a bitch," Shane muttered. He exited his vehicle and crossed the parking lot at a run. The adrenaline was already coursing through his veins. His hand was already on the gun at his hip.

Standing only a few feet away from Neil, Angela held up her hand. "Shane, stop. It's okay."

Not in his opinion. He didn't want Neil anywhere near her. She might think of this guy as a respected doctor, but

Shane saw a dangerous man who was accustomed to getting everything he wanted. "Show me your hands, Neil."

"Are you kidding?"

"That's an order," Shane barked.

Neil looked him up and down, taking in the obvious fact that Shane was an armed lawman. He raised both hands and turned in a circle. "Satisfied?"

"Not really." He'd like to arrest Neil for reckless driving, causing a public nuisance and being a general pain in the butt.

"Really," Angela said. "I can handle this."

"You've got five minutes."

"Would you mind stepping back?" Neil asked. "We'd like some privacy."

"Matter of fact," Shane drawled, "I do mind."

He stayed exactly where he was—about four feet away from them. His weight balanced on the balls of his feet, and his arms hung loose at his sides. At the slightest provocation, he would react with a vengeance.

Neil turned toward Angela. "I had hoped that you'd listen to reason and come along with Dr. Prentice."

"I'm actually glad you showed up," she said. "I gave Prentice a very clear message, but it's good to tell you in person so you can see my face and know that I'm serious."

"I'm listening," he said.

"Stay away from my son."

"That's not fair. I'd be a good father to Benjy. You know that. You know that I can give him everything he needs to develop into an extraordinary individual. He'd have the best tutors. He'd attend schools for gifted children."

"I know what my son needs."

"What?" He scoffed. "Peanut butter and jelly pancakes?"

"It's the same thing every child needs. The love of his parents."

Neil seemed taken aback. The muscle in his jaw worked as he tried to think of what to say next. In a tone of barely suppressed fury, he said, "You know I love Benjy."

"Not exactly," she said. "You value his intelligence. You want to show him off, to have him recite all the presidents like a trained monkey. He's more than a brain, more than potential. He's a little boy who needs to run around and get dirty and throw pebbles in a creek."

"Oh, I see. And I suppose you consider it a vital use of his time to hang around in a cheap breakfast restaurant."

"That's my decision. I'm his mother."

"Angela, please. I don't want to hurt you. We can work out our problems. For Benjy's sake."

She shook her head. "There's nothing to work out."

"I'm willing to forgive you."

Shane heard a note of desperation in Neil's voice—a sure indication that he was near the breaking point and, therefore, more of a threat. Shane cleared his throat as a reminder that he was still nearby. "Neil, it's time for you to move on."

"We don't need your interference." He wheeled around to face Shane. "You've done enough, poisoning her mind against me. Everything was fine until you came along."

"Fine?" Angela snapped. "Is it just fine for you to drug me? To have your little protégé stalk me?"

He swung back to face her. "Come back to me, Angela. We can still be married. There doesn't have to be a big ceremony. All we need is a justice of the peace."

She stuck out her chin. "Go to hell."

"You little bitch." He grabbed hold of her shoulders. "You can't say no to me. I won't let you."

Shane caught hold of his left arm, intending to separate

him from Angela. As he yanked them apart, Neil's right hand flicked out. If he hadn't been off balance, he would have slapped her face. As it was, he hit her shoulder. The force of his blow was enough to knock her backward into the car.

Shane twisted Neil's left arm behind his back and shoved hard. Neil stumbled and toppled forward. His knees collapsed. In seconds, he was lying facedown in the parking lot. Shane cuffed him.

He looked toward Angela. "Are you all right?"

Mutely, she nodded. She held her shoulder where Neil had made contact. Her eyes were wide and surprised as though she couldn't believe what had just taken place.

The other deputy joined them, and Shane left Neil to him as he went to Angela. "Are you sure you're not hurt?"

"I'm fine."

"I want you to take my car and follow us to the courthouse. We need to get you a restraining order." He checked her for symptoms of shock. Her breathing was regular and steady. Her pupils weren't dilated. "Are you okay to drive?"

"Totally fine," she repeated in a firm voice. She leaned closer to him and whispered, "You saved me again, my hero."

While she got in the car, Shane and the other deputy hauled Neil to his feet. With great satisfaction, Shane said, "Neil Revere, you're under arrest for assault."

"You won't get away with this," Neil snarled.

Shane dug into Neil's pocket for his car keys which he handed to the other deputy. "Would you mind moving the car? It's blocking the parking lot."

"No problem."

He escorted Neil to the police vehicle and stood facing

him. "Here's the deal. Angela is going to take out a restraining order. You can't come within a hundred feet of her."

"Do you think you can stop me?"

"A word of advice. Don't push me."

"What are you going to do?"

Constrained by his duty as a deputy, Shane fought the urge to drive his fist into Neil's gut. Beating a man in handcuffs wasn't his style, but he might be willing to make an exception for Neil.

"Someday," he said, "you and I are going to meet face-to-face, man-to-man. And I'll teach you what happens when you threaten women and children."

"You can't hurt me. I'll be out on bail within a few hours."

"Not until after you've gone through the booking process. You know the drill. The photograph. The fingerprinting. And the DNA swab."

"A DNA swab?"

"Standard procedure," Shane said, even though they seldom bothered with DNA. "Then you'll be locked in a holding cell along with the other local miscreants."

None too gently, he shoved his prisoner into the back of the car.

He glanced toward the far end of the parking lot. Prentice's fancy SUV was gone. A clean getaway.

SHANE WOULD BE WILLING to wager a month's salary that the arrest and booking process was unlike anything Neil Revere had ever experienced. Since everybody at the courthouse knew he'd attacked Angela and she happened to be their number one favorite chef, the officers treated him with as much disrespect as the law allowed. Their timing was such that Neil was assured of spending the night in a jail cell. Shane wished the accommodations had been more medieval—like a dungeon.

After Angela had filed her restraining order, they headed out toward the horse ranch where Benjy had been spending the afternoon. Their route navigated a maze of side roads to get there. Shane had chosen this place because it was off the beaten path.

While he drove, Angela filled him in on her meeting with Prentice. She mentioned that Prentice owned property in this general area and that Carlson had lived in Aspen at one time. Both of these leads would help in getting to the bottom of Neil's motives and the scheme he had intended to carry out.

"Anything else?" he asked.

Her shoulder twitched as though she wanted to dodge the question. "I don't think so."

Her high ponytail was unfastened and her hair tumbled around her face, shielding her expression, but she couldn't hide her feelings. Not only was she a lousy liar but he knew her well enough to sense her moods and her attitudes.

"You might as well tell me," he said.

"Tell you what?"

"You're holding something back. And it's going to eat at you until you finally blurt it out." He knew how her mind worked. "The more information I have, the sooner we get to the bottom of this."

"His eyes," she said. "Prentice took off his glasses and I saw the color of his eyes. Blue-gray. Exactly the same color as Benjy's."

It took a moment for him to absorb the weight of her observation. Prentice was involved in genetic engineering and had created the frozen embryo used in Angela's IVF procedure. Could he have used his own sperm? "We need to talk to Eve again. She might know where we can access Prentice's DNA profile."

"What if he's Benjy's biological father?" The twin worry lines between her brows appeared as her eyes narrowed. "I know it shouldn't bother me. I know that Benjy is my son no matter what the genetics. But damn!"

"We'll figure it out. I promise we'll find the truth."

"Maybe it's better if I don't know," she said.

Eve and her husband had come to the same conclusion. After they'd learned that all the babies in the Prentice-Jantzen study were not the biological offspring of the parents who raised them, they decided against making that information public.

Shane didn't agree. He would have arrested Prentice for fraud and informed the injured parties. At least Eve and her husband had insisted that Prentice close down his practice in Aspen and retire so he couldn't cause further harm.

Shane turned onto a two-lane gravel road. They were only a few miles from the horse ranch. "Prentice should have to pay for his crime. He experimented without your permission, violated your trust."

"Violated," she said. "That's a good word for how I feel."

"When Benjy's DNA test comes back—"

"I won't prosecute," she said. "I don't want to go through a trial. Prentice is a well-connected man who can hire good lawyers. I'm sure this case would be tied up in court for years, and the process would be more hurtful for me than for him. No way. As long as Prentice can't hurt anybody else, I don't care what he does."

Her reaction reminded him of a rape victim refusing to testify. Angela hadn't been assaulted, but the result was the same. Gently, he said, "This isn't your fault."

"Pull over," she said. "I need to take a minute to calm

down before I see Benjy. He's a smart little guy. As soon as he sees me, he'll know I'm upset."

He parked. On one side of the road was a forested hillside. The other was fenced.

Angela left the car and went toward the trees. Without a word, she hiked up the sloping hill, picking her way through pines and shrubs. She moved at a quick pace for a flatlander who wasn't acclimated to the altitude, but that didn't surprise him. She'd always been an avid runner.

They were almost out of sight of his vehicle when she turned and faced him. Her cheeks flushed red. Her breasts rose and fell as she sucked down one deep breath after another.

He couldn't tell if she was going to burst into tears or scream or let go with a string of curses. Whatever her response, he was here for her.

"If it weren't for you," she said, "I'd be falling apart right now."

"Give yourself some credit." He stepped up beside her. "You're plenty strong enough to stand on your own two feet."

She went up on tiptoe to kiss his cheek. At the last minute, she changed directions. Her soft, full lips pressed against his.

In that moment, everything changed.

Chapter Seventeen

Angela hadn't meant to kiss Shane, hadn't meant to touch him, hadn't meant to feel this burst of attraction. He was her best friend, someone she could trust, someone she cared for deeply. She loved him. *But not this way.*

Intending to apologize for overstepping an unspoken boundary, she tilted her head back and looked up. The boughs of the tall pines formed a ladder reaching into the skies. But all she saw was the blue of his eyes, and in them her desire reflected.

Deliberately, she glided her hand up his chest and around his neck. She pulled him close and kissed him for real. Her lips parted, and she drew his breath into her mouth.

He didn't move. His body was like granite, strong and steady. Even if she'd had a momentary lapse of judgment, he would resist.

She stammered, "I…I'm sorry."

"I'm not."

His hand clasped her waist, and he molded her body against his. They fit perfectly, as though they were meant to be joined. He kissed her back.

There was nothing gentle about the way his mouth worked over hers. Nothing timid about his hard, muscular body. Nothing reserved about the pure masculine energy sweeping over her.

In his arms, her heart was singing. A strange and wonderful heat coursed through her veins. He lifted her off the ground, and her legs wrapped around him. She clenched her thighs and held on, never wanting to let go.

Her back was against the trunk of a tree. They twined together so tightly that it seemed as if they were part of the forest. They had grown together.

Coming up for air, she inhaled a sharp gasp. A first kiss was supposed to be clumsy and hesitant, but Shane was masterful in his passion. His gaze penetrated deep inside her.

"I've waited so long," he murmured.

"Me, too." And here he was—a man she already loved as a friend. A lover? "I didn't know, didn't even know that I was waiting. Did you? Did you know?"

"In my dreams."

He eased his grasp and her legs slipped free. Her toes touched the ground. "You dreamed about me?"

"Being with you was more than I could hope for."

She tasted his mouth again. His kiss was magic, sparking tremors and shivers that she'd never experienced before. Her entire body—from the roots of her hair to her toenails—seemed to shimmer. "I don't want to stop."

"We don't have to."

But she knew better. Not matter how much she wanted to tear off his clothes and make love right here and now, she was a responsible person. They both were. "We're already late to pick up Benjy."

He dropped a light kiss on her forehead. "This isn't over."

"I certainly hope not."

She rested her head against his chest. She'd been in this position a thousand times before—hugging him when she was happy and crying on his shoulder when her life had shattered. Shane was always there for her. He was her rock.

But this moment felt different. Instead of clinging to him, she caressed his back, tracing her fingertips along his spine. She was aware, suddenly aware, that her best friend was a desirable man. His scent aroused her. Through his deputy uniform shirt, she heard the beating of his heart as a primal rhythm, summoning her.

Over the years, she'd seen the way other women threw themselves at Shane. Angela knew he was hot; she'd have to be blind not to notice how handsome he was. But she never imagined that he would be her lover.

He took her shoulders and held her apart from him. The blue of his eyes intoxicated her. She stared at his lips, wanting another kiss or two...or twenty.

"Angela," he said, calling her back to reality. "You're still my buddy. Understand?"

"Mmm." At the moment, friendship wasn't the first thing on her mind. "Tell me about those dreams."

"Can't. It's a guy thing."

She teased, "You fantasized about me. You think I'm pretty. You think I'm sexy."

He kissed the smirk off her lips, leaving her breathless. Then it was his turn to laugh. "I think you're a brat. Just as you've always been."

"Life goes on."

As they climbed down the hill and got back into his car, she wondered how her new vision of Shane would alter their relationship. Earlier, she'd been worried that Benjy would see anger and frustration in her manner. Her son would probably notice that she was glowing like a hot ember.

She tore her gaze away from Shane and stared through the car window as they approached the horse ranch. Beside the road, a log fence enclosed a huge field. Tucked into the pine forest that descended from the rocky foothills was a two-story house and a couple of outbuildings that she assumed were stables. Several horses lounged beside a trough like office workers taking a break at the water cooler.

The man who owned this ranch, Calvin Pratt, was an old friend of Shane's family and the head of a huge extended family. He had six of his grandchildren—ranging in age from three to twelve—staying with him for the summer, and he had a live-in housekeeper to help take care of them. Angela couldn't have asked for a better place to leave her son.

"You're quiet," Shane said.

Uncomfortable silences had never been a problem before.

Trying to slip back into friendship mode, she said, "I called Yvonne from the courthouse. I figured I should take the chance to use a phone since you disabled my cell and won't let me use it."

"For your own safely," he said.

"Yvonne told me that everything at Waffles is fine. They were already prepared for me to be gone for a couple of weeks on my honeymoon."

"You were going to Baja to swim with dolphins."

"Not my number one choice." She felt herself begin to loosen up. When all was said and done, he was still Shane. Her best friend. "Neil said I'd love Baja. Ha! He probably wanted to push me off a cliff onto jagged rocks."

"What did Yvonne have to say about the wedding?"

"A lot. After we took off, she drove across town and went to the chapel."

She'd made it her business to be present, mostly because she took a perverse delight in seeing Neil brought down. If Angela had listened to her friend, she never would have agreed to Neil's proposal.

"What happened?"

"Prentice stood at the front of the chapel and announced that the wedding was off. Yvonne said he made it sound like I'd had a nervous breakdown."

"I'll bet she set the record straight," he said. "Yvonne isn't exactly shy."

"She marched down the aisle—which she said was decorated very nicely with daisy bouquets and ribbons. Then she told everybody to save their get-well cards because I was absolutely fine, and I had a very good reason to call off the wedding. Neil had deceived me."

"Ouch," Shane said. "When one party accuses the other of deception, most people assume infidelity was involved."

"Oh, I'm sure that's what they thought, especially those with dirty minds."

And she had no desire to set the record straight. Explaining about Dr. Prentice and the DNA nightmare wasn't something she was looking forward to. She continued, "Later, Yvonne made arrangements to have all the food that was already prepared and paid for at the reception dinner to be delivered to homeless shelters. I was glad to hear that."

"What about the rest of it? Any regrets?"

"Only that I agreed to marry Neil in the first place."

In that doomed relationship, she'd gotten it so wrong. Could she trust her judgment when it came to Shane? The last thing she wanted was to make another heart-wrenching mistake.

AFTER SHANE DROPPED HER and Benjy off at the cabin, Angela had time to think. When she needed to concentrate, she cooked. Using the meager supplies they'd purchased at the local market, she baked pies and cakes for the gang at the courthouse.

Benjy acted as sous-chef, washing veggies and helping her add ingredients. "A pinch of salt," she said.

He poured a bit from the shaker into his little hand and held it up so she could see. "This much?"

"Perfect," she said.

He threw the salt into the mixture with a flourish. Then he adjusted the brim of the cowboy hat that appeared to be a permanent fixture on his head. "I'm not big enough to ride on the horses by myself."

"Not yet," she agreed.

"But the grandpa let me sit on the saddle with him. And I got to hold the reins. Grandpa's name is Calvin, like Calvin Coolidge." Benjy made the immediate reference, but instead of his usual listing of all presidents before and after Coolidge, he said, "I love horses. Mustangs are wild horses."

"How many does Calvin have?"

He yawned. "A whole bunch."

She shifted from baking to preparing dinner—chicken cacciatore and a creamy, bacon-flavored potato salad that would work for lunch on the following day. Benjy kept up with her, even though he was obviously tired. Tonight, he'd fall into bed early. She and Shane would have some privacy.

Her gaze drifted toward the hide-a-bed sofa in the living room where Shane had been sleeping, and she imagined the two of them lying there naked and tangled up in the quilts and sheets that were neatly folded on the floor.

Apparently, Shane had nothing on her when it came to fantasies. She could hardly wait for this daydream to become reality.

Holding her desires in check, she concentrated on everyday tasks, finishing the preparations for dinner. When Shane returned to the cabin, Benjy told him all about his adventures at the horse ranch. By the time they finished their meal, it was obvious that her son was tired. By eight-thirty, he was in bed. She sat beside him, holding his little hand.

He yawned. "Mommy, are you going to get married?"

She smoothed her hair off his forehead. "I might get married someday. But not to Neil. We don't get along anymore."

That might be the understatement of the century. She still had strong feelings for Neil Revere. All of them negative.

"You don't love him," Benjy said. "Mommies and daddies gotta be in love."

"That's right." She wasn't sure how much to explain. "I bet you have other questions."

"Some." He wrinkled his nose as he snuggled under the homemade patchwork quilt. The artful pattern of blue and green swatches bespoke the excellent craftsmanship of Shane's mother. He'd told Angela that he'd given the quilt to the owner of the cabin in exchange for computer services.

"You can ask me anything, pumpkin."

"Does Neil love me?"

Her automatic response would be to tell her son that everybody loved him, but she wouldn't lie. She couldn't truthfully say anything about Neil's feelings. Though he seemed to love Benjy, his overriding goal was to possess this genius child as evidence of his own cleverness.

"I don't know Neil's feelings," she said honestly. "The reason I called off the wedding was about my feelings. I don't love him."

"Do you love Shane?"

"You bet."

"Are you going to marry Shane?"

A simple question with a complicated answer. She was

ready to take up where they left off this afternoon. More kissing was most certainly in order. But marriage was a whole other thing.

"There are all kinds of love." She picked up his stuffed green dinosaur. "I love this T-Rex because he makes you giggle. And I love ice cream with hot fudge. And I love Yvonne. But I'm not going to marry any of them."

"You can't marry ice cream."

She leaned down to kiss his forehead. "Most of all, I love you."

He flung his little arms around her neck and planted a wet, sloppy kiss on her cheek.

Leaving him to sleep, she closed the door. As she entered the living room, Shane motioned to her. Together, they went outside onto the front porch.

The light from a full moon shone on the surrounding pine trees, chokecherry bushes and rocks. She went to the railing, and Shane stood beside her.

"I was on the computer," he said, "and I couldn't help overhearing what you said to Benjy. Nice job. You didn't lie, but you didn't say too much. You're a good mom."

"You heard Benjy ask if I'd marry you."

"I've wondered the same thing myself. I get along better with you than any other woman I've ever known. You're not half-bad to look at. And you're a great cook."

"If we were living in the 1950s, that's all you'd need for a wife."

"What's different about the 2010s?"

"Check any dating Web site and you'll find a million questions that indicate compatibility, goals, accomplishments and so on." She gave him a playful jab in the ribs. "Not to mention sex."

"Are you propositioning me?"

She looked him up and down. "I sure as hell am."

Chapter Eighteen

For a long time, Shane had admired Angela from afar. He remembered the day Tom introduced them, remembered the way her nose crinkled when she laughed, remembered the daisy she'd stuck into her ponytail. A pretty girl. That went without saying. But Angela had more than a bright smile and a trim body. When he looked in her eyes, he saw an unexpected depth of character, and he couldn't help but wonder what kind of storms she'd weathered in her young life.

From the start, she'd had an effect on Tom. He quit drinking and signed up for AA. He turned into a responsible man and a good husband. Shane had never seen his cousin happier, and he'd wished Tom and Angela the best. He'd taught himself not to yearn for her.

After Tom died, Angela had needed Shane as a friend; her heart had been too broken to think of him in any other way. And they had grieved together.

At the point when he'd begun to hope there might be something more than friendship between them, she brought a new man into her life: Benjy.

When she'd told him that she was getting married to Neil, he'd finally given up hope and accepted that Angela would never be his.

Now she stood before him and demanded the intimacy

that he'd always wanted. In the moonlight, her eyes shimmered. The summer breeze tossed the pine boughs, and the distance between them seemed to shrink as though they were being blown closer together.

He stroked her cheek, pushed a strand of hair behind her ear and said, "I want you to be sure about this."

"I know what you mean." Her voice was breathless, as though she'd just finished a ten-mile run. "Are we moving too fast?"

"We've known each other for seven years," he drawled. "Doesn't seem like a rush to me."

"What if this goes wrong? Oh, Shane. You have to promise me that you'll never stop being my friend. I can't imagine what my life would be like without you."

When she clasped his arm, her touch set off a chemical chain reaction that felt like an adrenaline surge. It was all he could do to restrain himself.

He took her hand and raised it to his lips. Her fingers trembled. He promised, "You'll never get rid of me."

"What if I'm rebounding?"

"What?"

"A rebound," she said. "When one relationship ends, there's a tendency to jump into another before you've resolved all your feelings. It's like a fling."

"Did you read about this in one of those online surveys?"

"Rebounding is a valid issue."

He wished he could take all the self-help articles in the world and torch them in a huge bonfire. "Okay, let's talk about your unresolved feelings for Neil."

She made a sour face. "I don't like him, don't respect him and he scares me a little bit."

"Sounds about right," he said.

"It does." She nodded. "Nothing unresolved there."

"And when we kissed, did it feel like a fling?"

She moved closer. "It felt right. I want to be with you, Shane. Maybe I always have."

That was all the affirmation he needed. He gathered her into his arms and kissed her. He took his time, lingering on her mouth. His hand slid inside her sweater and climbed her slender torso. She was slim but solid with the well-toned muscles of an athlete. At the same time, her curves were one hundred percent feminine. Her hips flared from her waist. When he cupped the fullness of her breast, she made a soft moaning sound that faded into a purr.

Savoring every moment, he opened his eyes and gazed into her lovely face. "Do you know that your eyes look different depending on your mood?"

"People have mentioned that before."

"I've always wondered what color your eyes were when you made love."

"And?"

"Darkest green. Like jade." He took her hand. "Come with me."

She glanced back at the cabin. "I can't leave Benjy."

"We're not going far. And the security alarm is set."

He hadn't wanted the first time they made love to be on a hide-a-bed with her son in the next room. This night would be special. Even if he couldn't treat her to satin sheets and a king-size bed, he'd give her starlight and the fresh scent of pine.

Ten yards up the hill behind the cabin, he'd assembled a nest of sleeping bags inside a circle of trees with a granite stone for a headboard.

She jumped into the center of the sleeping bags. "You were pretty sure I'd say yes."

"From the way you kissed me this afternoon, I had

reason to hope." He stretched out beside her. "But I never take your decisions for granted."

"I'm not capricious."

"But you're not predictable, either. That's one of the things I like about you."

She reached down and started efficiently unbuttoning his shirt. "Don't make it sound like I'm some exotic creature. You know I'm practical and hardworking."

"Stop." He stayed her fingers. "You, Angela, are a force of nature. Exotic doesn't begin to describe you. You're more rare than an orchid. More precious than diamonds."

She gave a snort and sat back on her heels. In a few quick moves, she peeled off her sweater and pulled her T-shirt up and over her head, revealing her no-nonsense zip-front sports bra. "I'm a cook."

"Chef," he corrected her. "You're an artist."

From the businesslike way she was tearing off her clothes, he could tell that she hadn't been properly seduced. The time had come for him to take charge and show her how truly special she was. He rolled over her and pinned her shoulders on the sleeping bag. "Let me undress you."

She gave him a curious look. "But it's always so clumsy when—"

He silenced her with a kiss. Slowly, he lavished attention on the sensitive parts of her body. Her earlobes. The hollow at the base of her throat. The soft skin on the inside of her elbow. And her breasts. Through the fabric of her bra, he teased her nipples into tight buds. When he finally unzipped the front of her bra, she gave a feral yelp that made him glad they weren't in the living room of the cabin.

Her impatience turned to arousal as she responded to the slow, deliberate rhythm of his lovemaking. Her hands explored his body. She was aggressive, as though she'd been programmed to follow certain steps. Though his need for her was rising to an intense level, he paused. He didn't want to be another lover. He would be her *only* lover.

Straddling her hips, he caught both her hands in his grasp. "Lie still, Angela."

She wriggled beneath him. "Why?"

Her long hair fanned out. "I want to see you. To appreciate how beautiful you are."

Her eyes, her jade eyes, gazed up at him, and she smiled. "Do I live up to your fantasy?"

"You're better than I dreamed."

He lay beside her on his back, looking up through the trees at the shimmering pinpricks of distant stars. When she linked her hand with him, a bond formed between them. They were the only people on the planet.

"I like what you said," she whispered, "about seeing me. I want to be seen."

"After all these years, it seems like we ought to know everything about each other. But there's always more."

"Another mood." She sighed. "A secret we haven't yet shared."

"This night is only the start."

And they took their time. Each touch was a new discovery as though neither of them had ever made love before. Their passion developed by degrees until the urgency overwhelmed him, and he lost himself in her.

UNDER THE DOWN COMFORTER he'd brought from the cabin, Angela snuggled against his naked chest. Her body trembled with delicious aftershocks from their lovemaking. She felt as if she'd eaten a seven-course gourmet dinner prepared by a master chef, worthy of the coveted three-star Michelin rating.

She'd always assumed that Shane was a good lover, but tonight surpassed anything she could fantasize about.

When he reached behind the granite rock beside them and pulled out a picnic basket, she wasn't surprised. The man had finesse. He unpacked a bottle of burgundy and two glasses.

"You thought of everything," she said.

"I want the best for you."

When he uncorked the wine, she noticed that he'd gotten wineglasses. She held one up. "We didn't have these glasses in the cabin before."

"I picked them up in town."

The goose-down comforter covered him from the waist down, but his chest was bare. He had just the right amount of springy black hair. As far as she could tell, he didn't have an ounce of flab. He was all muscle, all man.

Though the night breeze cooled her back and shoulders, she didn't feel the need for a sweater. The heat of their passion still kept her warm. "What else have you picked up?"

"Is there something I need to get?"

"I'm asking if you've done any more investigating."

"Are you sure you want to talk about this?"

"It's not the usual pillow talk." She gestured to the surrounding forest. "But this isn't a usual pillow. The sooner we figure out what's going on with Prentice and Neil, the sooner we can get back to our normal lives."

"I don't have much to go on." He poured the wine and handed her a glass. "I dropped off the swab for Benjy's DNA profile. And, here's a bonus, I can have Neil tested as well. They took DNA when he was booked."

"Is that standard procedure?"

"It's within the parameters of the law. We ought to have results in a couple of days."

She held up her glass, aware that she was completely

naked and not feeling in the least self-conscious. When he touched his glass with hers, she said, "To the first night."

"But not the last," he concluded her thought.

The wine aroused her taste buds and slid down her throat. All her senses seemed to be heightened. And her mind felt sharp. "What else are you working on?"

"You told me that Prentice has a cabin in this area, and I want to locate it."

"Why?" She grinned over the rim of her glass. "Are you hoping to find skeletons in his closet?"

"I won't know what I'm looking for until I see it. There's a lot that can be learned from the way a person lives." He licked a drop of wine from his lips. "When I was at the courthouse, I checked some property records. Prentice's house in Aspen is a multimillion-dollar chalet. Plus, he owns a smaller Aspen house that he rents out. And another in Glenwood Springs that's also occupied by renters."

It wasn't unusual for longtime mountain residents to own several properties. Deals became available, and people bought at a good price. In the West, land was always considered a good investment. "But Prentice doesn't have a cabin in this area?"

"Not in his name."

"What else are you investigating?"

"Carlson. I want to find out how much dirty work he's done for Neil."

"What have you turned up so far?" she asked.

"Not much. His academic records are marginal. Right now, he's only taking a part-time course load. He sure as hell doesn't seem like somebody Neil would handpick as his protégé. How much do you know about him?"

She'd never paid much attention to Carlson. He was ubiquitous, part of the background. "He's a snowboarder. Prentice said that he knew Carlson in Aspen."

"A couple of years ago," Shane said, "Carlson had a drunk and disorderly charge in Aspen. Since then, all he's had are a couple of traffic citations."

The pine boughs rustled in the wind, and she gave a little shiver. "It's chilly."

"Come over here and lean on me. I'll keep you warm."

She rested against his chest and pulled the comforter up to cover herself. With Shane holding her, she felt as if she was wrapped inside a cozy cocoon.

"The third issue I'm looking into," he said, "is Neil's mother."

"What does his mother have to do with anything?"

"Have you ever heard of the 'curious incident of the dog in the night'?"

She sipped her wine. "Doesn't ring any bells."

"Not a Sherlock Holmes fan, huh? Well, Holmes solved a case based on the fact that while the crime was taking place the dogs did *not* bark. No barking meant the dogs knew the intruder."

She twisted her head to look up at him. Moonlight shone on the strong, masculine planes of his face. In his features, she saw a younger version of Shane—a boy who savored Sherlock Holmes adventures. "I didn't know you liked detective stories."

"It was one of the reasons I became a deputy. I liked the idea of putting together the clues and coming up with a solution that led to an arrest."

"Are you sure you want to leave that job and work for PRESS?"

"Oh, yeah. Real-life law enforcement seldom involves a mystery. It's pretty much cut-and-dried. You see the bad guy and lock him up."

"So this chance to investigate must be interesting for you."

"I'm pretty sure that once we have all the pieces, the puzzle won't be that complicated," he said. "Anyway, Neil's mother is like the dog not barking. Nobody in his family says much about her, and that makes me think she might be important. What can you tell me about Janice Revere?"

"She and Roger are divorced. Obviously. And I guess it was a really bloody separation. Neil is estranged from her. Prentice told me that she has serious mental problems and has been hospitalized as a schizophrenic."

"That's not what I heard from Dr. Em. She recalled something about Neil's mother working as a psychiatrist at a hospital back east. Anyway, I looked her up online and came up with several women named Janice Revere. None were the right age."

"She could be using her maiden name."

"Or she could be married again. Dr. Em didn't know anything else about her."

Angela didn't bother wondering about why Prentice would lie about Neil's mother. Or why Neil never revealed anything about his estrangement from her. The two of them had done nothing but lie. "What's next?"

"I'll ask around and see if I can gather more information."

"Can I help?"

He gave her a squeeze and kissed the top of her head. "The number one priority is keeping you and Benjy safe. Neil's going to be out of jail by tomorrow, and he might come looking for you."

"But I have a restraining order."

As soon as the words left her lips, she knew a piece of paper wouldn't stop Neil from doing exactly as he wanted. He'd meant what he said about not letting her go.

She'd like to believe that she could handle herself, but when he'd lashed out at her in the parking lot, she'd been startled. Never before had she been struck by a man. The only fights she'd gotten into were playground shoving matches.

His blow had chipped away at her self-confidence, even though it hadn't caused any actual physical harm. Neil had shown himself to be capable of physical violence, and that scared her.

"This cabin is secure," Shane said. "But I don't want you to be here alone. During the day, it's best if you and Benjy stay with Calvin at the horse ranch where there are plenty of people around."

She finished her wine and set the glass aside. Turning around in his embrace, she wrapped her arms around him. "But I want to be with you."

"As much as possible."

"And as often as possible."

He kissed her, and she tasted wine on his lips. Though she had been completely satisfied, she wanted to make love again. She wished this night could last forever.

Chapter Nineteen

Over the next couple of days, Angela settled into a routine. First, she'd go for a morning run on the gravel road outside the cabin. Then, Shane would take her and Benjy to the horse ranch where they'd spend most of the day. After dinner, the night belonged to her and Shane.

This morning she'd already done her exercise and showered. In the cabin kitchen, she prepared cheese omelets to go with the muffins she'd made the night before, and her mind wandered. Last night, they'd made love beside the creek, bathed in moonlight and serenaded by the rush of water.

When they had climbed the hill back to the cabin so they'd be nearby in case Benjy woke up, they had seen intruders: a family of elk crossed in front of the cabin at a stately pace.

Though it had been close to midnight, she hadn't been ready for sleep, so she made them chamomile tea flavored with a stick of cinnamon. They went onto the porch to sip and talk. After all these years, it didn't seem as if they'd have much to say, but there were endless stories of their pasts and even more plans for the future. He encouraged her to write that cookbook of her breakfast recipes—something Neil would have put down as unimportant. And she promised to fly with him as soon as he was a certified helicopter pilot.

Her fears about losing him as a friend had been utterly unfounded. Their friendship hadn't changed; it had grown.

The morning light through the cabin window held the promise of another beautiful day. Though there was still much to be settled, she was beginning to feel safe. After he got out of jail, Neil hadn't tried to contact her. Nor had Prentice. Their precaution of keeping their location a secret seemed to be working.

She looked up from the stove as Shane and Benjy tromped through the front door of the cabin. Benjy dashed to the table. "I'm starving, Mommy."

"You're just in time." She prepared his plate and carried it to the coffee table in the living room, which was the only place they could all sit together and eat in this small cabin.

In the kitchen, Shane dished up his own food. He gave her a little kiss on the cheek before he joined Benjy. She liked the way their intimacy spilled over into their regular life. Casual kisses, hugs and holding hands felt perfectly natural, and Benjy seemed to accept their deepening relationship without question.

Her son was doing well in this mountain environment. Wearing his ever-present cowboy hat, he blended in with the other kids at the horse ranch. The only place he was a know-it-all was in the kitchen at the ranch house.

Angela had taken over the cooking chores to help out at the ranch, which was fine with her. She preferred keeping her hands busy and enjoyed coming up with new recipes for farm-fresh produce and the lusciously marbled beef from a nearby ranch. Every afternoon, she baked something sweet—cookies or a pie—and the children gathered around. Benjy was the self-appointed supervisor, telling all the other kids how to hold a spoon and how to measure.

She sat at the table and looked at her two men. "This is nice," she said. "Being together. Having breakfast. I could do this forever, until I grow old and gray."

Shane shot her a glance. "Speak for yourself, Grandma."

Benjy laughed. "Yeah, Grandma."

"We've got a lot to do today," Shane said. "I just got a phone call, and I'm going to need your help, Angela. I want you to come into town with me."

She looked at Benjy. "Will you be okay at the ranch?"

"I gotta be there," he said. "One of the mares is having a baby, and I have to help."

"Well, then, I guess I won't be missed."

She wondered about Shane's phone call. It was time for the DNA profiles for Benjy and Neil to have come back from the lab. Though she was fairly sure that she wouldn't like the results, she needed answers.

AFTER THEY DROPPED OFF Benjy, Shane held the car door for Angela and went around his Land Rover to slide behind the steering wheel. Though he was wearing his uniform, he doubted he'd be doing much work for Clear Creek County. His status as a lame-duck deputy allowed him free rein to pursue his investigation into Neil and Prentice.

Due to budget restrictions, the higher-ups had already decided that his position wouldn't be filled after he left to work for PRESS. The rest of the deputies said they'd miss him, but were also relieved that none of them would be laid off to trim costs.

As they drove away from the ranch, Angela peppered him with questions. "Who called you this morning? It was the lab, wasn't it? Should we contact Eve to interpret the DNA profiles?"

"Sorry," he said. "My call this morning wasn't about the DNA."

She flopped back in her seat. "Thank goodness."

"I thought you were anxious to find out."

"Of course, I want to know." Her slender hand rested near her throat as she exhaled a giant sigh. "At the same time, I don't."

"Because you have to face the problem and deal with it."

She nodded. "If the phone call wasn't about the DNA, what was it?"

"I've got a location for Prentice's cabin." He'd wasted a lot of time with computer searches, interviews with the county assessor's office and phone calls. Yesterday, he drove all the way to Fairplay in Park County to search through property records. "I'm guessing that this place is where Prentice goes to get away from it all. His hideaway. His name isn't on any of the records."

"If his name isn't on it, how did you figure it out?"

"The old-fashioned way," he said. "I talked to our local postmistress, and she referred me to somebody else and somebody else. This morning, she finally got information and called me. One of the rural delivery drivers had a note to deliver a package addressed to Dr. Prentice at a cabin belonging to J. Stilton."

"The name doesn't ring any bells," she said. "Why did you want me to come along?"

Partly because he wanted to spend more time with her. When they were apart, she filled his mind and he couldn't wait to get back to her. "I need your help to figure out what Neil and Prentice are up to. Our easygoing lifestyle won't stay this way forever."

Her eyes widened in alarm. "Have there been threats? Is there something you're not telling me?"

For a moment, he took his eyes off the road and met her gaze. Honesty had always been the cornerstone of their relationship. Though he had dedicated himself to protecting her, he wouldn't lie to her. "I'm not keeping secrets, and I never will. If there's a need for worry, you'll know about it."

"Good." She emphasized the word with a nod. "You don't have to treat me like a precious hothouse orchid."

"You are precious, but you're sturdy, too."

"A sturdy orchid?"

"A daisy," he said. "I want you to know that Neil hasn't given up. He and Prentice have both been sighted in this area. I reckon they're doing the same thing we are, but in reverse. They're trying to find our hideout."

"But they can't," she said. "Right?"

"I sure as hell hope not."

Though he didn't think Neil would physically harm her or Benjy, he wouldn't be surprised by a kidnapping scheme. Neil was arrogant enough to think that if he got Angela alone, he could still win her back.

"Tell me how to help," she said. "What are we looking for at this cabin?"

"You know these people better than I do. That's why I wanted you with me."

He concentrated on the road. Though he knew his way around Clear Creek County, he'd never been in this area and he was glad he had the GPS navigator to show him the way. Rural routes could be tricky; there were few road signs or markings to show where you were.

When they got close, he started reading the names on mailboxes at the side of the road. On a battered metal box, he could just make out the name *Stilton.*

Angela saw it, too. "There."

A fence that had once been white marked off a property that looked to be about two acres. A gray, ranch-style house with a sloped roof stood at the end of the gravel driveway. The detached garage was almost as big as the house.

"Doesn't look like anybody's home," he said. "No cars. But they could be parked in that garage."

"The house and grounds seem too dilapidated for Prentice. He's got expensive taste."

He drove to a crossroads and turned. Behind a stand of trees, he parked the car. "Let's do a little trespassing."

They made their way across another larger property that also appeared to be deserted. Though the forest was sparse and plain, the mountain views were attractive. He reckoned this area was filled mostly with vacation homes that were used only in summer or for weekend getaways. Or they could be rentals left vacant by the sluggish economy. Not many people could afford to live in solitude; they needed jobs and the price of gas made it impractical to make the commute from the mountains.

The morning sun beat down on his back. He could feel himself starting to sweat. Breaking into the Stilton house wasn't the way he usually pursued his duties. As a duly appointed law enforcement official, he could justify his actions as part of an ongoing investigation. Dr. Prentice had committed fraud many years ago when Angela was born. But Shane knew he was stepping outside the boundaries of legality into a gray area.

A tall spruce tree stood beside the house, and he crept into its shadow. Angela was right beside him. "What do we do now?" she asked.

"We hope that Prentice isn't sitting behind the door with a shotgun."

"He'd never dirty his hands with something so crude," she said. "But Carlson would."

Shane moved across the dried prairie grass to the back-door and tried to turn the knob. The good news was that Prentice didn't appear to have an alarm system. The bad news? The door was locked.

Angela peeked into the window beside the door. "This is a kitchen. I can hardly see through this filthy glass, but it's kind of cute inside. There's a vintage honey bear cookie jar."

He could have kicked down the door, but it was smarter to use finesse so Prentice wouldn't know they'd been here. He squatted down to eye level with the lock and took out a set of picks.

She hovered beside him. "Interesting skill. Are you a deputy or a cat burglar?"

"We patrol a lot of areas with empty houses," he said as he maneuvered the picks. "It's handy to be able to get inside."

After a few minutes, he had the lock unfastened. As Angela had noted, the kitchen seemed pleasant and wel-coming, with cherry-patterned wallpaper and red vinyl covers on the breakfast nook. Though dust lay thick on the windowsill, the counter had been wiped down. "Someone has been here recently."

Angela gave no sign of fear as she explored. Her first move was to open the refrigerator. "Whoever has been stay-ing here likes beer. Three six-packs."

The circular oak table in the dining area was covered with dust, and he saw footprints on the dusty hardwood floor. The pattern was common to work boots. Not the kind of footwear he expected Prentice to wear. Nothing about the furniture or the lamps or the knickknacks suggested the expensive taste of Dr. Prentice.

He pulled up the top on a rolltop desk. There was nothing inside but a couple of advertising flyers. He was beginning to think they'd come to the wrong house when Angela took a framed photograph off the mantel and studied it. "That's Neil."

The picture showed a skinny kid, probably eleven or twelve years old, dressed in a soccer uniform and proudly displaying a trophy. "How can you tell it's him?"

"He has the same picture at his house."

Other photos showed Neil as a toddler and in a Halloween costume. "There's nothing about the older Neil. You'd think somebody like Prentice would find more value in graduation pictures than in kid stuff."

Angela turned on her heel and strolled around the room. "I don't think he lives here. This place looks like it was decorated by a woman."

"A woman named Stilton."

"Prentice never married," she said. "I always thought it was odd for an ob-gyn who specialized in fertility treatments. He never had children of his own."

"He could have had a mistress, and this was her house." He went down the hallway. The doors stood open to two bedrooms and a bath. A rumpled comforter covered one of the bare mattresses. "This bed has been slept in."

"Recently?" she asked.

"I can't say for sure. From all the dust, I'd guess that this house has been closed up for a long time. But it's been lived in."

"By somebody who likes beer and didn't bother to sweep all the floors. That doesn't seem like Prentice or Neil."

He raised an eyebrow. "Are they both good housekeepers?"

"They wouldn't tolerate the dirt." She glanced with disgust at the floors and the dirty windows. "Not that either of them would pick up a broom. They'd hire somebody to get the place tidied up."

He'd been smart to bring Angela along; she noticed things that he wouldn't have seen. "You know," he said, "if Prentice used this place as a hideaway for his mistress, it would explain all the secrecy. He wouldn't want his name on this property."

"But that doesn't make sense. He's a single man. He doesn't need to hide his relationship."

"Unless she was married." He put the pieces together. "A married woman with an interest in Neil."

"Oh, my God. He was having an affair with Neil's mother."

Shane had been drifting toward the same conclusion. Prentice and Shane's father had been lifelong friends. Prentice would want to hide his involvement with the mysterious Mrs. Revere. Now that he had a name for the woman—Janice Stilton—he could locate her. "Do you think Neil found out?"

"If he did, why would he be friends with Prentice?"

"You met his father," he said. "Roger Revere isn't a real warm and likable guy."

"And Neil would blame his mother." She gave a snort of disgust. "That's why they were estranged and he refused to talk about her."

Tires crunched on the gravel outside the house. Someone was coming. Shane went to the bedroom window and looked out. He saw a black truck.

Chapter Twenty

Before Angela had a chance to think, Shane rushed her through the house. "Somebody's coming. Run."

She dashed into the living room. Her foot slipped and she stumbled. She tried to catch herself on the back of the wood chair beside the desk, but she was off balance. Both she and the chair hit the floor with a crash. Panic raced through her. If anyone was standing outside the front door, they'd hear.

As she scrambled to her feet, Shane yanked the chair upright and shoved it toward the desk. She would have straightened it out, but there wasn't time.

He grabbed her hand and pulled her through the kitchen and into the backyard. He closed the door. Under his breath, he muttered, "We should have covered our tracks."

"What do you mean?"

"The chair is off kilter. I opened the rolltop desk. You moved photos on the mantel."

"Do you think they'll notice?"

"Let's hope not."

Instead of racing back the way they came, he signaled her to be quiet and eased toward the side of the house. He was moving in the direction opposite the way they'd come when they approached the cabin. What was he thinking? Did he want to be caught?

Following him closer than his own shadow, she bumped into his back when he halted at the front of the house.

"What are you doing?" she whispered.

"We're okay. He didn't hear us inside the house because he was parking in the garage."

"Who is it?"

"Carlson." Shane pressed his back against the side of the house. "Quiet."

She stood beside him. Her heart thumped so loudly that she couldn't hear anything else. Fear ripped through her, and she hated that she was afraid of Carlson. During the whole time she'd known him, Neil's protégé had been a nonpresence. He'd faded into the wallpaper, seldom speaking and never making a scene.

But Carlson had put her through hell with his late-at-night whispered messages and his creepy stalking. He was probably responsible for slashing her wedding gown, and she knew that he'd do *anything* for Neil.

She heard the front door of the house slam. To Shane, she whispered, "Now do we run?"

"There's something I need to check out. Stick with me."

He dodged across the open space that separated the house and the garage, frequently looking over his shoulder to make sure Carlson hadn't spotted them. At the three-car garage, he opened the side door, pulled her inside and closed it.

Darkness surrounded them. Her nostrils twitched with the stink of grime and oil. Shane hit the light switch by the door, and a couple of bare bulbs cast a dim light.

Against the back wall was a workbench with an array of tools. Underneath were two five-gallon gas cans. She looked past the typical clutter that accumulates in a garage—trash cans and stuffed black garbage bags, an old television set, a broken rocking chair, a snowblower.

At the far end of the garage was a black truck—the same type of vehicle that had killed Tom five years ago.

The sight of it shocked her. *Was this the same truck?* Her throat tightened; she was unable to breathe. In her mind, she replayed the moment of his death. The clock read ten twenty-three. Through her phone, she heard the violent, fatal crash and Tom's whispered last words: *Love you, too.* Then silence.

Shane crossed the garage and went to the front of the truck. His hand rested on the fender. He leaned close, studying the joint between the fender and the door. When he looked at her, his gaze was stricken.

In a deathly calm voice, he said, "It's a '97 or '98. This fender has been replaced. The paint doesn't match the rest of the truck. There's no way of knowing if this is the original bumper or not."

This was the truck. She knew it. She sensed it.

Furious, she charged forward. With both fists, she hammered at the wall of the truck bed. She lashed out again and again as though she could destroy this damn thing with her bare hands. Overwhelmed with incomprehensible rage, she staggered backward until she bumped against the workbench. Her hands flew up to cover her face.

She should have been sobbing, but the tears didn't come. Her eyes squeezed shut. Her vision went dark. She could see the headlights of the truck coming toward her, not slowing down. The truck careened, faster and faster.

Shane wrapped her in his embrace. Wordlessly, he held her. She knew he was struggling, too. She could feel the tension in his arms. Tom had been his cousin, his best friend.

"I should have known it was Carlson," she said. "As

soon as we figured out that he was stalking me, I should have known. He always woke me up at ten twenty-three. On the night when you came to the house, I thought I saw truck lights through the kitchen window."

Carlson had been acting out Tom's death, night after night. He used that tragedy to haunt her.

She shivered and buried her face against Shane's chest. "You have to arrest him."

"First, I need proof." He gently stroked her back. "This truck says something to you and me, but I doubt there's going to be anything in the way of forensic evidence. It was five years ago, and the truck has been repaired."

"What about records of the repair job? Receipts from a body shop? There's got to be something."

"There is," he assured her. "Carlson won't get away with murder. And when he confesses, I'll arrest the man who put him up to it."

Carlson wasn't acting alone. He was a stooge—a stupid, pathetic toady who was capable only of following instructions. "It was Neil, wasn't it?"

"Neil or Prentice. Or both of them."

The whole terrible plot became clear. Neil and Prentice had manipulated Tom so he would insist on having their embryos frozen. Then they killed Tom to get control of her. She'd readily agreed to the IVF procedure. "I fell right into their trap."

"Don't blame yourself. You had no way of knowing what they were doing."

"Because I didn't know about the Prentice-Jantzen study, didn't know that I had been genetically engineered."

Eve had told her that there were only two females from that study. Prentice needed her to create the second generation: Benjy. She shook herself. "They can't get away with this."

"They won't," he assured her. "They're all going to jail."

Those were the words she wanted to hear. She wanted to know that Tom's death would be avenged.

ON THE DRIVE BACK TO THE sheriff's office, Angela fidgeted in the passenger seat, wishing she could make Shane's car move faster. "Are you sure the deputy you left watching the house won't let Carlson get away?"

"You heard my instructions. Don't let anyone leave but if somebody else shows up, don't stop them. Let them enter."

"Why do we have to go to the courthouse?"

"I need to coordinate the evidence, inform the sheriff and get a warrant. I'm making this arrest by the book. The worst thing that could happen now is to have these guys get off on a technicality."

Earlier, she hadn't wanted to press charges against Prentice because he could afford a dream team of lawyers. But this was different. They were talking about murder—Tom's murder.

She looked over at Shane. With his jaw set and his eyes focused straight ahead, he looked like a man on a mission—strong and determined. "I can always trust you to do the right thing."

"It's my job."

"For now," she said. "But you're not going to be a deputy much longer."

"And this arrest is one hell of a fine way to end my law enforcement career. I'll finally get justice for Tom."

A rush of gratitude went through her. She was so glad that he was in her life. In the midst of sorrow and rage, Shane had always stood beside her. The love she felt for him grew deeper every day, and she wanted to tell him what was in her heart.

But now probably wasn't the best time.

He glanced toward her. "When we get to the courthouse, I'll arrange for someone to take you to the horse ranch so you can be with Benjy."

"I want to come with you."

"It's police business."

She had a stake in what happened—perhaps the biggest stake, but she didn't want to get in the way. "Is there anything I can do?"

"Talk to Neil's mother."

Shane's phone calls to headquarters had already produced results. A search of records showed that Stilton was the maiden name of Janice Revere's mother. After her divorce, Janice Revere used the name Janice Stilton until she remarried and added a hyphen. She was now Janice Stilton-Parke, and she worked as a psychologist at a private clinic in Vermont.

Shane said, "I don't think she'll be useful as a witness. She left Colorado twenty-four years ago."

"When Neil was only twelve." Though Angela couldn't imagine how any mother could leave her child, she wouldn't pass judgment until she'd heard the whole story.

SHORTLY AFTER THEY ARRIVED at the courthouse, Shane directed her into an office that wasn't being used. There was an empty desk, a chair and a telephone. He placed a piece of paper with the phone numbers for Neil's mother on the desk.

He sat her in the swivel chair, turned her toward him and leaned down to kiss her on the lips.

She pulled back. "We shouldn't. I don't want people to get the wrong idea."

"Too late," he drawled. "Most people already think we're sleeping together. I mean, we're a couple of consenting adults, staying in a secluded cabin without a television."

"Why does a TV make a difference?"

"I'm easily distracted."

"Are you telling me that you'd find television more interesting than making love?"

"That depends. If we had the satellite sports network, I might be—"

She rose to her feet, held his face in her hands and kissed him hard and long. Just as she felt him beginning to respond, she ended the kiss. "Make no mistake, Shane. I'm way better than ESPN."

He gave her a pat on the butt and headed toward the door. "Take your time with the phone call."

His joking around had been just what she needed to relax. She sat behind the desk and dialed.

When a woman answered, Angela asked, "Is this Janice Stilton-Parke?"

"Yes, it is. Who's calling?"

"My name is Angela Hawthorne. I need to ask you a few questions about your son, Neil Revere. This is very important. Please don't hang up."

"I don't think I can help you." Her voice was calm and reasonable—exactly what Angela would expect from a psychologist. "I'm estranged from my son and haven't seen him in years."

"Neil and I were engaged."

"Past tense," Janice noted. "I have a few minutes, Angela. Go ahead and ask your questions."

It would be the height of cruelty to call this woman out of the blue and tell her that her son had turned into a murderer. Angela chose her words carefully. "When were you divorced from Roger?"

"Over twenty years ago."

"Was there a pre-nup?"

"No, but Roger is a lawyer. He used the courts to his advantage and obtained full custody of Neil. I tried to stay in contact. Made every effort. Until Neil told me he wanted nothing more to do with me."

"Do you remember Dr. Edgar Prentice?"

"Yes." Her answer was clipped, terse.

Angela asked, "What was your relationship with him?"

"Edgar was a friend of Roger's. They knew each other for years, even before we were married."

"Do you own property in Clear Creek County?"

There was a pause. "I suppose my name is on the property. Edgar purchased the land and cabin. He pays all the taxes and bills."

"Did you ever live on that property?"

"You're being very circumspect, Angela. It's not necessary. Long ago, I made peace with the feelings I have about my first marriage and my estrangement from Neil. I was foolish. I made a mistake, and I paid for it."

"The mistake," Angela said. "Was it Dr. Prentice?"

"I had an affair with him. That was why we were so clandestine about the cabin. I didn't want my husband to know that I'd betrayed him. He suspected that I had a lover, but I never told him that I was sleeping with his best friend."

Uncomfortable, Angela stared at the blank wall opposite the desk in the empty office. It wasn't her style to pry into another woman's life, but Janice seemed to be forthcoming and honest. "When did your affair with Prentice start?"

"I know the answer you're looking for, Angela. I never acknowledged this to Neil or his father, but it should have been obvious. They look nothing alike. Over the years, I've followed my son's career. It was no accident that he went into the field of medicine."

Angela knew what was coming next. "Like his father?"

"That's right," Janice said. "Edgar Prentice is Neil's biological father."

Chapter Twenty-One

In the courthouse, Shane paced the hallway outside the sheriff's office while the logistics of Carlson's arrest were being worked out. Since the murder took place in Park County, the sheriff in that jurisdiction needed to be advised. Shane was glad they had good reciprocal relations with Park County. He'd been there just a couple of days ago looking for information about Prentice's cabin.

Five years ago, when Tom was murdered, Shane had frequently conferred with the Park County investigators assigned to the case. He'd studied the photographs of the crime scene and reviewed the meager evidence, including the bloody fingerprint on Tom's SUV.

Five years ago, they found no match for the fingerprint. Since then Carlson had gotten himself arrested in Aspen for being drunk and disorderly. Now his prints were in the system. And Carlson's prints matched those found at the scene of the crime.

Shane had laid out his murder theory for the sheriff who agreed that they should be on the lookout for Prentice and Neil. At the very least, they were witnesses.

Sticking to the letter of the law helped Shane control his need for revenge. The minute he saw that damn truck, he wanted to rip Carlson's head off. That little bastard had killed a good man; he should suffer the ultimate punishment. But Shane didn't want this to end with Carlson. Neil and Prentice were equally culpable.

Down the hallway, he saw Angela leave the office where she'd been talking on the phone. She walked toward him with her head held high. Her cheeks flamed with color. She stepped into his arms and held on tight. Though the shape of her body had become familiar during their nights of lovemaking, the sensation of holding her still amazed him. After all these years, they'd found their fit as lovers.

"How was the phone call?" he asked.

"Tragic. I feel bad for Neil's mother."

"Before you tell me about her, I should show you this." He took an envelope from his back pocket. "The DNA results."

"It's still sealed."

"I thought you should be the one to open it."

She shook her head. "I don't think I can take any more shocks today. You read it and tell me what it says."

He escorted her to the wooden bench against the wall outside the sheriff's office, and he sat close beside her. Her posture was erect, as though her spine were a steel rod. He knew she was tense. If Benjy wasn't her biological child, she might be better off not knowing. "Are you ready for this?"

"Just get it over with."

Using his thumb, he opened the envelope and took out four sheets of paper. One was a copy of Angela's DNA profile that Eve had sent. There were two other similar sheets for Benjy and Neil. Shane didn't have the scientific know-how to interpret the results, but the technician had enclosed a cover letter to explain.

He skimmed the letter until he found the pertinent sentences which he read aloud. "The accuracy is 97.8 percent.

Subject A (Angela) and Subject N (Neil) are the genetic parents of Subject B (Benjy)."

"Neil," she said. "Neil is Benjy's father?"

"Maybe not. It's only 97.8 percent accurate."

"No wonder he was so determined to get custody. Benjy is his son."

"That's the biological part," he said. "As far as I'm concerned, Benjy is the child born from the love between you and Tom. You both planned for him. You went through the frozen embryo process together. He's Tom's boy."

"That's a good way for me to think of it."

But he could tell that she wasn't convinced. The fraud Prentice had perpetrated on her was particularly cruel. He'd lured her and Tom to his clinic, had extracted her egg and fertilized it with Neil's sperm. All without her consent or knowledge.

He held her chin and turned her face toward him. In her eyes, he saw pain and anger and other emotions he couldn't identify. "You're going to be all right with this."

"You don't know the worst part," she said. "Neil's mother had an affair with Prentice. He's Neil's biological father."

And Benjy's grandfather.

IN THE PARKING LOT behind the courthouse, Angela watched as Shane and three other deputies headed toward two vehicles. They'd broken out the bulletproof vests and heavy weaponry. Shane had told her that they were going to arrest Carlson, but he'd be taken to Park County where he'd be formally charged and incarcerated.

Shane strode over to where she was standing. "This is going to be over soon."

"I still don't understand why I can't come with you."

"Taking a murder suspect into custody is official police business. Not a spectator sport."

She leaned close and whispered, "You didn't mind having me along when we broke into the Stilton house."

"And we almost got caught." He handed over the keys to his Land Rover. "Take my car and wait for me at Calvin's horse ranch. But I don't want you driving alone. Get one of the dispatch officers to go with you."

"I don't need a babysitter."

"And you don't need to take risks," he said. "As long as Neil and Prentice are still at large, you're in danger."

One of the deputies motioned to Shane. She knew he had to hurry, but she hated being left behind. Seeing Carlson in handcuffs would bring her much-needed satisfaction. "Please let me come along."

He slapped a cell phone into her hand. "I'll call you and tell you everything that happens."

After giving her a peck on the cheek, he went to join the others. He looked good walking away. She'd always thought his uniform was sexy.

Resigned to her passive role, she juggled the car keys in her hand. In spite of Shane's warning, she figured she could manage the drive to Calvin's ranch by herself. Riding alone would give her time to think and absorb all that had happened today.

She went to his Land Rover and got behind the wheel. After adjusting the seat and the rearview mirror, she fastened her seat belt and drove away from the courthouse. The route to Calvin's horse ranch led away from town into the forest. These untraveled roads were pleasant; she did some of her best thinking when she was driving.

Knowing the truth about Benjy's DNA worried her. Though she took solace in the fact that he was genetically engineered to be a genius, she hated to think that he might inherit Prentice's lack of ethics or Neil's arrogance. Surely, those traits were learned behavior. She couldn't imagine her little guy being cruel in any way.

But Janice Revere must have felt the same way about her son. When Neil rejected her and sided with his father and Prentice, she must have been hurt.

Later, Angela might contact Janice and tell her about Benjy, offer her the chance to know her grandson. Benjy didn't have other grandparents. The closest thing to extended family he had was Shane's parents. And Eve, she reminded herself. Her half sister.

As she took a sharp turn onto a gravel road, the SUV seemed to wobble as though it was unstable.

The cell phone rang and she answered, "Hello, Shane."

"How are you doing?"

"I'm on the way to Calvin's." She decided to tell him the truth. "And I didn't drag anyone along with me. I'm fine."

"Are there any other cars on the road?"

She hadn't been watching the mirrors, but took a glance now. "Nobody in sight. And when did you get to be such a mother hen?"

"I think that happened right after I fell in love with you."

She pulled the phone away from her ear and stared at it. Did he just say that he loved her? He must have because the L-word echoed inside her head. How could he make that declaration over the phone? So casual. So calm.

"Angela, just be careful. If you have any trouble at all, hit the redial button and I'll answer."

Before she could respond, he disconnected the call.

Of course, she loved Shane as a friend. And she loved the way he seduced her. But was she in love with him?

She yanked at the wheel. The ride over this gravel road

was worse than it had ever been before. Something was wrong with this car.

A flat tire.

Her fingers clenched the steering wheel. *No! This can't be happening!* A flat tire led to Tom's death. She wouldn't let them kill her, too. Through the windshield, she saw the surrounding forest. There were no houses in sight. No other cars.

The car jostled wildly. She knew she should pull off onto the shoulder, but her foot wouldn't come off the accelerator. If she could keep going, she wouldn't be stuck here.

In her rearview mirror, she saw another car approaching. Sunlight gleamed on the chrome of the other vehicle. The front grill looked like shark's teeth.

She had to change directions. Couldn't risk leading them to Benjy. She'd rather die than let Neil get his hands on her son. But there was nowhere to turn on this road. No escape.

The other car pulled up to her back bumper. She couldn't outrun him with a flat tire. She had a better chance on foot. Every morning, she'd been running. All that training might pay off.

She swerved, and the other car gave her a little more room. He didn't want to put a dent in his expensive grill. If only she could get some distance, she'd have a better chance.

She unfastened her seat belt and tucked the cell phone into her sports bra. The phone was her only link to Shane. She slammed on the brakes. Shane's Land Rover swiveled to a stop.

Immediately, she threw open the door and dashed around the front of the car. Following her instincts, she sprinted across a rock-strewn open space toward a thick stand of aspen. Pumping hard, her legs accelerated as she ascended a rise.

Someone called her name, but she didn't stop, didn't look back. All her energy focused on getting away from them, running like hell.

A sharp pain stabbed into the center of her back and she fell forward. Her hands scraped on the rocky soil. Struggling, she forced herself to get up and lurched forward.

Her vision blurred. Her knees folded, and she hit the ground. Desperately, she tried to move. It was no use. She'd been shot.

Chapter Twenty-Two

Guns drawn, Shane and the others approached the Stilton house where Carlson was holed up. The deputy who had been watching the house reported that there had been no movement. Carlson hadn't attempted to leave.

At the front door, two men held a battering ram in case they needed to crash through the door. Shane reached out and tried the handle. It was unlocked.

Something was wrong with this setup. Why would Carlson sit here for two hours in the afternoon? He had to be following Neil's orders. Why did Neil want him there?

Shane threw open the door and rushed inside, followed by two other men. They didn't have far to go.

The television set in the front room showed a commercial for shampoo. Carlson was sprawled on the sofa facing the screen. He wasn't moving.

His mouth hung open. His skin was mottled. His sightless eyes bulged in their sockets.

Shane felt at the base of the man's throat for a pulse. Nothing. Standard procedure was to try CPR, but there was no point. "He's dead."

The deputy who had been watching the house spoke up, "I swear nobody got in here. I didn't just sit in my car. I was out, prowling around the house."

On the coffee table in front of the sofa were the contents

of a grease-stained carryout bag: a half-eaten hamburger, fries and a soft drink.

Shane was willing to bet that Carlson had been poisoned by something in the food or drink. Neil and Prentice must have decided that their protégé was a liability. And they had taken him out of the picture.

Deputy Keller—a gray-haired man whose beer belly pushed the limits of his Kevlar vest—took charge. "This here is a crime scene, boys. We need to handle things right. I'll call the sheriff."

Shane stepped back. He should have been glad to see the man who murdered Tom lying dead before him, but this wasn't the way he wanted this situation to play out. With Carlson dead, there was no one to point the finger at Prentice and Neil. And he was damn sure that those two doctors knew how to administer a poison that couldn't be traced back to them. They were about to get away with murder. Again.

His cell phone buzzed. Caller ID showed it was Angela.

She whispered, "Flat tire. Neil grabbed me."

His heart stopped. This was his greatest fear come true. "Where are you?"

"An SUV. In the back." Her voice was barely audible. "Can't talk."

"Angela, are you all right?"

"I was shot."

God, no. He couldn't lose her.

"Can you see through a window. Do you know where you are?"

"Can't tell."

If it was the last thing he ever did, he would get to her in time. Goddammit, he wouldn't let her die. "Leave this phone line open. Give me clues whenever you can."

He clipped his phone onto his ear and strode toward the exit.

"Hey," Keller called after him. "Where the hell do you think you're going?"

"Angela needs me."

ANGELA CURLED INTO A BALL on the floor of Prentice's SUV between the two front seats and the bench seat in the rear. The middle seats were pulled up. It was a strange prison—one that still had a new car smell.

Her only chance to survive this capture was the cell phone. She was lucky that Neil hadn't found it tucked inside her bra. If she could keep feeding information to Shane, he'd find her. Leaving the line open, she returned the phone to her bra.

Though her hands were tied in front of her, she still had a range of motion. Her back ached where she'd been shot. It wasn't as painful as she would have thought. As she became more alert, she seemed to be regaining her strength, rather than fading.

And she didn't see blood.

Twisting around, she dragged herself toward the front of the vehicle.

From the passenger seat, Neil glanced back at her. "You're feeling better already. I knew you would. The dose in the tranquilizer dart was minimal."

"You shot me with a trank gun?" The inside of her mouth tasted as if she'd been chewing on dirty socks. "How could you?"

"It was the best way to control you without hurting you. Why did you take off running?"

"Flat tire. That was how you—" She stopped herself before saying too much. Neil wasn't aware that she knew about Carlson and the black truck parked in Prentice's garage. "That was how Tom died."

"Easy now." He reached between the seats and held a water bottle toward her. "Drink some of this. You'll have a bit of a headache, but otherwise you'll be fine."

When she inched forward to reach the water, she realized that her ankles were bound together. "Untie me. Now."

"The restraints are for your own good. So you won't try something foolish. I don't want to hurt you, Angela."

She took the water bottle from him and drank. He'd been right about the headache, but her mind was clear. The most important thing was to let Shane know where they were.

"Where are you taking me, Neil?"

"I'm going to finish what we started. I'm aware that this isn't the best way to start a marriage, but—"

"I'll never marry you."

From the driver's seat, Prentice gave a short laugh. "You don't have a choice. We already have the marriage license. Obtained by proxy. All we need is a quick blessing, the signature of a minister and it's done."

These two men were crazy, obsessed. And dangerous. She got up on her knees so she could see through the window and look for landmarks. She had to say something to give Shane a clue to their whereabouts. She recognized the road they were on and the body of water beside it. "No wedding. It's not going to happen. I'd rather throw myself out of the car and drown in Beaver Lake."

"Try to be reasonable," Neil said. "We can work things out. For Benjy's sake. The boy needs a father."

"Never mention my son again."

"Oh, please," Prentice said. "You're not a moron, Angela. I'm sure you've figured out by now that I matched your DNA with someone of equal caliber. You must know that Neil is the biological father of your son."

After all their subterfuge, she didn't expect Prentice to be so direct. "I know. I had Benjy's DNA tested."

Neil smiled at her, actually smiled. "So many times, I wanted to tell you. I'm so proud of our son."

Our son? The words sounded obscene when he spoke them. Her anger exploded. "You bastard! You think you're so damn smart. Book smart. But you don't understand a thing about people, about real life. I'll never be your wife. And Benjy will never be your son."

"There's no reasoning with her," Prentice said to Neil. "I told you we'd have to do this the hard way."

Her jaw clenched. "What are you going to do? Kill me?"

"Of course not," Neil said. "But it might be necessary for you to disappear for a while. We have a convenient minister who will sign the certificate with or without you. Ironically, his name is Money. Pastor Money."

"Pastor Money," she repeated, hoping that Shane was listening.

Neil continued, "We'll tell everyone that we went on our honeymoon, and then you'll be hospitalized. It won't be a surprise. Everyone saw how erratic you've been acting, calling off the wedding at the last minute."

And Neil would use a biological claim to solidify his claim for custody. Benjy would fall into his hands. They thought there was nothing she could do to stop them, but she knew better. Carlson would be blamed for Tom's murder, and he would implicate both Prentice and Neil. Ultimately, they'd be in jail, and she'd be free of them.

But she needed to survive long enough for justice to take its course. She decided it was best to let them think she was going along with their insane plan. "It seems as if I don't have a choice."

"Then it's settled," Neil said. "We'll be married."

There was no way of sorting or understanding the avalanche of emotion that crashed over her. Her anger was matched by hopelessness. Her fear overwhelmed by hatred.

More than ever before, she needed Shane's help. One more time, she needed him to ride to her rescue. But she had to give him more to go on.

She played for time. "Can I, at least, clean up before this wedding?"

"I'm sure there's a washroom at the Chapel by the Creek."

"What's that? Chapel by the Creek?"

"Sounds idyllic, doesn't it? That's where we'll be wed." Neil seemed determined to put a good face on the situation. Could he really be so blind? So arrogant that he couldn't for one minute put himself in her shoes? "One day, this will all be a funny story to tell our grandchildren."

She prayed that Shane could hear her, that he would know the location.

CHAPEL BY THE CREEK. Shane knew where it was. And he also knew that Prentice's SUV was approaching on a winding back road that circled Beaver Lake.

He switched on the sirens and the flashing lights atop the official vehicle, and he hit the accelerator. Taking a direct highway route, he could arrive at the chapel before them.

Though backup would be helpful, he couldn't coordinate their arrivals and didn't want to take a chance on spooking Prentice into running.

Plus, he needed to keep listening to Angela's voice on the cell phone. The other voices were muffled and indistinct, but she came through loud and clear. When he'd heard her say that she'd been shot by a trank gun, he felt a sense of relief and he had known, without a doubt, that when this was over he wanted to live every day with her.

Through his phone, he heard her ask how long before they got there. She repeated the answer. "Twenty minutes, more or less."

He flew down the road, careening past the other traffic. He was close to the chapel. It made sense that Prentice would go there. Pastor Money was a nondenominational weirdo who would marry a goat to a chicken if you paid his fee.

He turned off the siren as he neared the chapel, skidded into the parking lot and drove around to the back. Now was the time to call for backup.

WHEN PRENTICE PARKED in front of a white chapel in need of a new paint job, Angela did everything she could to stall. Neil untied the cords around her ankles and helped her to her feet.

She groaned. "I'm a little dizzy. Give me a minute to get my bearings."

"Hurry it up," Prentice snapped. He didn't bother hiding his hostility toward her. "Let's get this over with."

She glared at him. "What's the big rush?"

"I think you know," he said with a sneer. "Carlson called me and told me that someone had broken into my cabin. I'm sure that your boyfriend, Shane, is trying to put together some kind of bogus evidence."

Bogus? Oh, how she wanted to accuse him! She wanted to throw his crimes in his face, but she tried to sound innocent. "I don't know what you're talking about."

"You can't make a case against me without Carlson," he said.

That was true. Their only solid evidence was Carlson's fingerprint at the scene of Tom's murder.

Prentice continued. "Poor Carlson. He has a bad ticker, you know. I wouldn't be surprised if he keeled over from a heart attack at any moment."

"My God, did you kill him, too?"

Neil had finished untying her hands. "Angela, please. I thought you were done with these paranoid delusions."

She stared at him in disbelief. "Are you saying that you don't know about Tom's murder?"

"Your husband was killed in a hit-and-run accident." He took her arm and led her toward the chapel. "I'm beginning to think that you really do need treatment."

She tried to jerk free, and he clamped down more tightly. Prentice held her other arm. Together, they marched her through the door.

The interior of the chapel was as run-down as the outside. The pews were scratched and worn. The carpet runner down the center aisle was a dark, dirty brown. At the front was a simple podium and a table with a white cloth. A man in a long, black robe fussed with a candle arrangement on the table.

"Pastor Money," Neil called to him. "We're here to be married."

Without turning around to face them, he waved them forward. "Yes, yes, get up here."

She dug in her heels, but it was no use. They dragged her down the aisle. She made one last appeal. "You've got to listen to me, Neil. Prentice arranged for Tom's murder. It was Carlson driving the black truck. And now Prentice has probably killed Carlson as well."

Halfway down the aisle, Neil came to a halt. His gaze rested on Prentice, and she saw a flicker of comprehension. "Is she telling the truth?"

"We're scientists, son. There are no facts to back up what she's saying."

Neil dropped her arm and stepped back. "My God, what have you done?"

"I did it for you. And for Benjy."

From outside the chapel, she heard an approaching siren. The man in the black robe whirled around.

It was Shane. His right arm extended straight out from his body. The nose of his gun pointed directly at the center of Prentice's forehead. He growled, "Let her go."

Prentice tried to hide behind her. His hand slipped on her arm, and Angela took advantage of the situation. With all the rage that had been building inside her since they grabbed her, she lashed out. Prentice staggered backward.

She ran toward Shane. In his black robe, he was an impressive figure. He told her to get behind the podium. The approaching sirens got louder.

He stared at Neil. "Are you armed?"

Neil held both hands in the air. "No."

Unwavering, Shane held his aim on Prentice. "You have a gun. Go ahead, make your move."

"If I do, you'll shoot me."

"We call that justifiable homicide," Shane drawled.

Three other lawmen charged through the door at the back of the chapel, and Shane stepped down, willing to leave the arrests to them.

When he turned toward her, she flung her arms around his neck and held on for all she was worth. He was her hero, coming to her rescue again. "I love you, Shane."

He smiled down at her. "It occurs to me that we're standing in a chapel, and Pastor Money is in the back room, ready to perform a wedding."

"Is that a proposition?"

"Marry me, Angela."

Without hesitation, she answered, "I will, but not here. Not today."

"When?"

"Soon enough."

THE NEXT YEAR ON Valentine's Day, Angela stood at the back of a Denver church and waited to marry the man she'd loved as a friend and adored as a lover. Ever since Shane moved into her Denver house, her life had been just about perfect. He loved his work at PRESS. She loved Waffles. In her spare time, she was writing her breakfast recipe cookbook.

Benjy had adapted without a qualm. They were a family, no matter what their DNA makeup.

The trials for Neil and Prentice were still going through appeals, but both men were in jail. Because they'd abducted her, they were denied bail and deemed to be a danger to others.

This would be a small ceremony with only a few good friends and a dinner at Waffles afterward.

She peeked through the open door leading down the aisle and saw Shane standing there in his black suit, looking like the most handsome man on earth. Beside him was his best man, Josh LaMotta, who was still dating Marie, the cake baker.

An infant wailed, and Angela turned toward her half sister, Eve, who had returned to the States with her newborn and her macho military husband.

"Are we ready?" Eve asked.

Benjy stepped up in front of her. "The baby is being loud. We can't start until the baby gets quiet."

Eve leaned down so Benjy was at eye level with the infant. "You tell her."

Benjy kissed the baby on the nose. "Shh."

Miraculously, the child settled down. Eve handed her

daughter off to her husband. She leaned close to Angela and whispered, "Am I noticing a little bulge under that suit?"

"A three-month-old bulge." Angela patted her tummy. "And the best part is that we got pregnant the old-fashioned way."

Yvonne signaled the organist.

Joyfully, Angela went down the aisle.

* * * * *

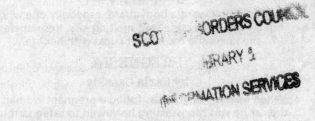

INTRIGUE..

INTRIGUE...

2 FREE BOOKS
AND A SURPRISE GIFT

We would like to take this opportunity to thank you for reading this Mills & Boon® book by offering you the chance to take TWO more specially selected books from the Intrigue series absolutely FREE! We're also making this offer to introduce you to the benefits of the Mills & Boon® Book Club™—

- **FREE home delivery**
- **FREE gifts and competitions**
- **FREE monthly Newsletter**
- **Exclusive Mills & Boon Book Club offers**
- **Books available before they're in the shops**

Accepting these FREE books and gift places you under no obligation to buy, you may cancel at any time, even after receiving your free books. Simply complete your details below and return the entire page to the address below. You don't even need a stamp!

YES Please send me 2 free Intrigue books and a surprise gift. I understand that unless you hear from me, I will receive 5 superb new stories every month, including two 2-in-1 books priced at £5.30 each and a single book priced at £3.30, postage and packing free. I am under no obligation to purchase any books and may cancel my subscription at any time. The free books and gift will be mine to keep in any case.

Ms/Mrs/Miss/Mr _____ Initials _____

Surname _____

Address _____

_____

_____ Postcode _____

E-mail _____

Send this whole page to: Mills & Boon Book Club, Free Book Offer, FREEPOST NAT 10298, Richmond, TW9 1BR